The Story of a Love That Was Just Beginning ...in a World That Was Coming To An End

They were an unlikely pair: a footloose untitled Englishman whose dangerous trade was espionage, and the beautiful, untouched daughter of the last Czar of Russia.

John Kirby and Olga, daughter of Nicholas and Alexandra, were destined to play out their doomed romance against the tragic drama of a society on the brink of revolution. Because the year was 1911, and a way of life was about to come to an abrupt end: a life of glittering palaces and summer villas, of dazzling gowns and opulent ballrooms, of Imperial grandeur and innocent young love.

Only the memories remain. And the images so hauntingly evoked by R. T. Stevens of this last sunlit summer of the Czars—im____ that will remain vivid in your mem___ ___ ____er the last page of this extrao_____ __ ____en turned.

"...A _____ ... a haunting _____ a ballroom nov_____ ___terary Guild

The Summer Day Is Done

R.T. Stevens

WARNER BOOKS

A Warner Communications Company

WARNER BOOKS EDITION

Copyright © 1976 by Souvenir Press Ltd.
All rights reserved

Library of Congress Catalog Card Number: 76-2822

ISBN 0-446-89270-X

This Warner Books Edition is published by
arrangement with Doubleday & Company, Inc.

Warner Books, Inc., 75 Rockefeller Plaza, New York, N.Y. 10019

W A Warner Communications Company

Printed in the United States of America

Not associated with Warner Press, Inc. of Anderson, Indiana

First Printing: June, 1977

10 9 8 7 6 5 4 3 2 1

THE SUMMER DAY IS DONE

I

Tranquillity

ONE

The main station of the Ukrainian seaport Niko-layev was more active than usual that morning. It was the activity of anticipation, a buzz, a bustle, a shouldering of neighbours. It had to do not with catching a train, but with seeing one. The Imperial train, carrying the Tsar and his family, was due to pass through.

Having discovered this, John Kirby detached himself from the bustle and strolled to the farthest point of the station, where he ran less risk of being jostled by the crowd. In addition, it was cooler at the far end. There the breeze from the Black Sea sneaked around the station buildings and relieved the enervating heat.

He was twenty-eight, tall and sinewy, with hair of deep brown and a beard flecked with gold. He wore light brown twill trousers, a white silk shirt open at the neck and a straw boater tipped to shade his grey eyes. He carried a belted jacket under his arm.

He heard the approaching rumble. The bustling people became a spreading mass, their excitement and curiosity infectious. The rumble increased to a rolling thunder and the iron monster steamed slowly through. The Imperial train, in any case, never travelled fast. It liked to give unfriendly anarchists the impression it was on the lookout.

The huge engine pulled gleaming coaches of royal-blue, each coach adorned with the double-eagled

Imperial crest. The whole was an engineering master-piece of iron, steel and wood, aptly designated a royal palace on wheels.

They called out, the people of Nikolayev who had crowded into the station, and some threw flowers and others knelt in a gesture of reverence. They did not know if the Tsar would show himself but hoped he would. Suddenly he did, and the day was blessed for them. The curtains of a coach drew aside and there he was, in uniform and standing at the window to acknowledge their greetings. He was bearded, hand-some and smiling. He was visible only for the short time it took the train to rumble through, but it was enough to make it an occasion of delight for the people. In their enthusiasm they almost pushed a raptly hypno-tised woman under the massively-rolling locomotive.

Not until the train was passing the end of the station did Kirby, standing unhampered and alone, see another curtain move.

A young girl looked out.

Startled blue eyes met his. He was aware of a girl soft with colour and enchantment. The warm sunlight danced on the window, was reflected in her eyes and made a shining cloud of her chestnut-blonde hair. He felt the strangest sense of indefinable communication as in shy, suspended animation she returned his gaze, the train bringing her to him, taking her away. The fleeting seconds stretched. He could not resist smiling. And at the very last moment before she vanished, she gave him the shyest of smiles in response.

He stared after the train until it was no more than a blue smudge.

It was 1911 and he had been in Russia three years. His British passport identified him as an English gentleman of independent means. In three years he had travelled extensively over the country, and it had left him with the impression that no one man could live long enough to discover the full extent of Russia's immensity or unravel more than one of its complexities. Millions of its people were simple and devout, thou-

10

sands were sophisticated and cynical. Some Russians were extravagantly passionate, others religiously fatalistic. Thousands made a banquet of every supper. Thousands more starved. There were freezing, bitter winters and hot, cloudless summers. There was incalculable wealth and unendurable poverty. The wealthy used the Tsar and the poor revered him.

Ubiquitous, interested, involved, Kirby had seen the unimpressive, unpaved indifference of Vladivostock in muddy autumn, the white brilliance of Siberia in dry, sub-zero winter. He had experienced the forbidding atmosphere of Moscow in a grey dawn and the fragrance of the Crimea in spring. He had tired of the limitless flatness of the Ukraine, been depressed by the industrial towns of the Urals and perpetually fascinated by the people in all places. Most recently, he had lived in St. Petersburg, the beautiful capital where the arts flourished and the gifted poured out their genius.

But the aristocrats of the capital deserted it *en masse* during the summer and autumn. They went to the South of France, to Italy and to the Crimea. Kirby himself was on his way to the Crimea. He had been invited there by Count Andrei Mikhailovich Purishkin. Kirby knew the Crimea and loved it. It was the least Russian of all the provinces of the Empire, but uncompromisingly loyal to the Tsar.

He thought again of blue eyes and a shy, enchanting smile.

A hand came to rest languidly on his shoulder. He turned. Count Andrei Mikhailovich Purishkin smiled at him. Nearly thirty, rakishly handsome in a light suit, white hat and sporting a slender malacca cane, Andrei was a good-natured representative of his kind. Amiable and indolent, he owned to a dislike of mental or physical effort. God had bequeathed him a silver spoon and who was he to challenge the whims of the Almighty? He was as he had been born, and Russia was as God and the Tsars had made it. Andrei thought far more of the accident of his noble birth than he

11

did of his wealth, but, Kirby reflected, if he had had only as much as a civil servant to live on he would have perished within a year. He would not have complained, however, he would merely have lapsed into incurable fragility.

"So you walked," he said to Kirby. He spoke in French, the language of the capital's nobility, although he could have used Russian, for Kirby was fluent in that language.

"Yes," he said, "it was warm but I needed the exercise. Your delightful aunt never let me out of my chair once in three days."

"She does it to every visitor. She dotes on an audience. Gregory saw to your luggage and has it here somewhere."

Gregory was the Count's secretary, a man of invaluable work capacity.

"He's a fine fellow," said Kirby. "What a good friend you are, Andrei Mikhailovich. Your servants are my servants. As a compulsive traveller I find the occasional use of another man's servants an excessive boon."

"Most of the time," observed Andrei, "you are disgustingly self-sufficient. What it is to be an Englishman and so sure of oneself. It isn't a virtue, you know, it's an intimidation. It can exhaust the weak."

There was always an air of ease and good fellowship about Kirby which appealed to the languid aristocrat, the suggestion of a man always curious about others, a man always looking for something new in life. They had met at the turn of the year in St. Petersburg, at a reception where Andrei had been intensely bored by its respectability and its demands on his feet. They became friends, and Andrei invited Kirby to leave his hotel and stay instead at the Purishkin family house overlooking the Neva. Now they were on their way to spend a month or two on Andrei's estate in the Crimea.

Many of the people on the platform had dispersed after the Imperial train had passed out of sight, and

12

most of those still there were awaiting the arrival of the Sevastopol connection, late because it had been held up by the stately Imperial progress. A few passengers were milling around the station samovar, drinking tea. Andrei looked and felt limp. He never exuded virility. Nevertheless, women adored him.

He remembered something.

"Do you mind company to Sevastopol, dear fellow?" he said.

"Whose?" asked Kirby .

"Not an unreasonable question, but is there something on your mind?"

"I was thinking."

"I do myself occasionally," said Andrei. "Our company won't be boring, I assure you, unless she talks politics. Then she'll be wearing. She's in her carriage outside and won't put a foot from it until the train arrives. She dislikes railway stations. Gregory is somewhere seeing to our luggage. I must find him, I suppose, and tell him of our changes of coaches. We've been invited to share hers. I hope you won't find it fretful. She is Princess Karinshka, the exquisitely formidable Aleka Petrovna."

"Is she more formidable than all the others?"

"Frequently," said Andrei and sighed. "She can scratch and draw blood. She has a passion for politics of the wrong kind. She's one of us but not one of us. It's despairing. But you will have to make up your own mind. Where the devil is Gregory?"

"You were going to look," said Kirby, who knew Andrei hoped he would make the search. A bell rang, a train whistled. The locomotive began its run in. Andrei wandered limply in search of Gregory.

Suddenly the platform was all babble and confusion. Kirby thought that this, at least, was common to all Russia. Wherever one went, whatever kind of people one was among, a quite ordinary incident could induce an apparent crisis. Even two people boarding a tramcar or two men putting up a poster seemed to crowd each other. It was a national malaise.

But the train would happily wait until everything sorted itself out. Kirby looked around for Andrei. When he saw him, he was with a woman. She was striking. Despite the heat she wore a long, black kaftan-style coat with a silky sheen to it and black laced boots that gleamed beneath the coat's swinging hem. Her hat with its half-veil was also black and she wore it like a crown on her massed auburn hair. She walked in gliding freedom, attended by a retinue of luggage-carrying porters. She stopped at the entrance to a coach and Andrei beckoned to Kirby. The woman looked at him. Her complexion was pale, her mouth only lightly touched with rouge, and her eyes were so dark that they almost matched the smoky black of her veil. Her face was oval, European rather than Russian. She was, thought Kirby, distinctively beautiful.

"You're English?" she said. Her voice was cool, low-keyed, slightly husky.

"And a traveller," said Andrei, "he's walking around Russia, dearest."

She glanced down at Kirby's brown shoes. They were dusty.

"Yes, I see," she said. She was speaking in Russian. She was opposed to the affectation of Russians speaking French.

Kirby, looking down at the dust on his shoes, said, "It's just something I picked up in Nikolayev, Highness."

She made a gesture of dissent with her hand. Steam was whistling, people hurrying, porters loading luggage. But Princess Karinshka was not a woman to let a standing train worry her.

"Mr. Kirby," she said in English, "there are more princesses in Russia than churches even. They mean nothing. It's Grand Duchesses you should beware of. I don't wish to be called 'Highness.' Will you share my coach to Sevastopol?"

"With delight," he said.

Andrei gave her his hand. She took it with some affection, smiling sleepily at him from behind her half-

14

veil as she climbed aboard. Even Princess Karinshka, a known society tigress, liked the lazy, agreeable Count. His ennui was a challenge to women.

The interior of the coach was all gilt and pearwood, the adjoining coupé fitted with luxurious sleeping berths. The whole was reserved for the Princess Karinshka, although the train was destined to reach Sevastopol before nightfall. Porters and officials were aboard, seeing to the stowing of luggage for the Princess and her two companions. She ignored it all. She took her seat and became immersed in conversation with Andrei, who, lounging contentedly, assured her that for the last nine months life had been empty without her. She obviously did not believe him but at least it amused her.

"What a dreadful liar you are, darling," she said.

"My dear," said Andrei, "it's true. Ask my good friend John if I have been myself this year."

"John?" Her pronunciation of the English name was like a husky cough. "Who is John?"

"Come, darling, you can do better than that," said Andrei. "You two have just met and will, I hope, be friends for life. It would be intolerable," he added in a murmur, "if you became more than that. I should have to think about ending it all. My life, I mean."

"You ridiculous man," said Princess Karinshka, "you could not even make the effort to load the pistol, let alone fire it."

"He could lean from a window and let himself fall," said Kirby.

"Oh," she said, lifting the veil and turning her dark eyes on Kirby, "that's a brilliant summing-up of all that Andrei Mikhailovich is capable of."

She stood up and removed her coat but not her hat. She wore a dress of dove-grey silk, collared and cuffed with lace, its high neck of almost Victorian modesty if one discounted the curving swell of the bodice.

As she sat down again the train jerked, jolted and pulled away, the tender piled high with the timber logs that fed the engine. Slowly, erratically, it began to move out of the station.

Andrei settled into luxurious inertia.

"We'll have champagne with our lunch," he said.

"You have a brain like a drawn cork," said the Princess.

With her veil turned up over her hat, she was regarding Kirby dispassionately now. Then suddenly she said to him, "Is it your opinion that England is a democracy?"

"Be careful how you answer that, dear man," said Andrei, "for you are facing the hammer of Russian Socialism."

"Well," said Kirby.

"Well what?" she said.

"The principles are democratic," he said.

"Is that an implication that it isn't democratic in practice?"

"Dearest one," said Andrei, "this is all very pleasant and comfortable. *Must* we have politics? Tell me where you have been these last nine months. Had you been naughty again?" He took out a gold cigar case. Princess Aleka accepted a long thin cigar, so did Kirby. They smoked. "Well, Aleka Petrovna?" Andrei was faintly insistent. Aleka blew smoke rings. Kirby watched her. She was catlike, her posture a silken grace. She would not be silent for long. Through the blue haze her eyes looked smoky black.

"If you must know," she said, "I've been in France and England."

"Ah, so you were caught distributing Socialist pamphlets again," said Andrei. "She's always doing it," he said to Kirby, "and I expect the secret police suggested to her father that if he didn't send her somewhere far away for a while, they would send her even farther for even longer. So he sent her to France and England."

"It was very educational," said Aleka. She smiled reminiscently. "In France democracy is corrupt, in England it doesn't really exist. England's political system, whatever it is, is no better than Tsarism because there are only rich people and poor people. I made many friends among the poor, but how strange some of them were. They would keep asking me why the Tsar let so many Russians starve, and so I said it was because he was probably like their King, who let so many of them starve. They seemed quite astonished at that, especially as I was always so amused. It would have been useless to tell them I was a Socialist, they would not have believed any princess could be."

"Socialism," said Kirby, extremely relaxed, "is for idealists, surely."

"Socialism is equality," she said, "and is for everyone."

"Unfortunately," said Kirby, "it pre-supposes that people are equal to equality. They're not. People are human beings. There are always those who are better, more adaptable, more inventive and harder-working. I am for the basic rights of the individual, for the right of equal opportunities, the right to be free, the right of the labourer to be worthy of his hire, the right of all to say what we like about anything we like. I am against exploitation, oppression, armed police, female soldiers and censorship of the press. Socialism implies that poverty is a virtue. It isn't. It's a regrettable condition and a matter——"

"Oh, damn it," she fumed, "are you reading me a speech? It sounds like it and it's all rubbish. You aren't talking about Socialism——"

"I know I'm not," he said.

"Oh, you are damnably English, aren't you?"

"Well, of course he is, my love," said Andrei placatingly, "and it would be so nice for all of us if you'd remember there are two things completely incompatible. Politics and peace. You can have one, you can't have both. I'd rather have peace. Darling, life is so infernally brief. You don't really want a revolution, do you?"

"Go to sleep," she said crossly, "and yes, I do. I

17

want a democratic system of government, not a Tsarist Council of fat old Ministers."

"Under a democracy, what would happen to the Tsar?" asked Kirby.

Andrei shuddered. "Not so loud, dear fellow," he said.

"But nothing will happen to him," said Aleka. "He'll still be the Tsar but not an autocratic one. You're against our Tsar? There, you see, Andrei, that's an Englishman for you. He'll hear nothing against his own royalty but wishes to do away with ours. Isn't that outrageous?"

"My sweet chicken," said Andrei, "why not let him speak for himself?"

"Why don't you?" she demanded, her silk dress whispering as she moved restlessly. "You can't be a nothing for ever."

"It's my earnest wish," said Andrei, "for all of us to mind our own business and not make life discomforting for our neighbours."

"Poor, ridiculous Andrei Mikhailovich," she said, "you'll be swept away one day when there are no more corners to sit in. Mr. Kirby, when you are in England do you belong to the rich or the poor?"

"Comfortably off is the expression," he said. "In Russia I borrow Andrei's servants."

"Oh, pooh," she said. "One day there will be no servants in Russia. One day it will all be very different. But not for a long time. Shall I tell you why?"

"Don't insist, dear chap," said Andrei.

"Because you can't change any system as autocratic as ours without first changing the people," said Aleka, "and Russian people will be harder to change than any others. They're ridiculously bound by what they think is the will of God. It isn't the will of God at all, it's the will of the Boyars."

"You're a Boyar," said Andrei.

"I disown them," said Aleka. "Mr. Kirby, I could dislike all my servants, not for being servants but for not wanting to change their lot."

"Why not give them each an acre of land and let them become their own masters?" said Kirby.

"They would sit on it and die," she said. "They would die of shame. They would say I was trying to make peasants of them."

"Dear me," he said.

"So I keep them," she said, "but I don't apologize for it. I too am trapped by the system."

"Never mind," he said cheerfully, "under the system as it is Andrei is able to order champagne with our lunch."

Princess Aleka thought little of that nonsense.

"It's easy for you," she said. "You can play the uninvolved observer full of complacency because whatever you see is not your responsibility."

She was a paradox, an aristocrat desirous of making a backward Russia look forward. She favoured the elimination of privilege which she herself enjoyed. It was privilege which most of all held Russia back. Kirby did not see how she and others of a similar mind could replace Tsarist autocracy with a people's democracy except by a miracle. Autocracy in Russia was immovably entrenched and was, moreover, accepted rather than objected to by the people. Such opposition as had been bold enough to take violent action, notably in the uprising of 1905, had always been localised and easy to crush.

Nevertheless, there had been some attempt to appease insistent and growing demands for the people's representatives to be heard in the halls of autocratic power. So in 1905 the country was allowed an elected parliament, the Duma. But the Tsar did not relinquish his right to appoint ministers and to control defence and foreign policy. He also retained the power to boot the Duma into the street, although Nicholas II, being the mild man he was, would never have made it look exactly like that.

Nicholas was inflexible in only one thing, his belief in the divine right of the Tsars. He could not allow the Duma to introduce and pass legislation which impinged on this divinity. He dissolved the first Duma after seventy-three days, applying the boot more in sorrow than anger. He genuinely believed, in any case, that the rapport between himself and his people made an intermediary organisation, such as the Duma, an anachronism. However, he was willing to try, to be generous. The second Duma came into being and lasted one hundred and three days. The third Duma was, in 1911, in its fourth year of office, its mandate being for five years. So there was hope.

Kirby had not come to Russia ignorant of its politics, its problems and its anomalies, and he had come to know more of these during his three years in various parts of the country. He could afford to linger. His father, an artillery colonel, had been killed in the Boer War. His mother, passionately devoted to her gay and flamboyant husband, did not long survive him and in 1905 Kirby at twenty-two suddenly found himself at the mercy of two possessive spinster aunts, who adored him. It was no great ordeal, for Emma and Charlotte Kirby were too lovable to make their possessiveness an irritation.

Emma, the elder, owned a Georgian cottage at Walton-on-Thames. There both sisters lived and Kirby spent most of his time with them. When Emma died in 1909 she left her not inconsiderable investments to her nephew. She also bequeathed him the cottage, with the stipulation that his Aunt Charlotte should be in residence for her lifetime. As he had also inherited several thousand pounds from his mother, Kirby became an English gentleman in that he had independent means and did not spit in public places.

Academically, he was the product of different schools and tutors, since his parents had disdained the normal practice of sending him to a public school, preferring to have him with them wherever his father's postings took them. He had seen the world while he was growing up, acquired a cosmopolitan outlook and an understanding of people.

He was observant. This trait had come to the

notice of others. He was not as entirely uninvolved as Princess Aleka had suggested.

Quite suddenly the brakes of the train screeched, and the train rocked and shuddered. They were thrown into a disorderly heap on the floor. Shouts and screams sounded from one end of the train to the other.

Kirby, conscious of slim legs in pale grey silk stockings, wanted to say, "Anyone for tennis?" but decided they would think he was hysterical. He pulled himself up and helped Aleka to her feet. She dusted herself down angrily. Andrei unfolded himself disgustedly.

"Really," he said to Kirby, "what must you think of our railways?"

"Oh, don't be a fool," said Aleka, "go and see what has happened, both of you."

That autocratic command coming from a professed Socialist was, thought Kirby, not quite what a democrat would have expected.

"Is your leg broken? Are you in pain?" he asked.

"Don't be so damned whimsical," she said.

"We'd better go," sighed Andrei, "she'll be unpleasant if we don't."

They left the coach, climbing down on to the track and mingling with passengers from other coaches. The engine was a roar of steam. Princess Aleka put her head out of the window. Kirby smiled up at her. Her hat was askew. Train officials hurried by. Andrei detained one of them to enquire what it was all about.

"It is nothing, nothing," said the official and hurried on. Kirby followed, Andrei picked his leisurely way. The engine stood in huge, steaming aloofness. It had come to a halt only a few yards from the beginning of a sweeping bend. A collection of timber baulks had been jammed into its path and in such a way as almost certainly to ride the front wheels off the lines. The driver was down on the track, grimacing at the near miss. Officials and passengers seethed around him. The driver, grimy from wood smoke, did not

21

like being shouted at. He had not been at fault, he had not placed the obstruction there. It was not his job to clear it, he had more than enough responsibilities as it was. Had he not been alert and perceptive the train would have been wrecked. Officials who were demanding action from him were peasants. He refused to labour at removing the baulks. That was work for others.

Kirby knew they would argue interminably unless someone did something. He set to and with the help of passengers in more of a hurry to get to Sevastopol than the officials seemed to be, began to loosen the jammed timbers. The driver looked on approvingly.

"Now there's a man who's not a dying bag of wind," he said to the officials. "You should be ashamed to stand aside and watch someone who has paid for his seat do your work for you."

"This was meant for the Tsar's train," said one official, paling a little.

"What?" said the driver. "Can't they tell the difference between my train and the Tsar's? Do I show the Imperial standard? Do I pull coaches of blue and gold? What are things coming to when shortsighted fools put me at this kind of risk? When you find them I'll feed them to my engine. All they're good for is making fuel." He climbed back into his cab. "Here," he called to Kirby seconds later and the Englishman came to take the enormous crowbar the driver offered. It made easier and shorter work of prising the timbers free.

Andrei looked on as if he were going to faint. Close proximity to manual labour always gave him a sick headache.

"I'm simply no good at this sort of thing, old fellow," he said to the sweating Kirby.

"I know," said Kirby, levering with the crowbar, "but you're a good friend, Andrei. Go and lie down somewhere."

When they returned to the coach Princess Aleka could not believe what she saw. The Englishman's

22

white silk shirt was smudged with dust and dirt, wet with patches of perspiration. And his hands were filthy. Andrei, still immaculate, sank into his seat, thankful it was all over.

"What is all this?" said Aleka, referring to the sweat and grime.

"It's something I keep picking up," said Kirby. She regarded the man behind the dirt. He returned her look with gravity. It made her sure he was laughing at her. "Shall I wash and change for lunch, do you think?" he said.

"I don't mind whether you do or not," she said. Loudly, over Andrei's head, she added, "It's always nice to meet a man who is not afraid to sweat."

"It's exhausting to others," said Andrei.

Over the meal in the dining-car Princess Aleka sparkled with life. The ornate, gilded car was full of diners and Kirby wondered if, in a compulsive desire to draw attention to herself, she was deliberately theatrical. She did not need to be. Her striking beauty alone was enough. The car was bright with colourful women, it hummed with conversation and was gay with laughter. Russians were never more alive than when they were eating and drinking.

The champagne induced increased vivacity in Aleka, brought a delicate flush to her paleness.

She looked at him. He wore a jacket with collar and tie now. He was not going to amuse her, she thought, he was only going to be politely charming. He seemed very sure of himself.

"What is your name now?" she said. "In English it's John? Yes, I think that was it. I shall call you Ivan. What is your father's name?"

"His name was John too."

His use of the past tense did not evoke an enquiry.

"Delicious," she said. "So you are Ivan Ivanovich. I am Aleka Petrovna. Now we know each other very well. When do you return to England?"

"I haven't made any plans," he said. The prawns

23

were succulent. She only toyed with hers, making more of the champagne than the food.

"It will be when you've walked all over Russia, I expect," she said. "Ah, then you'll find England so insignificant you'll take two strides and fall into the sea. What a ridiculous way to have an accident. Now that is very amusing."

She laughed.

"You're making people look, my dear," said Andrei, "and Ivan Ivanovich is English and therefore sensitive about such things."

"No one is looking at him," said Aleka, superb in her black-crowned auburn regality.

"Some of the women are," said Andrei.

"Pooh," she said, "old bitches will look at any dog." She forked a prawn and pointed it at Kirby above the gleaming tableware. "That was to insult them, not you, darling."

"I think I missed it," he said, "it's all the noise."

"Oh, you are a woodenhead, like all Englishmen."

"Ah well, dear man," said Andrei, "take comfort in the fact that if you have a wooden head she says I have an empty one."

The uniformed waiter came to refill their glasses. His servility and deference displeased the Socialist in Princess Aleka. She gave him a disdainful look. He replaced the bottle in its bucket and bowed low in exaggerated recognition of her disdain. She liked the cynicism of that riposte and smiled at him.

The scenery had changed, the train pulling them rapidly into the Crimea. The landscapes had lost their flatness, they were beginning to be greenly undulating. The sky was cloudless. Kirby did not know why she was still on his mind but as the sunlight danced on the window, casting reflections tinted with gold, he thought again of the girl with blue eyes.

When they were back in the coach after lunch it emerged that Aleka had made up her mind about something. She had decided, she said, that Andrei and his good friend Ivan Ivanovich should stay with

24

her at the Karinshka Palace near Yalta. Andrei, who had already closed his eyes, was shocked into opening them. He looked at Kirby. Kirby, who was to be Andrei's own guest, did not feel he could comment. He only smiled non-committally. It was Andrei's problem. Andrei realised he would either have to stay awake to make Aleka see reason or feign sleep and let her designs pass over him.

He sank back and closed his eyes once more.

"You will come, of course, Andrei. You too, Ivan. You will like Karinshka, Ivan. We will all have fun. It's not at all necessary for you to go to your own place, Andrei, it will only make your life empty again. Andrei, for God's sake, I'm talking to you."

Andre, without opening his eyes, mumbled his way into expressions of flattered delight but begged his little chicken to forgive him for his inability to accept. He was already committed to so many things on his estate.

"Don't talk rubbish," said Aleka.

"You are the dearest, loveliest lady," murmured Andrei, "but it's the arrangements, you see. What an extremely excellent lunch it was."

"Please kick him awake," said Aleka to Kirby. "If you don't I will."

"I'm not asleep, darling," said Andrei placatingly, "only at rest. Why don't you go into the coupé and get into something comfortable? Call if you need me."

"You ridiculous man," said Aleka, "what are arrangements to do with you? Gregory will see to all of them and without falling over you all the time. You won't do anything except indulge your passion for lying around. You can lie around at Karinshka. I've invited you. Do you wish to insult me? In front of Ivan? Worse, do you wish me to be bored? You know I can't stand my own company for more than a day."

"My dearest——"

"He is arguing with me," she said to Kirby, "he has no damned manners at all."

"Heaven forgive me," said Andrei.

"Good," she said, "it is settled, then."

"I meant——"

"What are you doing to me?" She was suddenly in a temper. "You have always come to Karinshka, is it some woman keeping you away this time? It had better not be. And what about Ivan Ivanovich? Don't be so damned selfish. He would like to come, but no, you are so concerned with yourself that his wishes don't count. Andrei Mikhailovich, I insist, do you hear?"

"Dearest," sighed Andrei, "we shall both be there and it will be enchanting."

And as the train carried them through the profusion of Crimean hills, woods and colour, he went to sleep.

TWO

The following morning, after spending the night at a hotel in Sevastopol, they took a small steamer over the bright waters of the Black Sea to Yalta. There they were met by servants from Karinshka Palace and from Andrei's estate, together with carriages. Only Gregory, the secretary, took Andrei's carriage. Andrei, reluctantly resigning himself to the whims of the temperamental Princess, took his seat with Kirby. His valet followed in a second carriage with the servants and the luggage.

The Karinshka Palace was several miles from Yalta. It was on this coast that many of Russia's most privileged aristocrats had built their great houses or palaces. Somewhere in the vicinity was the enormous estate of the Tsar himself, crowned by the Livadia Palace. At this time of year the Imperial family were almost always in residence. Livadia was adored by the Empress Alexandra. Only at Livadia did she find the complete peace so necessary to her spiritual well-being.

The road was white and dusty, the scenery breathtakingly beautiful, the hills and the valleys a riot of colour. Wild roses, wild grapes and every other kind of natural vegetation clothed the earth with heaven's abundance. Princess Aleka, fully veiled to protect herself from the dust, was in a mood of sweet satisfaction.

A woman tossed a flower into her lap. She took it up and gestured her thanks to the woman.

27

"You see," she said to Kirby, "they are real people here, not incurable serfs or priest-ridden peasants. All people should be real, should be proud. No one should be a servant."

He thought she probably had a hundred servants herself and said so. She received that in contemptuous scorn.

"I mean," she said bitingly, "that nobody should have a humble mind. One can serve without being at all humble. How can a man profess to have a brain if he can't see that?"

"I do see it. I took you literally, that's all. I'm a woodenhead."

"Well, we'll hope you get over it," she said, "but it's here, in the Crimea, that we might start the revolution, because here the people aren't humble."

When they arrived at last at the Karinshka Palace, Kirby thought he had never seen anything so expansively soaring. It was built on a high green hill overlooking the sea. Cupolas gleamed in the sunshine, were outlined against the blue sky. It had been left to Princess Aleka by her father's brother, an unprogressive old bachelor who had been murdered in the 1905 rebellion, and it was held in trust for her by her father, thereby overcoming the restriction placed on female inheritance.

Inside everything had a lofty vastness, walls and ceilings of gold and white, chandeliers immense and yet fragile. The wide central staircase was Russian Baroque, winding and floating towards the upper floors. Princess Aleka, restless and subject to boredom, often no sooner arrived in one place than she was fidgeting to be elsewhere. But Karinshka was different. After nine months in France and England she had longed for it. She swept through, her pale green silk coat swirling. Servants bowed or curtseyed.

Aleka herself showed Andrei and Kirby to their rooms on the first floor. It was a huge suite, fit for a king, the wallpapers like fragrant water-colour murals. Aleka had perhaps wanted to impress her English guest a little, for she waited on his reactions as he surveyed

28

the sumptuously-furnished drawing-room with its tall windows that opened on to the wide, sweeping balcony.

"Will you be comfortable enough?" she asked.

"Comfortable? I shall drown in velvet magnificence."

"Oh? You would prefer, perhaps, to look for a tent in the garden?"

"In the garden," he said, "I've only ever found the pen of my aunt."

She had removed her veil. Her dark eyes were full of merriment.

"Yes, when I was learning I heard that joke too," she said.

"I shall like it here," he said.

She turned as a servant came in. She said, "Ah, here is Karita. She is to look after you. She is a jewel. Karita, here is Ivan Ivanovich Kirby from England. You must see that he doesn't find fault. The English are very critical of the rest of us. But there, he's not too bad himself. Now I must go and see that Andrei Mikhailovich is happy. He's a little sulky at the moment. Poor Andrei."

She glided out.

Karita, the serving girl, floated a graceful curtsey to the Englishman. She wore a dress of sea blue, the colour of the Karinshka livery. The moulded bodice would have displayed a roundness had it not been covered by a crisp, white front with pockets for house keys. Beneath the wide skirt petticoats rustled. Kirby smiled. He saw a girl in blue and white, with golden hair burnished and braided, without a cap. She had huge brown eyes, was slim-waisted and composed. She could not have been more than nineteen. She clapped her hands. Two other servants in blue livery appeared, dark and muscular men. They bore his luggage. There were two portmanteaux and a valise.

"Just put them in there," said Kirby, indicating the bedroom, "I can manage."

Brown eyes looked at him in horror.

"But your Highness——"

"I'm not a Highness, I'm an English traveller."

29

Karita looked calmly resolute. He knew she would insist that the servants did everything and he nothing. He had been in the houses of other aristocrats, in Andrei's palatial St. Petersburg residence. One did not do things for oneself. It upset the servants. The less one did the closer one was to the All-Highest in the eyes of servants.

"Egor and Rudolf will see to your luggage, Highness, and I will unpack it," she said. He was very tall, very distinguished. He was obviously incognito, as many of Princess Aleka's guests liked to be at times. A man so distinguished and with such fine eyes must be much more than a traveller. Egor and Rudolf came out of the bedroom, she nodded to them and they left. "Will you have Tanya run your bath now?"

"Thank you. Who will put me in it?"

He was teasing her. Well! Karita drew herself up, clapped her hands again. Tanya, a maid, came hurrying in, she too in blue with a white front, but wearing a cap. She bobbed to Kirby, went through to the bedroom and into the bathroom. Kirby looked on indulgently. Sumptuousness and service were the keynotes of Karinshka. The blue and white elegance of the furniture, the walls adorned with paintings, enhanced the beauty of the bright, spacious drawing-room. And Karita was not unornamental. Positively pretty.

"Highness——"

"I am only Ivan Ivanovich," he said, using both names in the Russian way.

"Yes, indeed, Highness," she said. She regarded him a little cautiously. She had heard of England but had never seen anyone from that strange country. She had imagined all Englishmen to be dressed as soldiers and carrying swords, because they were always at war with someone. They were the warriors of Western Europe and carried their swords to the far corners of the world. She had heard that if an Englishman did not like the colour of a man's hair or the sound of his voice, he considered either a good enough reason to take the man's head off.

This Englishman was not in uniform but all the same Karita looked cautiously for a sword. He was without one.

"Something is wrong with me?" he said.

"Oh, your most gracious Highness," she said, blushing, "you must forgive me for staring so."

"You are Karita and in charge of this suite?" he said.

"Yes, Highness."

"Well, Karita, don't call me Highness or I'll have your head off."

Karita turned pale. Holy saints, it was true, then. She would lose her head. Not because of the colour of her hair but because of the way she spoke.

"Monsieur," she said, coming to terms with the problem, and using the courtesy title accorded to someone who bore no other, "have you killed many people?"

He thought about it.

"No, not very many," he said gravely. "Hardly any, in fact. Almost none, I think. Well, none that I can remember."

"None?" She did not know whether to be relieved or dubious. "None at all, monsieur?"

"I don't think so." He thought more about it, giving it weightier consideration. "Well, if there are any I can remember, I'll let you know. How will that do?"

She blushed because she knew he was amused. He was remarkably handsome. But he could not be telling the truth. She hoped he would never get angry with her. She was sure it would be terrible if he did.

"It's only what I've heard, your—only what I've heard, monsieur," she said.

"What, about me?" He was completely intrigued, finding her quaintness bewitching.

"About the English," said Karita. It was a blessed diversion when Tanya came to say the bath was ready and old Amarov wheeled in the trolley containing the silver samovar and dishes of savouries. Karita filled a glass with tea, Kirby took the glass and a savoury and carried them through to the bathroom. The colour of the bath gave a blueness to the steaming water and

31

Tanya had laid out what looked like masses of huge towels. He went into the bedroom, drank the tea and ate the savoury while he undressed.

In the drawing-room Karita glanced over her shoulder.

"You can leave the trolley, old one," she said, "his Highness will have what he wants when he's finished his bath."

Old Amarov, a retainer who had known many years of service with the Karinshka family, was white of eyebrow, sparse of hair.

"He's no Highness," he grumbled, "he's only an Englishman. My father fought them at Balaclava."

"Your father fought everyone," said Karita. "Don't let the Englishman hear you deny his nobility, he has slain a thousand men in his time. You've only to look at him to see that. It's true he's pretending to be ordinary but you can see he's not. And he's very kind."

"The wit of a woman is sharp indeed," said old Amarov, growling around, "and only a brainless donkey would question why someone who has slain a thousand men could be called kind."

"It was not out of kindness," said Karita composedly, "but in defence of his Tsar."

"Fool of a girl, England has no Tsar, only a king."

"Old one," said Karita, a little smile showing, "do you think her Highness favours him?"

"What is the world coming to?" Old Amarov was disgusted. "Go about your business, girl, and don't let your nose grow longer than it is."

Karita wrinkled a nose which she knew was not long at all. She sang as she whisked about the suite, seeing to this and that. With the Englishman in his bath she went into the bedroom and unpacked for him. She caressed the fine material of his English shirts, admired the soft strong leather of his footwear. Tanya helped her, stowing garments in the wardrobes as Karita handed them to her. She was careless with the leather case containing the Englishman's comb, hairbrush and mirror and the hairbrush fell to the floor,

32

hitting the corner of an open drawer on the way. Karita smacked her.

When Kirby, wearing a dressing-gown, came in from the bathroom, Tanya was still tearful. She fled when Kirby appeared. "He will take your head off for your clumsiness," Karita had said. Karita apologised to him for what had happened and was distressed, she said, that Tanya's carelessness had cracked the hairbrush.

"Oh?" he said.

She showed him the hairbrush. The back was of polished wood, inlaid with ivory. She pointed out a hairline crack.

"Dear me, that is bad," he said.

Karita blushed with mortification. Oh, that Tanya! She lifted her worried brown eyes. But he was smiling. He was not being terrible at all.

"If there's anything else you want, you will ring, monsieur?"

"What a treasure you are," he said.

Pink pleasure tinted her cheeks.

"Her Highness doesn't dine until nine," she said, "but there is food on the trolley if you wish it. I may go now, monsieur?"

"Yes," he said, "but I think I shall miss you."

She was used to being teased by the irrepressible friends of Princess Aleka but was never disconcerted by it. She was just a little disconcerted now.

Alone, Kirby took up the hairbrush. He twisted it, the ivory inlay was divorced from the polished wood and the back came away. He turned it over. What had been carefully inserted was still there, undisturbed.

He sat for a long while by the drawing-room window, watching the sun in its slow, evening descent. He had enjoyed his bath, his feeling was one of relaxed well-being. The view was a panorama of sky and sea, of garden magic where the hillsides swarmed with greens and golds.

He thought about a man he had to see in Yalta. But it was not easy to concentrate when images of shy innocence were so intrusive. How young she had

33

looked. He had glanced into the faces of a thousand girls, on the street, in restaurants and theatres, and everywhere else, but he could not call one of them clearly to mind. Except this one.

Karita returned to his suite at a little after eight.

"I am to tell you her Highness expects you in the dining-room at nine, monsieur."

"Then I'd better get dressed before then."

"It would not be out of place, monsieur." Karita too had a sense of humour. It was nice to see his smile of appreciation. She was beginning to find him unusually intriguing. It would not be at all unpleasant to be in charge of his comfort while he was here. If Englishmen were aggressive and quarrelsome, this one was not. It was better to make up one's own mind than to listen open-mouthed to others.

She went into the bedroom and came out carrying his white-jacketed evening suit.

"I will press it for you, Highness." It slipped out because she could not dissociate impulse from instinct.

She returned with the suit immaculately pressed and brushed within half-an-hour. It was warm and sleek from her attentions.

"Karita," he said when he had thanked her, "try not to be too indispensable, it will only destroy my self-reliance. How would you like it if, when I had finished my stay here, I couldn't even button up my own jacket?"

"Monsieur," she said, the braids of her hair like beaten gold, "what a fuss to make over such a little thing as pressing your clothes."

He laughed. She really was the prettiest and most self-possessed of young women.

She waited outside his door while he dressed. When he emerged just before nine Karita was quite delighted. He did her great credit. She curtseyed, then preceding him along the wide landing she led the way to the staircase. Slowly she descended. She found him by her side. She stopped in a little confusion.

"Your Highness——"

34

"If you call me that again I'll do something terrible," he said.

She knew he would not, but it did sound alarming. "Monsieur, I'm so sorry, but I am to go first, you see."

"Very well. We must all do as Romans do, of course." He followed her down. There were liveried servants standing like sentries at their posts in the shining hall used for balls. Karita's petticoats whispered and rustled. Footmen opened the doors to the dining-room. Kirby saw the illuminating enchantment of one single vast chandelier, the colour of paintings and the resplendence of a long table laid for dinner. Silver sparkled, glasses reflected brilliance. Princess Aleka stood at the head of the table talking to Andrei, Andrei a sartorial elegance in a cream-coloured jacket and midnight-blue trousers. Princess Aleka was a revelation. Her low-bodiced brocaded gown was a shimmer of silver and gold. Her bosom was unashamedly, curvingly opulent, her white shoulders smoothly bare. Her piled auburn hair was jewelled. In warm marble, thought Kirby, she would have looked like a sculptured goddess.

"Monsieur Ivan Ivanovich, your Highness," announced Karita.

Aleka turned.

"Why, Karita, such formality," she said, "but how prettily you do it. You have more feeling for an occasion than I have. It is an occasion, isn't it, when we have a handsome Englishman to dine with us?"

"Indeed, Highness," murmured Karita. Aleka laughed and Karita smiled, then whisked away.

Looking after her Aleka said, "You're pleased with her, Ivan? You have the best servant here. Andrei has his own valet, of course, but no one is quite as invaluable as Karita. Am I not good to you? You're comfortable? Everything is to your liking? Of course. What silly questions we do put to each other at times."

She sat at the head of the table, Kirby one place down on her right, Andrei opposite him. The enormously long table was fully laid although there were only the three of them. Aleka explained to Kirby that it was not necessary for him to think every evening would be as quiet and boring as this, for she would have the most entertaining friends to dinner each night from tomorrow onwards.

Andrei winced. Kirby said, "I give you my word, Princess, in a world revolving as giddily as ours there's nothing I enjoy more than quietude and boredom."

"I couldn't have put it better myself," said Andrei, "although I must say one's enjoyment is governed by whom one is sharing the boredom with. There's no boredom I couldn't enjoy with you, dear Aleka."

"Imbeciles," said Aleka. She was not bored herself, not at the moment. She was at Karinshka and her guests were exclusively her own. She knew many intelligent women but much preferred her love-hate relationships with men. Love, arguments and quarrels all exhilarated her.

Blue-liveried retainers began to serve dinner. Kirby found himself involved with a stuffed egg sitting on a bed of caviare. Aleka, like all aristocrats, behaved as if the servants were only deaf shadows, naming names and places with the abandon of an unimpeachable Bohemian as she told Andrei what she thought of some of his St. Petersburg friends.

"Good Lord, darling," said Andrei, "you must have looked through a thousand keyholes in your time."

"Indeed I've not," said Aleka, "I'm speaking of my personal knowledge of libertines. You have some frightful friends, Andrei."

"Horrifying," said Andrei, "and I do hope your personal knowledge was acquired as a result of victories and not defeats. To picture you trying to fight off Sergius Pavlich raises the most appalling images. The man is as hairy as a bear. Ghastly."

Vodka was served with the first courses. Aleka wanted to hear more of England and the English from Kirby, but interrupted him frequently to remind him that she had been there far more recently than he had, and that therefore her impressions of things were fresher than his were. Eventually Kirby mildly observed over a dish of tenderly white fish that it was a pity she raised questions to which she knew all the answers. It made him feel unnecessary.

"Darling, nobody is unnecessary," she said. They had been speaking of the separate Houses of Parliament and she was determined to put her point. "It's just that you forget I've attended both Houses and that it's not a question of my knowing the answers but of having opinions. Do you know what my opinion is of your Houses of Parliament?"

Her scent was delicately exotic and he was sure her bosom was powdered.

"I know you're going to tell me," he said.

"One House," she said, "is nothing to do with the people, it's full of lords and dukes and ancient nobodies. The other House is full of monkey-faced politicians who are supposed to have everything to do with the people but don't give a damn for them."

"We try to believe," said Kirby, "that the House of Lords protects us from the indifference of the Commons."

"Impossible," said Aleka, "because your House of Lords is full of aristocrats like Andrei. Andrei couldn't protect a dog from a flea, he couldn't even protect himself from one. Forgive me, Andrei, but that is so, isn't it?"

"Perfectly so, my little peahen," said Andrei.

She regarded him with exasperated affection.

"Sometimes, Andrei, I love you because you're like a rich man lost in a jungle, all your gold helpless to save you from the cannibals. And sometimes I don't know why I love you at all."

"To be loved for any reason is uplifting," said Kirby, "but to be loved for no reason at all is destructive to any man."

"Why?" she demanded.

"He assumes himself to be an indescribable perfection and surrounds himself with mirrors so that his perfection is always a delight to his own eyes. He dies the death of Narcissus. I think, by the way, that I read that in a book."

"Then it was a very stupid and badly-written book," said Aleka.

The vodka was followed by a Crimean wine, full-bodied and heady.

"Tomorrow," said Aleka, "it will all be much more exhilarating."

"God forbid," said Andrei, shuddering. "I have to tell you," he said to Kirby, "that Aleka Petrovna has an extraordinary liking for loud voices."

"Oh?" said Kirby. He reflected. "Shall I speak up a little, Princess?"

"Ivan," she said, "I should be very disappointed if you really did turn out to be a fool. It would be just my luck. Almost all my friends are idiots. But it'll be exhilarating, all the same. There'll be people here every day from now on. They'll come calling tomorrow and never stop. You'll find much to talk to them about."

As a servant refilled his wine glass Kirby said with an air of disarming sincerity, "I shall look forward to it. But how does one talk to idiots, Princess?"

"Idiots? Oh," she flashed, "that should be easy for you, it will simply be as one fool to another."

"Touché, darling," said Andrei.

A girl of sixteen stood on a balcony of the Imperial Palace at Livadia. The night was warm, the sky bright with stars, a velvet indigo encrusted with jewels. She wondered why she was thinking of a man she had glimpsed for no more than a few seconds, of his warm, friendly eyes and the smile he had given her.

It was silly.

Her sister came, putting an arm around her.

"Olga, what are you dreaming of out here?"

"Do you dream when you're awake, Tatiana?"

"Goose," said her sister, "when I'm awake I'm full of wishes, I only dream when I'm asleep."

38

"It's you who are the goose. Wishes are dreams too, silly."

Karita brought Kirby his breakfast.

He was awake, lying on his back, his hands folded behind his head. The huge windows let in the bright morning. Karita opened them and there came the scent of gardens, hills and sea. She herself was even brighter than the morning.

"Good morning," he said.

"My lord," she began, then blushed at his laughter.

"Karita, my lamb, you've been deceived again. Who has done it this time?"

"I asked Count Purishkin and he said you could not be less than a duke. A duke is an English lord, isn't he? You see, I knew I was not mistaken, but I've kept it to myself in case you wanted no one else to know."

"Well, lords and dukes of course are very funny about who should know and who shouldn't," he said seriously. "Your mind is made up that I'm a duke?"

"Highness, who was to tell Count Purishkin he was wrong? It would not have been proper for me to do so."

"Karita, I'm not a duke, so don't call me my lord or anything else. That would be even less proper? What's all this you've brought me?"

The breakfast trolley was mountainous with food. Karita began to itemise the dishes. Kirby sat up, shook his head and told her to take it all away, leaving only fruit and bread. Karita, a picture in her bright blue and immaculate white front, stood her ground.

"Her Highness said—well, she said——"

"Yes?" He thought her quick little smile delicious.

"She said that Count Purishkin had been starving you, monsieur."

"I must tell Andrei Mikhailovich that. So her Highness wishes to fatten me up. Are her friends coming to eat me, then?"

Karita could not restrain a gurgle. He was in such good humour again. And he did not really need to be

39

fattened up, he was very sinewy and that was how a man should be. The open neck of his silk pyjamas showed flesh brown and hard.

"You need only eat what you wish, monsieur," she said. "Also, her Highness said that if you would like to bathe in the sea this morning she will be ready for you to accompany her at eleven."

"Is it recommended, Karita?"

Karita's smile flirted around her lips, then she said, "It's recommended that you be ready by eleven, monsieur."

He smiled.

"How old are you, Karita?"

"Nineteen, my lord. I mean monsieur. Oh dear, because of one thing and another and Count Purishkin, I don't know what I do mean."

"We won't go into all that again. Nineteen is lovely, Karita. Thank you for my breakfast."

Karita went away feeling pleasantly disconcerted. He was very teasing. He was quite unlike Oravio, who was so serious and earnest. Oravio was a senior footman. It was understood by their families that in a year or two he and Karita would marry. Karita herself had not said yes or no. Oravio said she did not have to. It was something their families would decide. Karita did not tell him that her mother had said she could do better for herself than that. Her mother did not consider Oravio would be a monumental catch.

Certainly Oravio was dark and handsome. But he was not gifted with laughter. He admired his own seriousness, he said there was little to laugh at in Russia, anyway.

Karita did not know why, when she saw him on the landing, his sober, swarthy handsomeness suddenly seemed unexciting. He glanced at the door she had closed behind her.

"Why are you so pleased with yourself this morning?" he asked.

"It's my lord Ivan Ivanovich," she said, "he's making comical faces over his breakfast."

"Why do you call him 'lord'? He's no lord, he's only another arrogant Englishman."

There, thought Karita, there is someone else trying to think for me.

"He's not a bit like that," she said.

"They're all like that," said Oravio sternly, "keep away from him." He passed on. Karita tossed her head, tilted her nose and looked into a huge wall mirror. Well, you do not look all dark and intense, she said to herself. She went happily on her way.

"Ah," said old Amarov when she entered the kitchens, "what has tickled you today, my bright one?"

"See?" said Karita, pointing to his chest. He looked down and Karita brought her hand up and tweaked his flowing white moustache.

"Chit of an impudence," he shouted, "where is your respect for your betters?"

"You are a lovely old man, old one," said Karita and kissed his cheek.

"What are things coming to," muttered the old one, "what are they coming to?"

Later that morning Princess Aleka, Andrei and Kirby bathed from the golden beach exclusive to Karinshka. They changed in the beach hut, which to Kirby had all the size and amenities of a miniature mansion. It stood back on the bluff, it had a terrace and was pleasantly suitable for lunch to be taken there if desired. But Aleka was expecting visitors at the Palace.

She appeared in a blue costume, the skirt edged with white, and she wore a blue bathing hat with a white band. The legs of the costume were shamelessly short, buttoned only just below the knees. Her limbs were smooth, shapely, her skin white. She looked hard at Kirby in his black costume.

"How nice," she said slyly, "you aren't as thin as I thought, Ivan."

"Princess," he said, "I'm still full of breakfast."

Andrei emerged, a figure of fashionable beachwear in striped red and white.

41

"Goodness," murmured Aleka, "you are almost formidably beautiful, Andrei."

"Has the sun turned blue?" he said. "No, it is divinity in the shape of Aleka Petrovna. Must we go into the sea? It is a pity to spoil the way we look."

"You see?" said Aleka to Kirby. "He is even a coward about getting wet."

She was expressively graceful in the water, her breast stroke fluent and effortless. Kirby was entirely physical, distressing Andrei with his foaming, sea-beating crawl. Andrei himself merely floated on his back.

"Really, my dear chap," he murmured to the sky as Kirby splashed by. Aleka plummeted above him and pushed him under. "Dear God," he gasped on emerging, "the whole sea is ours and three is still a crowd. I'm going to lie on the beach. Ask Ivan to avoid treading on me when he comes out."

She pushed him under again.

"Andrei, are we not to be lovers any more?" she asked.

Andrei spat water.

"That is disgusting," she said, "I don't spit in the sea, why should you?"

"Perhaps when I'm half-drowned I have spit to spare," said Andrei.

"Andrei, speak to me of love," she said, treading water.

"Dearest angel, last night I was exhausted. The tiresome journey, you know."

"Is there another woman, you cad?"

Andrei, drifting languidly on his back again, said, "Darling, what was I to do for nearly a year? A desolate man must be comforted. Where is Ivan?"

"Trying to carve a divide in the Black Sea," she said. "Andrei . . ." She went close to him, he straightened up in alarm and they both trod water. She reached long white arms under the translucent blue. "Andrei . . ."

"By every precious saint," said Andrei faintly, "is this love?"

"Andrei, I am starved, starved, I tell you."

"Well, darling," he said, treading water sensitively, "you're making quite a meal of the first course."

In a flash of temper she pushed him away. She swam. She found Kirby. He too was now floating on the warm, caressing water. Irritably she placed a hand over his face and pushed his head under. The water was suddenly alive and she screamed as she was lifted and tossed. She smacked into the sea. She rose to the surface in a fury, kicking and scratching.

"Swine! How dare you!"

"My mistake," said Kirby, holding her off, "I thought it was a game for two."

She was still in a temper when they returned to the Palace but brightened when she saw there were visitors waiting. There were cries of delight at her appearance. Expansively Aleka invited them all to stay for lunch. It was no more than they expected, anyway. Lunch was noisy, merry and prolonged. The visitors gay and boisterous, restless and insatiable, talked and ate, ate and talked. Aleka's friends were like herself, temperamental, volatile and intensely Russian. Every emotion was uninhibitedly declared, expressed, revealed. They knew of Aleka's political views, they teased her, mocked her, derided her. Aleka herself did not seem to mind that everything she said battered vainly against the opposing flow, was drowned and swept back to die. There was such exhilaration in flinging sarcasm at derision, logic at mockery. She loved every moment. Her dark eyes flashed, she smote the table and broke her wine glass. Kirby watched her. Her pale face glowed, her body vibrated. She revelled in their company, despised their outlook.

Not until a little exhaustion set in among some did others make themselves heard. A young man with a jewelled tiepin and lips as glistening as a woman's said he had never seen a Socialist who did not look like a tram conductor in search of a non-paying passenger.

Aleka eyed him as if he had been born under rotting timber.

"Alexis, foolishness is bad enough, ignorance is worse," she said. "Russia is groaning and what do you do? Plaster ignorance all over your foolishness. Poor Alexis. How does it feel to be unforgivably stupid? Privilege is bleeding the people to death and you're indifferent to it. The Tsar's ministers are either corrupt or incompetent and you're grinning about it. It wouldn't be so bad if grinning suited you, but never have I seen anyone who looks more like a laughing donkey. There, it isn't your fault. You can't help your face and your teeth. If you wish you can leave the table and hide yourself in the cellars. Old Amarov will pour wine over you and you can grin and soak all day."

They laughed at the young man. He grinned the more.

"Come, Aleka Petrovna," said a smiling man, "in Russia it's always as bad as you say but never turns out worse than it was before. It's always an exaggeration."

"When it's not an exaggeration and the people are skinning you with sickles," said Aleka, "you'll all say why didn't someone tell you."

"Darling, you tell me," murmured a blonde woman to Kirby. She was festooned with ropes of pearls and sat next to him. Her features were cosmetically cared for, her eyes speculative and hungry.

"About Russia?" he said. "Alas, as Princess Aleka will tell you, I know so little about my own country that it would be regrettably inappropriate for me to set myself up as an observer of Russia."

"Oh, Aleka Petrovna is vastly amusing," she said, "but there's no need to take her seriously. I am always interested in what the English have to say about us. I have been interested ever since Aleka introduced us before lunch. I shan't mind if you're dreadfully rude about everybody, everyone else is." She went on and became so immersed in the game of claiming his attention that she quite lost the thread of her original

44

gambit and any desire she had to hear opinions that really did not matter. She passed on to the international flavour of Paris which, she declared, was the only capital city in Europe where foreigners felt themselves incipiently at home. Since everyone else seemed to have resumed talking as well Kirby gave up trying to listen to her alone and let the whole become a tableau of mouths that never closed.

It was like that for days.

They bathed in the mornings, they returned to become embroiled in marathon, noisy lunches. The visitors took their carriages back to their own estates late in the afternoon and most of them appeared for dinner at night. The dinners were even more exhilarating than the lunches, excepting only to Kirby and Andrei.

"The trouble with Russians, dear man," said the exhausted Andrei, "is that we're all so infernally egoistic. We're so frightfully Russian."

"Well, perhaps that's better than being frightfully Chinese."

"Are you sure you aren't doing the Chinese an injustice?"

"No, I'm not sure at all."

Kirby wanted to go into Yalta. He asked Karita about the possibility of taking a carriage. Karita passed the request on to old Amarov. Old Amarov asked the Princess. She was still in bed. Kirby was requested to make a personal appearance. Karita took him to Aleka's suite and through to the bedroom. She lay in a bed huge enough to accommodate six voluptuous concubines. His feet sank into the thick pile of a deep red carpet. There were enough slender-backed chairs to suggest she sometimes held court there. She sat up, her silken nightdress off her shoulders, her auburn hair a luxuriant disorder, her face at its palest.

"Why do you want to go into Yalta?" she asked.

"To see friends I know there."

"Can't you invite them here?" She sounded a little annoyed.

"You're kindness itself, Princess, but my friends are

45

workers and couldn't leave their jobs. Is there a carriage I might take?"

"Workers?" She looked at him disbelievingly, while Karita in dutiful attendance by the door looked anywhere but at the Princess. Unconventional though she knew Boyar women were, Karita thought that the Princess, in choosing to appear as if she were emerging nakedly from her nightdress, was going a little too far. The black silk seemed dangerously insecure against the white curving flesh, the wide, ruched neckline with its plunging front loosely low around both arms. But the Englishman did not look embarrassed, only casual as he regarded the Princess with an expression entirely pleasant. "Workers?" she said again. "You have friends among workers in Yalta?"

"At the British consulate," he said. "Princess, you only need to say yes or no. If it's inconvenient——"

"Of course it isn't," she said crossly. He thought she was perhaps liverish. It would not be surprising. "Heavens, it's not a crime to be interested in the movements of one's friends, is it? You aren't going because you're bored here, are you?"

His smile was an immediate denial.

"I haven't been bored at all and I'm certainly not now. Have you been painted in oils lately, Princess? Stay like that and I'll ask Andrei to come in and put you on canvas while I'm in Yalta."

Long lashes lifted. She looked challenging, as if daring him to exercise impropriety, to lower his gaze. Then she said, "Karita is to take a carriage in thirty minutes, she has a free day and is going to see her parents. You can ride with her and then take the carriage on to Yalta. But you're not to forget to return. Ivan, if I thought you really were bored——"

"I'll be back later," he said. He took her hand and kissed it. Aleka made a little face, but was not displeased.

The carriage did not arrive promptly but it was there in the end. Karita, in bright blouse, flowing skirt and linen bonnet, said she would sit up with the groom.

46

Kirby said he would prefer her company himself as the groom had the horses to talk to.

"Monsieur, it's not proper for me to sit with you," she said. She looked remarkably attractive.

"Well, let's be improper for once, no one will notice," said Kirby.

Her smile came, brightening her golden face. She sat up with him, her back very straight, her attitude as proper as it could be under the circumstances. He talked to her, asked her about her parents. She said her father farmed the land and her mother was very wise. She always went to see them when she had a free day.

She alighted when they had gone three miles. She thanked Kirby, said goodbye to the groom, and Kirby watched her turn off the road into a narrow lane, flanked on both sides by rolling carpets of colour. He saw the white rooftops of the village of Karka in the distance, where Karita's parents lived. She turned and waved. She looked as colourful as the landscapes.

Yalta was balmy with autumnal warmth. Holiday Russians were strolling and shopping. Kirby stepped out and asked the groom to return with the carriage in a couple of hours. He sauntered in the sunshine, the town brown and mellow. The atmosphere was one of peace, although in St. Petersburg there was another minor crisis and there had been unrest in the Urals. He had coffee, black and strong and sweet. He felt a sense of freedom. Princess Aleka did not make friends, she possessed them. In his meandering abstraction, he almost collided with a rather dumpy woman as she emerged from a shop. She stepping hastily back, dropped her folded parasol. He picked it up and offered it to her with apologies for his clumsiness. As he did so a slender woman, accompanied by a girl in summery white, also emerged from the shop. She looked at Kirby, at the woman he had brushed, and said in enquiry, "Anna?"

"Oh, it's nothing." The woman Anna, pleasant-faced,

smiled away any suggestion of importunity on the part of Kirby.

"Only that I was clumsy," he said in his faultless Russian. "I am terribly sorry, madam."

"Really, it was nothing," she said again, taking the parasol and shaking it out.

He felt a peculiar consciousness of the familiar. He turned his head and looked into blue eyes regarding him in curiosity. Immediately her shyness rushed into pink, startled recognition. Her chestnut-gold hair was a profusion beneath her white, ribboned bonnet, her youth an almost absurd enchantment to him. Their glances touched, held and were broken. She dropped her eyes at his ghost of a smile and went on her way with the slender woman and the dumpy one, parasols opening, swirling and perching. The girl seemed to float, her white dress a whispering caress.

He went on his own way and took with him a new image of a girl as sweet as dawn itself. He entered a building and found the offices he wanted. He went in. A clerk looked up. He asked for Mr. Anstruther, a consular representative of His Britannic Majesty. Mr. Anstruther came out. He was middle-aged and fatherly.

"Oh, yes," he said, seeing Kirby, "come through, will you?"

His office was brown. Brown leather chairs, ancient brown desk and mahogany paintwork. The curtains were of brown velvet and wooden filing cabinets stained brown. And Anstruther himself was brown.

"I was expecting you two days ago," he said, indicating a chair. Kirby sat down. "I hope nothing cropped up."

"It was only that I came under the ownership of Aleka Petrovna, the Princess Karinshka," said Kirby.

"Oh?" said Anstruther, looking interested.

"It took a few days to free myself. To have come before would have looked impolite."

"To whom?" Anstruther was slightly sarcastic.

"I understand your impatience."

48

"Not impatience, Mr. Kirby," said Anstruther mildly, "we can always wait as long as we're put in the picture. Worry is the word when we aren't. However, you're here. Have you got what you promised?"

"Yes," said Kirby. He brought out the wafer-thin rice papers that had lain within the cavity of his hairbrush and laid them on the table. "The information covers location of plants, factories, depots and so on. There are calculated yearly outputs, estimated stocks, types of armament, factors of obsolescence and everything else I could get. My estimation is that they're short of every essential, particularly ammunition. They could fight a war on manpower alone but how the devil they could successfully take on a major power I don't know. By the way, it cost me a dickens of a lot to get certain of the information. That's been included in the report and perhaps you'll have it credited to my account at Coutts'."

Carefully Anstruther studied the papers. Figures were construable but all else was in code. He looked up, his expression cautiously agreeable.

"Major power? Mmmm," he said, "you must have sensed the situation is changing. Rapidly. We don't anticipate being in dispute with Russia in the foreseeable future. Russia in the foreseeable future is more likely to be an ally. Either way, however, these figures should be invaluable. How reliable are they?"

"Only as much as I am. How reliable is that in the minds of our masters?"

"I hope you're being facetious," said Anstruther. He put the papers into an envelope, slid the envelope into a drawer and locked it. "You know, with the way things are going at the moment, if there is a war it could only be with Germany."

"Is that reliable?" asked Kirby.

"We think so."

"Russia," said Kirby, "is opposed in all things to Germany. It's traditional and it's incurable."

"Is it?" Anstruther stroked his chin. "There is the Tsarina to be reckoned with. An extremely good and religious woman, I believe, but German and with her own ways of influencing the Tsar. However, much as the Kaiser seeks to foster a closer personal relationship with the Tsar, Nicholas will never forgive him the fiasco of the Bjorko treaty. The Kaiser browbeat Nicholas into it and made them both look fools. It ran counter to the Russian alliance with France."

"And Willy and Nicholas have since cooled off?"

"Considerably. The Kaiser still tries but Nicholas manages to stand aloof when they meet. He does it most agreeably." Anstruther got up and walked about. "But things are changing every day. You know, everything that can be done to make your figures look vastly better than you suggest would almost certainly coincide with the official line now."

"Well, will you add a few noughts or shall I?"

"I mean," said Anstruther testily, "we'd approve an increased Russian output."

"You'd better talk to the Tsar about that," said Kirby. "I'd like a holiday myself. I've poked my nose into so many places these last three years that all I want for the next three is to mind my own business."

Anstruther permitted himself a brown, fatherly smile. He looked at Kirby, comfortably at ease in his chair. That was the man's *forte*, his ability to be at ease, to make friends and invite confidences. He was a better observer of a country than the finest official ambassador. He was invaluable in Russia.

"Well, your time is your own for the moment. We might get you back to England for a vacation if you like."

Kirby mused on that, then said, "Thanks all the same but no, not yet."

"You mentioned—let me see, who was it now? Princess Karinshka? Mmmm, I think we've got a file on her."

"On Princess Karinshka?"

"Let me see." Anstruther unlocked a cabinet, extracted a file, returned to his desk. He opened the file, perused a few entries. He looked up. "Did you know she's a Socialist?"

"She says she is. She doesn't live like one."

"That's not uncommon. Convert her," said Anstruther briskly, "a revolution in Russia would be no help to any of us at the moment."

"Except to the people. Well, except to some of the people."

Anstruther brushed that aside.

"One revolutionary aristocrat is worth ten thousand conventional revolutionaries in a country like this. It might only mean containing her particular pocket of trouble, but I'm sure you'll do your best. We'll leave it to you."

"Princess Karinshka could eat me," said Kirby, "so I'll leave it to you. I'm going to take that holiday. If you want me for anything really important, I'm staying at the Karinshka Palace. I don't know for how long. She's not a woman who can put up with the same faces indefinitely." He got to his feet.

"I'll get your report sent," said Anstruther, "and let you know sometime what they think of it."

"If they want to show enormous gratitude," said Kirby, "tell them to make me a lord. It will please a friend of mine and make me look more proper to her."

He got back to Karinshka quite late. He wandered with the groom around Crimean villages, intensely interested in the Tartar people and all the bargains they had to offer him. He accepted a great deal of hospitality, drinking their black coffee and their Tartar liqueurs. The groom, a Tartar himself, drove the carriage in lazy happiness, stopping whenever Kirby wished and joining the bargaining, the drinking and the establishing of friendship. He did not drink much coffee, however, he opted for something more infectiously convivial. He was singing when they arrived at Karinshka. Old Amarov kicked him all the way to the stables for being drunk.

The sky was purple, the descending sun slashing

the colour over the horizon. Karita appeared when Kirby reached the door of his suite and followed him in.

"It's not my place to say so, monsieur," she said, "but her Highness is dreadfully put out."

How quaint she was. He was warm with *bonhomie*.

"Is she?" he said. "What has Andrei Mikhailovich done now?"

"It isn't Count Purishkin, monsieur," said Karita, her brown eyes slightly reproving. "Who could be put out by so inoffensive a gentleman as he is?"

"Her Highness, perhaps?"

"Indeed no, monsieur, never. Well, almost never. It is you. You have been gone all day. You see, she is so sensitive. She thinks you must be bored here. Monsieur, are you?" She seemed touchingly anxious to hear that he wasn't.

"Never, little one."

"I am so glad. Monsieur, you must be ready by nine or she will not permit you to dine with her."

"Dear me," he said. "Well, never mind. You can bring me something up on a tray. If her Highness is having her usual visitors she won't miss me."

"Monsieur!" Karita was aghast. "She would kill us both."

"I must save you from that," he said. "I'll get ready, then. Did you enjoy seeing your parents?"

"Oh, yes." She looked pleased at his interest. "I spoke to my mother of you. It was because you're English and I wanted to tell her you didn't go around fighting everyone."

"I didn't realise she suffered such anxieties about us," he said. "I hope she believed you."

"Monsieur," said Karita, "you tease me dreadfully. But see, my mother has given me an ikon for you." She slipped a hand into the pocket of her dress beneath her white front and brought out a tiny bas-relief of polished wood. "She said it would bring you closer to God."

"Oh, she thought I was a heathen too, did she?"

"She didn't say so, only that she would like you to have it. Of course, if you don't wish it——"

"I wish it very much," he said. He studied the ikon, carved to delineate the head of the Virgin Mary. "I will value it very much. Thank your mother for me. And thank you, Karita."

He bent and kissed her. Karita felt the momentary pressure of warm, firm lips and then an intensely disconcerting confusion. She looked up at him, her face hot. She saw laughter but kindness too, and affection.

"Oh, goodness," she said, then the door opened to a knock and Princess Aleka swept in. She was gowned in deep green, her auburn hair brilliant, her jewels a radiance.

"Ivan, you utterly deplorable man," she cried, "where have you been? Andrei and I have been off our heads about you."

"I'm sorry I'm so late——"

"Yes, old Amarov told me how drunk the groom was. You aren't drunk too, I hope. No. How nice to have a friend who can drink in a hundred villages and still remain sober. But we thought we had lost you. Andrei said you had probably gone walking from Yalta to Kerch, it's only a hundred and fifty miles." She was apparently not a bit put out, she was in her most vivacious mood. He glanced at Karita, edging her way towards the bedroom, intent on running his bath. Karita gave a very expressive shrug. It clearly said that she could not understand her Highness any more than he could. "Ivan," Aleka went on, "I'm sorry but it will be quiet tonight. There will be none of our friends to dinner, I have had to put them all off. It is Andrei's fault. Can you imagine it, he said I am turning Karinshka into a zoo and that if I didn't give him a rest from the monkey house tonight he would hang himself! Oh yes, you can smile, but Andrei is like that. You simply could not trust him not to hang himself if he could find someone to knot the rope. So I have invited no one to dine with us. I hope you will be able to bear the awful silence. How nice that you're back in time to join Andrei and me. You and I must talk him into realising that a monkey house is far more entertaining than a cemetery. Do you know, he said he would always prefer a cemetery as long as there were dancing girls around and their *embonpoint* was sufficiently diverting. Yes, that is the ridiculous kind of man he is."

"Voluptuousness in a cemetery would be diverting," observed Kirby.

"There is no need for you to be ridiculous too," she said, but she was laughing. "Ivan, what is that you have?" He showed her the ikon, she regarded it in light curiosity, her bosom a warm fullness seeking to escape from the half-hearted embrace of her bodice. "Did you buy this in Yalta?"

"It was given to me by a friend."

"Oh?" Her dark eyes danced. "So, you have a friend in Yalta who cares for your spiritual graces? It's a Crimean ikon, so you have a Crimean sweetheart. Invite her, she shall stay with us. You'll be late for dinner if you don't hurry." She turned as Karita came to say his bath was ready. "Heavens, you grow prettier every day, child. Oravio is the luckiest of men."

She glided out in a shimmer of green.

"Karita," said Kirby, slipping off his jacket and undoing his tie, "I thought you said she was displeased with me."

"Monsieur, truly, she is up and down, down and up. It can be very confusing."

"Well, she is up now. Who is Oravio?"

"Oh, he is one of the footmen, we are supposed to have an arrangement. It is all only perhaps."

"Well," said Princess Aleka to Oravio a few minutes before she went down to dinner, "where did he go?"

"To Yalta, to the British consulate there," said

54

Oravio. "Then he seemed to wander all over the Crimea, doing nothing except talk to people and drink with them. It was a good day for him, it was execrable for me. Only for the party would I spend all day following a long-legged Englishman."

"He met no one of importance?"

"I don't know who he saw at his consulate. Elsewhere he met only peasants." Oravio was darkly contemptuous, and not of Kirby alone it seemed. Aleka's mouth tightened for a moment in anger.

"Be careful how you talk to me," she said.

"Yes, Highness. Always, Highness." His voice was a sneer, his bow an impertinence.

Andrei liked to be entertained. But he did not consider Aleka's dinner parties entertaining at all. They sapped his powers of endurance. Aleka in the past had never been as restless as this, wanting always to have people and noise around her. It was a concession indeed to have dinner proceed in civilised quietness that evening, but Andrei suspected the respite to be extremely temporary. Something must be done to enable placid life to pour back into him. He must go to his own estate for a few days. He could not take Kirby. Aleka would never stand to be robbed of both guests. It would not matter to Kirby. He could manage admirably, being a man of adaptability.

The next day Andrei spoke on the telephone to Gregory, his secretary. It was, he said afterwards to Aleka, the most damnable thing, but there was a crisis on his estate and Gregory had implored him to go there for a few days. Aleka said it was more than damnable, it was a Machiavellian ruse to go off and consort with one of his aristocratic whores. Andrei declared he had an undying love for her alone, begged her understanding of circumstances beyond his control and slipped away. She was furious.

"What about Livadia?" she shouted after him as he hurried down the steps to the waiting carriage.

"Perhaps, perhaps, but if not, beg their Highnesses to accept Ivan in my place," he called.

Aleka, absolutely livid for a while, almost had a standup fight with old Amarov. He gave her his notice. She accepted it but an hour later implored him to rescind it.

"It's impossible, old one," she said, "why, without you Karinshka would fall to the ground. Who else can I trust when I'm not here? Who else but you could command the servants? Look, I am on my knees. Stay, old ram, you shall have a horse of your very own. See, here are my tears as witness of all that you mean to us."

Old Amarov peered. He saw soft, cajoling brightness but no tears. However, the last thing to trust in any woman were tears.

"Your Highness, everything is as it was and there's no need to give me a horse."

"I insist. It's yours, old faithful. Bring me some tea and I'll know all is well between us again. And tell Monsieur Kirby to join me. He's hiding away somewhere. I don't know why it is, old Amarov, but some men have a damned indecent aptitude for avoiding a woman when she is most in need."

"What are you in need of, Highness?"

"I don't know," she said. "Tea at the moment, I suppose."

"Ivan Ivanovich." She had just arrived on the terrace to find him stretched out on a long cane chair, reading a book he had borrowed from her library. The sea lay like a placid blue lake in the distance, the air was lazily warming. He was a deep, even brown, the flecks of gold in his beard intensified by the sun. She looked broodingly at him.

"Princess?"

"Talk to me," she said, lowering her white-clad body on to an adjacent chair.

"How peaceful it is," he said.

"God," she said, "that's brilliant, isn't it? What's

the matter with you? Don't you like women? Don't you like me?"

He had liked a number of women, had thought he loved more than one of them. He could not remember why. The only clear picture he had in his mind these days was the face of an enchanting girl.

"You aren't serious, are you?" he said.

"Of course I damn well am," said Aleka.

"Then I love you," he said,

"Must you be an echo of Andrei? Andrei is always declaring his devotion and backing away from it. You would do the same. It's not necessary to love me, you know, only to like me. Ivan, put that book down. Look at me."

He looked at her. Her dark eyes were soft. Her white dress, high-waisted, gave her an unusual air of virginal charm. White was the purest and yet the most illusory of colours.

"You're excessively beautiful," he said.

"Do you know," she said, "I have the strangest feeling that although you're saying that to me you're thinking of someone else. Is it the God-fearing woman who gave you that ikon? Do you want to go and join Andrei on his estate? You can be quite frank, I shan't lose my temper."

"My dear Princess, I like it here," he said in relaxed satisfaction. "There's everything to do or there's nothing to do, and you don't mind either way. Who could be a more agreeable hostess than that? Is there something perhaps that you would like to do?"

"Yes," she said, "let's go down to the beach."

They went. They bathed. Aleka loved the water, its warm embrace dispelled her resentment of Andrei's desertion. Once immersed she was active and sinuous, her cotton costume clinging to her, wetly sheathing her curving body as she swam. Her blue-capped head rose above the water, her eyes as mischievous as a child's as Kirby came close. She jack-knifed and dived under him. She glided beneath him, came to the surface, rolled on to her back and kicked water.

57

"Ivan," she called. He swam around her, Aleka a figure of buoyancy, her breasts a convex of wet, glistening blue. "Love me," she laughed.

"Here? Impossible," he said.

She flirted water into his face.

"Well, kiss me at least," she said. He stood, his feet touching bottom, as she floated. He kissed her. As his mouth pressed down on hers she sank. She came up gasping and outraged. "Oh, animal!" she cried.

"What is my wet lady's wish then? Shall you sink again or swim?"

Sometimes, she thought, his eyes were damnably devilish, and he was always so good-humoured he was almost complacent. She floated again, looking up at him. His brown beard was wet, his teeth white in the sun.

"I think," she murmured, "I think I'll risk being sunk again. But please, Ivan, more gently this time."

The water was so caressing. She lay passively upon it. He bent above her, her expression mocking, provoking, her mouth wet from the sea. There was the faintest smile on Kirby's face. Her lips pursed. He kissed her again, gently, his mouth moving over hers. Her white legs stirred, rippling the water. Her arms reached up, wound around his neck. His mouth was warm, vibrant. It pressed. She sank, unwinding her arms to beat wildly at the enclosing water. She re-emerged in a fountainous flurry.

She gasped and coughed up salt sea.

"Ivan! You pig! Am I to be drowned by a kiss?"

He was laughing. She stretched her legs, linked them around his beneath the surface and heaved her body to pull him from his feet. He went backwards amid splashing, tumbling water. They both bobbed upwards. He was still laughing. Aleka burst into laughter of her own.

"Ivan, I love you." It was entirely playful. "Oh, what fun you are. There's nothing one can do with Andrei, but you and I can be children again. Who is to care? Kiss me."

"Is that being children?" he asked.

"But of course. Children kiss. Haven't you seen them? If it weren't for ridiculous and interfering adults, some of them would make love too."

They stood together, the water lapping their backs. She pressed close. He put his mouth to hers, their costumes merged wetly, revealingly. Spitefully, shrewishly, her fingers dug into his back and her nails raked his flesh through the cotton. He shuddered from the unexpected pain of it. He stooped, lifted her and flung her from him. She came up breathless, rageful.

"Ivan!" She trod water furiously. "Ivan, you pig of an Englishman!"

"What fun," said the pig of an Englishman.

Aleka laughed until the tears ran. They stayed long in the water, as active as porpoises until Aleka was tingling and exhausted. "There, aren't the real pleasures of life the simplest things?" she said on the way back to the Palace.

"Like drawing blood, you mean?"

"You deserved that," she said. "All God gave women to defend themselves were claws. Most women are afraid to use them but I'm not. Ivan, you don't dislike me, after all, do you?"

He was quite astonished. He said, "Dislike you? Princess, what have I ever said to make you think that?"

"Well," she said, "you are damnably stiff the way you will call me 'Princess.' I am Aleka Petrovna to my friends. Ivan, we are to be friends, aren't we?"

On either side of the winding ascent wild roses danced in the sun, nature was a fragrance and Russia seemed at eternal peace.

"That," said Kirby, "is a lovely thought, Aleka Petrovna."

"Who is the woman who gave you that ikon?"

"Someone's mother," he said.

"Ah," she mused, "is it the someone or is it the mother you have designs on? She had better be more than a promiscuous peasant. I don't like to lose my friends to women I don't approve of. I hate every one

59

of Andrei's women. Ivan, I forgot!" She was dramatic in her suddenness. "You are to meet the Tsar and Tsarina. Imagine that I didn't tell you. It is Andrei's fault. I have an invitation for Andrei and myself, there's to be a ball at Livadia in honour of Grand Duchess Olga Nicolaievna. It's her birthday. Although I'm not quite in favour from time to time because of my politics, I'm in favour at the moment. You see, I made myself pleasant to the Empress years ago. I was pleasant because so many others weren't. She's German, you know. But she's the kindest of persons and has always remembered that I was kind to her . . ."

"Can I interrupt?" said Kirby. "What's all this to do with me? How am I to meet their Imperial Highnesses?"

"But I've told you," she said. "Andrei has deserted me and I wouldn't let him escort me even if he were back in time. I telephoned the Empress this morning and explained that as Andrei Mikhailovich is suffering from nervous exhaustion I should like to have you escort me instead. She was very sweet and so you are invited in place of Andrei. It will be very magnificent but criminally sumptuous considering there are so many people who can't even get enough bread to eat. But I suppose if the Grand Duchess Olga can't have a birthday ball things would be sad indeed. What am I saying? They are sad. They are worse than sad. Ivan, we will go to the ball and you can help me convert the Tsar to democracy. Ivan, are you listening?"

THREE

Two nights later they went to Livadia, their carriage one of a multitude drawn up outside the steps of the Imperial Palace. Kirby had thought Karinshka Palace imposing. Livadia was breathtaking. Built of white limestone it overlooked the Black Sea and was a majestic example of man's genius for complementing nature. It was the constant joy of Empress Alexandra Fedorovna and she and Nicholas, Emperor of All the Russias, were never happier than when they were there. Tonight, to celebrate the sixteenth birthday of their eldest daughter, Grand Duchess Olga, their Imperial Majesties were giving a full-dress ball.

Caught up in the queue, it took time for Princess Aleka's carriage to reach the steps. Kirby spent the waiting period gazing entranced at the Palace. It was ablaze with lights, yet with its brilliance softly diffused in the evening light. There were columned balconies, cloistered walks and gardens of colour and magic. The air was heady with the scent of roses.

"Magnificent," he said.

"It's only another palace," said Aleka, magnificent herself in a tiara. She sat close to him in the carriage, the warmth of her body an allurement. "And it will be full of bores stuffed into uniforms and old harridans stuffed into corsets. Ivan, think of the poor and the starving. Then this will seem what it really is, an unforgivable extravagance."

"I thought of the poor and the starving when you gave your first dinner party," he said.

"You unspeakable cad," she said.

"Dear Aleka," he said placatingly.

At last they went in, gowned women and uniformed men preceding them, others following on as each carriage disgorged its occupants. Kirby felt himself caught in an immensity of glittering splendour. He smiled as by his side he heard Aleka humming the waltz from Tchaikovsky's *Sleeping Beauty*. Her cloak was taken, her pale golden gown bared her shoulders but for once her bosom was not threatening to escape. She knew the Empress well. Alexandra Fedorovna did not approve obtrusive exposure. Kirby, in black tails, was content to be effaced by her brilliance, her jewelled tiara an emblem of her rank, setting her glossy auburn hair on fire.

Karita had been overwhelmed with pleasure that he was to attend so splendid a ball, and she had seen to it that he had looked his best. But as for the implications of full dress, he could do no better than wear his tails. There were few men who were not richly ceremonial in their attire. White jackets hung with medals, honours and awards predominated. Well, he could not help that. He had nothing to hang. He hoped he would not look naked.

They were announced. Princess Aleka was well known. Palely, glitteringly she advanced, coolly enjoying being looked at. Already the state room was alive with people, the light of huge chandeliers reflected by the jewels of the women. With Kirby at her elbow Princess Aleka was received by their Imperial Majesties.

Nicholas was in uniform, decorations colourful, Imperial star resplendent. Aleka curtseyed, he took her hand, he smiled and spoke to her.

Between the Tsar and Tsarina stood a girl, a girl with the bluest of eyes, and with chestnut-gold hair

62

dressed high and lightly caressed by a sparkling tiara. Her gown was a flowing enchantment of coral pink. She was looking not at Aleka Petrovna but at the Princess's escort, a tall man with a gold-flecked beard and wide, deeply-grey eyes, a man who, in Western-styled evening tails, was so different from all the other men there. She came to as Aleka smiled at her, curtseyed to her and congratulated her.

Kirby bowed to the Tsar. Nicholas was not a tall man, but he was handsome, his beard giving him a similarity to his cousin, King George V of England. He had a simple, easy dignity and as he smiled he seemed to radiate genuine welcome and pleasure.

"It is good to see you, Mr. Kirby," he said in English, "for we have only the warmest memories of your country. If you don't enjoy the evening I don't know what my daughter will say. Will you give her your kindest wishes?"

"Willingly, your Imperial Highness, and thank you for the privilege of being able to do so."

He moved on and there she was, the Grand Duchess Olga Nicolaievna, sixteen and unbelievably sweet. He could not for the moment check the shock of surprise. Their little secret was in her eyes. She was the eldest daughter of the Tsar, yet for all that was breathlessly shy. She gave him her hand, he saw the bright ring worn over the gloved finger and he put his lips to it.

"Highness, I did not know it was you I saw," he said in Russian, "but now that I do, forgive me and let me wish you the happiest of birthdays."

"Forgive you?" Her voice soft and warm. "Oh no, it wasn't like that."

The Tsarina, who had received Aleka, glanced at her daughter and saw the flush on her face. There were other guests waiting and there was little time to give any of them more than a few brief words. Kirby moved to bow to Alexandra and to take the hand she extended.

Alexandra was a slender, beautiful woman, but she did not have it in her to dazzle her court, to establish

63

herself as a gay and evocative Empress. She was fervently religious, and had a mystique that made people think her remote and unapproachable.

Kirby, however, received no such impression now. He was conscious only of the kindest of smiles, even of warm responsiveness to his words of thanks.

"Why, Mr. Kirby," she said, speaking in English as Nicholas had, "we are delighted to meet you. If Russia has my love, England has more than a small part of my heart."

It was in England that she and Nicholas had spent their most idyllic days before they were married.

"Mama," broke in Olga, "he is English? I did not really catch his name."

"He is an English Ivan," said Princess Aleka, "and is the most terrible of men, dearest Olga. Have nothing whatever to do with him."

Blue eyes sought his, earnestly curious to discover whether signs of formidable failings were visible. He shook his head, smiling. In return she gave him her own shy smile to let him know she was sure he was not as terrible as that. He would have moved away with Aleka then but the Empress detained him. He had yet to discover that if Olga was endearingly shy, Alexandra was painfully so. It was something that made all state occasions, even this one, an ordeal. But she put her question.

"Mr. Kirby, where is your home in England?"

"By the river, your Highness. A place called Walton-on-Thames."

Alexandra shed her restraint, or rather, it slipped away to leave her in glowing pleasure.

"But that is where the Emperor and I—Mr. Kirby, I must find time to talk to you, perhaps."

"I should like that very much," he said simply.

She nodded, her eyes warm, and he withdrew to take the arm of the highly intrigued Aleka.

It did not help Alexandra to know that most eyes were on her and not on her daughter. It was always the same. Shyness not being a characteristic of the

Russians, there were few who understood how Alexandra suffered. Her inability to relax was construed as a Germanic restraint towards them. But nothing could have been farther from the truth. Alexandra had a great love for her adopted country and little love at all for Prussian Germany—she considered herself more English than German. Her mother had been Princess Alice, daughter of Queen Victoria, her language was English and England itself was her land of romance. She loved her husband passionately and adored her five children. Fundamentally she was honest and sincere, but it was a pity she was not the cleverest of Empresses instead of the most devout. Religion was her strength and her weakness.

With her spiritual fortitude and a courage that was the hallmark of the Hesse family she fought her public nervousness and every cruel turn of fortune's wheel. She did not consider herself the granddaughter of Queen Victoria for nothing. She faced up to the realisation that her only son, Alexis, was a haemophiliac, and on his behalf she put her trust in God and in that strange "holy man," Rasputin.

"Well?" whispered Aleka, her paleness tinted by an excitement she would have disowned if questioned.

"They could not have been kinder," said Kirby.

"That's not exactly an inspired comment. Can't you do better than that?"

"I'm reserving judgement. What do you feel about them, Aleka? They belong more to you than to me."

"I feel I can't be sentimental," she murmured, "that's too expensive a luxury in Russia today."

The state dining hall was a kaleidoscope of moving colour when the reception at last finished. Huge glass doors were opened and any guests who wished were free to wander in the gardens or view the majesty of Livadia from balconies. They could watch the sun setting in crimson glory over the Black Sea or later the rise of the autumn moon in silver radiance. There was a cotillion supper to enable guests to be served anytime during the dancing.

65

The dancing would go on until the small hours. Princess Aleka, now that she was here, had obviously decided not to let her principles interfere with her capacity for enjoying herself. This included exercises in the art of tormenting stuffed bores. They came her way soon enough, surrounding her, flattering her and eyeing her cleavage. They requested the privilege of her ball card. Aleka flirted with them, mocked them, denied them. Presented to her, wives or female companions returned her malicious smiles with chilling sweetness. Aleka refused to be chilled.

Kirby, quiet in dress and manner, was introduced by Aleka. The women, deep-bosomed, glittering with diamonds or sapphires or rubies, were not disinterested. The men, impeccably correct, were courteous but brief. They were single-minded in their pursuit of Aleka. She shrugged and made her ball card available. With her fan she tapped restrainingly at the hand of every man wishful to sign for more than one dance.

"I can't show favouritism, dear man," she said to a monocled officer, "or I myself will feel responsible when the others take you out and shoot you."

"Ah," he said, "the sublimity of such a death in such a cause."

"The man's a perfect fool," said Aleka, watching him return to his fuming wife. Her foot began to tap as the state orchestra began the opening bars of the first dance. "Oh, for God's sake, Ivan, don't act as if this is the first time you've been in a menagerie. You look like the man who is seeing his first elephant. Are you going to be dull all night? You let all those dressed-up apes breathe all over me and sign my card. Are you not going to dance with me yourself?"

He had been watching Grand Duchess Olga opening her ball in the arms of a young officer from the Tsar's suite. Graceful in her pink, regal in her tiara, there was still the shyness of a girl knowing a thousand eyes were on her.

"Princess, may I?" he said and took her card.

66

"I've left three dances for you," she said, pointing with her fan.

"That's favouritism, isn't it?"

"They won't shoot you. They can't have a diplomatic incident in front of the Tsar himself. Ivan, will you please wake up? You've signed for the first dance. I'm here. Don't you want the extravagant bliss of holding me?"

"I rather fancy that kind of sublimity. Princess, my arm."

They danced. Her dark eyes glowed, drawing his. Her smile was caressing, if a little shy. He enjoyed it all. All her facets were intriguing. Yet his sense of pleasure was not only because of Aleka. For the Tsar's daughter had caught his glance. She smiled. He felt the strangest and most sudden of emotions. It was as if his heart had turned over.

"Ivan?"

"Princess?"

"There you go again. Ivan, if you are looking at some other woman——"

"I'm immersed in extravagant bliss, dear one."

"Liar." But she laughed softly, circling, one hand on her lifted gown, the other on his shoulder. "Do you know, you're considerably good-looking tonight. And you're not in uniform, thank God. You need not stand about while I'm dancing with other men. You may present yourself to any of the women I've introduced you to. They'll be delighted to dance with you. Ivan, is there one you already have your eyes on? You are indecently far away."

"I'm not far away. I'm dancing with you," he murmured. "You're the most beautiful woman here. I shall almost certainly be shot."

"Darling," she breathed, "a compliment at last. Not an echo of Andrei. It would be delicious if you could pant a little over me. People are wondering who you are and if I'm in love with you. Who could think we were just good friends? That's not a bit exciting."

"Dearest Aleka," he said, "you are the loveliest of

women, the most imaginative of friends. Andrei will be sorry he missed this."

"Andrei," she said, "is deplorably inert, even at the gayest of balls. Even our Grand Duchess's sixteenth birthday could not tempt him. He is a man for the intimacy of a boudoir, not a ballroom. He's with some disgusting woman now."

"And I am here," said Kirby. "Thank you, Aleka Petrovna."

"Oh?" she said, curious because he sounded so earnest. It was not like Ivan Ivanovich. He was not to be taken seriously most of the time.

Afterwards Aleka danced with other men. He signed the cards of two or three other women. They were intrigued by his Englishness and his distinctive air of ease. They were willing to flirt outrageously with him. He responded but did not seek them out once he had danced with them. It was while he was watching Aleka in whirling movement with a Cossack officer that he was approached by an exquisitely uniformed personage whom he took to be a member of the Imperial suite.

"Her Imperial Highness presents her compliments, monsieur, and asks that if it is convenient she would like to see you."

He accompanied the man. The Tsar and Tsarina were seated in red and gold chairs at the far end, viewing the dancers with interest and pleasure. He bowed to the Tsarina. Alexandra smiled.

"Perhaps we might talk now, Mr. Kirby?" she said. She indicated a chair close to her own and he sat down. "Are you enjoying yourself?" Again she spoke in English. Her Russian was only moderate and all her family conversed mainly in English. She and Nicholas also used this language in their letters to each other. It was, to Alexandra, the language of her mother, of poets, of love.

"I'm enjoying myself immensely, Highness, and can't thank you enough for my being here," he said warmly. "I've heard of the Livadia Palace but I had no idea it was as beautiful as this."

It was not politeness, it was sincerity. Alexandra smiled again.

"I'm so glad you think that. It is beautiful, isn't it? We are blessed by Livadia. Nicholas?" She leaned towards Nicholas, who was lighting his inveterate cigarette. He was a compulsive smoker. "Here is Mr. Kirby from England, whose home is at Walton-on-Thames."

The Tsar's handsome face lit up. His smile was a warmth, a cordiality.

"My dear fellow," he said, "that is splendid. There's no place we speak of more often or with more affection."

"Has it changed at all, is it just the same?" asked Alexandra. Her red-gold hair was as thickly luxuriant as Aleka's. She was thirty-nine and as graceful as Olga at sixteen. "It's seventeen years since we were there, but I should like to think it's still as we remember it."

"I'm sure it is," said Kirby. "It never changes much, although I haven't seen it for three years myself. I've been in Russia."

"For three years?" Her interest deepened. "How much have you seen of our country, how much have you learned about it?"

"Your Highness, I've seen some of its infinite variations but I don't think I've learned anything. Except the extent of my own limitations. In Russia I only look and wonder." He felt self-distaste. The Empress was absorbed, Nicholas smiling and nodding. "Perhaps," he went on, "I've learned one thing. There are no people more friendly or more hospitable. I've travelled for three years and never wanted for anything. The poorest man will share his bread with you."

"Yes, the poor are with us," observed the Tsar, "but give us time."

"Imperial Highness," said Kirby, "I put that badly. I did not mean——"

69

"I know you didn't, my dear chap," said Nicholas, smiling, "but they are still there and it would only count against us if they couldn't be mentioned. I'm not sensitive on the subject, only concerned that we can't make it less of a problem overnight."

"It's with us in England too," said Kirby.

"Who are your family?" asked Alexandra. She did not put the question because of any social implications, only out of interest. She was charmed by the Englishman, delighted that she felt no restraint with him. That alone was a sweet pleasure to Alexandra, to be at ease with a comparative stranger.

"My father served in the British Army," said Kirby. "He was killed during the Boer War and my mother died soon afterwards. But I have an aunt who is very dear to me."

"I am so sorry about your parents," she said, "but very glad about your aunt. Tell me about your place in Walton."

"I own a small Georgian cottage there, its garden runs down to the river. It's misty in winter and beautiful in summer. It has an apple tree, of course, and the grass is very green, but the landing steps are always slippery and I have been known to bathe when actually dressed for tennis."

For a moment the Imperial couple were caught out. Then Alexandra let a little laugh of delight escape her and Nicholas followed.

"Oh, my dear fellow," he said, "that is the funniest thing."

The noise and rhythm of the dancers were something apart at that moment. They were sharing laughter. And people who were always more interested in the Imperial family than anything else looked on in curiosity, wondering what the Englishman had said so to amuse the Tsar and Tsarina.

"Nicky," said Alexandra, "I think Mr. Kirby is endeavouring to entertain us."

"Truthfully, Highness, it did happen once," said Kirby.

"Well, whether it did or didn't," said Nicholas, "I'm a great believer in tennis as a pastime, and if I had to fall off some landing steps I should probably be dressed for tennis too. We must have a game sometime, my dear chap."

"Well, whatever happens there, Walton is the loveliest place," murmured Alexandra reminiscently. "Mr. Kirby, this is our eldest daughter's sixteenth birthday. She is engaged to dance most of the evening with our young officers, but if you'd be excessively kind how nice it would be if for one dance at least England and Russia went hand-in-hand. I am sure she would like that very much."

It was neither a command nor a condescension, only a request that he might make his own contribution to the success of Olga's ball. The compliment astonished him. But it had been Olga herself who, fifteen minutes ago, had spoken to her mother.

"Mama, it is all tremendously exciting and my feet have left the floor a dozen times." Then casually, as she fanned herself, "Do you think I might dance with the Englishman, Mr. Kirby? It's only that I'd like to talk to him about Walton in England, where you and Papa were so happy, and to tell him it was Anna he bumped into the other day in Yalta."

"Oh yes, now I remember, he was the man," said Alexandra. "I thought I'd seen him before. What a curious coincidence. Darling, this is your own ball, your own birthday, and you may ask for anything you want. I will arrange it, I'm sure Mr. Kirby won't refuse."

"Mama," said Olga, who was not without wit inside her own circle, "he cannot refuse. I am a Grand Duchess."

"Oh, my sweet," said Alexandra in a rush of warm pride and affection, "you are more, much more. Isn't she, Nicky?"

"She's beautiful," said Nicholas, regarding his enchanting first-born smilingly, and Olga swept him a curtsey.

Kirby was still sitting beside Alexandra when Olga returned from a gay cotillion. She came in a rustle of silks and satins on the arm of her partner, an officer in full-dress blues, who bowed as he returned her to her parents. The flush on her face was of unusual excitement. Quiet and reserved, Olga took life in, loved it, but kept her joys, her delights and her curiosity shyly to herself. She sank into the chair between her parents, glanced at Kirby, who had risen, and glanced away.

"Your Highness?" He stood before her. She knew why. Her mother had spoken to him. Suddenly it was no longer an impulsive birthday wish that she might dance with him, but an obvious declaration of her interest in a man who had smiled at her. Embarrassment engulfed her. Alexandra saw the suffusing tide of pink. In her complete understanding of Olga's sensitivity, she prayed that Kirby would be neither too clever nor too obvious. "Your Highness," he said, "have you any idea of what I'd like to tell my grandchildren?"

The chestnut-gold head was bent, its tiara a caressing intricacy of light. It lifted.

"Your grandchildren?" said Olga in amazement.

"They are rather imaginative, aren't they, as I haven't even acquired a wife yet," he said, smiling. "But it could happen and when the time comes is it possible I'll be able to tell them I once danced with the Grand Duchess Olga Nicolaievna of Imperial Russia? They won't believe me, of course, but what will that matter?"

"Mama, listen to him!" Her shyness was still there, but she hid it in her laughing appeal to her mother. "Oh, Mr. Kirby, it would be terrible if they didn't believe you about such a little thing, so you must give them proof." She took her gilt-edged ball card from the tiny jewelled evening bag that dangled from her gloved wrist. She gave him the card. He saw that only the final dance was available. He signed it. She took the card back and signed it herself. "There, when the

72

ball is over I'll give it to you, although I think you are teasing me a little."

She was smiling, her soft wide mouth parted, her blue eyes deep pools of life.

"Thank you, your Highness," he said quietly, "and I am not teasing."

She watched him go. She said, "Mama, I was not too forward?"

"No, of course not, my love," said Alexandra, "nor was he too sauve. He is rather nice, I think. Perhaps Aleka Petrovna has found herself a man who will make her a very suitable husband and cure her of her restlessness."

Olga said nothing to that. She thought Aleka Petrovna so beautiful that it would not matter to a man what else she was.

Not until the ball was coming to its end did Kirby think about any further commitment to Aleka. He had danced twice with her. He remembered he was engaged for a third. He asked to see her card. It showed his signature against the last number. He began to explain how in a moment of forgetfulness he had complicated his life. Aleka was incredulous.

"What are you trying to say, that you have signed some other woman's card for the same dance?"

"It's the Grand Duchess Olga——"

"It's who?"

"Loveliest of friends, it's her birthday and I could not——"

"I am to sit out the waltz?" Incredulity turned to outrage. "Alone of all these people I'm to have no partner? I don't care if she's the Grand Duchess of Imperial Heaven or whose birthday it is! Go and tell her you were previously engaged! Oh, you infamous cad, do you think I'm a peasant? After I've brought you to a ball a thousand others would have paid a million roubles to attend, you will jilt me of the waltz? Never, do you hear, never!"

"I'm an utter swine, I know," he said, "but, my lovely sweet-hearted Princess, be forgiving."

73

"Forgiving!" She was as flashing as her jewels. "Oh, the humiliation. I am discarded! I shall be a waltz wallflower, a laughing-stock! She has a hundred officers she can command, why did you even ask her? Is it because you think the Tsar will decorate you? Oh, you have ruined everything for me. Even Andrei wouldn't insult me in this way. Dance with her, then, and I hope you're so clumsy that she falls over your feet. You won't get decorated for that!"

"Aleka, it was the Empress's request. I could not refuse."

People were looking, aware of the altercation. If he was a little disturbed by this, Aleka was not.

"Ah, now I have found you out," she said, "you are the worst kind of Englishman, a social snob. Go to her, then. Simper into her face. I shall find a partner. But I shall never forgive you, Ivan Ivanovich, we are no longer friends, we are no longer even speaking to each other!"

She became as proud as a martyr. She enjoyed it tremendously.

The final waltz came. Kirby made his way to the Imperial family around a cluster of generals and their wives, paid his respects to Alexandra and Nicholas and said to Olga, "Your Highness?" She laid her gloved hand on the arm he extended and the Tsar, the Tsarina and their suite watched the unknown Englishman escort the Grand Duchess Olga Nicolaievna into the last dance of her ball.

The music was such as to haunt him for many years to come, when he could never hear it without pain in his heart or pictures in his mind. He never forgot the brilliance of that ball, its enchantment, its colour, its gaiety.

Olga danced into his heart. How light she was, how adorably shy, her eyes lowered, her diamond tiara dazzling, her hair a shining crown. She was the Emperor's daughter, she was sixteen. He had never felt so old. He was a lifetime apart from her. He was treacherously apart from her. His trade was espionage.

"Mr. Kirby?" A whisper floated to his ears above the music.

"Highness?"

"You damaged Anna's parasol. It won't open properly."

"Oh dear me," he said.

She lifted her head. He felt delight to see that her eyes were warm with laughter.

"You'll have to bring her a new one, won't you?"

"I'll have to bring her a very special new one. Who is Anna?"

"Why our friend, Anna Vyrubova."

He had vaguely heard of Anna Vyrubova, personal friend and confidante of the Empress. Anna too was involved with the mystique of religion.

They danced on, the state room with its mirrors reflecting a revolving, shimmering whirl of movement. Olga's eyes were lowered again, she circled with him, then she looked up. She seemed very happy.

"Mr. Kirby?"

"Forgive me, Highness, I was thinking of my grandchildren."

"Oh, such stories you think up." She was deliciously amused. "This is my most wonderful birthday."

"And this," he said, "is my most unforgettable ball."

They circled close to the open glass doors. The night air, exotic with scent from the rose gardens, was an invitation. Olga stopped dancing and took his hand.

"It will go on and on until no one has any energy left," she said. "Have you been into the gardens?"

"Not yet."

"Wouldn't you like to?" She was diffident in her modesty. "It won't be cold but it won't be hot, either. It isn't because I'm not enjoying myself, indeed I am very much, but to go into the gardens at night is to feel you can return to dance on and on."

"I'd love it," he said and went with her into the warm Crimean night. She took him out on to one of the balconies first. It overlooked the cliffs and the sea. He was silent, absorbed in the wonder and tran-

75

quillity of the world at night. The moon was a huge disc of pure white, its light investing the Palace, the gardens and the silent sea with opalescence. The scent of flowers, of emergent buds and night-closed blooms, was like ambrosia. The rose gardens were justifiably the Empress's pride and joy.

Olga was as silent as he was as they let the beauty of the night embrace them.

Then she said, "Will we go down, Mr. Kirby?"

He had been received by the three of them, Nicholas, Alexandra and Olga. He had met them and talked with them, and he had found neither stiff formality nor grand aloofness in any of them, only friendly warmth and great charm. They did not command, they requested.

"I think we will, don't you?" he said, and Olga took his hand again as they left the balcony and made their way down into the gardens. There the moonlight turned the night into silvery day. Other people were there, strolling in every direction, the jewels of women a sparkling iridescence. Olga's gloved fingers were curled happily around his and she breathed in the scented atmosphere as if it was the sweetness of life itself. Kirby saw immense flowerbeds, expansive lawns and cloistered walks, all bathed in bright light. Livadia was a world of beauty and Kirby had no adequate words for it.

At last Olga said, "Did you ever know so lovely a night?"

"I've never known so lovely a place, Highness," he said.

"It was you at Nikolayev station, was it not?" she said shyly.

"Yes, and it was you on the train," he said. "I must have been half asleep not to realise who you were. Heavens, I didn't even raise my hat to you."

Grand Duchess Olga laughed. The opalescence silvered her tiara, made her white teeth shine.

"Mr. Kirby, oh, you are so funny," she said.

"For not raising my hat to you? But at least I did

to Anna Vyrubova. Now you'll think I only raise it to ladies I almost knock down."

"If you did, that wouldn't be funny, it would be eccentric," she said, "and usually that is the privilege of old gentlemen. You aren't quite an old gentleman yet, are you?"

Her shyness was gone. She was in unaffected pleasure of the moment, happy that she could talk to him and laugh with him.

"Your Highness," he said, "you are a most entertaining Grand Duchess. More it is you yourself who have made this a very beautiful ball indeed."

Olga flamed into colour. He thought for a moment he had said the wrong thing, been too personal, but then she whispered happily, "That was said for my birthday, was it not?"

"And for my grandchildren."

Her smile, impulsive, was that of a girl in delight.

"Mr. Kirby, you will bring Anna a new parasol, won't you?"

"I can't deny I owe her one."

She put her hand in his again as they returned to the ballroom where, as she had said, the waltz was going on and on.

"You see, I told you," she said, "and I should so much like to join in again now."

"Will you permit a not quite old gentleman, Highness?"

"Oh, I am sure you will hardly creak at all," said Olga demurely.

They danced again and she floated, floated in a whirl of pink. Those who knew her well remarked that they had never seen Grand Duchess Olga Nicolaievna look so unreservedly happy, although they could not quite understand why she had chosen to bring her ball to a close by dancing on and on with an unknown, untitled Englishman.

"A charming fellow," said Nicholas, observing his daughter in her exhilarating finale with Kirby, "but I wonder why she wished for him?"

77

"He is English," said Alexandra, tired now but tranquil, "and Olga is romantic about England, It's because of us, Nicky."

"My dearest love," he said.

Alexandra and Nicholas were always in love. They had a capacity for it. They gave their children love. Their children returned it.

Kirby brought Olga back to them at last. Princess Aleka had found a partner, a colonel of the Tsar's household troops. He was as mobile and as companionable as a stuffed ramrod. She wanted to go home. Impervious to unwritten rules she had made this obvious to Kirby by appearing in her cloak and her boredom. He could not ignore her, he owed her that much. And it was early morning. As he escorted Olga off the floor the orchestra strings died, the waltz died and her ball was over. But not before the orchestra had played *God Save The Tsar*, when the stillness after so many hours of gaiety was dramatic, and the singing an embodiment of both joy and tears.

Alexandra, always as affected as any by the national anthem, collected herself and said, "Thank you, Mr. Kirby, you have been immensely kind."

"Mama, he has been immensely tireless," said Olga breathlessly, "I am quite done up."

When she speaks like that, he thought, I could find her on any page in a Jane Austen book. She is as delicious as that.

"If I've been able to return a little of your own kindness, Imperial Highness, I am more than happy," he said. "Grand Duchess," he said to Olga, "my most grateful thanks. It is something to remember, Livadia."

He bowed to her, took the white-gloved hand she extended and put his lips to her ring.

"I have so enjoyed it," she said.

He had found her, discovered her and now had no more claim on her. He turned to go, then turned back and said, "I will have a new parasol sent to Anna."

"Oh no," she said impulsively, "you are not to

send it, you are to——" She broke off and the scarlet rushed. His heart was wrenched for her sensitivity and he blessed the arrival of Aleka then as the Princess came to take her leave of the Imperial family.

"I am glad you came, Aleka Petrovna," said Nicholas warmly, "and just as glad that you brought our new friend from England."

"Ah, but what you do not know, your Highness," said Aleka, her smile very fixed, "is that he is even more terrible than I thought. You would not believe how dreadful his behaviour can be."

Nicholas laughed like a boy. No one could take Aleka Petrovna seriously. Alexandra smiled. Olga, however, looked at Aleka in wondering curiosity. There was a glitter in the dark eyes of the Princess. Olga glanced up at Kirby. He smiled, he shook his head.

It was a long ride back to Karinshka and the sleepy groom was in no condition to drive fast. The night was almost over, giving way to the new day. Aleka was aloof, keeping her distance. He wondered when she would strike. But after twenty minutes she moved closer to him, she sighed and rested her head against his shoulder.

"I am a dreadful bitch, aren't I?" she murmured.

"No, it was my fault," he said.

"I should have been more gracious," she said, "because of course you couldn't refuse the Empress. There, I'm over it now and so tired. How nice you feel. You have put everyone into a flutter, dancing the waltz with Olga Nicolaievna. She is a pretty young thing but very shy with people she doesn't know." Her voice was a languid murmur now. "I hope they don't marry her off to some fat German. Do you know, I think I'm going to sleep." And she closed her eyes.

The only sound then was that of the carriage wheels bowling over the dusty road. It was the hour when the night was dying, the new day not yet awake.

"Aleka?" he murmured after a while.

Aleka was asleep on his shoulder.

Dawn was flushing the horizon when they reached Karinshka. He carried her up the steps and into her Palace. Old Amarov, in nightcap and ancient velvet dressing-gown that had belonged to his late master, emerged from grey shadows holding a lighted candelabra. He led the way up the staircase and preceded Kirby into the Princess's suite. Kirby carried her through to the bedroom and laid her on the vastness of her bed. Old Amarov switched on a single light and grumbling through his moustache went back to his own bed.

Aleka lay in shimmering repose. He removed her tiara. She did not stir. He carefully took off her silver satin slippers.

"Ivan?" Her voice a husky caress.

"You're home now."

"Stay with me," she murmured, "I am so lonely."

There was a rustle. Karita stood at the bedroom door. She was rosy from sleep and clad in a voluminous white nightgown, red-ribboned.

"Oh, I am sorry, monsieur," she whispered, "but Old Amarov woke me and said you were back and so I came to see to her Highness. But——" She did not finish, she disappeared. He went after her and caught her before she left the suite.

"See to her, then," he said quietly.

"Monsieur," she said, and he was sure she was laughing, "if you are able to manage——"

"Manage what, saucebox?"

"That is, if her Highness would prefer you——"

"I'll pinch your pretty nose for you, minx," he said and pulled one end of a red ribbon bow. The bow dissolved, the neck of the nightgown parted and Karita, stifling a shriek, clutched frantically.

"Monsieur!" she gasped.

The night, not the dawn, was in his eyes. Exhilarating, revelationary night. He bent his head, he kissed her.

"Goodnight, Karita, see to her," he said and left the suite.

Karita tingled deliciously. It would not do to tell Oravio.

In his own bedroom Kirby opened the windows wide and stepped out on to the balcony. The eastern sky was streaked with pearly-pink radiance, the sea an emergence of soft, misty grey. He thought of the girl he had danced with, a girl who belonged to the dawn.

FOUR

Some days later, with everything at Karinshka periodically harmonious—in that Aleka could not remain mentally tranquil all day every day—Andrei returned. He was fully convalesced, he said. The implication that after spending a few days at idyllic Karinshka a man needed to go away and recuperate so incensed Aleka that she slipped off a shoe and flung it at him. It passed him by and skittered along the terrace.

"Ah, the excitement of being loved," said Andrei, elegant in a cream suit with thin black stripes. "How have you been, dear man?" he asked Kirby.

Kirby, recumbent in a long cane chair and deeply browned by the Crimean sun, looked up with the smile of a man who had come to terms with his temperamental hostess.

"Very comfortable," he said.

"Quiet?" said Andrei cautiously.

"On and off," said Kirby. Aleka made a face.

"It's been extremely critical at my place," said Andrei.

"Liar," said Aleka, well-figured in shimmering silk. Its harmonious relationship with her body betrayed an unconventional lack of undergarments. "You know damned well you've done nothing but lie around with your Crimean concubines."

"Well, if not critical that could be very exhausting,"

said Kirby. "You had better sit down, Andrei old chap."

"I'll sit him down," said Aleka maliciously and she did. But she waited until lunch was served, by which time a host of vivacious women and ebullient men had turned up.

At lunch she placed Andrei between two adoringly possessive women and thereby had a little of her own back. He was numbed within minutes, their tongues seemed to lay hands on him. He was drained within an hour.

"Dear ladies," he said then, "why not carry me away now and do as you will with me? What is food when death is so welcome?"

"Darling Andrei," said one, "your impatience is delicious."

"Darling Anna," said the second to the first, "I shall be impatient myself as soon as lunch is over. Shall I go first or will you?"

"Dearest," said the first to the second, "I'm sure his bed is not as small as that. We will all go together."

"Dear God," said Andrei to Kirby across the table, "I think they mean it."

They drowned him with shrieks of laughter. He shuddered. They did mean it.

Old Amarov came to tell Aleka she was wanted on the telephone. She took the call in the library, the telephone itself a gold and white ornament rather than an instrument in its appearance. But not until the guests had departed, some invited to return for dinner, did Aleka tell Kirby what the phone call was about. They were on the terrace, Andrei sleeping with his chair in the shade.

"What has got into you, what have you done?" she said to Kirby. "It was the Empress herself who interrupted me at lunch."

"She had probably had hers by then," said Kirby, "you do dawdle a little over yours, Princess."

"I entertain my guests, I do not merely have them come and go," she said. "It was about you the Empress

83

telephoned. You've been invited to Livadia. It's unheard of. What have you done to make yourself so indispensable to her? Do you read the Bible well, is that it? I was invited too, of course, but she knew I'd have guests and that I couldn't go. I was put into an impossible position, I had to accept for you. She has been too kind for me to make the feeble excuse that I had as much right to your company as she had."

"Good heavens," said Kirby, "you don't think that would have sounded feeble to her, do you? Aleka, is this true? I'm invited to Livadia?"

"She said for a week or so." Aleka added maliciously, "Or so means they retain the privilege of kicking you out as soon as possible if you appear in the wrong trousers or say damn to the Tsarevich. What are you smiling about? It's quite sickening, I tell you. I am to be deprived just when I'd made plans for the three of us to cruise for a few days."

"Not entirely deprived, darling," murmured Andrei, who had woken up, "I shall still be here."

"Yes, darling," said Aleka, "I still have one friend who doesn't fall over himself to favour royalty. I am thankful for you, Andrei Mikhailovich. Ah well, you won't find it very exciting at Livadia, Ivan, you'll have to go to morning church and look holy. And all you'll be allowed to say apart from yes and no are your prayers. You are to go the day after tomorrow. Also, the Empress said that Grand Duchess Olga asked that you be reminded not to forget. Forget what?"

"A parasol," said Kirby. "I must go to Yalta tomorrow."

"You are completely ridiculous," said Aleka.

There was a letter for him later that day, delivered by hand from Yalta:

"Dear Kirby. We like your new friends. They are entirely respectable. Could you come and see me soon?"

It was not signed and it bore no address, but he knew it was from Anstruther.

Yalta was hot. But Anstruther seemed brown and temperate. Kirby tossed the letter on to his desk.

"What was that about?" he said. "I didn't like it."

"Overnight," said Anstruther, "you've become a man of substance. Not in the material things, but in your new friends. I understand they were very taken with you. I also hear they're thinking of inviting you to stay with them. Splendid."

"No," said Kirby flatly.

"No? No to what?"

"Whatever you're going to ask me. I'm on holiday."

"I'm not going to ask you anything," said Anstruther. "Do sit down. I'll have some tea sent in." Nothing more was said until the clerk had brought in the samovar, poured the tea and left. Then Anstruther remarked that friendship was a very happy thing. Kirby thought he had never heard anything so trite, and said so.

"Ambassadors work all their lives to make friends of king, emperors and presidents," said Anstruther. "They rarely succeed since their first loyalties are to their own heads of state and they are, therefore, suspect. You, my dear Kirby, have achieved more in a single evening than an ambassador in ten years. You have become a friend of the Romanovs. Now it would be interesting to know what the Tsar really thinks of the Russian alliance with France."

"I should imagine," said Kirby sarcastically, "that he sits up at night wondering if it entitles him to import the Can-Can."

Anstruther played that literally and said, "Really? I've always been under the impression he was the kind of man who could take the Can-Can or leave it alone. However, putting that to one side for the moment, take the extreme point. In the event of France going to war would Nicholas, no matter what the circumstances, keep to the full terms of the alliance?"

"Sir George Buchanan can find that out, that's his province, not mine."

"He might conceivably ask the Tsar's Minister of

War. He'd only get a diplomatic answer. We think the Tsar would honour the terms, but we'd like to know for certain. One likes to provide for certainties rather than possibilities."

"Well, provide for a certainty in this case, then," said Kirby, "and you'll be covered for both."

"Now your report," said Anstruther, pleasantly ignoring Kirby's suggestion, "indicates that Russia is simply not ready to go to war on behalf of any ally. Therefore, could the Tsar seriously commit Russia totally and unconditionally on the side of France and under any circumstances?"

"Why, are we thinking of sneaking up on the Republic?"

Anstruther looked just a little put out.

"Tut tut," he said. "Look here, it isn't much to ask. Nicholas and Alexandra confide in their friends. They might confide in you. It can't do any harm and it would let us know whether the ramifications of the alliance really are solid."

Kirby almost lost his temper.

"Damnation," he said, "of course they're solid. What do you think would happen to the Tsar if he pulled the bricks out? He'd never be able to look another head of state in the face. In any case, I'm having nothing to do with it. After I've had my holiday I'm resigning from the service. I want to be able to look people in the face myself."

"Resigning, you say?" Anstruther smiled bleakly. "Wishful thinking, I'm afraid, Mr. Kirby. You can't, not yet. And please don't mention it again, it might result in your being sent to China. We're badly in need of a man there who can make friends."

Damn that, thought Kirby. He had no wish to go to China or anywhere else now or in the immediate future.

Despite his introspective mood when he left Anstruther he did not forget to buy a parasol.

Princess Aleka, in a typical reversal of moods, compensated for her ungraciousness by being very gracious indeed the morning he left for Livadia. It was as if, thought Kirby, she had suddenly realised how much she appreciated that she and Andrei would be alone, if one discounted the presence of servants and the distractions of table guests.

She was sweetness itself. Not only did she insist that he should take the best carriage but Karita too. Karita would look after him very well at Livadia. He said that to take Karita would probably be very inconvenient for both her and Karita.

"Darling, it won't be a bit inconvenient for either of us," said Aleka, richly beautiful in a wide-sleeved morning gown of yellow, "and you simply cannot go to the Imperial Palace without a servant. Karita will be a treasure to you there. If she makes any fuss about going I'll box her ears."

That proved quite unnecessary. Karita glowed when the Princess informed her she was to go to Livadia with Ivan Ivanovich. She accompanied him in a trance of excitement. To be of service to the handsome, good-humoured Englishman at Livadia, well, that would be an unimaginable pleasure. She must be sure to do nothing wrong. It might not put him out, for he was neither exacting nor fussy, but she herself would be most upset. However, she would worry about that when it happened. Meanwhile, the prospect of seeing the Imperial family, even the Tsar himself, that was quite overwhelming.

Oravio had not been at all pleased at her going. He had looked very disapproving and said that the Englishman should have taken a manservant if he had to take any servant at all.

"That would not have been very flattering to me," said Karita, "it would have looked as if he hadn't found me satisfactory enough."

"How satisfactory is that?" said Oravio darkly. She smacked his face. She was not a girl to stomach an insinuation like that. The smack had left Oravio on glowering terms with her. It surprised her how little she cared.

Of course, everyone at Karinshka knew that the Englishman had been invited to Livadia by the Empress herself. It convinced Karita that he was certainly a man of some importance, despite his denials. The Princess had agreed with her.

"Yes, I'm sure you are right, Karita," she had said, "and it would be interesting to know what people he meets and talks to while he's at Livadia. You must keep your eyes and ears open and let me know, without, of course, his being aware of it. It will just be something interesting between you and me."

Karita thought that a rather uncomfortable commission. It sounded as if she was required to look through keyholes, to follow the Englishman about. She was going to do neither. What would he think of her if she did?

Kirby commanded her to sit in the carriage with him so that they might talk during the ride to Livadia. Karita said that would simply not look right when they arrived and that she would sit up with Dimitri, the groom.

"You're my personal servant," said Kirby, "and it will look quite right."

So she sat with him, but maintained the reserve she considered proper. The day was beautiful, the countryside lush and colourful as they drove around hills, through valleys and sometimes close to the sea. Karita sat with straight back, dressed in green skirt, white blouse and bonnet, its ribbons caught under her chin. Her brown eyes reflected her pleasure. Kirby was conversational but not familiarly so. He was not unaware of Karita's sense of propriety.

Suddenly, she said, "Tell me more of the ball and the Imperial Palace, monsieur. I can't hear enough about it all."

He discoursed on the ball, describing as best as he could all that was fascinating to her about the women and their gowns. He described how the

Emperor and Empress had looked, but he did not mention Grand Duchess Olga.

So Karita said at last, "But the Grand Duchess, monsieur, it was her ball, how did she look?"

Kirby let the jolting carriage run its course over a section of road in need of repair.

"She looked very sweet, I think," he said, "and very young."

Considering how he always had something telling to say about almost everything, Karita thought this disappointingly inadequate.

"But, monsieur, you danced with her," she said, "you must have noticed more than that. What was she wearing, how was her hair dressed, what jewels did she have?"

"She wore pink, her hair was up and she had a diamond tiara. She still looked very young."

"But it was her sixteenth birthday," said Karita, "she's grown up. Monsieur, I think you could hardly have seen her at all."

"I saw her very clearly," he said. The pictures came to his mind out of the morning air. There was a girl there, a girl who looked as if she would never grow up. "Actually, Karita, she was quite lovely. Look, there's Livadia."

When they were close Karita could not take her eyes off the white, shining Imperial Palace, majestic in the sunshine. It took her breath away, and she was sure that when she stepped from the carriage the weakness in her knees would prevent her legs from carrying her up the wide steps. She surprised herself. Indeed, Kirby thought as she entered the Palace that he had never seen the golden-haired Crimean girl look so composed. Magnificently adorned footmen appeared.

"Madame?" said one, mistaking her status.

"I am the personal servant of my lord duke Ivan Ivanovich Kirby," said Karita.

"Heaven be blessed," he said and gladly took her in charge before others could, while Kirby was ceremoniously escorted to his room on the first floor. As at Karinshka, it was a suite, but even more spacious. All its windows opened out on to a sunlit balcony. The drawing-room was blue-carpeted, its walls hung with paintings and ikons. The chairs were gilt and blue. Karinshka had impressed him, Livadia held him spellbound. The view was of the dancing blue sea, of green velvet lawns and beautifully colourful flowerbeds. The balcony itself seemed so high, poised far above the sounds of the earth and the murmurs of the sea. He felt in perfect peace.

Servants were in his suite, attending to the luggage he had brought, and in a remarkably short time Karita having established herself in the servants' quarters, arrived in her blue dress and white front. He heard her taking charge, supervising this and that in her efficient way. The servants left and she came out to him on the balcony.

"All is ready, monsieur," she said, "you are to be served lunch here in your suite, then afterwards you're to change and meet Countess Borodinsky."

"Who is she?"

"A lady-in-waiting." Karita already seemed as if matters and personages of the Imperial household were little to worry about, but the next moment she went on breathlessly. "Oh, it's all so beautiful but so confusing, I'm sure I'll lose myself a dozen times a day."

"I'll come and look for you and we'll get lost together," he said.

"And who will come and look for us?" she said gaily.

He had the lunch that was served in his suite. He was pleasantly surprised at the simplicity of the meal. Then he changed and an hour after lunch Karita took him to meet Countess Borodinsky. She was thirtyish, charming and put him entirely at his ease. Kirby in white flannels and blue jacket made his own impression on her. She liked his tall English look, his masculinity without the flamboyance of so many Russians.

They exchanged small talk on an easy, pleasant note and then she said, "Do you play tennis?"

"A little, Countess."

"A little will be enough to start with," she smiled. It was mid-afternoon and the Palace was quiet as she took him up to the Empress, who was writing letters in her boudoir. There, sitting at a table by the window, she received him. Her hair, deeply golden, showing only the minutest tints of grey, was lustrous, and he thought her quiet regally beautiful. Her smile was warmly welcoming.

"Mr. Kirby, how nice to see you, how good of you to leave Karinshka and be with us for a while."

"Imperial Highness," he said, "you must know that the pleasure is all on my side. You have built a place of wonder here. It's as beautiful by day as it is by night. I did not think it could be, but it is."

"Mr. Kirby, it was built to grace Holy Russia, it is not meant in any way to add lustre to me."

"It does, nevertheless," he said. "I cannot retract, Highness."

She smiled and shook her head. There was an air of devout modesty about her, the boudoir itself, with its numerous ikons and religious paintings, her spiritual sanctuary. Alexandra wanted only to serve her family and Russia, and would rather be known as Mother Tsarina than as Empress Alexandra, although as Empress she was conscious of all that her title entailed. She believed, as Nicholas did, in the divine right of Tsarist autocracy. God had called Nicholas to serve his people, to guide them and to administer for them.

Kirby sat and she talked to him. Her conversation was simply, homely, of her children, of Livadia and of England. Kirby's impression that she was the kindest of persons deepened. If she was neither brilliant nor devious, neither witty nor calculating, these were things, he thought, that might elevate some Empresses; but Alexandra, first and foremost a wife and mother, would not have been concerned to have been told she lacked them. She placed far greater importance on love and affection, and on Christian humility, only providing the Tsar's divinity was not called into question.

Finally she said, "You will excuse me now? I have so much correspondence to catch up with and we will be able to talk again while you're here. Countess Borodinsky will take you down into the gardens and introduce you to our dear Anna Vyrubova. I believe," she added with a shy smile not unlike Olga's, "that you and Anna met briefly before."

"I was clumsy then, I've been mortified since," he said.

Anna Vyrubova was in the gardens, seated at a white ornamental table and working with her needle. Behind her, in the distance, the mountains pointed their peaks at the blue sky. Comfortably plump, with pleasant features, she wagged her finger at Kirby as he was introduced to her.

"Ah," she said, "so you are the man who stepped on me."

"I've tried to think of it as a happy collision," he said, "and you were very kind about it. I must apologise for damaging your parasol and if my servant Karita—oh, yes."

Karita, watching from a position of advantage, moved as Kirby lifted his hand to her. She came hurrying up, petticoats peeping below swinging blue. She gave a long, wrapped package to Kirby, curtseyed and sped away, blushing just a little. Kirby handed the package to Anna, she unwrapped it, opened it up and exclaimed in pleasure at the colourful parasol. Countess Borodinsky excused herself and Kirby sat down. Anna was only too pleased to talk to him, and in conversation she was as pleasant and as uncomplicated as the Empress. She was genuinely devoted to Alexandra.

Kirby sat in relaxed enjoyment. The green lawns, the flowering shrubs and the profusion of roses, beautiful in the golden sunshine, lent enchantment to majesty and brought visual splendour to tranquillity. There was no noise save the murmur of hot autumn, no voice except Anna's. There were no children. He wondered about that.

A hand clapped him on the shoulder. He turned in his chair and saw the Tsar. He rose to his feet.

"My dear fellow," said Nicholas, his smile infectious, "how splendid to see you." He wore white and carried two tennis racquets. "You are just the man for me. Anna, what do you think, General Sikorski has cried off with a sore back. I suspect it's to do with his reluctance to take a beating. Generals are like that," he said to Kirby. "I hope you aren't. Anna, will it do if I borrow our English friend and play a set with him?"

Anna, teeth biting on a thread, nodded. It all spoke of free-and-easy informality. Livadia, thought Kirby, induced that. The Tsar put his hand on Kirby's arm and led him to the tennis court. Nicholas was an enthusiastic and capable player. Kirby had once been of county standard but was rusty. It had been years since he'd played. They knocked up. Kirby was completely out of touch and showed it.

"Don't worry, my dear man," called Nicholas as Kirby apologised for his lack of co-ordination, "it takes a little time if one hasn't played the game for a while."

They were quite alone. There were no guards, no obtrusive court officials, nobody at all except themselves. The Tsar was as carefree as a boy. Kirby hit a good forehand at last and Nicholas beamed in delight. He hit more, as well as a competent backhand or two.

"Ah, you're ready?" called Nicholas. "You serve, my dear chap, I insist."

Tennis in 1911 was a pastime rather than a sport. Strokes were made from the back of the court, and anything like a cunning drop shot or a vindictive volley was considered not quite the thing, unless one was playing for a championship. Volleying indeed was in its suspect infancy. Some men still served under-

93

hand. Not so the Tsar or Kirby. They served in a competitive spirit.

"My dear fellow," said the Tsar midway through the set, "I think you're winning. I must make you a general."

Kirby had been wondering whether it would be wise to win, if he could. If the Tsar had invited him here in order to indulge his Imperial passion for tennis, perhaps he also took an Imperial pleasure in winning. It would be a little ungrateful to beat him, perhaps. It might even be tactless. He decided, however, that the Tsar simply enjoyed playing and, as far as the result was concerned, differed from generals in his outlook. Yet few people, especially the exalted few, lost with the same relish as they won . . . oh well, he thought, just get on with the game and let it all happen naturally.

He clouted a few forehands out of court. He lost the set 7–5. The Tsar sank into a seat by the side of the court, wiping his forehead with a silk handkerchief. He wore another one around his neck. He was in very good humour.

"Absolutely first-class, Mr. Kirby. Splendid. We must play again. You're improving all the time."

"Another set now?" Kirby was hot himself.

"We'll have a drink first."

It was standard practice. Cool drinks appeared as if the liveried servant was a genie. Kirby let himself cool down. It was undeniably pleasant here. He was not quite sure how it had all happened, but he had just finished a most enjoyable set of tennis with the Tsar of All the Russias. His name would be in the papers if anyone at home found out. In the local papers.

He breathed in the warm air. A flutter caught his eye, a flutter of white whisking behind a shrub. It disappeared.

"Ready, my dear man?" said the Tsar, who liked to play tennis on and off all day.

They played again. Kirby got better. Lithe and

active in his white flannels he had the Tsar stretching to reach his returns. Nicholas muffed a shot, the ball just carried the net, it seemed to hover and drop dead. Kirby swooped, got his racquet to the ball as it died, but unable to check his diving impetus he plunged head-first into the net. The Tsar roared with laughter, it was echoed by the impulsive laughter of a delighted girl. She had stolen from her tutor to peep at the game.

"Oh, Mr. Kirby! Papa!" She was in pure merriment. Kirby disentangled himself and sat up. He saw her in a white dress, the waist sashed with wide red ribbon, and her hair was a cascading brightness, flowing to her shoulders. He smiled, not at all discomfited. It was worth ten falls to see the Grand Duchess Olga Nicolaievna in such merriment.

"Hm, that you should have come at so significant a moment for Mr. Kirby," said Nicholas to his delighted daughter. "Who's going to pick him up?" He advanced to the net, laughingly extending a helping hand over it. Kirby got to his feet, brushed his flannels. "You're not hurt, I hope, my dear fellow? Good. And there's no damage to the net. It was a splendid effort and all because of such a bad shot of mine. Did you see my bad shot, Olga?"

"Papa," said Olga demurely, "I only saw Mr. Kirby dive gallantly into the net." Kirby regarded her in pretended admonition. She responded with the happiest of smiles. "Well, it was so funny, you see," she explained.

"Your Highness," he said, "I don't do it for every Grand Duchess I meet, only for those celebrating a sixteenth birthday."

"Oh, that is *very* gallant," she said. Then, "Papa, I'll stay and pick up the balls for you and Mr. Kirby, shall I?"

The Tsar looked at his watch.

"Return to Monsieur Gilliard for a little longer, my love, otherwise he'll come shaking his head at all of us."

"Papa, you're dreadfully hard on me sometimes,"

said Olga, but she went. She stopped, turned round and said to Kirby, "Did you bring the parasol?"

"I did, Highness," he said.

"Now Anna will think she's had a birthday too," said Grand Duchess Olga.

He met all the children later, all five of them. Alexis, the Tsarevich, was an extraordinarily attractive boy of seven, his grey-blue eyes always eager, it seemed, to discover new entertainments. It was as if he sensed his life would be short and that he must enjoy all that he could while he could. Anastasia, gifted and tomboyish, was ten and still chubby with puppy fat. Marie was twelve, apple-cheeked, blue-eyed, pretty and already desperately romantic. Tatiana was fourteen, slender and vivacious, with impish grey eyes and beautiful auburn hair. Such was her zest for life, such the irresistible nature of her personality, that even at fourteen she was inclined to outshine and dominate Olga, her closest and dearest sister. Olga, the eldest, was to outsiders the quietest and shyest of the Grand Duchesses, but within her family and to her friends she had all the most endearing qualities: wit, charm, compassion and the same infinite capacity for loving as her mother.

They were all intensely interested in the tall Englishman. Alexis, always boyishly interested in military matters, asked him if he would have time to do some drilling.

"I'm quite good at all the commands, you know," he said.

"Well, I should think I could spare some time," said Kirby. He sat in a white garden chair, the children sat on the lawn around him, all except Olga who, having recently grown up, had decided it was more decorous to repose in a chair of her own. She had said she did not want to look part of the hooligan element. At which her sisters had threatened to plop her into a pool. It did not ruffle Olga. She was happy. She was always happy at Livadia. She was a reflection of its tranquillity. "Yes," Kirby continued, "I ought to do some drill, I've never done any at all. It should do me the world of good as long as I can sit down in between."

"Oh, that's jolly decent of you," said Alexis, elated at the prospect.

"Not at all," said Kirby.

"Well, you've asked for it now," said Marie, "Alexis is simply dreadful when he's got someone he can drill, he simply never stops."

"General Sikorski says he's insatiable," said Tatiana, "he orders his victims about night and day. You'll never get time to sit down at all."

"Oh, pooh," said Alexis, "they're just girls and they're awful at drill, they just fall about."

"I've a shocking feeling," said Kirby, "that as I'm new to it I'll probably fall about myself."

Alexis rocked with laughter, Marie giggled. Anastasia got up and very solemnly said, "Here is Ivan Ivanovich being drilled by Alexis and falling about." She began to stagger and reel around, and Anna Vyrubova came to see what all the hysterics were about.

"What's happening?" she asked.

"It's only Stasha being herself," said Olga.

"Stasha, love, get up," said Anna. Anastasia was rolling on the grass. "What *are* you doing?"

"I'm doing Ivan Ivanovich falling about." They were already using his Russian names.

"Actually," said Tatiana, "I think you're doing him falling down."

They wandered with him through the gardens and along cloistered avenues where the grape vines wound and curled. They were delighted with him, at his interest in everything, at his interest in them, at his responsiveness to their chatter. Alexis said he was going to make Ivan Ivanovich one of his very best friends.

"Olga," whispered Tatiana, taking her elder sister by the arm while the others showed Kirby the fish in a sunlit pool, "you are shockingly close, you didn't say a word about what he was like, only that you

97

danced with him and that Mama and Papa were very taken with him. And he's the handsomest man."

"Do you think so?" Olga was offhand. "I hadn't really noticed—well, yes, he's quite nice, I suppose."

Tatiana looked in curiosity at her sister. There was something new about Olga. She was not herself, she was apart from the rest of them. Her long, shining hair had been recently brushed and she held herself more carefully than usual. That was it, she was not romping with them as she normally did, she was sixteen and simulating the behaviour of a young woman, not a girl. Tatiana's eyes danced.

"Of course," she said seriously, "he's rather old———"

"He is not!" Olga's whispered denial was too quick, too impulsive. She knew it, she coloured up.

"Why, Olga, you're blushing," Tatiana teased, but she relented quickly and added, "Anyway, who cares how old he is? He is rather delicious, I think, don't you?"

"Tasha, he'll hear you," said Olga a little desperately. She glanced at Kirby. He was down on one knee at the edge of the pool, his hand on the shoulder of Alexis, who was pointing out the fish. Marie and Anastasia were both talking to him at once. He seemed completely at ease.

"When tea is served I shall make eyes at him over the bread and butter," said Tatiana, "I'll be the first one ever to make bread and butter romantic."

"Tasha, little one," said Olga, "you are not to."

"I'm almost as big as you," said Tatiana, "and what am I not to do?"

"You are not to be so forward."

Tatiana gurgled. Olga was so absurdly sensitive, she felt the mistakes of all of them.

"But, Olga, he's Mama's own guest and we simply can't neglect him, we must make the nicest fuss of him."

Olga smiled. Tatiana was irresistible.

They left the pool. Kirby sat under the trees, on the grass, his back against a broad trunk. Alexis showed him his personal possessions, including very useful bits of string, an onyx button and a glossy, shining chestnut. One never knew, he said, when a chestnut might not be just the thing. As man to man, Kirby agreed. If another chestnut could be found, then there'd be enough to play Conkers. It was a game, he informed them, that everyone in England played with chestnuts. And in the warm sunshine of the afternoon Kirby came to know the children of the Tsar. He thought them utterly natural, uninhibited and unspoiled. They took as much pleasure in simple things as all other children. This was how their parents governed their formative years.

Tatiana dropped to her knees, unable to resist the temptation of claiming his attention. Olga remained standing, quietly absorbed, looking when she knew his eyes were elsewhere and wondering how he came to be so brown and sinewy, so much in command of situations. His teeth were white when he smiled and he smiled often. He made Tatiana, Marie and Anastasia giggle until they were having fits.

"It can't be," Tatiana was saying.

"Yes, it's what they call a bunny-wobble," he said.

"What is?" asked Olga, who had missed the previous exchanges in her absorption of other things.

"What I was describing to Tatiana," he said, "a bustle on a stout lady at Ascot."

Marie shrieked, Anastasia rolled about.

"Ivan Ivanovich," cried Tatiana, "you're dreadful."

"Bustles," said Olga, "aren't worn any more, not by any ladies."

"Well, you see," he said, "it was the bunny-wobble look that did that."

He glanced up at her. She was standing in light and shade, the light caressing her, the shade softening her. Her blue eyes were bright with laughter, her face golden from the sun and framed by her shining hair. He had never seen a girl so young and so beautiful. Girls of sixteen were usually sweet but awkward, hesitating between youth and maturity. Olga was bewitching.

"Mr. Kirby," she said, "I don't think you've ever seen a bustle."

"Nor have I," said Alexis, "but uniforms are much better and I've seen heaps of those. Of course," he said to Kirby, "we don't have to be with girls all the time, you know. They can go and have their tea, we can have ours here."

"Alexis." A calm, modulated voice broke in. It was the Empress, cool in white linen, her parasol shading her from the sun. She was rarely without her parasol at Livadia, though her daughters lifted their faces to the sun day in, day out. "Alexis, where is Derevenko?"

Derevenko was a sailor whose one duty was to watch over the Tsarevich and prevent him tumbling and chasing about too energetically. The slightest knock could produce a haemophiliac condition of agonising duration.

"He's over there, Mama," said Alexis. Kirby had risen and Alexis took his hand to establish proprietary rights over their new friend. Alexandra did not miss the gesture. She smiled.

"Were you teasing your sisters, Aleky?" she asked.

"Only a little," the boy said, and he made it sound as if not every person his size could get the better of four girls all bigger than he was.

"And the girls were teasing you, I suppose, Mr. Kirby?" said Alexandra.

"Only a little," he said.

"Come, let's all have tea," said Alexandra.

It was served on one of the lawns. The Tsar joined them, so did Anna. Nicholas regaled his family with an amusing account of how Mr. Kirby had fallen into the tennis net. Olga, a hand smothering her mirth, caught Kirby's glance. He seemed as amused as any of them. She thought him the most agreeable and good-humoured of men.

Afterwards she managed to find him as he wandered round the rose beds.

"Mr. Kirby, there you are."

"Your Highness? Am I wanted?"

100

"Wanted? Oh, no," she said, "it's only that Papa is perhaps not very kind to make everyone laugh at your expense, but he doesn't mean to be. Truly, he couldn't be unkind to anyone."

"I know." He put out a hand and touched the richness of a red rosebud. "I didn't mind a bit."

"I think," she began and left it at that. She looked at the rose he was touching.

"What is it you think, Highness?"

"That it's nice you're here," she said, and was immediately in hot confusion at so committing her feelings. "Well," she hastened on, "the children are all going to watch Alexis drilling you tomorrow and——"

"And that should be very nice," he smiled. "That is," he added thoughtfully, "how nice will it be for me? Are there penalties involved for incompetence, do you know? Imagine being incompetent in front of Grand Duchesses."

Grand Duchess Olga permitted herself an impulsive indulgence. "And Anna too," she said, "as well as General Sikorski, Monsieur Gilliard and Countess Borodinsky. Alexis is inviting everyone to be there, Mama and Papa too."

"Oh good heavens," he said.

"Mr. Kirby," she said, "you simply can't be incompetent now, can you?"

"Not in front of General Sikorski, at least," he said. She was looking away, leaning a little in closer inspection of the red roses. "Your Highness, can you look me in the eye and tell me you're not pulling my leg?"

Olga straightened up. She was laughing.

"Oh, I'm awful, I couldn't resist it," she said. The evening sunlight touched her hair with red-gold fire. Then she said, "Did Princess Aleka Petrovna mind that you came? Mama invited her too but of course she could not leave her guests."

"She didn't mind a bit," he said.

"She is very beautiful," said Olga.

"Very," he said. She glimpsed his teeth as he smiled. "Frighteningly," he added.

101

Somehow she thought he was laughing at himself.

He found himself at dinner that evening with the Imperial family, in their own private dining-room. He knew this was a compliment, for apart from Anna Vyrubova he was the only outsider present. And Anna was not an outsider herself, she seemed one with the family. The younger children had had their supper and were at prayers before going to bed, only Olga being at dinner. But she was sixteen and incontestably a young lady in a gown of deep purple.

The meal was a pleasant surprise to Kirby after the sumptuous menus of Karinshka. The Tsar liked the plainest Russian dishes, soups, fish, bread and fruit. The conversation was simple and unaffected, and laughter was easily come by.

"Papa," said Olga demurely, "will General Sikorski be better tomorrow?"

"My love," said Nicholas, "the General has said that while there's a younger man to run about on the other side of the court, he'd prefer to rest his aching bones."

"My aching bones are at your service, sir," said Kirby.

"You can't deceive me like that, my dear fellow," said Nicholas, "you mean to have your revenge to-morrow. But you'll see, Olga, there's always some way to beat the enemy."

"Yes, I know, Papa, I've already seen your way," said Olga, "you play the most dreadful shot and he turns somersaults trying to get it back."

"My dear," said Nicholas to Alexandra, "do you hear that from our own child?"

"I'm not quite sure what it all means," said Alexandra, "but it sounds very unfair to poor Mr. Kirby."

"I think," said Kirby in a theatrical aside to Anna, "that I now know why General Sikorski keeps out of the way."

Olga could hardly suppress her merriment. Her shyness was forgotten. She only felt very happy.

Livadia was idyllic. Its atmosphere of tranquillity and graciousness enchanted Kirby, the Imperial family charmed him. Their modesty, their warmth and their total lack of affectation were constant. He played tennis with Nicholas and whenever she could Alexandra showed her liking for him by requesting that he come and talk with her. The Grand Duchesses and the Tsarevich escaped from their tutor immediately at the end of every lesson to look for him and have him play games with them. He drilled with Alexis. This put the younger girls into fits, Alexis so important and the tall Englishman so drily comical. He swore he would never know his right from his left. Alexis told him not to worry, it would come to him in the end. Old General Sikorski, a great favorite who was always at Livadia, looked on and said that as a soldier Ivan Ivanovich from England would make a very fine sailor.

Kirby bathed with the family off their private beach. Nicholas bathed whenever he could, so did the children. Alexandra did not, but sat on a beach chair under her parasol with Anna Vyrubova. The young girls were like nymphs in their bathing costumes. Tatiana was slender, Olga slender too but with perceptible shapeliness. In her costume of blue and white shyness returned. There was nowhere she could hide on the first occasion she presented herself to Kirby on the beach, but he made nothing of it, put out his hand, and they ran into the water together.

Nicholas liked the open air, he liked exercise and most of all he liked tennis. When he was not on the beach or attending to state business in his retreat, he found his way to the tennis court. Whenever he played with Kirby, Olga and Tatiana made every excuse they could to steal time off from their studies so that they could sit by the side of the court and watch. Not that they were onerously tutored at Livadia, only that there was always some subject they had to keep up with.

Tatiana was beginning to affect a sighing infatuation for the Englishman, declaring him to be soulfully disturbing to a girl. Olga's reaction was to suggest to Tatiana that she should not make remarks he might overhear.

"I wish he would hear," said Tatiana, as they sat on the bench by the court, "but he is shockingly oblivious."

"And you are shockingly yourself."

"What a pity he isn't a prince," said Tatiana, swinging her legs and displaying ankles amid frothy white, "he would do very well for me."

"That is silly."

"It isn't," insisted Tatiana. "One has to think about these things when one is a growing young woman as I am."

"You aren't, you're only cheeky. Besides, even if he were a prince he'd never marry a chatterbox like you."

"Yes, he would," said Tatiana, "my chatter would amuse him and he likes being amused. You would never do for him."

"Oh, monkey!" cried Olga and tweaked a tress of her sister's auburn hair.

"Is the zoo now open?" asked a masculine voice. Olga hastily let go. Kirby was there, picking up a wandering ball.

"It's all because I'm a chatterbox," Tatiana said to him.

"I like chatterboxes," said Kirby and returned to the court.

"There, didn't I say so?" said Tatiana in triumph.

"He only meant that he likes children," said Olga sweetly.

This time it was Olga who had her hair pulled. Then Tatiana fled, Olga in swift pursuit. Shrieks pierced the tranquillity. Olga returned sedately, seated herself on the white bench again, put her elbows on her knees, cupped her chin in her hands and watched the game to its end.

In the gardens one day Alexandra said to Kirby. "We must all do as the children do and call you Ivan

104

Ivanovich. It's impossible to keep calling you Mr. Kirby when you are so much our friend now and when you've been very kind to a rather tedious woman who has enjoyed your conversation so much. One day I'm sure the Tsar and I will visit England again and you shall receive us at Walton if you're there and if you will."

"Your Highness," he said, "there are times, you know, when your own kindness leaves me absolutely nothing to say. What is there I can say except that you and all the Imperial family make Livadia what it is, and that I love it very much. Your friendship I cherish and always will."

"You are the nicest man, Ivan Ivanovich," said Alexandra.

He was known as Ivan Ivanovich to all the Imperial family then. To all, that is, except Olga. She still addressed him as Mr. Kirby. He did not comment on it. Her ways and her reasons were her own. They made her what she was, herself.

She came running one afternoon in chase of Tatiana, who knew only too well how deliciously to outrage her elder sister. As he turned the corner of the balustraded terrace Olga ran straight into his arms. For one unrehearsed moment she was a breathless warmth and softness against him. He was conscious of innocence in confusion. He released her almost at once.

Her blood rushed. She turned so that her tumbled, sunbright hair hid her scarlet.

"I thought for a moment that Anna Vyrubova and I had collided again," he said lightly. "If you're looking for Tatiana, she's gone that way, but don't say I said so. She and I are friends at the moment."

"Mr. Kirby, I'm so sorry," she said, the breathlessness in her voice. "I'm no better than the children, rushing about like that."

"Highness, suppose we rush about together and surround your sister? I never act my age, either, I like to forget it."

He put out his hand, and Anna Vyrubova, coming

on to the terrace to look for Alexis, saw Olga flying over green lawns hand-in-hand with Ivan Ivanovich, her face turned to the sun and radiant with the joy of being alive.

How happy the Grand Duchess was. How kind Ivan Ivanovich was, spending so much of his time in company with all the children.

Livadia seemed even lovelier these days.

"Olga darling," said Alexandra, "why do you still call him Mr. Kirby? It sounds so formal now."

"Does it, Mama? I hadn't thought."

"Well, it does, my sweet. Don't you like him?"

"Oh, he is quite nice and very good at tennis." Olga went to the window of her mother's boudoir and looked at the distant mountain tops.

"Oh dear, that sounds as if you don't like him," said Alexandra.

"Mama, one could not dislike Mr. Kirby. Do you know, I think there's still some snow on the mountains."

It was very unlike Olga, thought Alexandra, to turn her back when one was speaking to her.

"Olga my love, come here."

Olga came slowly from the window and Alexandra saw that pink was burning her cheeks. If Alexandra was not an intellectual she did not lack perception where her family was concerned. A little dismay attacked her. She covered it with a warm, affectionate smile.

"Darling, you're growing up, aren't you?" she said. "Soon, in a few years Papa and I will have to think about——"

"Oh, Mama, no! I am happy with you and Papa, I am not to be married, not even in a few years— not for many years—Mama, please."

Alexandra felt heartache. She too had been young, she too had had her dreams.

"Of course you don't want to get married, darling. Who does at sixteen?"

106

It was well that Mr. Kirby's visit was ending in a few days.

That evening Alexandra said to Nicholas, "What do you think of our new English friend now that you know him so well?"

"Utterly splendid fellow," said Nicholas, enjoying his cigarette. "Plays a devilishly sporting game of tennis and is never a bore. Doesn't push himself, either. Extremely discreet on politics in case he offends."

"Yes, he's always very gracious," said Alexandra. "Nicky, you don't think perhaps he has his own reasons for being ingratiating, do you?"

"My love," said Nicholas, "we invited him here ourselves, he didn't arrive on our doorstep with an ingratiating smile."

"I confess I like him very much," said Alexandra, "but would it be terribly unkind of us if we find out a little more about him? We really know nothing at all."

"Ah," smiled Nicholas, "you've a reason for asking that."

"Oh, it's nothing important," said Alexandra, not wanting even with Nicholas to embroil Olga in something she herself could have been mistaken about. "It's just that it would be nice to know more about him."

"Well, he seems the most decent chap to me," said Nicholas, "but perhaps you're right, especially if we're to see more of him."

"I'll leave it all to you, my love," said Alexandra contentedly.

Nicholas spoke later to one of his secretaries. Several weeks afterwards he received a written report, emanating from England. It was entirely satisfactory. John Kirby owned a cottage at Walton-on-Thames, occupied by a relative of his called Charlotte Kirby. He was the son of a deceased Army colonel and was a man of independent means who had travelled extensively.

It pleased Alexandra. She liked him very much and although it was entirely unsuitable for Olga to conceive an excessive liking for him, she was sure that

Olga would never forget she was the daughter of the Tsar.

It had been ten days of pure pleasure for Kirby. And it had been a revelationary and blissful ten days for Karita. She adored Livadia. It was beautiful, peaceful, and warm with charm and friendliness. Karinshka had its excitement and gaiety, its lovely and temperamental Princess, but it did not have such beauty, such grandeur and yet such simplicity. Nor did it have the Imperial family.

The Emperor had spoken to her, smiled at her, complimented her. The Empress was kindness itself. And the children. Adorable. Karita loved every one of them. Because, to them, she belonged to Ivan Ivanovich, their newest best friend, she too was their friend, and sometimes they came to her and asked her to do this or that for them.

Kirby found her in his suite once with tears in her eyes.

"Who has upset you?" he asked.

"Oh, no one has," she said. "It's the children. Monsieur, I've heard people say things about the Imperial family and I know now they were ignorant people. Never, never, will I ever believe what people tell me, only what I see with my own eyes. Oh, I'm so glad I came with you, it has taught me so much, it has taught me that our Tsar is a good man who loves people. Now I know what I shall say to ignorant ones when they speak lies to me. I shall——"

"Karita, you're making a speech, but I love you for it."

She blushed a little. It was possible, he thought, that many people would consider themselves neither ignorant nor liars when laying the blame for Russia's ills at the Tsar's door.

"Monsieur," said Karita, "it's because of you that I've met the Imperial family, I am so fortunate to be here with you. Of course, that isn't to say it isn't beautiful at Karinshka, only that——"

"Only that there are more ups and downs at Karinshka," he said.

"I wasn't going to say that at all," said Karita loyally.

"Of course you weren't," he said, "you are a treasure, Karita."

He kissed her. Karita tingled. It was a very agreeable sensation.

His visit was nearly over now. He was drilling for the last time with Alexis. Alexis was giving the commands and Kirby was doing his very best. At last, he said, he knew his left from his right, and he owed it all to Alexis.

"Oh, you've been jolly good, you know," beamed the boy.

The Grand Duchesses, white-bloused and blue-skirted, were as usual an hilarious and irreverent audience. Marie declared that Ivan Ivanovich really was the most comical driller poor Alexis had ever had to contend with. Tatiana said that he was fascinatingly droll and that she was head over heels in love with him.

"When I'm married to the King of Denmark," she said, "I shall invite him to dinner every night."

"Darling," said Olga, "I'm sure nothing would please the King of Denmark more than being invited to dinner every night by his own wife."

"Goose," said Tatiana, "I meant I'd invite Ivan, then he'd spend all evening kissing my hand."

"Mama and Papa wouldn't think much of that," said Marie.

"Nor would the King of Denmark," said Olga.

"And how awful for Ivan Ivanovich," said Anastasia, "fancy having to kiss someone's hand while everyone else was eating all that scrumptious food."

"Not just someone's hand," said Tatiana, "mine."

"Oh, help," said Anastasia.

"Tasha, are you dreadfully, dreadfully in love?" asked Marie.

"She's dreadfully everything," said Olga.

109

"No one, simply no one," declared Tatiana, "has any idea of how terribly one suffers when one is in love." She waved gaily to Kirby. He waved back. Alexis was aghast. Didn't Ivan Ivanovich understand that at drill a fellow simply didn't wave at people, especially girls?

"Great Scott, what a trial I am to both of us, Alexis," said Kirby.

"Oh, I don't mind too much," said Alexis magnanimously.

"Oh, jolly good," said the much-improved recruit, "and I tell you what, give me a right incline and a couple of about-turns and then I'll be too dizzy to wave to anyone."

There was hysteria at that. Olga murmured, "Oh, dear delicious Mr. Kirby," and then blushed crimson as Tatiana slyly peeped at her.

"What does love really feel like?" Anastasia asked earnestly of Tatiana.

"One just can't eat," said Tatiana. "Isn't that awful, being quite starving and yet unable to eat a thing because of love?"

"Never mind," said Olga, "when your love has departed you'll be able to go back to eating like a horse."

"When he's gone I shall be quite inconsolable," said Tatiana, who could remain immune to teasing, "but we shall write long passionate letters to each other, of course."

"How lovely," said Marie with a sigh, and Anastasia, who had a gift for histrionics, gave a very creditable imitation of love awaiting a passionate post.

Olga was suddenly wistful. He was leaving tomorrow.

He was going. The Tsar had already said a friendly goodbye to him. The rest of the Imperial family, together with Anna Vyrubova, were on the broad terrace at the top of the steps to see him on his way. Karita, having made her curtsey, stood to one side while he said goodbye to all of them. Anna was charming. Alexis kissed him. Tatiana gave him her hand and

110

sighed. Marie was sweetly affectionate. Anastasia, giggling, kissed him too. Olga wanted to smile but her lips were stiff. Alexandra was gracious.

"Perhaps you'll be able to come and see us again before you return to England," she said.

"Oh yes, you must," cried the younger children.

Olga's blue eyes darkened. He had said nothing to her about returning to England.

"Wherever I am, I shan't forget Livadia," he said. He smiled. "It's the loveliest place, full of the very nicest people. Bless you all."

They waved to him and to Karita as he went down the white, shining steps with her to the carriage ordered to take him back to Karinshka.

"Goodbye, Ivan Ivanovich, come again!"

Only Olga was quiet. When he had finally gone she disappeared.

FIVE

Princess Aleka seemed happier to have Karita back than Kirby. She fussed over the girl as Kirby made his way up to his suite. Karita was bubbling, full of Livadia and its splendours, enthusiastic about the Imperial family. Aleka let her go on, then boredom raised its head and she interrupted.

"Who did he meet, Karita?"

"Oh, everyone, the Tsar and Tsarina and all the children, Highness. You would never believe how much they all liked him and he was so good with them. All the Grand Duchesses are lovely and so sweet."

"Simpering angels, yes, I know."

"No, Highness." Karita risked her position with her quiet but firm contradiction. "They aren't like that, truly."

"Oh, very well. There." She patted Karita's cheek. "But I'm not interested in the Romanovs. What men did he meet? There are always the most intriguing ones who come and go at Livadia."

"There was old General Sikorski and officers of the Tsar's guard," said Karita, "but he met no one else, Highness. He spent all his time playing tennis with the Tsar or bathing with the family or being with the children."

"Oh, was it as boring as that for him?" Aleka laughed. "He is the soul of innocence and uneventfulness, poor man. Go along, Karita, and see if he wishes someone to run an uneventful bath for him."

She went up herself a little later. He was writing a letter in his drawing-room. He rose.

"So," she said, "you have returned to the poor relations."

"Princess," he said, smiling, "it's good to see you're still yourself. But lovelier."

Andrei came languidly in.

"Welcome back, dear man," he said, "it's gladdening to see you. You must tell us all about it."

"Must he?" said Aleka. "It will only be about playing tennis with the Tsar and games with children. When that by itself has been said, what more is there?"

"There are those delicious ladies of the court," said Andrei.

"What is delicious about the virgin matrons of Alexandra?" asked Aleka.

"But, my chicken, surely you understand that their very respectability makes their conquest an esoteric journey into the unknown?" said Andrei. "Surely they were included in Ivan's games?"

"Darling," said Aleka, her paleness overlaid by honey unavoidably caught from the sun, "do you seriously think our virtuous Ivan would play games with court ladies under the nose of his beloved Alexandra? I'll swear he didn't attempt to unlace the most willing of them."

"I didn't have time," said Kirby, "I had so much drilling to do."

"Drilling?" said Andrei faintly. "Drilling?"

"I'll tell you all about it at dinner," said Kirby.

Aleka looked hard at him. God, how insufferably pleased he was with himself, he was the damnedest man to shake out of self-satisfaction. "I think we can manage without being patronised," she said. "Do you imagine you're the only man who's knelt at the feet of our autocrats and been patted on the head? Ah, I suppose that next you expect to winter at Tsarskoe Selo?"

113

"You are the sweetest friend to have, Princess," he said.

It sounded like a pat on the head.

"Andrei," she said, "when you first picked this dreadful man out of his little pond why didn't you throw him back?"

"My dearest," said Andrei, "I would have if I'd known you were going to adore him."

That brought laughter from her.

"Ivan Ivanovich," she said, "it's nice you're back. Don't go away again. It makes me cross."

"I can't stay for ever," said Kirby, "I must return to England fairly soon."

"England? That little place? Why, you ridiculous man, it will give you claustrophobia."

That gave her the last word. She glided out happily then. Andrei winked and followed. Left to himself again Kirby finished his letter of thanks to Alexandra.

Several days later he went into Yalta. Anstruther made him fairly welcome. Kirby wrote out an official letter of resignation and pushed it across to Anstruther. Anstruther read it in his fatherly way, scrawled "Unacceptable" over it and pushed it back. He then brought up the subject of leave. Kirby had had virtually none for more than three years. Anstruther informed him he had now been given six months, and that this stood even though Kirby had been disappointingly negative over the question of how totally Russia was committed in her alliance with France. Kirby insisted he had never had any intention of stepping on that ground.

Anstruther took it manfully and told him to enjoy his leave.

The Crimean autumn was still warm and beautiful when he made up his mind to return to England. But there were shadows in his mind and an image of the impossible, and the bright, fragrant days only reminded him of young, breathless loveliness. He must leave Russia, where he was so dangerously close to being haunted by a child of the dawn. She was sixteen. Sixteen. A Grand Duchess. The moon could not have been

114

more unassailable. In a few years she would marry one of her own kind. She could not escape, would not wish to, for as the Tsar's daughter she could not trade in fairy stories.

Aleka was incensed when he told her. She had been remarkably equable since his return and had become so affectionately tolerant of Andrei's indolence that Andrei confided to Kirby that he was sure he was experiencing a loving prelude to a proposal. It would be entirely consistent in Aleka to take this initiative. How, said Andrei, could a man say no to Aleka and not end up with his throat cut?

Kirby had a feeling that the Princess now would willingly take the knife to him.

"So, you wish to leave us! You're so drunk from drinking with Romanovs that we're too dull for you! Go back to England, then. You're bored with us. I'm not so self-centered that I haven't noticed that."

"Aleka, I swear that isn't true," he said. "I swear that you know it isn't. You and Andrei are the least boring people I know. Isn't it possible that I can want to return home for a while without you thinking I'm trying to insult you? Sweet Princess, you are the most stimulating woman in Russia and one of the loveliest. When I come back you'll be the first person I'll look for." That was a lie but he had to say it. Temperamental and outrageous, the Princess had still been fascinating and generous, she had given him friendship, provocation and the freedom of Karinshka.

Her mood changed. Sweetness replaced anger.

"Ivan, you aren't compelled to go. You are free to do as you like. You have no responsibilities to anyone, have you?"

"It's not that," he said, "only that I haven't seen my own country for over three years. And I do have an aunt who likes to see me once in a while."

"But she has had so much of you in the past," said Aleka, "and here we are just beginning to know you, to like you. Ivan, stay with us, come to St. Petersburg with us when we go there."

He was in her suite, where Aleka had been dressing for dinner. She had draped a green silk negligee over her petticoats, and her unbraided hair was a spilling auburn richness. He could not deny her loveliness. She only lacked innocence. Ruefully he wondered what he was coming to that he should be in such absurd consciousness of innocence, which sat so coyly and uncomfortably on so many women.

"I'll come to St. Petersburg after I've been to England."

"Oh, thank you for that crumb," she said, "how generous of you. Oh, why must you go? Together we could turn everything upside-down in St. Petersburg and outrage everyone. You'd be able to meet far more interesting people than you've met here, you'd become a lion instead of going back to England and only being a mouse."

"Well, let me be a mouse for a while and turn me into a lion later."

"Oh, stop trying to be clever and amusing." Then a sudden intuition sprang. "Ivan, you're in love, that's what it is."

"You're easy to fall in love with, Aleka Petrovna."

"I wish you wouldn't be so damned fatuous. It isn't me, it's someone else. Why, I know now, you were already in love the day I met you on the station at Nikolayev. It showed then. You were a thousand miles away all that day. Is it this woman in Yalta?"

"It's no one."

"Imagine you lying about so sacred a thing as love." She was a little mocking. "Don't you trust me?"

"Not altogether, love."

"God, you can be a cad sometimes," she said. She flung back her hair. "Oh, if your mind is made up, I suppose it's because she's in England herself. Ivan, you're a dreadful disappointment to me."

"I'm sorry," he said. "Aleka, thank you. Karinshka has been wonderful."

"Yes, but I wish you hadn't been thinking of someone else all the time," she said. She shrugged, she smiled, she shook her head. She laughed.

Karita was undisguisedly upset. When she had superintended his packing the next morning and the other servants had gone she said to him, "I am to say goodbye to you, monsieur?"

"I hope not, Karita." He was dressed for travel, in light cord trousers and belted jacket, white shirt and velvet tie of brown. "I hope to be back if her Highness invites me."

Her brown eyes were unhappy. Her relationship with him had been entirely without friction, it had become something that gave her a warm pleasure. She had almost come to feel a permanency about it and now it wasn't permanent at all. It was very silly, but his departure made her feel unwanted, unnecessary. Worst of all, his good humour and his affectionate treatment of her had spoiled the special relationship she had had with Oravio. She knew indeed that she did not want to marry Oravio at all. She would only become someone to whom Oravio would say, "Woman, do this," or "Woman, do that."

"It will be very nice if you do come back, monsieur," she said.

"Karita?" He put a hand under her chin and lifted her face. Her eyes were brimming, "Karita, what's this?"

"Oh, monsieur, forgive me, but you've been so kind to me and it was so lovely at Livadia."

"Yes, Karita," he said gently, "we share that, you and I. We know Livadia. That we will never forget, will we?"

"Never," said Karita.

"Sweet one, what will I do without you? I'll misplace everything I own." He kissed her. His mouth was warm and firm, the kiss not light but lingering and affection-ate. She trembled, the tingling rushed through her body. "There, that was to tell you I'll be back again." He smiled, not without regret. Karita was the prettiest and most companionable of persons. She smelled of

117

the woods and the fields, the flowers and the sun, and she was the personification of all that was best about the Crimea.

"Oh, monsieur," she cried and rushed from the suite.

He said goodbye to old Amarov and then to Aleka and Andrei. Andrei was exhibiting a faintly forlorn look. He liked Kirby unreservedly. Kirby did not make demands on a man. He minded his own business about things. He was a good fellow.

Aleka was not deceived by the kiss Kirby gave her. She was sure he was relieved to be going. It made her feel very dissatisfied and she suffered the pressure of his lips stiffly and unresponsively. She could bring herself to say no more than, "Goodbye." It was irritating to listen to Andrei professing he would miss Ivan confoundedly. Good God, anyone would think he was in love with the man himself.

When Kirby had gone she became furiously in need of action and stimulation.

"To the beach," she cried to Andrei, "now, at once, this instant."

"Dearest angel," he said, "as we are, without that which will keep us decent?"

"Without anything, anything," she said, running down the steps.

Naked in the warm blue sea, the beach a golden desert, Aleka plunged and frisked, Andrei gently bobbed. Aleka rose from the depths, hair streaming, white body flashing, breasts gleamingly wet.

"Oh, dear heaven," murmured Andrei.

"Tonight you shall make love to me, darling," she said.

"My own," said Andrei. And, as he let himself float, "My God."

SIX

Lenin, the most inflexible revolutionary of them all, who considered that if a man had logic he did not need emotions, was active in exile. He argued systems. It was systems that Russia required. It did not require compassion, charity or humanitarianism. It did not even require politics. He was a headache to many of his fellow exiles. He talked for hours on end. He was unanswerable, uncontradictable. A man of logic was like that.

The Duma seemed agreeably reasonable to the Tsar one day, disagreeably unreasonable the next.

Peter Stolypin, the far-seeing prime minister who might have saved everything for everyone given time, was dead. Assassinated. The assassin, as usual, had been a man of passion and little sense. He thought, as all assassins do, that violence was superior to argument.

Gregor Rasputin was in bad odour again. The belching old fool, for this was what his addictive gormandising and his loud mouth made him at times, had only himself to blame. He had seduced an Imperial servant. But his Imperial champion, Alexandra, would hear no word against him. He was a holy man. The suggestion by her mother-in-law, the Dowager Empress Marie, that everything would be rosy again if the holy man was kicked all the way back to his Siberian village, was received coldly and rejected firmly.

"Olga, my lamb, you always seem to be looking for someone or something."

Grand Duchess Olga Nicolaievna turned from the rail of the *Standart,* the Imperial yacht. She had been observing the movements of people she could see on other vessels anchored at Reval on the Baltic coast. It was June, eight months and more since her birthday ball at Livadia. Always distinctive in the sincerity of her feelings, she was more physically distinctive now. She was a little taller, a little shapelier, and she had acquired a poise that gave a soft dignity to her charm. She smiled unaffectedly at Anna Vyrubova.

"Oh, I was just looking at people," she said, "there's always something to see about people."

In a blue and white yachting dress, with a round white hat banded in blue, she looked fresh and lovely, her skin creamy from the sun.

"Almost we're deserted," said Anna, "everyone has gone aboard the *Hohenzollern* to drink champagne with Emperor William."

The German Emperor had spent three days in Reval, inflicting his boisterous personality on Nicholas and becoming egoistically expansive in the welcome Reval had given him. Olga considered him well-meaning but overpowering. He wanted to manage everyone and everything.

There was a British yacht stately at anchor some distance away.

"See that one is from England," said Anna, pointing.

"Yes, I noticed," said Olga.

"Perhaps our Mr. Kirby is aboard," said Anna. "Do you remember him? He was the Englishman who bought me this parasol and was so nice with Alexis."

"Mr. Kirby? Oh, yes." Olga did not affect a great deal of interest. "He played a lot of tennis with Papa. They're all very gay aboard the *Hohenzollern,* Anna, you can hear them."

Kaiser William's white and gold yacht was anchored close to the *Standart.* A hum of revelry buzzed from

120

it. The sun, rising to its midday peak, brought lustre to the vessel's immaculate brightness. But Olga was proud of the *Standart*, which outshone the *Hohenzollern* in almost every way. It was the most graceful, the most beautiful vessel afloat.

"I should really be on my way to join your Mama under the awning," said Anna.

"Well, of course, Anna. You mustn't let me keep you."

Anna went. Tatiana stole softly up on her sister. Graceful and willowy at fifteen, Tatiana was a physical echo of her elegant mother but her temperamental opposite. She had a gay and inexhaustible vitality, a lively mind and a teasing approach to all her sisters, especially to Olga. But it did not prevent the two of them being as close as they could be. They could not have enough of each other's company.

"Boo, goose," said Tatiana. Olga, elbows on rail, chin in hands, her round white hat on the back of her head, only said, "Go away, child."

"Oh, listen to grandmamma," said Tatiana. "What are you doing? You're dreaming again."

"I'm looking," said Olga.

"What at?"

"There, where Russia is dancing," said Olga.

"I knew it," said Tatiana, "you are dreaming."

"But see," said Olga, "everything is reflected in the sea and everything is dancing. That shows I am looking, that I'm not dreaming."

But she was.

"Yes, but it's only reflections of yachts and things," said Tatiana. She surveyed the sunlit, sparkling waters and then saw what Olga had seen. The waters were a dancing reflection of heaven and earth. "Olga, you're so strange sometimes." She put an arm around her. Adoring Olga, she could not bear to be shut out.

"You silly, it isn't strange to see things in waters," said Olga, "you can see them in fires too. I think I'll go down to the piano and practise my Bach. I'm dreadful at Bach."

"You're dreadful at Tchaikovsky and all the others too," said Tatiana.

"That," said Olga, "isn't as bad as being dreadful all over, as you are, Tatiana Nicolaievna."

Tatiana laughed. It was always a happiness when Olga was being droll. Suddenly, animatedly, she rushed into an item of news. "Olga, listen. I heard Mama say that Crown Prince Carol of Rumania has asked if he might have a photograph of you. He's seen your picture in a paper and is most *terribly* impressed. I hope it wasn't the one where your hat was over your face. But what do you think, do you think he'll ask to come and meet you?"

"Perhaps," said Olga quietly.

The sun was a golden glow, the harbour gay with flags and bunting. Somewhere a ship's orchestra was playing. But Olga Nicolaievna was pale beneath her summer tan, cold inside her fluttering dress.

The weeks were long, the months interminable. England did not help a bit. Kirby wasted his six months of leave doing nothing worth remembering. His Aunt Charlotte, formidably acute for all her reactionary Victorianism, offered the opinion that his restlessness was a natural consequence of rushing all over the globe and that more rushing would only make it worse. His best course was to settle down in a worthwhile job. A cousin of hers could probably find him a very worthwhile one in the Admiralty. Alternatively, he could get married. It would not be before time.

He was saved from the Admiralty and from wedlock by being sent to Germany when his leave was up. They thought he could be useful there. Everything that was anything was happening in Germany at the moment. He went to Berlin. There he discovered he was one of so many that there was an air of duplication about his every movement. He traded with contacts who, he suspected, had already traded with shadowy colleagues of his. He could not help feeling that the quantity of agents in Berlin was more obvious than their quality. Inevitably the Germans would come to feel the Wilhemstrasse was being invaded.

He avoided buying the Russian newspapers that were available on the bookstands. He could not, however, avoid seeing reports in German papers of the Kaiser's visit to the Russian Baltic. In one he was suddenly confronted with a picture of the Russian Imperial family going aboard the *Hohenzollern*. Out of the black and white came the face of Grand Duchess Olga, seen over the shoulder of a sister and crowned by a white round hat.

She was smiling.

He put the paper down, left it on a bench in the Tiergarten.

His suspicions that his own people were overplaying their hand crystallised into fact. He received a message.

"We think they're on to you. Come home."

He returned to England. They told him to remain on call. He met a girl, Felicity Dawes, whose dark eyes and rich silks reminded him of Princess Aleka. He had written a letter of grateful thanks to the Princess. She had not replied. He became fairly involved with Felicity, who took him to Berkshire to meet her parents. They were charming. Felicity was charming too, but occasionally intense. He made love to her. She was very intense and passionately delighted to be compromised. She took it to mean they were engaged. Kirby, temporarily released from the accumulated pressures of a celibacy a man of his age found unnatural, did not, however, feel ecstatic enough to be as honourable as that. Felicity, fulminating against his elusiveness, wrote him a letter and had it delivered by hand.

It was an ultimatum and he might have reconsidered in her favour had it not coincided with the arrival of a letter from the Empress Alexandra.

He could not believe it.

The Imperial family intended to go to Livadia earlier this year, they had to be in Poland in the autumn.

Would he care to join them if he was free? The Empress wrote in her usual staccato style.

"It is a long way for you—but if you can come please do—all will be delighted to see you again—the children especially—we shall be there only for three weeks—this has been such a busy year——"

It was not a long letter but its sincerity shone.

He wondered how she had got hold of his Walton address. She had, perhaps, enquired of Princess Aleka.

He went, leaving behind a bewildered and outraged Felicity.

They gave him leave, they seemed interested that he was going to Russia again. He arrived three days after the Imperial family had installed themselves. He was received by a member of the Tsar's suite. Nicholas was on an outdoor excursion with the children and Alexandra, troubled by sciatica, was resting. Taken up to the rooms he had occupied last year the first person he saw in his suite was Karita.

"No," he said disbelievingly.

"But yes, monsieur." Her eyes were shining, she swooped into a glad curtsey. "You are back and at Livadia. Oh, everything is so nice. It was the Empress herself who arranged for me to come from Karinshka. She said you could not do without me."

She was golden, her braided hair a gleaming casque.

"How very nice, Karita," he said, "how very nice indeed."

The spacious suite was in impeccable order, the sun diffused its light warmly over comfort and graciousness. The tall windows of the drawing-room stood open on to the gleaming white balcony. Karita in excited happiness began to unpack his luggage.

"Karita," he called from the open windows. She went to him. He was just the same, and already the sun was putting the familiar flecks of gold into his trim, brown beard. His eyes showed pleasure, kindness, affection. He put his arm around her shoulders and looked at the view with her, at the blues, the reds, the greens, and at the melting transience of horizons.

"It's been the best part of a year, Karita. I've missed you, I've missed Russia."

"It is awfully agreeable that you're back again," she said.

"It's more agreeable to see you, little one." He kissed her. Karita accepted it naturally but it was still disturbing. It made her face flame. She returned to the unpacking. He followed her into the bedroom. "Princess Aleka, how is she?" he asked.

"She hasn't been to Karinshka yet, monsieur. She's been everywhere else and has let others use her Palace. It's full of them now. They're all very gay and enjoying themselves very much, but it isn't the same without her Highness. She is very gay herself but you don't hear her as much as you hear her friends. Oh, it is so nice to be here."

"I see." He watched her. She was unpacking carefully as if treasuring each moment of the task. She was in her Karinshka blue and white. He thought that in a year or two she would be quite lovely. She had character, grace and smooth, fine-boned features. "They've been running you off your feet, have they?"

"Oh, it's only been busy for me. It's old Amarov who is having headaches. He keeps asking what is Russia coming to when the nobility behave so loudly and so irresponsibly in someone else's house. But then he's always saying that about everybody. He is a lovely old man."

He heard noises, the sound of scampering feet and youthful voices, and then into the suite ran the children. Alexis, Anastasia, Marie and Tatiana, sun-flushed and heated from the excursion with the Tsar, but still with the unlimited energy of the young and joyful. There were delighted shrieks.

"Ivan Ivanovich!"

They surrounded him, touched him, hugged his arms, laughed up at him.

He had never had such a welcome. Its effect momentarily robbed him of speech. Karita, glancing at him, had the oddest feeling that Ivan Ivanovich was

125

painfully overwhelmed. Then lightly he said to the excited children, "Let me see, who are you? Were you here before? Are you new children?"

"Ivan Ivanovich! It is us! See, this is me, Alexis!"

"And me, I'm Marie, you know I'm Marie."

"My word," said Tatiana to Anastasia, "he's shockingly forgetful when you consider how beautiful we all are. At least, I am."

"Oh, yes, goodness gracious me," said eleven-year-old Anastasia, trying to sound like her mother in surprise.

"Why, of course," said Kirby, "now I know you. Good lord, here you all are. What a coincidence." He shook hands with Anastasia. "How are you, General Sikorski?"

Anastasia doubled up.

"She's not him," cried Alexis, hopping about in delight, "she's Stasha."

"No, go on," said Kirby, "well, I never." He smiled at Tatiana. "Ah, Irena Vladinova, I can't mistake you, at least. You never change."

Marie and Anastasia shrieked. Irena Vladinova worked in the kitchens. She was very jolly. She was also very fat.

"Oh, Ivan Ivanovich, you wretch," cried Tatiana. Then she sighed, "Oh, you're still so scandalously endangering to a fair maid."

"I'm what?"

"Oh, they're just some words I picked up," said Tatiana, already strikingly attractive. She was fifteen.

"Well, try not to pick up too many more," he said.

They romped around him. They took Karita by the hand and made her join in. A lady-in-waiting looked in to see what all the noise was about. Karita blushed. She suggested their young Highnesses should go down to the gardens and he would join them there soon. They begged him not to be long and danced out. Karita said that people who said unkind things about them deserved to bite out their own tongues.

"It's a habit of centuries for the best to be stoned by the worst, Karita."

"Oh, everyone is so happy now that you're back," she said, and then for some reason hurried out, leaving the unpacking only half done. It did not bother him, he began to attend to it himself. He looked up at a new sound. It was the merest whispering rustle. He saw her, the one who hadn't come with the others, the one so much on his mind. She was at the open door, but holding back as if her entrance would be an intrusion. She had one hand on the door frame, from the other hung a white straw hat. Her dress was a soft, waisted whiteness. Her chestnut-blonde hair seemed a deep, burnished gold. Olga Nicolaievna was almost seventeen, she was not afraid of life but she could still be shy.

"Well," he said, "well." She thought that very English. A Russian friend would have offered a prolific flourish of words at seeing her again after so long an absence.

"The children ran back," she said, "Papa and I walked."

"And here you are," he said. "Highness, I'm having a day of the nicest surprises."

"Are you?" Her voice was a little unsure of itself. "I didn't know if you—that is, Mama received your telegram but no one knew if you'd really come."

"But I sent another telegram from Moscow as soon as I got there."

"Did you? Oh yes." She seemed to be searching for words. She found some. "Papa would have stayed out all day if Tatiana and I hadn't reminded him we should miss your arrival. I expect you're awfully fatigued, you've had such a tiring journey."

He had been affected by the exuberant joy of the others. He was just as affected by Olga's quiet diffidence.

"To arrive at Livadia makes any journey worthwhile."

"You've been in England," she said, and then saw

the open and unopened luggage. "Isn't there anyone to help you? Shall I?"

She came in then. Unlike the others she did not look heated from the excursion, she was cool and fresh, as if she had laved her face and brushed her hair. And changed her dress.

"Highness——"

"It isn't necessary to call me that," she said, clicking open the locks of a case, "it's only in public that I'm supposed to be grand."

"Olga Nicolaievna, you're very grand in the very best way, but Karita will be back to attend to this."

"Mr. Kirby, I'm not incapable, you know." She was still a little unsure of herself, her shyness obvious. And she knew it was obvious and that made it worse. To overcome her self-consciousness she took out a white shirt and held it up against her front, saying lightly, "See, this is what you wear when you're playing tennis with Papa, isn't it?"

"And when I fall about," he smiled.

She shot him a quick glance. He was just the same, so relaxed. He was always able to say something that eased her out of her restraint. She suddenly found confidence in herself.

"Mr. Kirby, oh, I'm so happy you could come. We all are. It will be such fun again."

Her smile was impulsive, full of the winning charm of her father's. She was lovelier, more endearing than ever.

He hid an intensely emotional reaction by saying, "Karita won't think so when she sees the state of these things." He indicated the contents of the newly-opened case. The clothes were tumbled and creased.

"Oh, that's nothing," said Olga, "it's only important that you've come all this way to see us again. Papa will be delighted."

Karita returned. She was dismayed to see the Grand Duchess actually unpacking clothes. The Grand Duchess even appeared to be happy about it, but it was the improperest activity for her young Imperial Highness.

It was even more improper for Mr. Kirby to stand by and let her.

"Your Highness——"

"Karita, I'm not in the way, am I?" said Olga. "I'm not at all busy and can help, really. Are you seeing to refreshment? Mr. Kirby has creaking bones, you know, and I expect all of them are aching shockingly after his journey. And look, just see how he's packed some of his things. You should look after him always and go to England with him, and then you'll be able to see he doesn't stay away from us so long. Think, he's been away nearly a whole year and didn't write to us once. Isn't that terrible?"

"I did write to her Imperial Majesty," said Kirby.

"Oh yes, to Mama," said Olga as if that was of no account at all.

"But he has made up for it now," said Karita, taking things as Olga unpacked them. She put aside items that needed pressing and hung others in the capacious wardrobe or placed them on shelves.

"Yes, but you should still go with him next time," said Olga, "no one could look after him better than you, Karita."

"Would you like to do that?" asked Kirby.

Karita stood in open-mouthed astonishment.

"Oh," she gasped.

"There, you see, Olga Nicolaievna," he said, "you've stunned her with thoughts of the awful responsibility of it."

"Oh no," said Karita, "I'd like it immensely. But you're teasing me, and I can't speak English."

"I'll teach you on the way," he said.

"Oh, now I'm frightened to death," said Karita and sat heavily down. Olga laughed.

"Karita, you must," she said delightedly, "it will be simply famous."

Karita could not think of anything more famous, that would please her more. She looked up at Kirby. He did not seem a bit teasing, only very interested.

"You'll have to ask the Princess Karinshka," she said,

"and then my parents and also Karita Katerinova———"

"Who is Karita Katerinova?"

"My grandmother," said Karita, "and then there's old Amarov, he would be like an old bear with fleas if you didn't ask his approval too, but it's Her Highness the Princess Karinshka who is most important."

"Naturally, we'll ask them all," said Kirby.

Olga stole a look at him. There was nothing to say how important the Princess was in his eyes. He just seemed very pleased about the prospects of Karita becoming his own servant. It would be the happiest arrangement. Karita would not let him forget Russia. Karita would write to her and tell her all that he was doing.

Olga felt uncommonly pleased with herself.

The Empress Alexandra also seemed pleased. Stiff and in pain as she often was with sciatica, she was never irritable with it. And at Livadia she could almost forget it, for here she was always at her most contented, close to her family, close to peace and beauty. Although state affairs frequently took up much of the Tsar's time, there were still many hours of leisure, of happiness and of remoteness from the narrow and critical environment of St. Petersburg.

In the atmosphere of the capital things never got better. It was invariably the fault of incompetent politicians. Without the burden of politicians the people could happily have left everything entirely to the Tsar and his own picked ministers. The Tsar thought first of the people. Politicians thought first of self-advancement and self-glorification. The Tsar did not have to consider his own advancement and was not interested in glory.

Tenderness was the keynote of all Alexandra's feelings towards her beloved husband. How blessed they were in their family, and if God had chosen to visit Alexis with weakness He had also sent them His elect to ease the boy's sufferings.

Alexandra gave Kirby a welcome not only kind, it was almost affectionate. She knew how his company delighted the children and that was sufficient in itself to earn her regard. And Nicholas, who seemed to dislike no one except disagreeable members of the Duma and people who threw bombs that maimed the innocent, was extremely partial towards the Englishman. He could not wait to get him on the tennis court again.

The children quickly resumed possession of Kirby whenever they could. They had no lack of playmates, including grown-ups, but it was Kirby they loved. He drilled with Alexis, who still had an enthusiasm for this particular activity, and they took turns to be officer and soldier. He introduced English games to all of them, and during the heat of afternoons, when most of the sensible adults retired to cooler quarters, the green lawns of Livadia sighed under romping, scampering feet and the bright air echoed to shrieks and laughter.

Olga seemed not quite to know how to conduct herself when games were afoot. She was balanced on the brink. She was a young lady who could not join unruly, exuberant children without looking like one herself. Yet the gaiety and the infectiousness of the games called to her. And Mr. Kirby himself always played and no one could say he was not grown up. So sometimes she watched and sometimes she joined in, and when she joined in she was exquisitely caught up in the merriment, flushed, laughing, flying, slim ankles glimpsed amid swirling petticoats.

When she was watching, Alexis, always adoringly teased by the girls, would call on her for help.

"Olga, take them away!"

"They're nothing to do with me," Olga would say, "they're really too dreadful to belong to anyone."

One day she responded to his appeal by saying, "Alexis, I'm still catching my breath from the other game, ask Mr. Kirby to help you."

"He can't help," said Anastasia, "Marie and I are sitting on him."

Olga, who had been leaning back, fanning herself,

sat up. Mr. Kirby lay flat on his back. He seemed quite comfortable and was softly whistling a tune she had heard from him before, but Anastasia and Marie were indeed sitting on him.

"Oh, you ruffians," cried Olga, "if Mama were to see you—get up!"

Alexis was shouting with laughter, Tatiana in hysterics.

"It's all right," said Kirby, "it's just a new game."

"It's Ivan's own fault," said Tatiana, "he's always lying down in the middle of some game or other."

This was usually when he was requested to take sides. He avoided showing partiality by lying down and closing his eyes. More often than not they'd dance around him, singing a song of Georgian peasants at harvest time. And then, "Arise, Ivan Ivanovich, the corn is all cut and the grapes all gathered. Arise!"

Kirby would open his eyes and say, "Good. With the work all done who needs me?" And he'd close his eyes again, they'd drop to their knees around him and shout him awake. It was a made-up game they adored, and in the flowering vitality of the girls and merriment of the boy, Kirby renewed his enchanted relationship with the children of the Tsar. He came to love them all, Anastasia the gifted, Marie the romantic, Tatiana the gay and Alexis the brave.

And Olga?

He loved Olga in a way that alarmed him.

Dearest of them all, grave in her moments of reserve, endearingly shy when caught off guard, wide-mouthed and blue-eyed, with her tumbling hair always lustrous and alive, Grand Duchess Olga Nicolaievna took renewed possession of his heart

The days were hot and glorious. Olga loved it when, except for her mother, they all went off together on countryside excursions. The Tsar was an outdoor addict. On these occasions there was no need for her to consider whether to frolic or sit, there was only the pleasure of walking with her family, with Kirby and any others who cared to join them. They explored woods, looked for berries, wandered over flower-carpeted slopes and meadows, and grew brown and happy and hungry.

Olga, perhaps, was desperate to grow up at this stage, to be a young woman. The excursions helped, made conversation easy, for there were always so many things to talk about, the abundant variety of nature being all around them. She could talk to Kirby about the colour of wild blooms, the call of a bird and each different view. Sometimes if there was a ridge or slope to climb and he was near he took her hand. It was never anything but a natural gesture to which she responded naturally, his clasp friendly and sure. She could not help herself, each time it happened her fingers closed around his and clung.

"Mr. Kirby—see?"

It was the tiniest and most delicate of wild blue flowers, peeping from a bed of moss.

"And all alone," he said as they stooped to inspect it together.

"Why do you say that?" she asked, seeing his face in profile, its expression absorbed. "You aren't alone, are you? You have friends and a home in England?"

"No, I'm not alone, Olga. I'll never be alone."

"What does that mean?" She straightened up, regarding him a little seriously. He was bare-headed, wearing open-necked white shirt and blue flannel trousers. The sun was in his eyes.

"That I'm very fortunate," he said, "some people can be lonely in the most crowded places."

"Yes, if they have no one who belongs to them," said Olga.

"Yes," he agreed. "Come on, the others are leaving us behind. Shall we walk or run?"

If there were the intriguing complexities of growing up to consider, there was also the joy of still being young. The others were well ahead, the woods were bright with sunshine, the leaves glossy on the trees, dry on the ground. There was silence. It was broken by a whoop in the distance.

"Run," said Grand Duchess Olga, and they ran, the leaves dancing around their feet. She laughed, an unseen twig caught her hat and pulled it from her head. "Oh!" she said. They stopped, he picked up her hat and she stood quite still as gravely he put it on the back of her head where it perched like a white halo. Her blue eyes held his, hers full of life's simple wonders.

"There, now you're grand again, Highness," he said.

"Mr. Kirby, please don't call me that."

She was a summer fragrance in green and white, her snowy blouse buttoned high to the neck, her skirt the colour of Livadia's velvet lawns, her look one of wistful entreaty.

"Sometimes it can't be helped," he smiled.

They went on, walking this time. They saw the others in the distance. Tatiana had stopped to wait for them. She was waving.

Olga said, "You know, of course, that Tatiana is passionately in love with you."

"No, is she?" He considered it whimsically. "What d'you think, shall I wait for her to declare herself or what shall I do?"

"Well," said Olga demurely, "I think you should know she's also madly in love with the first officer of our yacht and terribly enamoured of a captain in our own regiment in St. Petersburg. So, really, it would be better to do nothing."

"I'll just wait," he said, "it may all blow over."

They came up with Tatiana, who took his hand. They began to talk of books. Olga was an avid reader. The conversation flowed. Tatiana had never known her sister so unrestrained outside the family. She talked and talked. Well, thought Tatiana, imagine that.

When they finally got back to the Palace that day Olga said to him, "Mr. Kirby, I've never enjoyed myself so much, except perhaps——" The pink came.

"Except perhaps when Anastasia and Marie sat on me?"

"Except at my birthday ball," she said.

134

"Well, that was exceptional, wasn't it? That was an unforgettable experience for everybody."

Her eyes danced.

"Oh, dear Mr. Kirby," she said and flew.

Never, he thought, had there been innocence entirely without artifice or primness. Never until Olga Nicolaievna.

He took tea in the gardens with the Tsar and the children. Olga did not appear, she had her tea with her mother and Anna Vyrubova in Alexandra's boudoir. Alexandra observed how well Olga looked, how healthy from her walk.

"Child, lamb," she smiled, "you've brought the sun indoors with you."

"It was lovely," said Olga, helping herself to bread and butter, "and Papa went on and on as usual. He'd walk off the face of the earth if you didn't hold him back."

"Where did you go?"

"Where? Oh, everywhere. Oh, thank you, Anna, I'm in such need of that." She took the glass of tea from Anna. The boudoir was an entirely feminine room, restful and quiet. Olga relaxed, sipping her hot tea. Alexandra discerned the soft, glowing happiness. She remembered again her own dreamy years at Darmstadt.

"What are you thinking about, darling?" she asked.

"Mama, wouldn't it be wonderful if today could go on for ever?" said Olga. "Then we would always be with you and Papa. Nothing could be more perfect."

How young she was, thought Alexandra with heartache, how very young.

"We should need some sleep," said Anna practically.

"No, we shouldn't," said Olga, "it would always be day, we'd never be tired, there'd be no tomorrow, only today, going on and on. What do you say to that, Mama?"

"I say my sweet darling is very happy." Alexandra paused, then said, "And how did our friend Mr. Kirby enjoy himself?"

135

Olga bent her head lower to her glass of tea.

"Oh, very well, I think. Alexis says Papa must make him a general."

"What would you like Papa to make him, my love?" asked Alexandra gently.

"I? Mama, what is it to do with me? I hadn't thought about it at all." But the blush was there, burning, the falling hair a bright curtain that could not quite hide the rising crimson. Olga could never be evasive without betraying herself.

Alexandra sighed. She frequently relived her own youthful dreams and the day when Nicholas appeared, a handsome embodiment of all she had ever desired. She had been so fortunate. Olga might not be. She could not spoil her daughter's dreams. They would fill her life for a year or two, would fade and be replaced by more practical considerations. It was only important that while her children were young they should be happy. They were none of them difficult, they were the best of children, devoted and good. They were intelligent, they knew who they were but they would never place material things before love and kindness.

Olga must have her dreams.

But she would never forget she was the Tsar's daughter. And Mr. Kirby could be relied on. At least, she felt he could.

"Ivan Ivanovich," said Tatiana one morning, "my mother says she would be exquisitely enchanted to receive you at your most loving convenience."

"What did she say?" he asked.

"Actually," said Tatiana, "she asked if you would like to go and see her."

"Quite the same thing, O Grand Duchess," he said. "*Avante*, I go to exquisitely enchant the Empress."

Tatiana watched him as he went long-leggedly on his way. The little sigh that escaped her was genuine. He really was the nicest man and so droll.

"Do you know," she said a few minutes later to Olga, "I think I'm going to become awfully incurable."

"Darling," said Olga soothingly, "you aren't to

worry. You are bound to develop some sort of brain later on and then you'll be just as normal as the rest of us. Well, almost."

"I'm speaking," said Tatiana haughtily, "of becoming incurable in my passion for Ivan."

"How fascinating," said Olga in awe and wonder. "Do you think it's going to be as incurable as your passion for Captain Mestaroy and your devotion to First Officer Paul Sahkov?"

"Heavens," said Tatiana, "how cutting you are." She bubbled. "But, Olga, isn't it delicious to have Ivan here? He's so droll. I'm sure those stiff Englishwomen swoon about for him. Tell Mama we simply must keep him."

"Keep him? Do you think he's a monkey, then?"

"Well," said Tatiana impishly, "no one could say he wouldn't make an adorable pet."

Olga turned away.

"That's not amusing," she said quietly, "that is only very silly."

Tatiana flew to her sister.

"Olga, oh, I'm sorry." She stared in disbelief and distress. There were tears in Olga's eyes. "Olga?"

"Oh, it's nothing," said Olga quickly, "it's just something in my eye. See if you can see it?"

But Tatiana could see nothing.

Alexandra thanked Kirby for coming to see her so quickly. She was gracious without being condescending. She spoke first of her family's pleasure in his company, of his continuing kindness towards the children. She asked about his own feelings, whether he still found Livadia enjoyable. He answered in the only possible way. Then she returned to the children, discussing with him the ways and characteristics of each. She spoke at length of Olga.

"Your Highness," he said then, "all your children are a delight. It would be gratuitous of me to speak of what they mean to you and his Imperial Highness, and what you mean to them. They are your children

137

and always will be. I know what the Grand Duchess Olga means to you, I know what she is and who she is. There's nothing I'd do to give you concern in any way. I am greatly privileged by the kindness you've shown me, and as much as an Englishman can be I'm your servant, Highness. I am also your friend. Always."

Alexandra, sensitive and responsive, regarded him with swimming eyes.

"Thank you, Ivan Ivanovich," she said and said no more.

The days began to pass more rapidly. It was still summer, the leaves still a bright green, the sun a brilliance. Alexis was not concerned with time, only with life, and Anastasia, Marie and Tatiana absorbed each day with careless rapture. Only Olga was wistfully counting the hours. And each hour saw her turn her back more consciously on adolescence to face maturity. If she did not have Tatiana's quick vitality, she was beautiful because of her colouring, her blue eyes and her inherent grace.

The gardens of Livadia were invaded that summer by every spirit that belonged to the realms of laughter and joy, and the presiding king was the jester of mirth and revelry.

Kirby burned to a deep brown, the sun drenching his hair and his beard with gold. Sometimes Olga could not take her eyes off him. Visitors in the shape of the occasional ministers, formal in frock coats, looked like museum effigies beside him. The Tsar rolled up the shirt sleeve on his serving arm at tennis. Kirby rolled up both of his. His arms were tanned, dark, sinewy. Olga thought of roving adventurers, piratical and free. She also thought of pale, elegant Crown Princes and the coldness came.

Stay as long as you like, Alexandra had said. But Kirby knew he could not stay until the family went, with himself as a last-minute embarrassment to his royal hosts. He told Karita he could not stay the full three weeks. She understood.

"Their Imperial Highnesses will be so busy when they leave," she said, "it wouldn't do for us to be in the way, monsieur." She hesitated, "You will not forget, I am to be in your service, yes?"

"Do you really wish that, Karita?"

"Oh, yes," she said.

She had no fears. Ivan Ivanovich would be her protector as well as her employer. Her parents had not only given her their blessing, they had said that to be in the service of an English lord and to go to England with him was to give her and all her family a standing never before achieved. They agreed with her that he was, of course, a lord. She would come back to Russia in time, but meanwhile would see the world and that was a good thing for anyone. She was to remain faithful to Russian Orthodoxy, count her beads and take her ikons. Oravio no longer mattered. He was to marry another girl, a more complaisant one than Karita.

Of course, it was all still dependent on whether Princess Aleka Petrovna would agree to release her. Kirby was to arrange to call on her in St. Petersburg. It was all very exciting and sometimes Karita could hardly sleep at night.

Kirby advised Alexandra that he must go. She did not attempt to dissuade him, she only said, "You don't mean immediately, I imagine?"

"I thought the day after tomorrow, Your Highness."

She nodded. It was difficult to fault him, except in that his presence did divert Olga's thoughts from the inescapable course her life must take. "Well, we ourselves will be leaving soon. Will you tell the children, Ivan? If I tell them they'll beg me until I'm distracted."

He told them, all of them, in the gardens. They did not hide their dismay. Alexis thought his going was something to do with having been drilled too much.

"No, Alexis," he said, "you've drilled me not too much, not too little, but just enough. Now I know my left from my right and my nose from my knees."

139

Alexis thought that splendid but very funny.

"Ivan," said Anastasia, "it's not a laughing matter. What will we do? Who will play 'I Spy' with us?"

"Only General Sikorski," said Tatiana, "and he'll get it all mixed up with 'Catch.' "

" 'Catch'?" said Marie.

"Yes," said Tatiana. "Catch my eyeglass, dear child, it's falling out again."

They shrieked, forgetting their dismay. Only Olga remained apart from the laughter.

The following morning she searched the gardens for him. She found only Anna Vyrubova.

"Anna," she said, "where is Mr. Kirby? Have you seen him?"

"I think he's already gone, sweet," said Anna.

"But he couldn't have," said Olga aghast, "he hasn't said goodbye and he wasn't to leave until tomorrow."

"He's only gone to Yalta," said Anna passively, "he's arranging a carriage now."

"I must see Mama." Olga was urgent. "Perhaps she'll let me go with him, I've things to get. Anna, please send someone to tell him to wait while I find Mama."

She ran. She found her mother. She smoothed her hair and dress, she explained that she had things to buy in Yalta.

"What things, darling?"

"Oh, a book for you, Mama. Please, may I go with Mr. Kirby? It would save two carriages and having to find someone else to go with me."

Alexandra could not resist the appeal. Olga could dream a little longer. Mr. Kirby would be gone tomorrow. She sent only a footman to accompany the coachman. Yalta was a friendly place. The family often shopped informally there.

The carriage was waiting when Olga came down the steps. She wore her best walking-out dress of summery white, with a blue-and-white beribboned bonnet, and carried a parasol. Kirby thought she looked young and sweetly lovely. He gave her his hand, assisting her into the open landau.

"It's not inconvenient for you, Mr. Kirby?" She was as composed as she could be.

"Inconvenient? I'm delighted," he said.

"Oh." She lowered her eyes demurely. "You see," she said, as he seated himself beside her, "I've things to buy and Mama said my French lesson was of no great importance."

"French lessons never are except to the French. But are you to have no lady-in-waiting?"

"You are to escort me," she said. "Oh, will that be a nuisance? You're going because you have things to do there. I shall be in the way."

"In the way?" he said as the carriage moved off with the wheels grinding a little. That, he thought, was typical of her modesty, and her presence typical of the informality of the family when they were at Livadia. "Olga Nicolaievna, when you're in the way the day will be a sad one. You'll be a great help, in fact. I'm going to buy presents, and you'll be able to tell me what everyone would like. Well, I am in luck, aren't I?"

"You're going to buy presents for the children?" She had put her parasol up. She looked like summer itself in her soft, warm enchantment.

"For everyone," he said.

"What fun," said Olga. She often accompanied her mother to Yalta. It was quite exhilarating to accompany Mr. Kirby. They bowled along at a spanking clip-clop, the air dry with heat and as heady as a vineyard. The wild grape foliage was dusty, the fruit glimmering among the leaves. "Buying presents *is* fun, isn't it?" she said.

"It was going to be a worrying responsibility buying the right ones until you came along," he said. "You'll be invaluable. Look, the hawk."

She followed his pointing finger, eyes tracing the falling descent of the bird. It dropped from the sky, a plummeting black against the blue, and disappeared behind a slope.

"How swiftly a hawk dives," she said, "almost as if it's given up life."

"Instead," he said, "it's actually gone to plunder the life of another. You are a very fine Grand Duchess today, Olga. Is it your hat, your dress, your parasol or you?"

He spoke lightly, with a smile. She looked at him, her eyes dancing.

"I think you're being nice to me because I'm going to be invaluable when you shop," she said.

He laughed. It evoked a happy response from Olga. They laughed together. Oh, how wonderful it was not to feel shy or constrained, to feel so much at ease with him. She liked it as he sat back in relaxed enjoyment of the ride, his straw boater tipped to shade his eyes from the sun, his blue linen jacket and white trousers cool-looking. The wheels threw up chips as they entered a village whose brightly-coloured cottages and houses were built on serrated slopes. A man on a horse loped towards them, the horse black, the man as dark as mahogany. He touched his hat and inclined his head to the Grand Duchess. The Tsar and his family were familiar figures in the area, the carriage with its Imperial crest easily recognisable. Olga gave the man a smile, inclining her own head shyly under her parasol. Kirby loved the way she made the gesture. He felt that here in the Crimea the Tsar, if not Tsarism, was as secure as he could be. He was sure that under no circumstances would Olga be allowed to ride through St. Petersburg as freely as she was riding to Yalta. Here the Imperial family went around without fuss. It was not like that in certain other places in Russia.

Before he had met the Imperial family he had been curious about them as autocrats, not as people. Now he was sure there were no people less equipped to be autocrats than they were. They had inherited autocracy, they were imprisoned by their heritage and governed by the edicts of their ancestors.

On this summer day it did not seem important.

"Mr. Kirby . . ." She turned to speak to him. He gave her a smile and she knew there was no need to make conversation, no need to think that on such a day he would regard silence as dull. It was enough for him that summer bequeathed its magic and the carriage wheels sang over the dusty road. She was not unused to the attentions of men, mainly the suitable young officers always in the background. They could engage in endless light flirtatiousness. It would be words, words. How nice that Mr. Kirby could get along without any words at all at times. Olga felt so free, so relaxed.

They alighted outside a square house in Yalta. Kirby said that he first had to see a consulate official. Did Olga mind if they did their shopping afterwards?

"It's whatever you wish," she said, "I only have to buy a book for Mama."

"Good," he said. He took her in with him and the clerk, with no idea who she was, only that she was deliciously charming, found her a chair. She was quite happy to sit and wait, making no fuss at being left while he went through into Anstruther's office. Anstruther had not missed a glimpse of the girl. She pleased him very much.

"No one coud say your Russian references aren't of the highest," he said.

"Do you mind if we don't discuss that?" said Kirby. "I'm not on a social visit. I had a letter from you. What is it you want?"

"Do sit down, I won't keep you long in view of the young lady waiting. But don't mistake me, let me explain my outlook. They say things about the Tsar in England and elsewhere and it's taught me to be careful about offering opinions on people I don't know personally. In my position as a very minor civil servant I've never been close to the Imperial family, but I know a little about them. I envy you. I wish I had

143

your capacity for making friends, and I don't necessarily mean influential friends."

"Don't be apologetic, it's making me feel uncomfortable," said Kirby, "but thanks all the same. Now, what have you brought me here for?"

"I hope you're not going to be touchy," said Anstruther reprovingly. "They aren't going to ask too much of you. You know Kiev well. There's a man there the Russians want and we'd like to do them a favour. We'd like to tell them where they can pick him up. You have friends and contacts in Kiev. The man's name is Spirokof. We know he's in Kiev. We don't know exactly where. They want you to go there, talk to people and find out."

"That's not my branch of the profession," said Kirby, "I'm an observer not an informer."

Anstruther tried his most fatherly smile.

"Spirokof," he said, "is a maker and thrower of bombs. He intends to make one for the Tsar. He's going to Poland in October. So is the Tsar. The Russians will be watching for Spirokof there but it would do us the world of good if we helped them to pick him up in Kiev."

"Damn it," said Kirby.

"Good, you'll go, then? Good. Then they'd like you to remain in Russia for a while, in St. Petersburg. You could do your best work from now on. You get on with Russians, and with the international situation as it is we need people like you. You'll probably be instructed in St. Petersburg to make love to the whole nation. I wish," Anstruther concluded drily, "I had your ability and your job."

"You can have my job. You have your own qualifications." Kirby made for the door. "You'll excuse my hurry. With the international situation as it is I'd be out of my mind if I kept the Tsar's eldest daughter waiting any longer."

"Good luck in Kiev," said Anstruther.

Olga had composed herself to a patient wait and Kirby's reappearance came as a happy surprise. He did not seem to have been long at all. She rose with a smile.

"Just an extension to my passport," said Kirby. The clerk jumped up to open the door. Olga's smile entranced him. He bowed. It delighted her because she knew he did not know who she was. Therefore the bow was for herself. Out in the street she walked by Kirby's side, a girl in a flowing white dress and parasol, with a grace that made people look.

She loved shops. She forgot all her self-consciousness in the pleasure of knowing the Yalta shops better than he did. They looked in windows, they entered cool, shady interiors.

"First," he said, "something for your mother."

"Why, a book," she said, forgetting that that was what she had said she wanted to buy.

Kirby did not intend to be ostentatious, to go in search of the expensive. That would impress neither Olga nor her parents. It was the suitable, not the expensive, they would appreciate. He and Olga did not discuss prices at all, they simply looked at everything that was interesting. Finally, on Olga's earnest recommendation, he bought Alexandra a book of English poetry.

"Mama will love that," she said as it was being wrapped, "and I shall enjoy it too, so it's really a present for both of us."

"Well, one present for two people is as good as two presents for the price of one," he said. "What a very invaluable start, Olga."

"Oh, pray don't mention it," she said gravely but with a smile peeping.

He smiled too and began softly to whistle that tune. He looked very tall under the low ceiling of the bookshop. They went into other shops. He bought a new tennis racquet for the Tsar, again with Olga's approval.

"That will please Papa immensely," she said, "he just uses any old racquet that comes to hand, sometimes one with a broken string. He says he can't afford a new one."

145

For Marie, they chose a glass ball which when shaken showed a snowstorm in London. It was colourful and fascinating, and Olga said it would be a gift from England. For Alexis they chose a boy's peaked blue cap of canvas and linen, for Anastasia a bright headscarf to protect her hair from the dust. For Tatiana a pair of winter gloves made of sealskin.

Then he said to Olga, who was enjoying it all so much, "And what for you, Olga Nicolaievna?" They were in a shop full of glass cabinets containing Crimean wood carvings and pottery, much of it religious. Olga was absorbed in the contents of one cabinet.

"Oh, but there's Mama's book," she said, "it's for both of us as we agreed."

"I didn't agree."

Suddenly she was pink. He turned away, not wanting to embarrass her more. He looked at a wall lined with shelves, each shelf full of beautifully-bound books. Some were prayer books. His eyes passed them over. The Imperial family were deeply religious, their observance of evening prayers had not escaped him. It was not uncommon in the evenings to see one or more of the children with a prayer book. He did not think, therefore, that Olga was in need of more religion.

"Olga, do you have a Shakespeare?" he asked.

She turned from the cabinet. He was holding a book bound in soft black leather, a volume of Shakespeare's plays in English. There was a Shakespeare at Tsarskoe Selo. It belonged to the family, not to her. Olga, well-read in the classics, had not yet become serious about Shakespeare. She removed her gloves, took the book from him, opened it and glanced through the preface pages. It was English, it had been printed and bound in England.

She lifted shining blue eyes to his. The pink was there, a warm blissful pink.

"Oh, I'd like something from England," she said, "especially this. I would cherish it, truly I would."

"Then have it, won't you?"

She nodded, not knowing what else to say in her

146

delight. There were people who said the Imperial family had the wealth of Croesus. He wondered what they would say to see Olga in such glowing pleasure over this gift of a book. He paid for it. Olga did not want it wrapped, she would take it as it was, except that she drew Kirby aside and shyly whispered, "Please, will you write in it for me?"

He took a fountain pen from his inside pocket, laid the book on top of a cabinet and opened it up. On the blank flyleaf he wrote, "*To Olga Nicolaievna, in gratitude for so much sunshine—J. Kirby, Livadia 1912.*" She read it. He had not put Ivan Ivanovich. He had put himself. He understood, he was not Ivan Ivanovich to her because he was not Russian. She did not ask for him to be Russian or to behave other than as an Englishman.

She wanted to thank him very much but the right words eluded her. Her dark lashes blinked away her sentiment as they emerged from the shade of the shop into the bright day. She stopped and he took the book from her to let her put up her parasol. Her parasol up, she happily took the book back from him. "Mr. Kirby, I—oh, you are so kind." Then suddenly the right words came. She smiled up at him from beneath the parasol. "It isn't at all surprising that Tatiana is so passionately devoted to you."

"Great Scott," he said, "hasn't that all blown over yet?"

"Oh, she's quite incurable at the moment," said Olga. Her eyes sparkled and they walked together down the street to pick up their carriage, to return to Livadia, he with the other gifts swinging from fingers hooked inside strings. Then she said, "Oh, how forgetful I am, I came to buy Mama a book and you have bought it instead. Never mind, I'll buy her an embroidery cover. Do you have some money I might borrow? I forgot that too. I'll pay you back, I promise."

"Olga Nicolaievna," he said, "just how forgetful are you?"

"Well, if I do forget to pay you back," said Olga,

"I suppose you could say I was shockingly remiss."

He loved her for that. He loved everything about her. He went with her to make her purchase. Olga was quick. She selected a pattern of primroses and forget-me-nots. He laughed at the forget-me-nots. So did Olga.

They talked easily on the drive back. Occasionally Olga pointed out a white gleaming house or palace and told him who owned it. He took in, as he had many times before, the warm lushness of grass, the wild, untouched slopes, the scent of the ever-present roses and the purity of the air that mingled with the dancing wind from the sea. And he took in too the enchantment of a girl unspoiled and precious.

Lunch awaited them at the Imperial Palace. They were late but no one minded. They were crowded by the children, their meal interrupted, and Kirby gave them their presents. They were overwhelmed.

They played their last games with their friend Ivan Ivanovich that afternoon, but in the spiritedly resilient way of the young they did not let their regret at his imminent departure mitigate their enthusiasms of the moment. The Empress and Anna were there, needle-work on their laps. Alexandra's eyes turned oftenest on Alexis. He had the energy of two normal boys. Few people knew of the Tsarevich's inherited weakness. It was something Alexandra did not want people to know.

She had been delighted with the book of poetry, requesting Kirby to inscribe the flyleaf with his name and the date. The Tsar had beamed at the acquisition of a new racquet.

"Absolutely capital, my dear fellow," he said, "and be sure that although I'm plagued with reports today, I'll find time for a set or two later. You are the most generous chap."

Olga stood near, sharing her father's pleasure. She was closer to Nicholas than any of his other children.

The white Palace was touched by a pink glow as that bright day turned into evening and the sun reddened. The long afternoon was over, the lawns, the gardens, the cloistered walks and the courtyards became silent. The laughter, the play, the high voices and deep voices, the fluttering dresses, the young and the adult, all had retreated, vanished. The white chairs were empty, the garden tables brushed clean, and only lengthening shadows came to invade the green grass that had known so many dancing feet.

Life itself seemed suspended. But where an old thick vine curled and crept over a high wall and the path was a tiled surface of soft colour, a girl in a white dress walked alone. Her face was wistful, her blue eyes full of dreams. A young officer emerged from the Palace and came looking for her.

"Olga Nicolaievna, it's evening time and they're wondering where you are."

"Yes, the day has gone, Vasily. It could not last, could it?"

"It will be the same tomorrow."

He had said goodbye to the Tsar and now the rest of the family were at the top of the steps to see him on his way, as they had last year. Karita was with him, composed and self-possessed, but just a little sad.

"Come again, Ivan, come again!" The children were as exuberant in their goodbyes as in their play. "Come to Tsarskoe Selo, you must!"

He thanked Alexandra in simple terms, putting his lips to the hand she extended. Olga, by her mother's side and apart from the noisy children, was very quiet, her hands, clasped in front of her. The children were around him again, delaying him with further goodbyes.

"Don't crowd him so," said Olga, "you're all such ruffians."

He glanced up from them and smiled at her. Then he teased Marie's curl, winked at Alexis.

"Farewell, then, children, sweet ruffians, grand Grand Duchesses, all," he said.

"Oh, must you go, must you?" cried Anastasia.

"I must," he said, "I'm quite done up."

It was a favourite expression of Olga's. They burst into final hilarious laughter and waved and called to him as with Karita he went down to the carriage put at his disposal. He turned at the bottom, waved his responses and then assisted Karita into the carriage.

Olga, eyes wide and incredulous, trembled. Alexandra slid her hand inside her daughter's arm, gently restraining her from an impulsive flight downwards.

"Mama, oh, Mama," gasped Olga, "he did not say goodbye to me."

"Yes, he did, my love," murmured Alexandra, "in his own way."

Olga did not wait to see the carriage drive off, she turned and ran along the terrace and into the gardens. Alexandra sighed. Olga's dream was over, as many of her own dreams had been over when she herself was a romantic girl. But Olga would recover. She would forget. There would be so many other things.

She lifted her hand, her white lawn handkerchief fluttering in goodbye to the moving carriage.

Karita was quite mutinous. Ivan Ivanovich was to go to Kiev for a while. Without her. She was to be dropped off at Karinshka, he to take the carriage on to Yalta and proceed from there to Sevastopol and Kiev. He would return to Karinshka when he could and take her to St. Petersburg then, where they would see Princess Aleka together and discuss her release from the Princess's service.

"That is not what was agreed," said Karita. She felt horribly disappointed and let down. They would laugh at her at Karinshka, for she had spoken on the telephone to old Amarov and it had been understood she would not be coming back.

"Then let's make a new agreement," said Kirby. He looked quiet and sombre, and for once was not alive to all that they passed. "I'm sorry, Karita, but it's only for a while, then I promise to come and fetch you from Karinshka, see your parents and take you to St. Petersburg."

150

"It is not what was said," she insisted.

"Oh dear," said Kirby.

"Monsieur, it makes me look so foolish."

He understood then. He took her hand. She stiffened, sat very upright.

"I'm sorry, Karita, forgive me," he said, "but let us have this new agreement. If you feel foolish, I feel unhappy. So we're both suffering together. But you and I can't fall out, that would never do. Karita?"

Her profile was extraordinarily sweet, but her mouth was set. She looked straight in front of her. He saw her swallow.

Then she said, "You promise, monsieur? You'll come for me later?"

"Yes, Karita."

She reconciled herself. He would not let her down again. Would he? She looked at him. He was all affection, his smile reassuring.

"Very well, monsieur," she said. "Oh, I have something for you. Her Highness the Grand Duchess Olga Nicolaievna asked me to give it to you after we left."

She gave him a little flat package. He opened it as the carriage swayed and jostled over the road. It was a snapshot in a small gilt frame, a snapshot of Olga and Tatiana in the gardens of Livadia. Tatiana looked gay and alive, even in sepia. Olga's shy smile peeped amid her flowing hair. The sun caught it, the picture flashed and danced. She had written across the bottom of the photograph.

"So that you shan't forget us—Olga Nicolaievna."

He had not realised just how much he loved her until that moment.

Olga was sobbing her heart out. Only Tatiana, closest and dearest to her, found her. She lay full length on leafy ground amid the trees, face down, her head pillowed on her arms, the sobs racking her.

"Olga, oh dearest, sweetest sister, what is it, what is it?"

"Tasha . . . oh, I'm in such pain."

151

"See, don't move. I'll run for Doctor Botkin."

"Oh no, do not. Don't bring anyone, please."

"Then don't cry so, you'll break my heart. Do you want to break my heart?" Tatiana was in anxiety and distress. "Olga, don't. Tell me what it is, tell me."

The slim, rounded body shuddered and still the sobs came.

"Tasha, don't tell anyone, please don't."

"Dear dear Olga, never, never."

"I'll be all right." She strove to check her despair. "I'm better—better already."

"There, we'll go to Monsieur Gilliard together in a moment. He'll be pleased Ivan Ivanovich has gone, not because he doesn't like him but because we'll attend better to our French lessons now."

"Tatiana?"

"Oh, sweet sister, do you think I don't know? I'm not as young as all that."

She lay quiet then. She turned and sat up in a while. She was pale beneath her creamy tan, her face streaked with tears. She dabbed at them with a tiny handkerchief already soaked.

"Tasha, he didn't say goodbye to me, he didn't say one word to me, not one."

"He did. Oh, you silly, he did." Tatiana was earnestly comforting. "He said goodbye to all of us, all of us together. He couldn't say anything specially to you, he couldn't. You know he couldn't. He's not like the very proper Englishmen we hear about, he is proper in the very nicest way. Listen, yesterday I said to him, 'Ivan, who is the fairest of us all?' And he laughed and said, 'Tatiana Nicolaievna is the fairest, of course, Anastasia the cheekiest and Marie the nicest.' So you see?"

"See?" Olga could only see that he had gone lightly and left her in pain.

"He wouldn't even say your name, and that's it, don't you understand? Oh, you goose, it's in his eyes all the time, the way he looks at you and he's always looking at you. When we're both old and our husbands are rather bald and fat, we'll tell our grandchildren all about a handsome English prince who adored you and danced at your birthday ball with you."

"Our grandchildren?" Olga's laugh was fragile, half-hearted. "Tasha, he talked of *his* grandchildren. But he's not a prince."

"He's our prince, dearest sister, yours to remember and mine to talk to you about. There, we'll always have each other, always."

She was consoled but the pain was still there.

He had gone and Livadia had lost its enchantment.

SEVEN

Kiev, capital of the Ukraine, had been of fascinating interest to him on previous visits. It had lost its interest for him now. Now it was only a cloudy city harbouring a man called Spirokof, and until he located this man Kiev imprisoned him.

He missed Karita, missed her busy concern for his daily life. He missed all the familiarities of the new existence Empress Alexandra had created for him, the children, the laughter, the tranquillity of evenings bathed by red-gold. He missed Olga. He could not think of how far apart she was from him in every way without emptiness forming like a gaping darkness in his mind.

But he had an assignment to pursue in Kiev. It was a grey, monotonous pursuit to engage in. Its only redemption was in its connection with the Tsar.

He seemed detached from reality in Kiev, for what he had thought very unreal, his regard for a daughter of Nicholas, had come home to roost as an unarguable fact. It was unreal to emerge into light each day and not be able to see her.

He found friends he had made on earlier trips to Kiev, and one by one he renewed contact with men he had used years ago for obtaining information. It was a slow tedious business. It meant the renewal of goodwill, the re-establishment of their confidence in him and the asking of questions. The questions brought blank faces, lifted eyebrows, or even a glance over a shoulder and an excuse to leave. Spirokof? Who was he?

It took weeks, it took what seemed like an eternity. But in the end there was a man whose acquisitiveness was more obsessive than his caution and who silently put out his hand and flexed covetous fingers. It was only a question of how much after that. Kirby went to a bank. It was not his inclination to haggle on this occasion, nor was it part of any personal fortune he was giving away.

He checked the information and sent to Anstruther a description of a man whom he saw entering and leaving a house twice in one day. Anstruther telegraphed an affirmative. Kirby had no intention of visiting the Okhrana, the secret police, to give them the information himself. They would ask questions of their own, scrutinise his passport, his background, enquire after his reasons and remember his face. He sent them the information in block letters on plain paper. For his own amusement he signed it in Lenin's name.

Then he left Kiev and returned to the Crimea, going to Karinshka. It was quiet there, the best of autumn gone. But Karita was golden and glowing, enormously happy to see him. Old Amarov shook his head and said he wondered what it was all coming to. Kirby went with Karita to her home in the village of Karka and there he met her parents, the most dignified people he had ever known. They talked with him, they did not mention Karita directly but spoke circuitously about the mutual responsibilities of servant and master. It seemed to Kirby after a while that the responsibilities of the latter far exceeded those of the former.

He had to sign a document. When this was done they at last smiled, touched their foreheads with clasped fingertips and bowed in acknowledgement of the fact that they had given Karita into his service and care, providing Princess Karinshka also signed the document.

"Now," said Karita, who had said nothing at all so far, "you are my father and mother, Ivan Ivanovich."

155

"And in time you will return her to us as good and as unspoiled as she is today," said her father.

Kirby put his hand on the document and inclined his head. He knew what was meant by unspoiled.

All the way to St. Petersburg Kirby tried to teach Karita the basics of English. They had a first-class compartment but not a private coach. The other passengers became extremely curious and put Karita in some embarrassment. Not so her new master. He was quite himself all the time. Karita thought there were occasions when he gave the impression that the world belonged to him, that it had been made for his convenience, except that this was not to inconvenience others.

He did not actually ignore the fascinated audience but certainly he did not let anyone distract him. And of course it wasn't long before some of them wanted to join in, and then it was very distracting and rather like turmoil. However, Kirby assured them it was all a very serious business and that if Karita Katerinova Sergova did not know the difference in English between "yes" and "no" by the time they reached St. Petersburg, her life there would become intolerable with confusion and complexity. This so impressed the other passengers that they were nearly models of rectitude and co-operation from then on, except for the times when her flummoxed pronunciation brought gales of Russian laughter from them.

Karita bore this with dignity. It did not matter who laughed at her as long as Ivan Ivanovich didn't.

It became colder as the train steamed farther and farther north-west and when they reached St. Petersburg it was snowing. Karita was entranced but shocked. Entranced by the huge, drifting flakes, shocked by the damp cold. They procured a droshky, Karita wrapped in all the coats she had. Porters loaded the luggage.

"We can't have this," said Kirby, seeing her nose turn pink and observing her little shivers.

"Ivan Ivanovich, it's dreadful," she gasped, blowing flakes from her lips.

He wore a warm check cape over his suit and a soft check hat.

"It isn't like Livadia very much, is it?" he said and had the droshky driver take them to the shops.

The afternoon was already darkening. The lights began to go on and almost at once the leaden flakes became spiralling swirls of glittering white. It was a bright wintry revelation to the Crimean girl.

They stopped adjacent a shop whose windows were a splendour of shining furs. Kirby took her in, Karita numb in more ways than one. She was to have a fur coat and hat, he said. She crimsoned.

"Monsieur, I can't, you can't, it isn't proper," she whispered frantically at the approach of a gowned assistant. But how warm the shop was, how enormous, and how ready he was to take no notice of her dismay.

"You can, I can and we must," he said. "If you freeze, sweet child, what will be said about me?" He spoke to the assistant who seemed grander than the Empress in her manner. Whatever it was he said to her, her grandness melted. She looked at Karita, smiled in totally committed admiration of the girl's colouring and led her up three carpeted steps to a wide, deep alcove sumptuous with padded chairs and tall mirrors. The next thing Karita knew was that she was being helped into a thick sable coat, deeply, glossily black. Oh, the warmth, the enclosing warmth and richness, the sensation of comfort and elegance. Kirby did not ask the price. It was not that kind of establishment. He merely said it would do very nicely.

"That is, if it will also do for you, Karita. Will it?"

Every mirror told her it would, and her shining brown eyes told him. She was gold and black. Madame herself joined them and was enraptured. She had a girl bring fur hats and they found one to match the sable coat. Karita pulled it on over her braided hair. The sable coat and the Cossack-style hat eliminated Karita the maid and presented her as a vivid, radiant beauty. Kirby felt an immense pleasure.

"Ivan Ivanovich?" she said faintly and in entreaty.

157

"Look at yourself," he smiled and she turned and the mirrors reflected the rich, glossy picture that was herself.

"Beautiful, oh so beautiful," said the gowned assistant.

"Enchantée, enchantée," said Madame to show she was on speaking terms with the nobility. She clapped her hands discreetly and the inevitable samovar appeared. The hot, steaming tea was drunk and the transaction settled most congenially, the cost not being mentioned until the very last moment and then confided in no more than a murmur. Karita was dumb now as well as numb. She was to keep the sable on, her damp coats carefully wrapped and put into a silver-coloured box.

They went to another shop and he bought her warm, winter boots. And when they were in the droshky again, Karita, booted and furred, was warm and beautifully snug, except for the tip of her nose. But the cold on her face was an exhilarating tingle now that she was so warm everywhere else.

However, her situation needed thinking about. She was not a simple girl and the Karinshka Palace had never been a rest home for the purely conventional. Princess Aleka and her guests had always been far from that. Karita knew that when some men gave expensive gifts to girls it was not in unconditional benefaction. What she did not know was whether the Englishman would require payment for gifts rendered.

If he turned out to be such a man as that she would rather give the gifts back. And it would never be the same after that.

The droshky swished over the snow, the horse's clop-clopping muffled. The city was alive now, bright with lights, a white fairyland under a black sky. People walked about in brisk defiance of the cold.

"Karita, are you all right?"

"I'm in amazement at you, Ivan Ivanovich."

"Are you really, now. Will you tell me why it's monsieur one moment and Ivan Ivanovich the next?"

"It's new to me to have you for my father and mother," she said, "I'm not used to it yet."

"Naturally, it doesn't confuse me," he said. "What are you in amazement at, about me?"

"You've spent a fortune on me," she said.

"Well, as your father and mother I've a right to. And you look lovely, little pink nose."

Her eyes shone, the flakes melting as they touched her lashes. The droshky went on to the east side of the Neva, taking them to the apartment which his people had selected and rented for him. The driver pulled up outside the tall, five-storey building, its many windows soft with curtained light. As Kirby helped Karita descend to the pavement a closed carriage came along. Its passenger, a woman, peered through the falling snow. She called out and the carriage braked to a halt, the horse slithering a little. The door swung open, she almost leapt from the vehicle and came swiftly over the snow, her furs glistening, her pale face alight.

"Ivan! Oh, Ivan Ivanovich!"

Ignoring Karita and caring nothing for the droshky driver, who had descended to help with the luggage, she flung herself into Kirby's arms. She pressed close, her dark eyes like black shadows, her auburn hair enclosed by her fur hat.

"Well I never," said Kirby, "my good fortune, I presume, Highness?"

"Devil, monster!" cried joyful Princess Aleka and kissed him resoundingly. Her mouth was warm from her closed carriage, his had been touched by the damp cold, and the contact was a tingling, emotive sensation for each. "Oh, how happy I am, Russia has reclaimed you. I've reclaimed you. Russia and I are both irresistible. I——" She broke off, conscious now that the person she had ignored was a girl in a rich, black sable coat. "Who is this?" she asked disgustedly.

"Your Highness," said Karita, "we have come to see you."

Aleka peered incredulously.

"Karita? What are you doing here, for God's sake?" The sky rained snow on them as Aleka stared at Karita's furs, at the elegance and beauty they gave her. She swung round on Kirby. The driver was torn between wanting payment and wanting to witness. He coughed. Aleka ignored him. "How dare you," she said to Kirby in fury, "oh, how dare you!"

"Her Highness," observed Kirby to Karita, "is already up and down."

"Libertine!" hissed Aleka. "You have torn this innocent from my protection and from her loved ones! I will have you shot!"

"Highness, no," cried Karita, "oh no!"

It was intensely interesting, thought the driver, but it was the sort of thing that could go on indefinitely and cost a man money. Didn't they realise how competitive it was plying for hire? No, the fact was they were the kind of people who didn't have to ply for hire. Theirs was a world of comfort and talk. Talk, talk, talk. And here they were now, going at it in the snow and having the time of their lives. He shifted crunchingly from one foot to the other.

"Oh," sneered Aleka, "you've run off with him, have you, girl? The seducer has won you with a fur coat, has he? Karita, I blush for you. You whom I've seen grow from a child. Oh, fool of a girl. Do you think a fur coat can make you happy? Do you think a man can? Karita, I blush for your lost innoncence and your stupidity."

"Your Highness, you are blushing very unnecessarily," said Karita.

"Oh, my word," said Kirby and found it difficult to keep his face straight. "Let me pay the driver and deal with the luggage, and then we can all talk about it in my apartment."

The driver had lumbered off the luggage, it stood bulkily in the snow. Kirby paid him off so handsomely that the man took back all he had said to himself and to clear his conscience he spoke out.

"God go with you, Highness," he said to Kirby,

"and may He do more than that. You're in for a fiery time with these two and will need all the help you can get."

"You insolence!" shouted Aleka. He touched his whip to his shaggy hat, mounted and drove off grinning and happy. Kirby brought the apartment porter out to deal with his luggage and then went up. The apartment was on the second floor. Karita was in immediate approval. She had been afraid he would not do himself justice and could not think why he had not taken a magnificent house. But she could not fault the spaciousness of the apartment, the number of rooms and the effects and furnishings. The drawing-room was laid with a deep red carpet, spaced with red-padded chairs. There were warm velvets and brocades, rugs and tapestries, a dining-room of panelled walls and two bedrooms.

He and she looked it over. Princess Aleka followed them about, a vision of pale, accusatory beauty. She was ready to cry with temper.

"Princess," said Kirby at last, "please sit down. There's nothing wrong, I assure you."

"Oh, damnation," she said, "are you married to her, then?"

"Your Highness!" Karita was inexpressibly shocked.

"What the devil are you doing here together, then?"

Kirby made her sit. The apartment was warm, she was stifled in her furs but refused to remove even her hat. She would suffer bodily discomfort as well as mental turmoil. Nothing would make her believe that Ivan Ivanovich had brought Karita to St. Petersburg for the good of her soul. The man was a swine. They all were.

Kirby explained. Karita helped. Aleka began to listen. The atmosphere became calmer. Kirby put it all very concisely. The swine sounded sincere enough. Karita looked angelically so.

"Oh, don't go on," Aleka said suddenly, "isn't it enough that you let me make a fool of myself? Ivan, you do some unspeakable things to me. And then you

161

wish me to do you a favour, to release Karita. Where did she get that sable?"

"She got it because she needed it. Aleka sweet, would you have her perish?"

"I only want to protect her."

He looked into her brooding, suspicious eyes. His look made her flush a little angrily.

"She'll be safe with me and from me," he said, "but if you say so, she must remain in your service and go back to Karinshka."

Karita seemed to wince. She turned and went into the main bedroom to unpack his luggage. Aleka regarded Kirby from under drooping lids. He was so bronzed that she felt anemic. He was seducing her from her resentment with that smile of his. She wrenched herself away from it, got up and flung her coat off, revealing a deep green dress that brought her paleness to life.

She turned to him. She was smiling. She took off her hat and tossed it on to a chair. Her auburn hair was dressed to softly shade her forehead.

"Ivan? You're pleased that we met tonight? You haven't said so."

"I'm always pleased to meet you, Aleka. You're an excitement."

She came forward and put her hands on his shoulders, her lightly rouged mouth provocative.

"You could not tolerate dull little England after Russia, could you?" she said. "You shouldn't have gone, I told you not to. I should have gone to Karinshka if I'd known you were at Livadia. Alexandra would not have refused to have me there too. Why didn't you let me know? Oh, of course, that wouldn't have suited you, would it? There was Alexandra Fedorovna to fetch and carry for. I should have been excessively in the way. It isn't very flattering to feel I'm less stimulating than she is. Although she's an Empress, she's not exactly pulsating."

"Do Empresses have to be?" he asked.

"Oh you, with your silly words." She smoothed

162

his shoulders, her hands lightly caressing. "I've been everywhere except to the Crimea. Ivan, everything is beginning to be tremendously active and I've been sticking pins into ministers. Tonight I'm having a late supper after the theatre. Come at half-past ten."

"What about Karita?"

She flashed into fire again.

"Oh, is she so indispensable that you have to bring her too?"

"I mean, what about releasing her to me? Will you, dear Princess?"

"Let us see," she said and she called Karita. Karita came from the bedroom, looking more as Aleka remembered her in a neat blue dress cuffed and collared with white. "Karita, you can't live with Ivan Ivanovich. What would people think?"

"Where else would his servant live, Highness?"

"But not just you alone, Karita, there must be others."

"Highness, it's not for me to decide about others."

"You have a great deal to learn, silly girl. Do you really wish this new life, to be away from the Crimea and old Amarov, and have Ivan Ivanovich walk your legs off? He has a habit of wandering far and wide, you know."

Yes, he had wandered off to Kiev, thought Karita. That had been upsetting. But what was that compared with other things? She would be serving a friend of the Tsar himself and the Grand Duchess Olga Nicolaievna had wished very much for her to do that. Then there was the obvious fact that Ivan Ivanovich needed her. He simply had no idea of the injustice he did himself—what must people have thought of him at times, a man of his position without a servant? Besides, he made her laugh, he teased her. It would be terrible if he engaged someone else instead of her. She would not go to England. That would make her parents look foolish as well as herself. And he would make someone else laugh in her place.

"Highness," she said, "if it doesn't upset you too

163

much I would like to be in his service. I'm to go to England with him if you agree."

"Are you indeed?" The Princess looked as if she had made the one discovery that mattered. "So that's it, is it? He's going back to England already, is he?"

"Before you go on to say I can't get her there quickly enough," said Kirby, "I've already explained I'll be in St. Petersburg for some time."

"Now he's cross with me," said Aleka. "That is what you'll have to put up with whenever you speak out of turn, Karita. But if this is what you really wish, then I'll agree. There, have I pleased you both?"

"Oh, your Highness," said Karita, grateful, "you've pleased me very much."

"Did you wish it as much as that?" said Aleka sweetly. "Be careful, child."

Karita, with a modestly innocent look, dropped a curtsey, bobbed her head to Kirby, and returned to her work in the bedroom. There she permitted herself a happy whirl or two in waltz time.

"Well, Ivan?" said Aleka.

"Thank you, Princess."

"Oh, how formidable you are to deal with! Am I myself to ask for a kiss when I've just released the sweetest girl in the Crimea to you?"

He kissed her, his arms around her, his mouth warm with friendship and gratitude. She closed her eyes, hiding the laughter in them, but it communicated itself physically in quivers.

"What are you laughing at?" he asked.

"At you, darling. At myself. At us. How silly we all are, and we are nothing compared with events. But how lovely to have friends, how sublime to laugh with them. Dear Ivan, that's what life is all about. You know it, I know it, Andrei almost knows it, but there are so few others."

"And the poor and oppressed?"

"That's the strength of the poor and oppressed, they can still laugh. That's what makes them worth every sacrifice."

164

"You might sacrifice your wealth," said Kirby, "but what else?"

She picked up her handsome fur, he took it and helped her into it.

"My friends, my scruples and my pity," she said. "Did you enjoy Livadia?"

"Very much."

"But of course. If you were a Russian I'd tell you it was healthier not to become too intimate with the Romanovs. But you're not. So." She shrugged. She smiled. "Ivan, we'll enjoy the season together in St. Petersburg."

"I enjoyed some of it last year with Andrei. Will it be different with you?"

"Much more stimulating, darling," she purred. "Andrei avoids people who matter. I like to meet them. Of course," she added thoughtfully, "my time isn't all my own, but we will see as much of each other as possible. You see, I have a new lover at the moment."

"Well, how delightful," he said very agreeably, "I hope he's stimulating. You deserve that, however new he is."

"Cad," she said. "But I thought I'd tell you."

"I appreciate it. Thank you."

"Most Englishmen are fairly civilised," she said, picking up her hat, "but you are damnable. You'll come to supper tonight?"

"I'll look forward to it very much." He saw her to the door.

As he opened it she said, "I lied, you know. I don't have a lover, not at the moment."

"Aleka Petrovna," he said, "that's anybody's fault but yours, and I'll do all I can to find you one."

She looked for a moment as if she would claw him. Then she burst into laughter.

"Oh, Ivan Ivanovich, how good that we've met again. There are only two men I adore, you and Andrei Mikhailovich. You'll see him tonight. Goodbye now."

She gave him her hand. He kissed it. She was laughing when he straightened up. It might, he thought, have been the democrat in her that was ridiculing the outmoded mumbo-jumbo of the privileged.

Later he went to Aleka's supper reception. Karita did not mind a bit at being left.

"Goodness, you are not to consider me," she said.

She was very quaint.

The reception reminded Kirby of the boisterous carousings at Karinshka last year. It took place in the magnificent drawing-room of her palatial house in the Prospekt Nevskiy, a hugely roaring fire adding heat to the fire of the conversation. It differed from the conversation at Karinshka in that it took place standing up. The supper was served buffet-style, but plates, forks and full mouths did not impede the flow of words. Nothing could get in the way of Russian voices. Forks indeed could emphasise the more telling points. The sound of discussion and argument rose and fell like surf around the eardrums.

At Karinshka the guests had all been of the nobility, the young, cynical and irresponsible kind. Here in St. Petersburg Aleka drew to her house a much more varied collection of individuals. She strove for an intellectual symposium, Kirby supposed, but the effect seemed just the same. There were young and burning progressives, whose command of political phraseology was such that every sentence was an oration.

"Only a combustible agglomeration of the most incorruptible ideals exploding as one will bring down the bastions of reactionary Philistines, only——"

"Yes, yes," roared a well-fed journalist with a face like a paunch, "but have you got a match? My cigar's gone out."

He had to roar. The din of discussion was indescribable. Even the burning young orator didn't quite catch the whole of the roar and passed him a clean fork instead.

There were intense students. They were either pale-faced young men or terribly earnest young women. They assailed the ears of writers and painters, and were assailed in their turn or out of their turn. Aleka moved from group to group, joining arguments and starting new ones. She was goddess-like in a gown of palest cream. In her excitement, her half-covered bosom rose and fell, and the paunch-faced journalist said he was damned if she had any right to introduce that factor into an aesthetic argument on the principles of inalienable factory rights for workers.

"What," he said in a loud aside, "has a bosom to do with any principles?"

"Well," said Kirby, who received the full force of the aside, "it does belong to our hostess. One must allow her some advantage."

"I suppose one could look at it in that light, but it's damned unnerving," said the journalist.

Andrei had found a chair. He reposed limply, gratefully. He had been delighted to see Kirby again. He lifted a languid hand in acknowledgment as the Englishman came to join him.

"Dear man, did you ever?" he said, his lazy handsomeness accentuated by a displaced lock of black hair. "The supper is beyond reproach, old boy, but how can one digest food in this atmosphere?"

Nobody else was having that kind of trouble. The more the guests talked the hungrier they became.

"I'm surprised you're here," said Kirby.

"Compulsive reaction of twitching limbs, my friend. She calls, my limbs obey."

"I can't think why you don't marry her, you'll suit each other perfectly."

"Love is one thing," said Andrei, "to be devoured is another. Is there some champagne?"

A liveried servant, self-trained to telepathic perfection for moments like this, bore down on them with a tray of filled glasses. They each took a glass. The golden liquid popped around the rims.

Not until the food had gone did the guests depart. They were as loquacious as ever and for minutes the street outside was full of loud voices and then all was quiet. Aleka slumped into a chair, stretched her legs in ecstasy. The room was littered. Cigarette smoke curled lazily around walls and ceiling. The roaring fire had subsided.

"Open a window," said Aleka.

Andrei paled.

A servant appeared, parted vast hanging curtains and opened a window. Damp, icy air rushed madly in to heat itself. Andrei shivered. Aleka breathed deeply. Earrings ruby red depended from her pierced lobes and three strands of matching stones rested like fire around her neck and over her bosom. Kirby put his head out of the window. The Prospekt Nevskiy was a cold, brilliant white.

"Man's inhumanity to man is a sad thing," said Andrei and retreated from the incoming cold to stand with his back to the fire.

"You can shut it now," said Aleka. Kirby closed the window. "Well, Ivan, what did you think of my guests?"

"Didn't I meet most of them at Karinshka last year?" he said.

"Are you mad?" she said.

"They sounded the same."

"Andrei, did you hear that?" She was reclining in feline content. "That is our Ivan come back to us, isn't it? Andrei, isn't he precious? How did we ever manage to be amused without him?"

"I haven't been amused," said Andrei, "not with everyone so distressingly agitated about everyone else. No one is taking the time to enjoy life, everyone is in a hurry to make things respectably dismal for the rest of us. They are all talking about saving Russia. Ah, poor innocents, in saving it their way they'll destroy it, and then they'll say, 'What happened?'"

"Andrei, you see," smiled Aleka, "is at last becoming involved. He's actually beginning to talk. We will all talk. It is nice now, just the three of us. Ivan, Socialism

168

is getting stronger all the time. We shall yet have it while we're still young."

"You won't like it," said Kirby.

"Oh, you are a Tsarist, of course. You can't see any good in Socialism."

"I can see it would work for others," he said, "but not for you, Aleka."

"Because I'm a Boyar and wealthy? Pooh," she said, "you think I wish to remain privileged? I am for a Socialist Russia and I can't make conditions to preserve this for myself or that for myself. I wouldn't want to. If I have to I'll work. I would not be ashamed to. I will work for the State."

She never could, thought Kirby. It would drive her mad. She would die if she were chained, and she had no idea of what work entailed, even less idea of what work for the State meant. Others could accept it, would accept it. Aleka could not. She wanted to think she could, but it would stupefy her, destroy her. She was born to invigorate people, to amuse, to shock, to entertain. When Rome burned, aristocrats turned to their fiddles. Socialists did away with fiddles. Cromwell did away with them in England. The people hated it.

Before Aleka could endure it in practice, Socialism would have to become sophisticated. It would have to grow up.

There was only one way she could work for the State. In the theatre. There she would make the workers laugh and cry.

"Become an actress," he suggested.

"My dear man," said Andrei, "she is already a prima donna."

"You see how Ivan can dislike me at times?" said Aleka. "I don't mind being beggared for the cause, but I do mind being disposed of. He'd dispose of me by putting me to work in the decadent theatre. That's all he thinks I'm good for, to paint my face, put on costume and prance about. I should hope I was more invaluable to Socialism than that. You see what love

169

has done for him, Andrei? It's made him sour. Poor Ivan, did you find her in love with another?"

Kirby thought of Felicity Dawes.

"I had an aberration," he said, "and now I daren't look her in the face again."

"How fortuitous," said Andrei, "and how convenient. But that, of course, is what aberrations are for. I have had a hundred."

Karita was extremely impressed by St. Petersburg. It was so different from any Crimean town, so much more expansive and inspiring. The snow might be cold and damp at the moment but by the turn of the year the atmosphere would become clear, sparkling and brilliant.

Kirby introduced his glowing, excited servant to the city, and Karita, snug and warm in her new furs, rode with him in droshkies or sleighs that sped over every fresh fall of snow to set her face tingling. The centre of the city was dominated by the ancient Admiralty buildings, constructed under the guiding hand of Peter the Great, and the wide streets radiated in long, straight prospect from this focal point. The theatres and opera houses were cultural monuments to the city's greatness, and Karita's eyes opened wide at their magnificent exteriors. She liked it best at night, when the frozen snow sparkled with a million eyes of reflected light under the lamps, when the capital came to glittering life and its privileged aristocracy rode on their swift, jingling sleighs to theatres, restaurants and clubs.

She did not mind the cold. She was healthy, the blood of her Tartar ancestors warm in her veins. In her fur hat and sable coat, her golden skin glowing, her brown eyes alive, she looked young, eager and beautiful. Kirby thought her the most attractive and companionable of persons. More, he found her interest in St. Petersburg a channel into which he could pour the attention he could not give to Olga. Sometimes she even reminded him of Olga. That was when she

170

was lost in wonder and curiosity, and when, because St. Petersburg contained so much that was awe-inspiring, she was a little unsure of herself. Sometimes she even seemed shy. Not in quite the way that Olga was, but in the way that many girls of the era were. They are a vanished species.

He had a tendency to tease her. Karita did not mind that a bit. He teased her because she always insisted on bringing breakfast to him in bed. Karita had never known any member of the nobility who got up for breakfast at Karinshka, and so she blushed at his suggestion that it would be easier and more convenient if they breakfasted together in the kitchen.

"But that would never do, never," she said.

"Why?"

"It's not proper to start with. It would look very odd."

"What else?"

"People would think I was neglecting my duties if you had to get up to eat."

"Very well," he said from the comfort of his bed, "from now on I'll take lunch and dinner in bed in addition to breakfast. We can't have people talking about you."

"Lunch and dinner aren't the same thing at all," said Karita primly, "and it's no good looking down your nose, I know when you're teasing me."

She was very upset one day at his suggestion that it might be desirable to engage a second servant, perhaps a cook.

"I'm not satisfactory? I cannot cook?"

"You're very satisfactory, and you cook beautifully. But you do every bit of the work."

"But you make no work, only a little," she said. "Is it because I've done something wrong?"

"No, little treasure, it's because you ought to have company," he said, "I leave you alone too much at night. At Karinshka you were never alone."

But she was sure he had found some fault in her. She did not mind too much if he engaged another

171

servant, but she would mind very much if it was because she was inadequate in some way.

"But I've made friends with other servants in the other apartments," she said, "and we often sit together in the evenings. However, monsieur, you must decide, of course."

He smiled. Monsieur was how she now addressed him when she was on her dignity. He put his hand under her chin, lifting her face. It was a familiar gesture of affection. It turned Karita rosy. He was going to kiss her.

"No, Karita, you decide," he said, "and if ever you want another servant to help with the work, I'll engage one. I'm more than happy to leave it to you. Are you moderately happy?"

"Oh, I'm very happy, Ivan Ivanovich," said Karita.

He smiled. But he didn't kiss her, after all. Nor had he ever said anything about her sable coat to indicate that she was expected to be generous herself.

The following day, in response to a message, he went to the offices of the Imperial Import & Export Company. Reflecting on the fact that the undercover administration of his trade was so often established behind the façade of this kind of business, he felt he couldn't be the only one who realised this. The manager, a man from Hampshire called Brown, received him genially, took him into another office and there he was welcomed in fatherly fashion by Anstruther.

"Yes, thank you," said Kirby, "but have you been promoted or demoted?"

"You will have your little joke," said Anstruther. St. Petersburg's winter had paled his brown face somewhat but to compensate he wore a chocolate-brown suit. "So you're interesting yourself in politics?"

"I've been meeting people while waiting for someone to call me," said Kirby, "but I've never been interested in politics. Politics benefit only politicians. I like people myself."

172

"Dear me," said Anstruther, "it's not like you to sound depressed."

"Dear me," said Kirby.

"But I agree with you, of course. Politicians must have their games to play. You and I are safer on the sidelines. Politics are made up of Utopian promises and unsatisfactory consequences. I must tell you that they think you're doing an excellent piece of liaison work with the Socialists here, but no one can trace the source of the assignment."

"It's not an assignment, as you well know. I've merely attended some receptions given by the Princess Karinshka. They've been very wearing."

Anstruther looked sympathetic.

"Yes, I can understand that," he said. "But interesting, all the same. And a fine piece of free-lance work. Write us a report, will you? It will be useful to know the current opinions of the radicals, it might give us some idea of whose side they'll be on in the event of an international crisis."

"What opinions d'you think I hear? People at a Russian reception all talk at once. You couldn't hear a bomb drop."

"Oh, come now," said Anstruther, toying with a sample tin of export pink salmon, "you must know what they're saying. Every little helps, you know. And it's for the benefit of the people in the long run. We'll expect something from you in a couple of days. Meanwhile, comfort yourself with some personally good news. You've been gazetted into the Army. It's in *The Times*. In the spring you'll join our mission of military observers at the Russian manoeuvres and so on. You'll like the fact that it's an entirely straightforward job, aside from the opportunity you'll have of checking certain aspects of that armament and munitions report we had from you. You'll make an ideal observer and we hope you'll like the uniform. We're committed now to being as friendly as possible towards Russia. We look upon them as our future allies. You can be nice to them without feeling the pangs of deceit. By the way, they've made you a colonel. There'll be red tabs as well. Your home regiment is the 14th Hussars. I don't suppose you'll quibble at that. I'll let you know when the uniform is ready. Until then just let us have a report now and again on how the radicals are thinking. I don't think we want a revolution here at the moment. It could drastically affect the balance of power."

"I feel," said Kirby, "that you've been reading all that from *The Boys' Friend*. It's full of good, clean fun and adventure. You don't, I suppose, know what happens in the next chapter?"

"We'll see, we'll see," said Anstruther briskly. "Is your apartment satisfactory? It was the best we could get."

"My servant thought a house overlooking the river would have been better."

"H'm," said Anstruther, "your servant must think you're a lord."

"She does," said Kirby, "I told you that before."

Princess Aleka was endeavouring to lionise him. He was her new interest for the moment, and she felt he was intriguing enough to do justice to her talent for finding social lions. He soon realised what she was up to. She was lionising herself. On one occasion she introduced him to a circle of acquaintances and hangers-on as an Englishman who had rubbed shoulders with radical notabilities like George Bernard Shaw.

He drew her aside.

"I've never met George Bernard Shaw and he wouldn't want to meet me."

"Don't be so modest," she said, "and please don't shout."

"Why not? Everybody else does."

"Don't be tiresome, darling." She was cool and decorous in light grey, highnecked. "What's the matter with you? Do you wish me to find you a woman?"

"I'm still trying to find you a man."

"You are an absolute pig," she said. "Everything

174

could so easily be perfect, we could make devastating love together, but no, you avoid me, you leave as soon as my receptions are over. Ivan, you aren't a bit nice to me."

He surveyed her grey-clad elegance. She was as sly and as fascinating as a red-headed witch at the moment. It was an afternoon *salon*, her guests mostly radical intellectuals who were already launched into their habitual monologues. The buzz began to rise and fall.

He had brought Karita with him. She was helping to look after the guests. Intellectuals were the most ravenous of them all. Karita's main responsibility, however, was to use any excuse she could to get her master away by five o'clock.

"Aleka," he said, "I can't make devastating love to a woman who passes me around."

"Oh, don't be so bourgeoise, you're acting like a shopkeeper who goes home at night to be respectable. And I'm not passing you round, I'm havnng you mcct people who matter. Please, darling, be a little intelligent this afternoon, there are people here who are dying to hear all about Sidney and Beatrice from you."

"Sidney and Beatrice?"

"Yes, you know, the Webbs of London. They've written books about a new social order and are very expert on the principles of gradual Socialism. They are greatly admired here, so I said, of course, that you'd talk about them."

"I don't know the first thing about them."

"Now, darling," she murmured, "you can be very impressive when you're in the mood, and you can make up whatever you like about them. You can talk about how you saved their lives when the House of Lords tried to assassinate them. There's no need to look like that, I know that's all a flight of my fancy, but you'll be able to make it sound beautiful. You need not be modest. Also, it's important that you emphasise how Russian Socialists have the support of their British comrades." She refused to waste any more time. She swung round, picked up a little silver bell and rang it. The buzzing stopped and Aleka said, "Dear friends, some of you have already met Ivan Ivanovich. He's from England, where he's active in the cause of the people. And how wonderful, he is actually intimate with such great international Socialists as Sidney and Beatrice Webb——"

"Ah." It was a sigh of appreciation, an encouragement rather than an interruption.

"Also," continued Aleka, "he has many times debated with George Bernard Shaw. I simply cannot tell you how delighted I am that he wishes to meet you all and speak with you all."

Good lord, thought Kirby, as he stepped into the vacated limelight and came up against an expectant hush, they're going to listen for once, only this time to someone with nothing to say.

He had better think of something.

"My friends," he said. "I think it must have been George Bernard Shaw who said that to conduct a successful circus you must first of all produce a lion. I'm not sure what happens if the lion fails to roar, however. Who would like to ask me some questions?"

Karita, glancing from across the room, thought he looked tall and very sure of himself, but what he had meant by his reference to circuses and lions she had no idea.

Yes, she had. She laughed to herself.

"Monsieur," said a blackbearded man, quite benign despite the hirsute ferocity of his appearance, "where at present do the estimable Sidney and Beatrice Webb place the influence of trade unionism in a wholly capitalist society? Isn't it true that they consider the confluence an anomaly and that healthy capitalism means weak trade unionism?"

"How delighted I am, sir," said Kirby, "that you've answered the question so well yourself. Are there any more?"

There were. Inevitably they all began asking at once. That is to say, the end of one question ran into the beginning of another, and all Kirby could do was to meet each question halfway.

"Yes, that's quite correct—no, the use of carrier pigeons for the importation of banned books for the masses is impractical because of the weight—madam, I've never seen Beatrice Webb in proletarian or non-proletarian hats—I'm sorry, sir, I lost the best part of your question—but to the gentleman on your left whose question is just arriving I'd say both Sidney and Beatrice are totally committed to the Japanese interpretations—yes, it's very confusing—yes, please do all speak together, it concertinas the questions most conveniently—madam, I assure you, George Bernard Shaw and I ride the same horse—well, do repeat the question if you get a chance——" And so he went on in a vein of continuing ridicule.

Princess Aleka was almost panting with the effort of controlling her hysteria as she retreated to hide herself among the servants.

"Will we serve tea now, Highness?" asked Karita.

Aleka leaned helplessly against the wall.

"Karita, oh that fiend, he really is turning my after-noon *salon* into a circus," she gasped.

"Highness?"

"That terrible Ivan Ivanovich—he's a monster of upside-down perfidy. Yes, you had better serve tea before I kill him." She choked with laughter. Karita permitted herself a gurgle.

The real questions were beginning to falter, the guests beginning to put fingers into their ears and to look glassily at him.

"I am sure," observed benign blackbeard to his neighbour, "that the fellow is mad."

"Egocentric, I'd say. Ah, here is the tea."

They swarmed around the samovars, glad to escape from the roaring lion. They munched cakes and pastries. Aleka took Kirby by the arm.

"Ah, my dearest friend," she whispered, "when they've gone I will kill you."

"Why?" He took the glass of tea Karita brought

177

him and gave her a smile. She was sure he winked as well. He was dreadful. "I thought I was impressive and I've still to tell them how I fought off the House of Lords single-handed while Sidney and Beatrice made their escape."

"Make a fool of yourself if you must," said Aleka, "but not of me. You are maddening. And it's so funny."

"Is it?"

"Darling, you'll find you've made yourself an enormous success. They will all go away and talk about you. Even so, don't you dare do it again. The cause is not to be ridiculed."

"Ah, there's Karita signalling me," he said, "I must go."

"Oh, you infamous coward, you dare!" Her eyes flashed. "When they've gone you and I will be alone—Ivan, you're to be nice to me——"

"I must definitely go," he said, "or I shan't be nice to you at all. Do you want your dress torn?"

"Yes, violently," she said.

But he left while her guests were still gulping and munching. He took Karita with him. Aleka fumed.

It was Andrei who told him he had heard the Tsarevich had been very ill since the autumn. Andrei mentioned it casually. Kirby took it to heart. The Imperial family, in residence at Tsarskoe Selo, were close enough for him to visit. He thought, however, that Alexandra might not want that. She had always been kind but it was reasonable enough for her to want to discourage his further association with Olga.

So he wrote Alexandra a letter of concern and sympathy. She replied some days later, briefly but in her usual sincere fashion, thanking him excessively for writing about Alexis and telling him the boy was better but still very weak. She did not say what had been wrong with him and she did not ask Kirby to visit them.

He understood.

178

EIGHT

It was mid-January and the season was in full swing. Alive and invigorating at this time of the year, St. Petersburg was a capital full of people in search of culture and pleasure. Its aristocrats were either oblivious of the country's unrest or untroubled by it. Any unrest in the city itself was always dealt with so speedily by the authorities that it was never more than a temporary headline. The power of the Okhrana, with its vast army of servants and informers active throughout Russia, was such that potential agitations and demonstrations were crushed before they could be publicly organised. The nobles were confident too that the Tsar, when he eventually came to his sense, would disband the Duma once and for all. Indeed, if he would only instruct its president, Rodzianko, then Rodzianko would smother it by the sheer formidability of his will and his weight. Rodzianko was an aristocrat of great size and competence.

Unfortunately, he was not altogether in favour with Alexandra.

He did not like Rasputin.

The holy man had prophesied that while he lived the Tsar and the throne would be safe. Whether he said this out of genuine mystic conviction or to keep people like Rodzianko off his back, only Rasputin knew. Nothing he did or said made clear, practical sense: there was always an element of ambivalence—

of "I alone know what I and God are talking about."

The only thing that was obvious about him was his uncomplicated passion for women. Singlemindedly, unashamedly, he bore down on them like a bull. They were either seduced or ravished, overwhelmed or numbed. Some of them enjoyed it immensely.

However, he was not in St. Petersburg at the moment and the city felt the better for his absence. On a white glittering night, clear and tinglingly sharp, the Imperial Opera House drew into its tiered auditorium patrons who had been privileged to acquire tickets for Tchaikovsky's ballet *Swan Lake*. The critics in their tendentious search for the vague and abstract scorned the traditional appeal of *Swan Lake*. They proclaimed it rubbish, thus following in the footsteps of equally enlightened critics who had declared many of Beethoven's works to be garbage. The people, in their simple rusticity, took Beethoven to their bosom and, in this later era, adored *Swan Lake*.

The Tsar was there that night with his two elder daughters (Alexandra rarely went to the opera or theatre). When he entered the Imperial box, the girls following, every member of the audience rose. The enthusiasm was emotional, the acclamation put a flush on to the faces of the Grand Duchesses. The national anthem was sung with roaring Russian fervour, and at the end the Tsar responded with smiling gestures and this evoked more enthusiasm. Not until he sat down did the brilliantly dressed audience subside. He looked handsome, happy and resplendent in his uniform, and Olga and Tatiana were almost tearfully proud.

They sat one on each side of him, behind them a small, select entourage. Tatiana was eager, alive. In her sixteenth year her elegance was superb. In white gown, long white gloves, her auburn hair up and crowned with a tiara, she responded to looks and stared with unselfconscious smiles and nods. Olga was also gowned in shimmering white, with a tiara in her bright hair. Outwardly she seemed composed but the pink began to tint her cheeks at the attention

180

focused on her. Whereas Tatiana looked around, hugely enjoying the atmosphere, her face expressive of her excitement, Olga took refuge in her programme and because of her genuine interest in the ballet soon became absorbed in the notes.

The lights faded, the overture began. And when the curtain rose to admit the audience to the ballet's magical world, Tatiana became entranced. Olga too lost herself heart and soul in the heaven of Tchaikovsky's music, and as the story of Odette unfolded her blue eyes dreamed and she was utterly still.

At the interval the Imperial party retired from their box to the reception room where Nicholas, never free from social trivia on occasions like this, received the manager of the Opera House and various members of the company before enjoying some refreshment. He was in his usual good form, charming everyone and showing not the faintest sign that his Empire, as always, was rocking.

Returning to their box Tatiana acknowledged a gesture from the box opposite with a little wave of her hand.

"Who is it you're waving to?" asked Olga.

"Aleka Petrovna," said Tatiana, seating herself, "she's here tonight with friends."

The lights were fading as Olga glanced across. Princess Aleka was very much there, her silvery gown worn with risqué abandon off her shoulders. There was another woman and some men, but the lights dimmed to leave the box in semi-darkness as the curtain went up. Olga sought her opera glasses but was too shy to use them until the audience had become absorbed again in the ballet. Indeed, she had never used glasses on an audience, only to magnify a stage view. Within the shadows of the box she raised the glasses to her eyes and picked out the ballerina, a fantasy of spinning *pas seul*. Olga held the magnified image of light and grace, the brilliance of the fixed stage smile, and then briefly focused the glasses on the opposite box. The profile of Aleka Petrovna emerged from the half shadows, relaxed and engrossed. But during the short seconds of her observance Olga could not distinguish who the men were.

When the ballet reached its melodic, haunting end, Tatiana emitted an ecstatic sigh. Olga sat in pure, dreamy bliss, and only when the bouquets were being presented to the prima ballerina and the audience was still noisy with rapturous applause did she glance again at the box opposite. There were three men. She did not know any of them.

Tsarskoe Selo, some fifteen miles south of St. Petersburg, was where the Imperial family spent most of the winter season. Removed from the life, opulence and political atmosphere of the capital, they created their own world of parochial detachment in well-guarded seclusion. At Tsarskoe Selo the antics of the Duma, the discontent of the people and the noise of revolutionaries were not intrusive. Here the family lived in united harmony, and the sounds of Olga or Tatiana at the piano created the atmosphere of happy Sundays in a middle-class home. The warmth and the peace within kept at bay the snow and the cold outside.

There were two palaces at Tsarskoe Selo. These were surrounded by the Imperial Park, and round the high iron railings of the Park scarlet-clad Cossacks patrolled in mounted vigilance night and day.

The old structure, the Catherine Palace, was a hugely ornate edifice. It was entirely characteristic of its flamboyant builder, Catherine the Great. The Alexander Palace, the smaller of the two, had been erected by Alexander I on a less pretentious scale, and it was typical of the modest Nicholas to use the smaller and simpler building. Even so, the Alexander Palace had more than one hundred rooms, each one exquisitely furnished. Porcelain stoves heated the rooms, the stoves fed with timber. And throughout the winter Empress Alexandra kept the Palace fragrant with a multitude of flowers, many of which were brought by train from her beloved Crimea.

Beyond the Imperial Park were the houses and mansions of the court nobility, making of Tsarskoe Selo an expansive Tsarist suburb.

It was warm, it was family in the Alexander Palace.

"Olga, there you are," said Tatiana, entering the music room. Olga was sitting at the piano. Her elbows were on depressed keys, her chin cupped in her hands, and there was an open book propped on the music stand. "What are you doing?"

"I am practicing Bach," said Olga.

"Do you think you're better at it when you play with your elbows?"

"I couldn't be worse," said Olga.

"But you aren't playing, you're reading. Move up." Tatiana pushed and made room for herself on the piano stool, achieving a precarious equality for both of them. "What is it you're reading?" She reached for the book. Olga reacted too late. Sisterly companionship turned into a whirl and scurry as Tatiana fled around the room with the book, Olga in pursuit.

"Tatiana! Give it back!"

Tatiana hared back to the piano, ducked behind it and feigned to go first one way, then the other. Olga darted. Tatiana emerged, Olga swooped. She caught her sister by the hair. Tatiana yelled, astonished that Olga could be so fierce.

"Olga, no! Oh, here is your old book, then, and could I please have my hair back?"

"There." Olga, no longer agitated now that she had retrieved the book, ruffled her sister's hair. The gesture was forgiving, affectionate.

"Such a fuss," said Tatiana, "and it's only that old Shakespeare of yours."

"It's my new Shakespeare, if you must know."

"Is it?" Tatiana sounded most interested. "So it is. Who would have thought Gregor would give you such a worldly book as that?"

"Gregor? Gregor Rasputin?" Olga knew she was being teased but for once she could not take it lightly. She tolerated Rasputin, she could not like him. Her mother passionately believed in his godliness, looked upon him as saintly and was sure it was by his hand that Alexis had recovered from the critical haemorrhage contracted in Poland during the autumn. Alexandra was Rasputin's most ardent disciple. And because of his son's weakness, that only Rasputin seemed to understand, and his wife's belief, Nicholas accepted him too. A man regarded as a saintly friend by their parents had also of course a right to the friendship of the four Grand Duchesses. And Rasputin could be amusing. But he could also be coarse and familiar. He had often been at Tsarskoe Selo and, taking typically uncouth advantage of his influence with Alexandra, roamed in and out of every room as if he owned not only the Palace but the Imperial family as well. He made remarks that shocked Marie, turned Anastasia pink, induced coolness in Tatiana and coldness in Olga. But because of their parents they bore with him. Olga only suffered him. He had once attempted to stroke her arm, she had removed herself immediately.

For all else that has been said about him, Rasputin was a fool. He made no secret of his belief that he was smarter than anyone else and that he had more foresight than presidents and prime ministers. Yet he could not see that as much as the health of Alexis and the security of Tsarism depended on him, he was even more dependent for his life and fortunes on the prestige and standing of the Emperor and Empress. For all his belief in his own superiority, he was too obtuse to realise that he himself was slowly destroying the reputation and credibility of the Imperial couple. In his stupidity he had even seduced the Grand Duchesses' nurse. Alexandra refused to believe the woman and Nicholas would not even attempt to weigh the woman's word against his wife's convictions. But St. Petersburg would and did, and it was Alexandra and Nicholas they found wanting.

None of Tatiana's teasing made Olga more unresponsive than that which touched on Rasputin.

184

"You're having one of your silly days," she said quietly.

Tatiana always knew when Olga was hurt. She felt the pangs of immediate contrition.

"Olga—oh, you're so sensitive, you know I didn't mean it, you mustn't get cross. You know I know Gregor wouldn't give you any kind of book, he's never read one himself in his life, he wouldn't know the difference between a book and a candle. He's just as likely to light the book and read the candle."

"It doesn't matter," said Olga.

Tatiana felt she would like to cry a little. Olga was growing up so, on her dignity so, trying to be old while she was still young. It was ridiculous. Sometimes when the sunshine was on the snow and they could all romp and frolic in its frosty softness, Olga would shake and brush the snow from her coat and say something about being too old for that sort of thing. It took all the enthusiasm of the others to make her rejoin the fun.

Tatiana knew why Olga desperately wanted to be a woman. But Olga herself should know one couldn't hurry the process, and one shouldn't try to when it was for an illusion. It would only make it worse, not better.

"Olga," said Tatiana tenderly, "let me see." She put out a hand. Olga hesitated, then gave her the book. Tatiana opened it up and saw the inscribed flyleaf.

To Olga Nicolaievna, in gratitude for so much sunshine—J. Kirby, Livadia 1912.

"You know," said Tatiana, "I think Ivan Ivanovich is so very much nicer than Gregor, but don't tell——"

"No, don't tell Mama you said so," smiled Olga, and Tatiana smiled too. "Marie and Stasha are out with the sledge, shall we go too?"

"Oh yes," said Tatiana, "and, Olga, please please don't grow up without me."

"You'll grow up before any of us," said Olga. "Go on, darling, I'll follow you out in a moment."

Tatiana went, happy to join her sisters in the crisp February sunshine, happy that Olga would follow.

Olga tidied up the sheets of music on the piano. It was nearly March, Easter wasn't so far away, and at Easter they always went to Livadia. She did not think it would be quite so lovely this time.

Leaving the music room she walked through polished, shining rooms and then came out into a corridor. Advancing towards her was all the panoply of what was certainly an official presentation. There were braided court dignitaries, Russian officers in full dress and British officers too. The panoply was martial, boots gleaming, sword scabbards clinking, and the khaki uniforms of the British were adorned with red shoulder tabs, their caps red-banded, tucked under their arms. As they approached the Grand Duchess the Russian officers acknowledged her. Olga's response was a shy smile.

There was a smile too from one of the British officers. She caught it, she looked. She stopped, they all passed her. She gazed after them, at the officer who had smiled, he was taller than his colleagues. Her eyes were incredulous. But disbelief was in almost immediate conflict with delight, and disbelief lost. She hitched the skirt of her dress, the corridor was empty and Olga ran. It did not take her long to find out from the court chamberlain's office what she wanted to know.

A British military mission was to be presented to the Tsar.

The Tsar received them in formal but friendly splendour, in uniform himself. With his own officers at his back he shook hands with each member of the British team. One of them was tall, bearded, and with deep grey eyes. Nicholas recognised him immediately. He beamed, he clapped him on the shoulder.

"My dear fellow," he said, then shook Kirby's hand heartily. "My dear fellow, I couldn't be more pleased. This is excellent."

"It's excellent to see you, sir," said Kirby.

"Have you come to see how my generals play the game of war?" Nicholas laughed. The other British officers looked on in great curiosity. No one had said that this new fellow, Colonel Kirby, was on speaking terms with the Russian Emperor. "That reminds me," Nicholas went on, "I always felt you would make a general yourself, but I didn't see how I could arrange it. There would have been such jealousy, my dear chap. However, I now see that His Majesty has recognised your talents, although he's been more cautious than I'd have been. So, you're a colonel now. Ah, you're an intriguing fellow, we had no idea we'd see you in the British Army. A capital step, capital."

The senior British officer, Brigadier Rollinson, muttered to his aide-de-camp, "Well, I'm damned." Major Gerard, the aide-de-camp, knew that could have meant anything and was best responded to by a sound from the back of the throat. Still, it was a rum go with this Kirby chap. He had popped up out of the blue. No one had ever heard of him before. Odds on he was somebody's precious relative. Or somebody's embarrassment. He might have been shoved off on this Russian beano in order to keep him out of the way for a while. But where the fellow was all wrong was in having a beard. It showed he was out of the blue all right, he must have upset an Admiral's daughter and been transferred from the Navy. Never been known before. Already Brigadier Rollinson had looked at his beard with a cold eye. It would have to come off soner or later.

It did not offend Nicholas, of course. He clapped Kirby on the shoulder again and said, "Delighted to have met you again, we must play some more tennis, eh? But not in this weather."

He was affable to all the British officers. Any of them who had pre-conceived ideas about autocrats were forced to revise them. Nicholas radiated good humour and kindness. The reception became one of easy informality, Russian officers mixing with the British and Nicholas moving around to talk to everyone. After the reception the Russians took charge of the British, having arranged to entertain them during the evening. They withdrew at the prescribed time, leaving the state room to pass through an ante-room.

There was a girl standing by one of the windows overlooking the white carpet of the snow-covered Park. She wore a cream linen dress. The sun, slanting in through the window, etched her within its winter framework of sharp light. She turned as the officers came from the state room. Kirby saw her at once. He hesitated, then murmured an excuse to Brigadier Rollinson and broke away. As he came towards her Olga thought him taller than ever in his tailored uniform, but he was no different really. The smile was the same, his air of easy assurance the same.

And if she was a little taller herself and a little shapelier, she still had shyness and diffidence, there was still a shy desire that he speak first.

"Your Highness, how lovely." He took her extended hand, bent and put his lips to her ring. "You are more the Grand Duchess than ever."

"Mr. Kirby, I was in such surprise to see you." Her voice had its inimitable touch of breathlessness, her face its inevitable touch of pink. "And in uniform—I didn't know you were in the British Army."

"It was a surprise to me too when it happened," he smiled, "but one must be of service to one's country sometimes. Am I not very agreeable in uniform?"

Impulsively she said, "Oh, you look——" She checked herself. "You look very correct."

"I don't think our senior officer quite agrees with that, he's given me the oddest looks." He looked out of the window and saw three winter-clad girls pulling a sledge over the snow. "That looks like your sisters, I wish I had the time to join them."

"They'd love it if you could." But she knew he couldn't stay long.

"I was so sorry to hear about Alexis," he said. "Is he better now?"

"He's better but not quite himself yet," she said. "I'll tell him I saw you. Mr. Kirby—oh, I suppose that isn't right now——"

"Colonel, then," he said. It was difficult to smile

into her blue eyes without giving something of his feelings away.

"Colonel Kirby," she said with an effort, "it will be Easter soon."

"Yes, I suppose it will."

Her shyness was so intense that she sounded breathless as she whispered, "Oh, come to Livadia ... come to Livadia ..."

"Is it just as beautiful at Easter?" His longing was as intense as her shyness. And the hopelessness of it all was a pain.

"Oh, more so," she breathed, "but for us, for all of us, it's so much nicer when you're there, and it would cheer Alexis so."

Didn't she realise that it was her mother who must ask him? He doubted if Alexandra would. However well disposed she was towards him she was not likely to encourage any further association with Olga.

"Highness———"

"Why do you call me that?" she said in a little hurt.

"It can't be helped at times, you know," he smiled. "Easter at Livadia would be wonderful but I'm not my own master now, Olga. I have to take orders. I must go, I'll be keeping them waiting. Forgive me? But remember me to the children, tell them I miss them. I'll think of you at Easter and be very envious. I'd like nothing better than to be there." He took her hand again. He put his lips to her fingertips. He heard her whisper breathlessly again.

"Come to Livadia ... please, Colonel Kirby."

She did not go out to join the others, she returned to the music room. She tried to practise Bach. She was awful. She had the wish, the will, but she did not have Tatiana's gifted fluency. And she could not read the music properly. It kept blurring.

Anna Vyrubova came. She found Olga sitting at the piano but not playing.

"Have you heard?" said Anna. "Our friend Ivan Ivanovich has been with other British officers. Would

189

you believe it, he's in the Army and is a colonel. Your Papa said it was very remiss of King George not to have made him a general."

"Did he?" said Olga, looking hard at the music. "And what did Mama say?"

"Only that it was very interesting."

"Anna," said Olga unhappily, "I am more dreadful at Bach all the time."

"What nonsense," said Anna, "you are very good. Your Mama says she will listen to you and Tatiana Nicolaievna later."

"Perhaps Tatiana had better play Bach and I'll play Beethoven."

She played Beethoven very well later but thought all the time of Livadia.

Princess Aleka was hysterical with laughter.

"Oh, Ivan Ivanovich! Andrei, come and see, they've made a soldier of him. How dashing, how sublime, how ridiculous! Andrei!"

Andrei entered the room, lazily casual in trousers and ruffed shirt. He looked at Kirby, groped for a chair and subsided astonished into it.

"Sweet angels," he murmured, "is it really you, dear man?"

"I thought you'd both approve," said Kirby, "I'm on honeymoon with the Russian Army later and this is my going-away outfit."

"Your bride will be enraptured," said Aleka, "you are deliciously irresistible, isn't he, Andrei?"

"Not to me," said Andrei. "That is one deviation I can fight against. Ah," he said more cheerfully as a servant came to announce that his carriage was below, "that means I can go home and recover. You've been a shock to me, Ivan."

It took him ten minutes to prepare for departure. When he had gone Aleka sighed.

"There, you see," she said, "Andrei feels as I do. You're a disappointment to both of us, Ivan. Armies, darling, are horribly anathematic. They're a perpetual menace to people. Now you're farther away from me than ever."

"It's only so that I can officially observe Russian manoeuvres," said Kirby, "I shall remain with you in spirit, dear Princess."

"There's no need to be like that now," she said, "come and sit with me." She was in soft black, chiffon-like, and disposed over a blue and gold chaise-longue. He sat beside her, her scent was delicately exotic. "Ivan?" She moved closer and traced his left eyebrow with a cool white finger. "Why won't you love me?"

"Well, there's Andrei," he said.

She drew back. She looked angry, offended.

"What is he to do with it? He and I are only very dear friends."

"Yes, I know. And I'm an officer and a gentleman now. I can't let Andrei down without staining the honour of the regiment."

"Oh, how amusing you are," she said cuttingly. "I am the one who is being let down if Andrei has talked about me." Her smile was sweetly bitter. "Is that why I'm distasteful to you, because of Andrei, because of other lovers?"

"Andrei hasn't said a word about you."

"Then you're only guessing."

"And you aren't at all distasteful, my sweet," he said.

"I'm sure some people would think you a prig," said Aleka, "but I think you are much more than you seem. Are you, Ivan?"

"I wonder about you too sometimes," he said.

Their smiles clashed a little.

"You treat me very badly, you know," said Aleka. "I don't ask you how many women you've made love to, but you, ah, you're saying a woman has to be a virgin if you're to grace her immaculate bed. That's just like a man. What does it matter what Andrei and I do? It need not be anything to do with you and me. Kiss me and you will see."

He kissed her. It took his mind off so much else. Aleka murmured and melted. The telephone rang. She

191

let it ring, her arms around his neck. He infuriated her by disengaging to get up and answer it himself. It was Karita. For him.

"There's a man here, an Englishman," she said, "and he says he's going to wait for you. He says his name is Brown. I told him I didn't know when you'd be back but he's waiting all the same, so I thought I'd telephone you."

"Of course, Karita. Tell him I'll be there in twenty minutes. If he wishes it, give him something to drink."

Aleka vibrated as he put the telephone back into its cradle.

"You wouldn't dare to go now," she said.

He stooped, he kissed her affectionately but without passion. She stared up at him, dark eyes smouldering.

"Perhaps another time, dear Princess?" he said.

"What a swine you are," she said.

The man Brown turned out to be Anstruther.

"I used my manager's name," he said, "I thought it better. One never knows. I didn't mind waiting. I'm not sure that the uniform wouldn't have looked more impressive if we'd arranged for you to wear a few medals with it, but it's difficult sometimes to think of everything. We can talk here, I suppose? Your maid is charming but not unsuspicious."

"You're safe," said Kirby, "she scorns keyholes."

"Good," said Anstruther. He settled himself comfortably in his chair and crossed his legs. "I must say, we seem to have fixed you up very comfortably here. When do the Russian manoeuvres take place?"

"April, as you know."

"Yes." Anstruther pursed his lips. He thought and then he said, "It seems you'll have to get rid of your beard. Do you mind?"

"I'll miss it, naturally, I've had it a long time."

"Well, at least it's had a good run," said Anstruther. "But Brigadier Rollinson doesn't like it and to save him the embarrassment of quoting regulations to you and spoiling the *esprit de corps* of the mission, we thought you might volunteer a sacrifice. Otherwise the Brigadier may insist that you be transferred back to the Navy. I know you've never been in the Navy, but he's convinced that you have and that there's some hanky-panky going on. Look, Kirby, my boy, you can keep the moustache, just take the beard off. Now, there's just one thing more. It's something else we'd like to help the Russians with. You did excellent work in Kiev, excellent. Do you think you're up to doing something quite different?"

"What is something quite different?" Kirby knew by now that Anstruther's brown fatherliness covered a multitude of whimsies that weren't fatherly at all.

"It's the question of your engagement to the Princess Karinshka."

"I think I'll have a brandy," said Kirby, "what would you like?"

"A brandy will be excellent," said Anstruther gratefully, "your maid gave me wine which, unfortunately, was corked."

Kirby did not bother to hide his smile. He poured brandies. Anstruther took his with murmured thanks. He began to explain. It was to do with co-operation, to help relieve the Russians of a minor embarrassment in the shape of Princess Karinshka. It was necessary to destroy her credibility as a serious Socialist. Indeed, she was more than a Socialist. She posed as that but she was, in fact, a committed revolutionary. Had she ever mentioned a trip to England and France?

"Yes," said Kirby, "the police wanted her out of the way for a while, so she looked around Europe. She wasn't very impressed."

"Wasn't she? For most of that time she was with Lenin and other revolutionaries." Anstruther sipped his brandy but did not miss Kirby's faint grimace.

It was necessary, Anstruther pointed out, to do something about the lady. She was attracting too much attention as a reformer. On the surface she appeared to be a political dilettante. This was merely a smoke-screen hiding the fact that she was secretly working with the most dangerous people. There was always Siberia, but to send her there would enhance her standing as a genuine radical. It would never do to advertise that an aristocrat of her rank was so strongly opposed to Tsarism that she had to be removed to Siberia. It would be better to convince the people, especially her revolutionary friends, that she was a fake.

"And the best way to do that," said Anstruther, "would be to announce her engagement to you, Colonel Kirby, an English aristocrat serving in His Majesty's Imperial Forces and a personal friend of the Tsar himself. Nicholas would be delighted at the news. The Princess is a great embarrassment to him at times."

"No more than you are to me," said Kirby, "and dammit, you don't expect me to agree to this, do you? She won't get sent to Siberia, she's been kind to the Empress and the Empress doesn't forget kindnesses."

"Really, Kirby," said Anstruther, shaking his head. "The Empress hasn't seen the latest report on her activities. She's in touch with the most dedicated of the exiled revolutionaries. If the Empress thought the Princess was herself just as dedicated to destroying Tsarism, nothing could save her. Naturally, you'll want to do your best for her. There have been rumors that you might marry her, you know. We hear she's extremely attached to you. Perhaps I didn't make it clear that you don't have to ask her. We arrange a *fait accompli* by having the newspapers announce the engagement with some interesting personal details. It will be a surprise to you as well as to her, although it's possible, from what we've heard, that she may consider it a happy surprise."

"Do you know the Princess?"

"Not socially," said Anstruther, "but in other fields. However, she has her weaknesses. There's a chance that you're one of them. We feel she won't rush to deny the announcement, she may in the way of a woman even be blind at first to its political consequences, which will destroy her reputation as a serious revolutionary. Because of her background that's always been suspect. You, of course, will neither deny nor confirm the announcement. To all enquirers you'll be non-committal. You'll talk to her. You may come to a happy arrangement with her. I must point out that we aren't actually asking that you marry her, but who knows? She may be delighted to consider it."

"She'll scream my head off," said Kirby.

"Oh, I don't know. You can play an extremely civilised and gallant part, and if it saves her from Siberia think how pleased you'll be. What we're after is convincing people that by her engagement to an English aristocrat the Princess has reverted to type. You'll then have helped the Tsar by discrediting a revolutionary and you'll also have helped a friend. She is your friend, isn't she?"

"Spasmodically. By the way, I'm not an aristocrat."

"You will be when the engagement is announced and the details printed," said Anstruther. "Leave it all to us and our Russian colleagues."

"There's one thing I've always been sure of," said Kirby, "this isn't the gentlemen's branch of the service."

"Gentlemen," said Anstruther, "never serve their King and country in the same way that we do, my dear Kirby."

The announcement appeared two days later. There were photographs, one of Princess Aleka, one of himself. The one of himself had been taken on the Prospekt Nevskiy, but who had taken it he did not know. Karita saw the papers and when she brought them in with his breakfast her congratulations seemed to carry reservations.

"You don't sound completely happy for us, Karita," he said. He looked at her, she returned his gaze quite composedly. In her position with him Karita had come to understand her rights and one of her rights was to speak her mind without, of course, being impertinent.

"Ivan Ivanovich," she said, "I'm not sure if you and Her Highness are suited. She is very lovely, of course, and very kind, but you are both very different."

"I see," he said, "you mean I'm neither lovely nor kind."

"You are very deceiving," said Karita, trim and attractive in dark blue. "All this time you've told me you're not an English lord, but in the papers it says you are."

He glanced through a paragraph or two.

"It doesn't say that at all," he said.

"It says you're an aristocrat, that's the same thing, isn't it?" Karita even shook her finger at him. "A fine time I've had trying to tell people who you are when you've confused me so, and now look, everyone will say the papers know more about you than I do."

He laughed. She never lost her quaintness. The St. Petersburg winter had given her a glow that freshened her honeyed Crimean look. She was not only an extremely personable part of his daily life now, she was also entirely entertaining.

"Run along, chicken," he said.

He ate his breakfast leisurely, waiting for Aleka to telephone. She normally slept late or rose late, but this morning she came through well before he'd finished his meal. She was in a husky-voiced frenzy.

"Ivan, what is this? You've seen it? It's damnable, I'm going to kill somebody."

"I don't blame you——"

"Shut up. I'll do the talking. How dare you do such a thing, how dare you have it put in the papers! You're always making a fool of me and this is the worst kind of way."

"I'm as innocent——"

"Shut up. I am coming round to your place to kick and scream. I woke up feeling lovely and now I have a shocking headache, everything is going thump, thump. Ah, it's you who will look the bigger fool and have a bigger headache when I have done with you."

"Yes, come round and we'll talk about it."

"Talk? I am going to shoot you."

She arrived in an hour, fur-clad and magnificently

196

dramatic. She stormed past Karita and met Kirby face-to-face in the drawing-room as he emerged from the bedroom. He wore a dressing-gown. This enraged her. He had not even bothered to dress decently to receive her, she could have been anybody. Then she stared at his face. He was freshly-shaved and had just taken his beard off, leaving only a moustache. He looked younger, but the now undisguised line of his chin was strong, masculine.

"You ridiculous man," she shouted, "did you take your beard off because you were afraid I'd pull it out bit by bit?"

"Oh, they're just a bit fussy about beards in our Army," he said. "Do sit down, my sweet."

"You cad," she cried and began to stride and swish about. She was quite alarming for a few minutes. He let her get on with it, knowing how much she was enjoying herself. One had to admire her performance, she was really not far short of superb if one discounted the occasional Russian swear word that lowered the tone a little. She flung her fur coat over a chair and rampaged around again in a long, high-waisted black dress with its short train sweeping the floor angrily.

"It's your doing, every word of it," she said.

"Upon my soul, Aleka love, I'm as innocent as you are," he said. "Indeed, I thought at first it was your doing."

"Mine?" She subjected him to flashing scorn. "Are you mad? If I wanted to marry a man I'd ask him, not tell the papers."

"What an interesting woman you are, Aleka."

She sat down. She got up again. She chose another chair. She looked up at him. A slightly malicious smile curved her lips.

"Are you suggesting someone has made a fool of both of us?" she said.

"I swear to you I'm sure of it," he said, and was able to look completely convincing.

She mused a little on this, her lashes flickering.

"Imagine that," she said.

"You do have some very unconventional friends," he said, "and in high places."

"Yes. And what sort of friends do you have?" Her smile was sweet.

"Well, I wonder about that now," he said.

"Mm," she said. "What are we going to do about it?"

"Don't you know? I'd have thought you'd have known immediately what we must do. Nothing. We'll let the announcement stand."

She stared. She laughed. It came bubbling.

"But of course," she said. "Oh, my clever Ivan. We will stun them all. We will be engaged. And we'll do the laughing. Of course, this isn't to suppose that we ourselves are serious, that you wish to marry me?"

"My dearest Princess," he said, "it need only mean we can be engaged for as long as you think the joke can last or perhaps until you find a good Ukrainian Socialist farmer——"

"Don't spoil yourself," she said. "So, we are engaged, then?"

"While at the same time you remain perfectly free not to marry me."

She mused on that too.

"Perhaps," she said, "I might wish to. But at least, now we're engaged we can be lovers. I think we would be exciting lovers, Ivan."

"We'll talk about it."

"Talk?" She pealed off a trill of ironic laughter. "Talking isn't loving, you fool."

He thought of Olga. Talking was loving. It was listening, observing, hearing and communicating. It was taking pleasure in the sight and sound of her. Love to Aleka meant bodies exquisitely juxtaposed in a bed. That could be fleetingly, tenderly beautiful, but it was not love itself, it was the ultimate consequence and the final consummation of love, a physical transience that had far less meaning than the desire to protect, to cherish, to hold. It would not be mirrored in the mind with the same unfading clarity as the memory of a fallen summer hat being replaced on a chestnut-blonde head while blue eyes smiled in shy wonder at life.

I am, he thought, ridiculously in love.

"Talking will at least lead us to bed," he said, "but you're under no obligation, Aleka."

"How superbly English you are," she smiled, "it's only the English who would speak of love and obligation together. Darling, love in this context is not an obligation, it's a condition of being engaged. And if we are to laugh louder than the jokers, our engagement must be complete and ecstatic. I'm not utterly consumed by impatience, however, and can wait until tonight. How clean and dashing you look without your beard. Shall we say tonight, then?"

"If you've nothing else on," he said.

"Darling, I shall have nothing on at all. Come at eleven. Andrei," she said, her smile a little malicious again, "will be gone by then."

But as Aleka drove out that afternoon on her way to an undisclosed rendezvous, a bitter and disillusioned student threw a bomb at her carriage. It wrecked the carriage, injured two passing women—innocent limbs are always expendable for a cause—and killed the horse. Aleka was pulled bleeding and unconscious from the smashed carriage and taken to hospital. She was bruised, cut, concussed and badly shocked. And extremely lucky. Kirby went to see her each day. On the third day she was sitting up, surrounded by flowers sent by Andrei, and receiving Kirby with a smile. Her head and forehead were bandaged. She looked palely lovely. Rather like a nun in a state of beatitude, he thought.

"Did someone think I was the prime minister?" she said.

He winced a little. She must surely by now have realised the political implications of her engagement to him. No one would believe she championed the rights of workers now.

"They're holding a student," he said.

"The silly boy," she said. "Tell me, how do I look?"

"Not as if you'd had a bomb thrown at you. Quite lovely, in fact. Karita sends you her most respectful wishes and blessings. She's a little angry. She doesn't like bomb-throwers, whoever they are."

"How sweet of her, but tell her I'm not angry so there's no need for her to be." Aleka, after two days of dulled and numbed nerves, sounded as if she had recovered enough to be charitable. "Ivan, you're almost depressingly healthy. Andrei comes in looking wan and nervous. You are always indecently equable. Can't you be just a little bit wan yourself? It would cheer me up enormously."

"Who has been to see you?" he asked.

"Oh, you and Andrei and people," she said. "It's too risky for some of my real friends. Isn't this an awfully despotic country when true patriots can only come out at night?"

"It is when students start throwing bombs at you."

"We're still engaged?" she said with the ghost of a smile.

"Yes, if you think we're still the ones who are laughing."

"Well, of course we are. Kiss me."

He leaned and put his mouth to hers. Hers was cool, soft and cleanly antiseptic. He stayed a while and they talked. She did not mention the bomb. She did mention his uniform. She didn't like it. It classed him as an aggressive tool of imperialism, she said. There should only be workers' armies.

"They'll probably be just as aggressive," he said.

"But with more justification," said Aleka. "I shall soon be home again and then you must buy me a ring. Our laugh at the expense of whoever was responsible for our engagement will cost you an awful lot of money, darling."

"I'm sure it will be worth it," he said, kissing her goodbye.

The snow was beginning to disappear. There were

spears of green grass pricking the fading white surface. Grand Duchess Olga Nicolaievna stood at the window of the music room, her face a little sombre in its expression, her eyes darkly blue.

Easter would soon be here. They would go to Livadia.

She put her mouth to the cold window. A little circle of mist formed. She erased it with her hand. Tatiana came in. Tatiana was always looking for her, always watching her elder sister. She put an arm around Olga's waist.

"It's gloomy outside today," she said. "Mama says that if you'd condescend, she'd like you to help her with some embroidery. I said I'd see how condescending you were."

"Oh, I'm excessively so today."

"Isn't it sad about Aleka Petrovna?" said Tatiana. "But already she's much better, Mama says. Mama says it was only by the grace of God she wasn't killed. Can you think why people should be so wicked?"

"I can think that people have a right to be angry sometimes," said Olga, keeping her eyes on the Park, "I can't think they have a right to kill, however angry. Poor Aleka Petrovna, but how glad she must be that she escaped."

"Yes, she's the kindest person and so amusing," said Tatiana. "She has promised to help me meet the nicest people when I make my debut and go out into society."

"You won't need any help," said Olga, "and isn't it to be supposed that she'll be in England with Colonel Kirby when you are in society?"

Tatiana essayed a cautious look at her sister. Olga's face, in profile, was soft with shadows. She had not been at all gay lately.

"Olga," said Tatiana, "don't you think we should all send Aleka Petrovna and Colonel Kirby our best wishes and felicitations?"

"Yes," said Olga evenly, "perhaps we should. We'll speak to Mama."

The snow was very much thinner. But it looked colder. It was because the skies were so grey.

He would not come to Livadia now.

NINE

Aleka was home and recovering. She was amused and intrigued to receive a letter sent by the Empress Alexandra on behalf of the Imperial family. It contained a most sympathetic reference to her "accident" with best wishes for a speedy return to health, and concluded with felicitations on her engagement to Colonel Kirby.

Resting in silken-limbed convalescence on a couch, she handed the letter, written on embossed Imperial notepaper, to Kirby.

"From your most high friends," she said, "and that is an exquisite embellishment of the joke, isn't it?"

He read the letter, then said, "An Imperial embellishment." Aleka did not seem further interested in it, so he slipped the letter casually into his pocket. It had been happily signed by all of them and it was something to have from the family he loved.

Aleka was paler than usual by reason of her time in hospital and had made up her mind to go to Karinshka to find the sunshine and warmth of the Crimean spring. She was satisfied with the state of the nation. It was growling and discordant, the workers underpaid, restless and mutinous. Things would come along very nicely while she was away, events would bring the collapse of autocracy nearer. She was not needed at the moment to hasten things along. Her bruised and battered body was weaker than she had realised. She needed a recuperative sojourn at Karinshka.

"You will come too, Ivan," she said.

"Next week Russia's Caucasian Army begins its spring manoeuvres," said Kirby, "and I have to be there."

"Well, of course," she said impatiently, "and they're taking place in the north of the Crimea. That is for the convenience of the Tsar, so that he can be at Livadia. He'll attend them from there. You can attend them from Karinshka. Manoeuvres are very stupid, everyone playing at being uniformed assassins. It isn't manoeuvres the people need, it's work and bread. All the generals will be full of vodka and champagne and have to be propped up on their horses. Yes, and you'll be drunk all the time yourself, you'll see. It will be a party for the officers, only the soldiers will have to manoeuvre. The Tsar will ride up and down on a hill, looking very happy and heroic, and when a gun goes off he'll say, 'My dear fellow, what was that? Nobody is to get hurt, you understand.' Pooh, that's Russian manoeuvres for you and you'll be able to tell your King what fun it was and he'll give you a medal for being as stupid as everyone else. Ivan, we will go to Karinshka tomorrow."

"Andrei will probably decline," said Kirby, "he's been feeling *de trop* lately."

She gave him a dark look.

"I'm not inviting him, you idiot man," she said, "and even if I did, of course he wouldn't come. He's not the man to want to be in the way. You know, you have a provoking way of sliding around corners. Remember, I'm still very frail, I'm to be spoiled, not provoked. Andrei has been very sweet about us, he has no idea it's a joke. Ivan, there's to be no sliding away at Karinshka—why, it's been ridiculous here, you've been so elusive you've made me run after you. Do you want me to think I'm a fate worse than death for you?"

"You're the loveliest creature," he said, "but I've had to remember how frail you are. I'll use your telephone, if I may, and see if I can get away in advance with you. Karinshka will be good for you. It will be good for Karita too. She can see her family again. She keeps asking me when she's to go to England with me, she'll be quite happy when I tell her we're going to Karinshka instead for a while."

"Come here," said Aleka, huskily imperious. She reached up and took hold of the lapels of his khaki jacket, she held his eyes in brooding suspicion. "What are you talking about Karita for? It's always Karita this or Karita that with you."

"I'm her mother and father," he said. She did not like his smile. It was too easy. He was always like that. One asked him something that was important or nearly important, and first he smiled to take one's mind off the answer and then when he did answer it was no answer at all.

"What rubbish," she said. "Is she the one you're always thinking about? And what is it you think about? How to seduce her? Or how you have seduced her?"

"I'm to return her in time to her parents as good as the day she left."

"Oh, that is more rubbish," said Aleka irritably, "don't you know what they meant by that? They meant that if you didn't you were to sit around a table with them and discuss the price you'd pay for having seduced their virgin."

"Extraordinary," he murmured.

"They are extraordinary?" she said, scornful that he should be so naïve.

"No, you are," he said.

She caught his hand and bit it.

She was quite proud of the teethmarks she made.

The Crimea had burst into flamboyant spring. The hills and valleys were green from rain, the blossoms bright under the sun. Nature, having lain dormant through the damp, cold winter, had come to eager life. Trees and plants were tender with leaf, breaking buds were tossing into colour. Soft clouds were rolling

205

back, uncovering the endless blue. The fields were scattered with gold.

In the north Russian divisions were moving into place for the forthcoming manoeuvres. Much to the relief of Princess Aleka there wasn't a general in sight in the south. She would not have minded soldiers too much, they were the unlucky conscripts who had been unable to avoid being dragged into the Tsar's service. Soldiers she would have entertained and mesmerised, as long as they weren't Cossacks. The Cossacks were the Tsar's devil-dancers, she said.

As much as her restlessness allowed, she relaxed at Karinshka. She convalesced in the balmy spring sunshine. Kirby lay around with her. It rained a little at times and drove them in from the terrace. She did not know whether to be infuriated or bored when it was wet. Kirby saved her from the latter state. He was good-tempered and amusing. There were moments when he was not, however. He had brought military manuals and notes with him, all to do with his present responsibilities as a military observer. He added to the notes, writing in the sunshine.

"Ah, you are going to turn into a stuffed bore like all the others," she said.

"Loosen your corset if it's making you uncomfortable, dearest," he returned.

She laughed.

"That's your privilege while we're engaged," she said, "come, I dare you."

Comfortable in his chair he looked up from his notes and mused on the blue sky.

"I wonder," he said, "if it's possible to make a reinforced corset that's bullet-proof? I'll borrow one of yours for an experiment if I may, Aleka love."

"My dear," purred Aleka, "they are all yours to shoot at as you desire, but you will have to come and get them."

Karita was delighted to be back in the Crimea for a while. She had been to see her parents. They had looked her up and down, had satisfied themselves that

206

she was in good hands but wanted to know why she had not yet been to England. Karita said she would go when Ivan Ivanovich took her, she could not go before. Her mother wanted to know if he had a castle in England. All English aristocrats lived in castles, as was well known. Karita said he had three.

Old Amarov was pleased to see her again. He patted her, pushed his moustache aside and kissed her. Karita hugged him and old Amarov wanted to know what girls were coming to.

Oravio had little to say to her but plenty of looks, all of them dark and lowering. He was to be married soon. Karita felt enormously relieved that it wasn't to her. How dull he was. He would never, never make anyone laugh. She was surprised one morning to see him in the suite. Her Highness and Ivan Ivanovich had gone down to the beach. Not to bathe, the sea still had winter's bite to it, but to bask in the sea air. Karita had come up to put the bedroom in order. She met Oravio coming out of it.

"What are you doing here?" she asked.

"What's that to do with you?"

"Anyone who puts his nose into these rooms is my business," said Karita.

"Mind your tongue," said Oravio, "I've been out on the balcony outside the bedroom window, making good some crumbling mortar." He pushed a trowel under her nose. "Next time I'll ask you for my orders, I don't think."

"Since when has that been your job?" Karita pushed the trowel aside and tossed her gold head. "You're putting your nose in, you're always doing that. How would you like Ivan Ivanovich to slice it off?"

Oravio showed teeth that, white as they were, seemed to scowl at her. He jabbed with the trowel, making severe gashes in the air.

"How would you like to have me slice yours off, lackey of an imperialist?" he said. "Yes, and worse than lackey, no doubt."

Karita's brown eyes seemed to burn a little, but it

207

was her contemptuous silence that was more impressive.

When Kirby returned from the beach a little before lunch the suite was in its usual state of immaculate splendour, the open windows bringing in soft air that drenched the rooms with fragrance. Karita came in, carrying one of his uniforms. He had put them aside for his week at Karinshka and was wearing a comfortable old shirt of faded blue cotton and light cord trousers. Already the sun had bronzed him and without his beard the deepening brown of his skin was more apparent.

"I've been cleaning and pressing this one," she said, "and will do the other one this afternoon."

"No, go out and play," he said.

"Play?"

"With a young man, with Oravio if you like. I'll ask Aleka Petrovna to spare him for the afternoon."

Karita wrinkled her nose. Really, as old Amarov would have said, what was Ivan Ivanovich coming to not to know how dull and dreary Oravio was?

"If I wanted to run through the grass with a man I would not choose Oravio," she said.

"Ah," said Kirby, and rubbed a sideburn. "Well, perhaps Oravio isn't exactly a pillar of light. There is Sergius, then."

"Sergius is very much nicer," said Karita, "and might do very well in five years time when he's grown up. This afternoon I shall be far too busy to take him by the hand."

He laughed aloud. Karita smiled. He was always in amusement about something. It made her feel very pleased.

"Karita," he said, "no one is ever going to do your thinking for you. But remember how pretty you are, remember it's spring and and that young men don't like growing up. Think of yourself sometimes and not of my shirts or socks or uniforms."

"But I like your shirts and uniforms," said Karita, "and I don't even mind your socks too much."

"Minx," he said and kissed her affectionately.

Well! thought Karita rosily. He had not done that all the time they had been in St. Petersburg. What possessed him to kiss her here but never in St. Petersburg? It was very confusing. Not that she minded. Ivan Ivanovich was always so agreeable. She was sure he would make Princess Aleka Petrovna very happy.

For about three months.

In her own suite Aleka was coldly observant of three wafer-thin buff cards Oravio produced from his pocket.

"They were in the Englishman's hairbrush," he said. "He's not very clever. Hiding-places like that are as old as Amarov."

"Why should he consider he has to be clever when he believes others are stupid?" Aleka sounded as if she would have preferred Oravio to have found nothing. "Let me see them."

"They'll have to be sent to Prolofski, he'll decode them," said Oravio.

"You don't give the orders here." She put out a hand. Oravio shrugged and handed the cards over. They were all neatly inscribed with small English lettering. She could decipher none of it.

"You realise what has been done to you and why?" said Oravio darkly. "The Okhrana know about you and this is their way of destroying you with the help of English pigs. Now no one trusts you. You'll be watched by everyone. But you've been lightly treated. That's because you can claim the tyrants' friendship. Otherwise you'd have had to suffer what true comrades have suffered."

"Hold your silly tongue," she said sharply, "of course I realise, I did from the beginning. Do you think I'm a fool? It's you who lack brains. These cards need not be sent to Prolofski. What is on them must be carefully and quickly copied and the copy sent. The cards must be put back before Colonel Kirby has a chance to miss them."

209

"I am at your service, naturally," said Oravio insolently.

"When Prolofski has decoded them we'll see if Colonel Kirby is not what he seems."

"He never has been," said Oravio.

"Ivan, you've got your nose in books again. Talk to me."

Aleka and Kirby were on the terrace. The weather was drier and warmer each day. There was the softest of golden hazes shimmering above the sea. Kirby had his manuals and his notes in page-flutttering profusion on a table and over his lap.

"You talk, Princess," he said, "and faithfully I promise to listen."

"What a terrible man you are," she murmured, "you're still far more interested in those stupid manoeuvres than you are in me. If I were to make your life a thing of misery for your indifference to me, it would be no more than you deserved."

He felt he had little to fear. She seemed to be indulging a temporary mania for doing nothing. It was so uncharacteristic that he wondered if, despite her lighthearted references to the incident, the attempt on her life had been more of a shock than she would admit.

"I'm not indifferent," he said, "but perhaps you and I feel it's more stimulating to progress than it is to arrive. Perhaps we enjoy anticipation so much that we prefer the event always to be ahead of us."

"Darling," she said, "I anticipate. You procrastinate. Procrastination is not at all stimulating, it's very uncomplimentary. It makes me feel that one day I shall be very odious to you."

She was almost absurdly Russian. She lived in phases, he thought, in brief devotion to lovers or causes. Andrei had been a phase. Now it was his turn, Kirby supposed. How long would he last once they became lovers? A week? And then she would be looking over her shoulder. He could not deny it might be an illuminating week. She was superbly beautiful. The sea air and the warm days had erased her pallor and given back to her skin its pampered lustre of pearly whiteness.

He was held back not by lack of natural desire but by his inescapable regard for Olga, by a feeling that to make love to Aleka would be to betray innocence. But since he could never be more to Olga than someone she knew, that feeling was an absurdity. Nevertheless, it was there.

"You must allow me to consider how delicate you still are," he said.

"My God," she said, "what a ridiculous man you are and what strange ideas you have about women. When a woman needs love do you think she wants to be regarded as delicate and untouchable? She wants to be subjected to fire, passion and conquest. Don't you know how primitive women are? Darling, put women into a jungle and they'd survive. Put men in and they'd perish."

"Eaten by the women, do you think?" he suggested.

She lifted her white hands to the sky and turned her eyes to its blue as if entreating the heavens to bear witness to the hopelessness and impossibility of men. He smiled. If she ever did marry she would at least never bore her husband, unless in one of her careless moods she picked a man who did not like theatricals.

The Russian manoeuvres, engaging divisions from the Army of the Caucasus, took place on a plateau in the north of the Crimea. They were for Kirby not too far removed from Aleka's descriptions. They consisted of movements which, to him, appeared unrelated to commonsense. Soldiers in their thousands marched across the line of guns, offering themselves, it seemed, as willing targets. The officers from generals downwards were immaculate, bemedalled models of martial *haute couture*. They rode horses just as immaculate. In groups they trotted elegantly from one point to another, expressing restrained consternation as marching brigades periodically collided with other formations marching from elsewhere.

Generals, omnipotently observing the scheme of things from places of high vantage, bristled at the incompetence of others or beamed in acknowledgement of their own genius according to whether confusion or cohesion was uppermost. The Tsar was there each day, surrounded by his staff, the only sober-hued note being struck by Nicholas himself and the massively austere Grand Duke Nicholas Nicolaievich, the Russian Commander-in-Chief.

The Tsar, a military enthusiast, enjoyed every moment. Masses of marching infantry aroused admiration in him. The power and potential of polished guns brought compliments from him. He watched from a high ridge one afternoon as limbered guns were raced into position, the carriages swaying and rocking, the horses pounding, the artillerymen shouting. It looked spectacular. But Brigadier Rollinson, senior British observer, grunted. And Kirby, who had no military experience but a knowledge of armaments, did not have to ride down to examine the guns before pronouncing them aged and inferior. However, if the quality of much of the Russian armament was unimpressive, the manpower that surged and poured over the immense plain each day had a swamping effect on the imagination.

Nicholas, whenever observers from friendly powers were close enough, never failed to exchange friendly words with them. Especially did he seem to appreciate Kirby's presence.

"Exciting, isn't it, my dear fellow?"

"It's new to me, sir," said Kirby.

"Ah, they're splendid soldiers, the very best," said Nicholas, leaning forward on his horse to embrace the columns of moving infantry with a wave of his arm. He looked around, smiled whimsically and murmured, "If only my generals could manoeuvre as well as my soldiers can march."

He was in his element.

Kirby began to get a little bored. Relatively his role was an inactive one, sitting his horse among men who spoke a jargon unfamiliar to him. As a diversion he tried to discover if he knew more than the Russian staff officers about what was afoot each day. But as manoeuvre followed manoeuvre he could only conclude that where the greatest weight of numbers engaged, there lay tactics of generals smothered by unmanageable quantities of men.

Each evening he and his fellow officers compared notes under the supervision of Brigadier Rollinson. Kirby felt these sessions were meaningless as they dealt with the obvious. And that was that Grand Duke Nicholas Nicolaievich could face an enemy with the most formidable array of manpower in the world. He said so. Brigadier Rollinson smiled bleakly at the implied criticism, which disregarded the formidability of the Grand Duke himself. In any war, he felt the Grand Duke would come to terms with quantity.

The Brigadier liked Kirby better now that the Navy-style beard had gone. He might lack experience but he did not lack a gift for communicating with Russians. It was an extremely useful gift.

At night the British and other foreign observers were entertained in Russian messes. Kirby was introduced to the fleshpots Aleka had spoken of. Whatever the Russians thought of their own manoeuvres they wholeheartedly embraced the nightly sorties into the wine cellars. Kirby avoided getting drunk. He merely achieved a state of glassy-eyed, stiff-backed immobility. The Russians got very drunk. They danced and sang until the early hours. Kirby sang too, and in Russian, but so solemnly and tunelessly that the Russians howled with delight. They slapped him on the back and told him that although he had a terrible voice he was a fine fellow.

"Frankly," said Kirby, cautiously sitting down again, "I sing better when I'm drunk."

They roared at this. Brigadier Rollinson made a

note that Colonel Kirby might have a future as a liaison officer.

On the final day of what Kirby considered a week of inconclusiveness, the Tsar was to review his troops. He arrived early that morning in an open automobile. He was greeted with unrestrained enthusiasm. He stood up in the motorcar and responded with smiles and salutes. There was a girl with him.

Grand Duchess Olga Nicolaievna was colonel-in-chief of a regiment in St. Petersburg. In this capacity she had come from Livadia with her father to be present at the review. Nicholas did not hide his pride in her as he assisted her from the automobile. Olga wore a white, golden-braided military jacket with skirt and boots. A red-and-white cap adorned her gleaming hair. She was shy at being so much the centre of attention for the moment, but responded to the gallantries of officers with quick smiles. Her horse was brought, together with the Tsar's, and they rode at a walk, Olga side-saddle, between lines of officers until they reached the front of a stand erected to seat privileged onlookers and observers. The stand was full, the women dressed colourfully, their whites and greens, yellows and blues alternating with the sober hues of formally-attired foreign attachés.

The Tsar turned, rode forward and halted, easy and relaxed on his mount, his pleasure in the occasion obvious. Olga stayed in a position behind him but to his right. Flanking her was Grand Duke Nicholas Nicolaievich, a soldier of integrity and ability, of stern kindness, and idolised by the troops. Over six feet tall he sat his horse majestically. Behind the group were massed senior officers of the Tsar's staff, as well as some foreign observers, Kirby among them.

He was some ten paces behind the Grand Duchess. Her horse shifted a little, she quietened it. He could only see her back. It was very straight, her jacket enhancing her slender waist. Beneath her cap her hair, thickly plaited and wound around her head, was like dark, burnished russet in the sunlight. He could not take his eyes off her.

The troops began to march past to the music of massed regimental bands. It was an acclamation as much as a parade as the Tsar saluted each regiment. Banners whipped and fluttered, and the thud of marching feet became a ceaseless rhythm. Olga sat in an attitude of composure and pride as her father took so many salutes.

The artillery appeared, guns and carriages heavily indenting the trampled earth. They were horse-drawn, the long traces black in the bright light, the men upright in their saddles. The long columns of horsed men and grey metal bruised the ground and threw up dust, the sun sent light running over gun barrels and spinning around wheels.

It was the Cossacks who brought the review to its emotional close. They came in a sweeping, thunderous gallop on their small horses. Their noise, their rhythm and their abandonment quickened the blood of every onlooker. Sabres glittered amid a sea of tossing manes and impulsively the crowded stand rose to the onrushing spectacle. Kirby saw Olga visibly quiver, so infectious was the excitement evoked by the galloping Cossacks. When they had finally passed there was an audible sigh from the women in the stand.

Kirby did not know if his regard was too obsessive, too intent, but suddenly as emotional bodies relaxed Olga turned in her saddle and looked directly back at him, as if she had felt his eyes upon her. She had not seen him without his beard but recognition was immediate. Blue eyes looked into grey. Kirby smiled. Colour rushed into her face, then she turned to her front again, her eyes bright with joy.

It was over. The Tsar turned, wheeling his horse. Olga moved close to him.

"Papa, did you know? Colonel Kirby is here—is he to be invited to Livadia? He——"

But there were so many voices, so much noise, with her father receiving the congratulations of his staff

215

and his generals, as well as the applause from the crowded stand. He rode back to the car with Olga, escorted by officers. She passed quite close to Kirby, gave him the shyest of glances, the quickest of smiles, and was then swallowed up in the tide of uniforms. At the car Nicholas was in no hurry to dismount. He had enjoyed it all far too much to give up the pleasure of exchanging further comments with the Grand Duke and others. He was in genial commendation of everything, his smile constantly lighting up his handsome face, while Olga shook her head at the extravagances of officers who declared they would suffer indescribable torment if she did not stay and dine with them. Cossack officers, returning from their ceremonial gallop, were pressing forward now to bring their own greetings to the Tsar and his daughter before they left for Livadia, where they were now in residence with the rest of the family.

Nicholas and Olga finally dismounted. Grand Duke Nicholas, commanding and courtly, handed her into the car at a moment when more Cossacks burst upon the crowded scene, swelling the numbers dangerously in their exuberantly reckless way. Kirby felt as if he was being squeezed by irresistible movement and weight. His mount, a mare, threw up her head. A compact but fiery Cossack stallion snapped its teeth at her. Rolling-eyed she backed, then reared in shrill fright from its odour and viciousness. Kirby toppled backwards, he lost stirrups and seat and thudded to the ground. Olga, standing in the car, saw it all. In paralysing horror she saw the mare wheel and plunge, bringing shod forefeet crashing down. The right hoof broke Kirby's left arm, the other hoof struck the peaked cap from his head.

The blood drained from Olga's face. Her gloved hands stifled a scream. There was a disorderly milling of men and horses, the mare shivering. But Nicholas was not as indecisive in a common crisis as in an Imperial one. He shouted a command that was surprisingly clear and authoritative.

"Nicholas Nicolaievich! Get them clear!"

Grand Duke Nicholas roared, "Rabble! Get back, you fools!" He struck out, a giant of a man undwarfed even by horsed men, and the *mêlée* broke apart. Noisy Cossacks sprang from saddles to see to the fallen, unconscious British colonel. They brought him out, one arm limp and dangling, his head bloody.

He awoke to a sense of drowsy comfort, to the light of the late afternoon sun streaming through open windows. Brocaded curtains hung back in soft, heavy folds. The room and its furnishings were in blue and gold, the walls adorned with ikons and pictures. Vases were filled with the spring flowers of the Crimea, each bloom fresh and new, and with its own delicate scent.

The atmosphere was quiet, beautiful.

He knew where he was.

He turned his head, he winced as the movement shattered his drowsiness and brought stabbing pain. It hammered at his temple for long seconds before subsiding to a sensitive ache. His left arm was heavy with plaster, the pain a dull, throbbing insistence. He was in blue pyjamas, the jacket embroidered with the Imperial crest. He lay there, recalling his fall, the breath-robbing impact as the ground rose to meet his back, the plunging forelegs of the frightened horse above him. That had been a moment of fine balance between life and death.

Someone came quietly in. It was Karita. She looked crisply delicious in her full-skirted blue dress with white front. Every golden hair was in place. She regarded him silently for a moment as if she could not make up her mind whether he had been unforgivably clumsy or excessively unfortunate. She must have given him the benefit of the doubt, for she smiled and said, "Poor Ivan Ivanovich, you're better now?"

"Better than—oh, great God," he said as speech imparted throbs to his skull. "What's happening to my head?"

"Nothing's happening now," said Karita, "the damage is already done. But there was only a small cut and a big bruise, so you haven't been bandaged. It's your arm that's bad, you've broken it."

"Not me, the horse," he said, speaking economically and with care.

"Well, never mind, you're all right now," said Karita.

"Thank you," he said.

"Well, at least you're better," she said. She hoped he was. The Imperial family had been most concerned, the Grand Duchess Olga Nicolaievna distressed. "Dr. Botkin himself attended to your arm," she went on. "They put it in splints after it happened and then you were brought here, and Dr. Botkin could not have served you better if you'd been the Tsar himself. The Empress telephoned Princess Karinshka and asked if I might come over, and Princess Karinshka too of course. But Her Highness said she'd come tomorrow as long as——"

"Yes," he said as Karita stopped to pat a pillow and hide a smile.

"As long as you weren't dying today. She said you were probably drunk, but not to Her Imperial Highness, of course."

"To you."

"She wasn't serious," said Karita. "Everyone here has been so kind and the children were in such a bother about you. The Tsarevich is not very well himself but he commanded all his sisters to be quiet and to only creep about, as if this was only a small house instead of a palace. The Empress said I'd be a great help to you if I could come and so I came at once. Ivan Ivanovich, you see, you need to be unfortunate to find out how lucky you are. They could not have been kinder to a Grand Duke."

"They don't have to be." He winced again. "Grand Dukes don't fall off their horses."

"I'll fetch you something to eat," said Karita.

"Nothing to eat, angel, just some tea. Thank you, Karita."

"It isn't me, it's our Father Tsar and all his family," she said. "You should be proud, I am very proud."

"Livadia," he said abstractedly. "Well, I never."

"Yes, Livadia," said Karita, looking at the open windows, the invading brightness "It's the loveliest place in the world, full of goodness and God. I'll fetch the tea."

He felt drowsy again when she'd gone. He felt at peace. The ache and the pain were unimportant.

He heard the sound of a trolley being wheeled in. He turned his head slowly, keeping the thumping contained to a bearable level. He saw the white trolley and the silver samovar, with the dish of lemon. He saw the skirt of a primrose yellow dress. That was odd. He raised his eyes and looked into the face of Olga. Her eyes were dark with concern, her soft wide mouth parted a little. Her dress was waisted by a red sash, her hair unbraided and flowing. She had sat her horse that day in quiet composure, in pride of her father. She had looked superb. Now she was as lovely as the blossoms of spring. And so young, so much beyond him because of her youth and her birth.

The intensity of his love was shattering.

"I'm absolutely sure you aren't Karita," he said. Each word he spoke seemed to thump in his head, but that was unimportant too.

"Oh, Mr. Kirby!" Olga was breathless with relief and gladness. "Karita said you'd woken up, that you were better—oh, I mean Colonel Kirby, of course. But you were unconscious for so long, are you really better?"

"Much," he said. "How is the horse?"

She stared down at him, unable for the moment to place his question in context. Then she understood and she laughed.

"Oh, I'm so relieved," she said, "and as for the horse Alexis says he'll give it a good talking to. Everyone is so sorry about your accident but, oh, you see, I said to Alexis days ago that you still might come. I didn't think it would be this way, which has been very painful for you, but now you're here Mama will see that you're well looked after. Your arm isn't going to matter at all and you'll have to stay until you're really better. Oh, I'm talking when I should be doing this."

She realised she had been rushing on. She turned to the trolley and filled a glass from the samovar. She floated a slice of lemon on the golden liquid.

"Your Highness——"

"Oh, no," she said swiftly, "you're not to call me that, you know you're not." She turned to him again, not too shy now to show him a little reproof.

He was using his right arm to lever himself up to a sitting position.

"I thought," he said, "that if you could punch the pillows up a little——"

"Oh, I'm so sorry." Olga leaned. She moved the pillows, heaping them. Her hair was a soft whisper close to him, her scent perceptible, her dress rustling. "There, how is that?"

The pillows were very comfortable. His broken arm throbbed, his head thumped. But he felt well looked after already.

"That," he said, "is fine. Thank you, Olga."

She carefully handed him the glass of tea. It looked good. He was parched. He took a mouthful. He gulped. It was scalding.

"What is wrong?" she asked, quick with anxiety.

"Too hot," he said.

Olga shook her head and her hair shimmered. "Oh, that's nothing compared with everything else. I thought —we thought—well, it was so frightening for a moment."

"It was my own fault," said Kirby, "I was paying too much attention to you, thinking how splendid you looked. Then there was a bump and I was absolutely sure I was going to miss my lunch."

"It looked much worse than your lunch," said Olga. "Papa was so good. When he saw how bad you seemed he said, 'This is infernally distressing, what's the best

220

thing to do now?' So I said, 'It's our fault in a way, Papa, so we'd better take him back to Livadia with us and let Dr. Botkin see to him.' And Papa said, 'Splendid,' and began to order everyone about in the most practical way until everything was arranged to his satisfaction. Then he began the drive home and we followed with you in another motorcar. Well, it was thought best that an army surgeon should be with you and I sat with you too. Papa was most agreeable about that. He said army surgeons were the most considerate of fellows but not quite as considerate as women."

"Oh, much less, Olga," he smiled. "Karita was right, you've all been wonderful and it was only my arm. Thank you for everything."

"But it wasn't only your arm," she said, "it was your head where the horse kicked you. There, at the side of your head, where you have the most awful bruise." She reached out, indicating with a characteristically shy gesture the livid bruise on his temple and spreading beneath his hair. "There was only a small cut but it bled such a lot, and you were so still in the car, so pale, and I was so——" She drew in breath. "Oh, I was very silly. See, you're sitting up now and we need not worry about you at all, need we? But I'm not being very good for you, I'm talking too much and Mama said you were to have quiet."

"No, Olga Nicolaievna," he said.

"I'm not being very good for you?"

"You're not talking too much."

Olga smiled happily at that. He did not know how happy she always was at finding how easy it was to talk to him. She could not help her shyness or the way it constrained her in conversation with people. She did not suffer in that way with Colonel Kirby.

Colonel Kirby drank the hot tea slowly. Olga regarded him. His dark brown hair was unusually tousled. He had no beard. She must ask him about that. Perhaps Aleka Petrovna was responsible, not liking him with a beard. It did make him look younger.

Tatiana would exclaim extravagantly over his hand-someness.

"Colonel Kirby?" Olga was suddenly aware that he was pale under his tan. "Oh, you aren't feeling too well, are you? But I'm sure you will be in a few days and then you'll be able to get up. The children can't wait to see you and you should hear Tatiana——"

"Ah, Tatiana," he said gravely.

"Yes, she's still quite devoted," said Olga, "but Mama says no one is to bother you yet, not even Tatiana."

"Will you thank Her Imperial Highness for me?" he said. "But tell her it could never be a bother. Olga, I could not be more favoured."

She was like her mother in her sensitivity and his sincerity had an alarmingly weakening effect on her. Covering up she said brightly, "You've taken off your beard. Why did you do that?"

"They don't like them in the British Army," he said, "I think they think beards get in the way."

"Well," said Olga, "I simply can't conceive what they could get in the way of, but I'm sure Tatiana will consider you extremely dashing with a moustache and a broken arm."

"And my heroic tendency to fall off a horse," he said.

Olga's smile was quick with delight.

"Oh, we're all so glad you're here," she said, "Livadia will be such fun again. Well, it will be when you can come down into the gardens. I must go now, I've tired you enough and Karita will come to serve you more tea if you wish it."

She did not want to go but her mother had said she could see Colonel Kirby for just five minutes. She could not stay longer, she gave him a smile and went. Kirby thought the room had been suddenly deprived of its brightest flower. He leaned back, his eyes turned towards the open windows.

Outside Livadia was greenly alive with the warm freshness of spring, a spring that was like soft summer.

He thought of Olga, of her unkissed mouth.

He thought of the sophisticated beauty of Princess Aleka Petrovna.

Olga had spoiled him for that.

He dropped into welcome sleep. He awoke when the night had come, velvet and dark. He was out of bed and in the bathroom when Karita looked in. She saw the light under the bathroom door. She returned to his bedside and switched on the light there. It gave a shaded golden glow. She talked to herself until he came out of the bathroom wearing the blue linen pyjamas that belonged to the Tsar. Nicholas did not wear silk.

"Well, you're a fine one," said Karita, seeing how awkwardly he held his plastered arm to his chest. "Dr. Botkin said you weren't to get up and walk about yet, he's not sure about your head."

"Sometimes, Karita, I must get up."

"You should ring first and I'll come and help you."

"My dear girl," he said, "I haven't lost a leg."

She ignored that. She saw him back into bed. She tucked in the bedclothes and straightened the pillows. He glowered at her. She ignored that too.

"If you can't sleep," she said, "Dr. Botkin says you're to take two drops of that in water." She showed him a small bottle next to a glass of water on the bedside table.

"Very well, Miss Nightingale," he said.

"Who is Miss Nightingale?" asked Karita. In the glow of the lamp she looked warmly golden.

"Someone lovely and compassionate. And strictly efficient. You're just like her."

Karita made a final adjustment to the bedclothes.

"You must go to sleep," she said. "Her Highness Princess Aleka Petrovna will be here tomorrow and you must be at your best for her."

"Is she coming to see if I'm dead or to see if I was drunk?"

"Ivan Ivanovich," said Karita, holding herself in so that her desire to gurgle was tightly constrained,

223

"that is not at all a nice thing to say. A man came to see her this morning."

The irrelevance of this penetrated his ache.

"Andrei Mikhailovich?" he offered.

"A different kind of man," said Karita, "who only looks at you and doesn't speak to you. He had eyes like a fish four days old. His name is Prolofski. He would only speak to her Highness."

"What about?"

"How should I know? It was while he was there that the Empress telephoned and I came here. Ivan Ivanovich, is there anything you want?"

"Yes, I want to know why you're telling me about a man called Prolofski," said Kirby.

"Oh," said Karita casually, "people have heard of Prolofski. He is against our Father Tsar."

"Thank you, Karita. And there's nothing else I want. Goodnight, sweet one."

She put out a hand to the light switch. He was lying on his back, his eyes open, reflective. She was in confusion at herself for a long time afterwards at what she did then, but impulsively she bent and kissed him on the mouth.

"Oh!" she gasped and switched out the light.

"How nice," said Ivan Ivanovich from out of the darkness and she heard a murmur of laughter, affectionate and comforting.

The Tsar looked in on Kirby the next morning and was delighted to see him sitting up and reading. Karita was quite beside herself with pride and pleasure as she brought Nicholas through and her curtsey as she left would have graced the most elegant women of the court.

"A charming girl," said Nicholas, "a credit to you, my dear man. Now, how are you? What a wretched business it was. You have the most violent-looking bruise, we were far more worried about your skull than your arm."

Kirby assured him it was nothing, although it had

224

been a sick pain when he woke. Now it was back to being a bearable ache again. Nicholas talked, his flow of words easy as he passed from one light subject to another. His greatest gift was his ability to charm people, to set aside any suggestion of high and unapproachable majesty. All his children had inherited something of his personality. It was his simplicity and his friendliness that softened the harshness of every gaoler the Bolsheviks vindictively thrust upon him after the October Revolution. That was until they found Yurovsky, the one gaoler whose sadistic brutality could not be softened by man or God.

Nicholas had only come to enquire after Kirby's health, to say a few cheerful words, but he stayed twenty minutes, talking of everything but the worries and problems which were never absent and on which he pondered conscientiously but indecisively day by day. His was the indecisiveness that afflicts every peaceable, good-natured man.

Finally he said, "Your arm is an inconvenience to you, Ivan, and a disappointment to me. There'll be no tennis except with generals or ministers. Whatever talents generals and ministers have, they leave them behind on a tennis court. You have no idea, my dear fellow."

"Perhaps I have a little idea, sir," said Kirby.

Nicholas chuckled.

Apart from the Tsar and Karita, who looked in from time to time to see to things, Kirby was left alone that morning. He supposed that Alexandra was being adamant in her insistence that he was to have quiet. It was very quiet. Even Karita, whenever she popped in, seemed elusively disinclined to converse. Karita, in fact, could not imagine what Ivan Ivanovich must think of her. It was not improper for him to kiss her, she supposed, but it was dreadfully improper for her to kiss him. Whenever she was in his bedroom she was confusedly aware of his eyes following her and laughing at her. It was quite the best thing to say nothing but to whisk about busily.

Princess Aleka arrived during the afternoon. First she paid her respects to Alexandra, whose sciatica had not improved and who spent more of her time in her boudoir. The Princess imparted news which astonished and displeased Alexandra.

"Ending your betrothal? Aleka Petrovna, I can't believe you to be serious."

"I am very serious, Your Highness," said Aleka, cool and striking in black. Alexandra thought it a most unfortunate colour, seeming as it did to convey sombre finality. Nor did a black half-veil help to dispel this impression.

"But you and Colonel Kirby, you are so well matched," said Alexandra. She knew Olga had not been overjoyed to hear of the engagement. How Olga would react to the news that it was off she could guess. She would begin to dream impossibly again. "The Emperor and I were so pleased for you, it seemed quite the happiest thing."

"Unfortunately," said Aleka unemotionally, "we are not in love. You will agree, Your Highness, that that is all-important? Yes. it was an engagement brought about by circumstances rather than by mutual affection."

"I am sorrier than I can say." Alexandra regarded Aleka with disappointment and regret. "Oh, I wish both of you would think this over."

Aleka, paler than usual and smoky-eyed, said, "When I tell him I've decided to end it, I'm sure he'll agree with me that to think it over would be a waste of time."

"When?" Alexandra was more astonished. "You mean it's your decision alone and that you have yet to tell him? Aleka Petrovna, you can't tell him now, not when he's so unwell. It was only by God's blessing that he didn't have his head kicked in. Dr. Botkin said his escape was miraculous, and only time will tell whether there is any real injury."

Aleka did not seem to be moved.

"I will see how it is, Your Highness," she said.

226

Alexandra sensed an inflexibility that was bitterly emotional. She thought of Olga and sighed.

Kirby greeted Aleka with a smile. He thought her appearance in sombrely soft black incongruously conspicuous. It was as if a pale-faced mourner had entered the brightness of Livadia. She did not sit down. She stood looking at him, almost with an air of disinterest.

"You didn't think I was dead, did you?" he said as she lifted her veil.

"I only heard that you fell off your horse," she said.

"And would you believe it, I was sober at the time."

She did not respond, she only said, "Are you better today and able to talk without groaning?"

"I felt better the moment I found I was still alive," he said. "But how attractively bereaved you look, Aleka love."

"Appearances can be deceptive," she said. "So can people. The joke is over, Ivan Ivanovich. Shall I surprise you by telling you it never began? Did you think I believed your professed innocence? As soon as I saw that announcement I knew it could not have been worked out without your help. My dear stupid man, it was all too obvious. You were all too obvious. No one would walk around Russia for three years for the mere fun of it. There are so many more exciting things to do if you have money. I did not believe you were genuine from the start. Sometimes I hoped you were because you're not an unexciting man. Sometimes I hoped you would love me. But you have always been in love with someone else and you have always had other things to do. You are a British Government agent. And as an agent, a spy, a man without principles even where friends are concerned, you tried to make me look a fool, tried to discredit me politically. But I am rooted in the cause and it would take a far better, a far more ingenious and persuasive man than you to pull up those roots." A little glitter appeared in her eyes. "I was your friend, Ivan, I was ready to be more than your friend. You betrayed me."

He was very still, his back against heaped pillows,

an open book on the bed.

"I thought it was a way of saving you from your other friends," he said, "they will only lead you to Siberia."

"Siberia would not be lonely, many of my associates are there already."

"We all have our causes to serve," he said, desperately conscious of how close he was to his own destruction. Accusation by itself would smear him. If she had proof destruction was inevitable. The Imperial family would look at him in horrified disbelief. The blue eyes would freeze.

"Causes?" Princess Aleka was savagely mocking. "Do you call yours a cause? Espionage? Espionage is for humanity's rejects, who are not fit for anything else. What friends have you made in Russia whom you have not sought to use or deceive? What did you do in your three years of travelling? What strengths and weaknesses of Tsarism did you discover? And now you have made a friend of the Tsar himself. Now you will use him, deceive him, and carry his very soul back to England in a locked box. What a triumph for you, Ivan Ivanovich. What a story you could write. A spy at the court of the Emperor of Russia. Have you looked into every cabinet, under every bed?"

He wondered if he was sweating. He felt he was.

"You have your beliefs, Aleka, I have mine. You believe in revolution and would do anything to achieve it. I believe you are wrong and would do what I could to save you and Russia. The Tsar needs time, help, tolerance. He will give you justice in the end. However I've served my own Government, I'd do nothing now to hurt Russia. How did you find out, by the way?"

"You're very calm," she said. "Is it because you have no real feelings? Yes, that's it, isn't it? People like you must be cold. It need not bother you how we found out. You were very suspect. You were always alone. Where is there any rich Englishman who travels without even one servant? Karita must have been an embarrassment to you at times. You were lucky that she isn't the kind to listen at doors, to spy on the spy. But we have the proof we need, all the names of your own special friends in Russia, everything necessary to have *you* sent to Siberia. Indeed, perhaps Alexandra Fedorovna will be so upset that she will have you shot."

"I see," he said. His head throbbed. Pain stabbed.

"Yes, that's a great worry to you, isn't it?" Her smile was bitter. "How our charming Imperial family will look at you when they know. It doesn't matter about lesser people, their feelings don't signify. But the Emperor and Empress, ah, they are different."

"They are better than you think, Aleka. That is why they should be offered something kinder than revolution. That is why I'm for them, not against them."

She made a gesture of rejection with her hand.

"Spare me your penitence," she said, "I'd like to think you were more of a man than that. And spare yourself tears for the moment. I'm not going to tell them. Those aren't my orders. You're safe on one condition. Oh, do you think I care about spies, who are really only very little men? I don't care about such men, not in the smallest way, whether they live or died or what happens to them. I don't care if you've stolen a million secrets from Russia, one person like old Amarov is worth a thousand people like you, all with a million secrets each. So don't think I care about what happens to you, whether you're caught and shot or caught and hanged. There are real tyrants we're concerned with, real wrongs, real betrayers, all vastly bigger than you. You are to go free, but only if you remember that you will work with us now. When we want you we will use *you*."

He had been mistaken about Princess Aleka. She was not a spoiled, capricious dilettante who took up causes to escape boredom. She was to be treated with the finest care and caution. Nothing mattered more to him than his relationship with the children of the Tsar. He would fight to preserve that above everything else. He would fight even harder to preserve Olga's friendship: in a few years she would make a suitable marriage, and after that he might never see her again, but he could not make do with less than memories unspoiled by exposure of his trade.

"In our work," he said, "we place little value on anything but expediency, as you would know, Princess. How will you want to use me?"

"You will be told—from time to time," she said. "Is it necessary for me to tell you not to be stupid?"

"No," he said.

"You will not hear from me," she said, "but a man called Peter Prolofski. Goodbye, Ivan Ivanovich."

"I am sorry, Aleka," he said.

She looked at him. She saw the savage mark at his temple, a dark, ugly blue. She saw regret on his face and something of sadness. She compressed her lips, fighting to discipline emotions she had always indulged. But her lips broke apart and she said huskily, "Ivan, is there anything more foolish than people?"

"I don't know," he said, "but you've always been generous and lovely."

"Oh, you damned stupid idiot," she said, "you could have had Aleka Petrovna but you threw her away." She stooped, she pressed her mouth to his, fiercely, tempestuously for long seconds. "That is the last of my generosity," she said and swept out like a rushing cloud of black.

He put his hand to his forehead. It was damp. Outside, floating up from a green lawn, he heard the laugh of a girl. He got up and went to the open windows. They overlooked tranquillity. He saw woods, the mountain peaks. To the left he saw the sea. Far in the distance it merged with the pale blue sky. The vistas were infinitely beautiful, infinitely peaceful.

"No, darling," said the Empress to her eldest daughter later that day.

"But, Mama," said Olga, "it's only that it must be so boring for him, and it would not inconvenience me in the slightest to read to him."

"Is it to be supposed he can't read to himself?"

"It's a dreadful strain, Mama, if one has a bad head," said Olga. "Dearest Mama, it wouldn't have happened if Papa and I had not allowed so many soldiers to crowd us so. It's simply impossible for Papa to spare time to sit with him but I shouldn't mind at all. And positively no one has been to see him all day, he'll think us dreadfully uncaring."

"He'll think nothing of the kind, my love," said Alexandra, in restful relaxation but soft determination. "Dr. Botkin has been to see him and so has Papa. And so has Aleka Petrovna." She hesitated a little at this. Olga had bent her head low over the book she held. "Darling, there's nothing you can do for him that Karita can't do more properly. Olga?" Olga had put her book aside and risen. "Oh, my precious, no more of this or I shan't be able to let him stay."

"You would not send him away?" Olga was quick with distress. "Mama, you couldn't, he is quite dangerously ill."

"Olga, you know he isn't. He might have been, but he isn't. Dr. Botkin is finally quite happy about him. He suffered severe concussion, nothing more, except for his broken arm."

Olga moved slowly to the window, her back to her mother.

"Mama," she said quietly, "you know I would never disobey you or Papa, never. Nor would I ever do anything to distress you. But please let him stay. Alexis would be so disappointed if you didn't. He's so looking forward to seeing him when he's up. It wouldn't be for long, in any case, because as soon as he's well enough he'll rejoin Aleka Petrovna at Karinshka."

Alexandra sighed. Physically she was more fragile, but her will to endure was tenacious. Morally she was scrupulous. She would not, could not, lie to any of her family, or deceive any of them.

"No, darling, he won't do that," she said. "They have broken their engagement, they won't be married, after all. I know no one more headstrong or foolish than Aleka Petrovna."

"Mama?" Olga had a hand to her throat and spoke faintly.

"Don't ask me why, my love." Alexandra's regret was undisguised. "It seems an awful pity to me, I thought him so much the right man for her. She had such prospects, homes in both Russia and England. Who could wish for more than that? Papa wasn't just pleased with the match, he was relieved. Aleka is so wild in her ways, so bewildering in her choice of friends. She so needs a strong, guiding hand. Colonel Kirby would have been *so* suitable, and now it is all off. Oh, it's very foolish and just when I'd thought— Olga, lamb, this is why you mustn't be foolish yourself but very discreet and proper in every way."

"Mama," said Olga breathlessly, "I think Aleka Petrovna—oh, how very very silly she is."

"Yes, very silly. Darling, if Dr. Botkin says he may, then our Ivan Ivanovich can come down into the gardens tomorrow, and then you can all cheer him up. Although," Alexandra added a little ruefully, "I don't know why Livadia seems to have become so much to do with him, do you?"

"I suppose," said Olga, "he has rather grown on us here."

Nicholas came in then to take tea with Alexandra. He was forty-five. Some of the strain of his responsibilities had begun to show, but already Livadia had cast its peaceful glow over him and he looked as if he was enjoying a sunny convalescence from the cares of the throne. Alexandra had not yet told him of the broken engagement. She did so now. Nicholas was obviously disappointed but did not take long to discover a consoling factor.

"Ah, well," he said happily, "at least our good friend Ivan Kirby now has no need to hurry away. I fancy he's the kind of man who in another week will try a one-armed game of tennis. What do you say to that, Olga?"

Olga went to her father, took his hand and put it to her cheek.

"I say, Papa, that you are the loveliest man," she said.

TEN

Kirby was up the next day. All his belongings had arrived from Karinshka and because one could always be so informal at Livadia and the day was so warm, he was comfortably attired in a cream cotton shirt and brown trousers. His arm was in a sling. He went down and out on to the terrace, Karita with him and fussing just a little.

"You're like an old hen," he said.

"An old hen looking after an old goose," she said.

They were coming to understand each other, these two. Each was necessary to the other. To Kirby her services were indispensable, her companionship a pleasure. To Karita his protective ownership of her gave her a satisfying sense of belonging. In the palace of Princess Karinshka she had only been one of many servants. With Ivan Ivanovich there was no one to argue her rights or her standing, she alone commanded his welfare. But she was neither possessive nor jealous. Instinctively she felt Ivan Ivanovich would be as loyal to her as she was to him.

She accompanied him into the gardens. There were a few people about, strolling with heads together and in weighty converse. The Imperial family kept guests to a minimum at Livadia, but there were always some notabilities around, some persons of ministerial or diplomatic consequence.

Kirby found a table and chairs on the quietest of

the velvet lawns. Karita saw him settled into one of the chairs before leaving him.

"Now you can enjoy the sun and your book," she said. "I'll know when the Grand Duchesses have found you because then there'll be so much noise."

"If you can't sleep, put a pillow over your head," he said.

Karita flirted the skirt of her dress at him, then whisked away.

It was quiet. He relaxed. He supposed the children were with Pierre Gilliard. The tranquillity, so much a part of Livadia, gave it an Arcadian remoteness from the economic and political storms of the Empire. It nurtured unreality in a world where existence for so many was an unending struggle against suffering and poverty. It was an oasis of plenty in a desert of fruitless, arid autocracy. Always there were promises of reforms, always bitter political quarrels about how to achieve them. There were the people looking to their Father Tsar for inspiration, and there was Nicholas loving his people but dedicated to the perpetuation of divine rights.

And there was Alexandra, assuring Nicholas that he alone was ordained by God to lead and guide Russia. More than ever, because of Rasputin's allusion to the security of the Empire going hand-in-hand with the preservation of Tsarism, she confirmed Nicholas's belief that concessions to radicals would undermine his God-given absolutism. Concessions, said Alexandra, were wanted only by self-seeking politicians, not by the people. The people were devoted and loyal.

But concessions must come. Kirby thought they might happen when the children were older, when Alexis was a man and he and his sisters, in their adult compassion, would see what their parents would not. They would exercise an influence which Alexandra and Nicholas, because of their love for their children, would be unable to dismiss.

There was a sigh in the air, a soft rustle, and his reverie was broken. Suddenly they were there. They had seen him, stolen silently up on him, and now they were around him, laughing and clapping their hands: Anastasia, Marie and Tatiana, young and lovely in pinafore dresses swirling in the sunshine. Marie salaamed and Anastasia indulged in a curtsey so extravagant that a slight nudge from Tatiana sent her sprawling on to the grass.

"Well," gasped Anastasia, her blue eyes as wide as Olga's, "did you see that, Ivan Ivanovich?"

"Yes, and I thought you did it beautifully," said Kirby.

"We've decided, you see," said Tatiana, "that Stasia must be your slave while you're here, and it's only proper for any slave to be prostrate in the presence of her master. Oh, Ivan, how good to see you. We're all shockingly unbridled about it."

"I am not," said Marie. "I am quite excited. Tatiana, what *is* shockingly unbridled?"

"Oh, just abandonedly blissful," said Tatiana. She was nearly sixteen. "Now," she said, "who is to kiss him first? Mama won't approve if we all do it together."

"Here's Alexis," said Marie, "he should be the first and then we can all talk about how we're going to look after Ivan's sad misfortunes. Oh, I hope your arm doesn't still hurt you." She bent to peer solicitously at Kirby's arm as Alexis arrived, carried by Nagorny, a sailor deputed with his comrade Derevenko to watch constantly over the Tsarevich.

Alexis was a little drawn. His left leg seemed crippled. He was taking a long time to recover from that fall, when he had been so critically ill that his parents thought there was little they could do except watch him die. Rasputin had interceded from afar, had sent a message saying Alexis would live. Alexas had lived. How, therefore, could anyone convince Alexandra that Rasputin was not a living saint?

Nagorny set the boy gently down in a chair. Alexis smiled at Kirby. He was not a youngster to feel eternally sorry for himself.

"Isn't it a nuisance, Ivan Ivanovich," he said, "you

with a crooked arm and me with a crooked leg? But it's awfully nice to see you, how d'you do?"

Kirby got up to shake Alexis by the hand. "Well, what's an arm and a leg? We can manage, I'll wager." The boy pulled at his arm, Kirby stooped and Alexis kissed him. Kirby sat down again and the Grand Duchesses simply insisted on taking their turn.

"Oh, Lord," said Alexis, "you're in for it now. Those girls, they're always kissing someone or something. They're always kissing me and I can tell you, it makes a fellow feel quite knocked out."

"We're only going to let Ivan Ivanovich see how nice it is to have him here again," said Marie.

"What do you think, now he has no beard?" asked Anastasia of Marie in an audible aside.

"Well, it's not like kissing Papa," said Marie.

A dress whispered behind Kirby. He knew they were all there then, the enchantment of Livadia indivisible from their completeness as a group.

"Children," said Olga, "what did Mama say?"

"Mama said I'm so perfect I make up for all her disappointments," said Anastasia, seating herself on the grass with Marie.

"Mama said to take care with Colonel Kirby," said Olga, "which meant you weren't to climb all over him." She came round from behind his chair. She was in a dress of pale blue, her long hair plaited and tied by ribbons of matching blue. "Good morning, Colonel Kirby," she smiled, "I trust you continue to improve?"

"Oh, help," murmured Anastasia.

"Your Highness," said Kirby, rising to bow low to Olga, "I'm remarkably vigorous today."

"Oh, your Magnificence," said Olga, dipping in gracefully exaggerated curtsey, "how exalted we are to hear it."

The younger Grand Duchesses groaned. Anastasia and Marie stood up to join with Tatiana in similar exaggerations, much to the delight of Alexis.

"Oh, your Eminence," sighed Tatiana to Marie.

237

"Oh, your Graciousness," murmured Marie to Tatiana.

"Oh, your Good Heavens Above," said Anastasia to no one in particular.

"I trust you are getting over your spots?" said Tatiana to Anastasia.

"Goodness, yes," said Anastasia, "what a dreadful shame that yours still show."

Alexis shook with merriment, then to Olga, "You needn't worry about Ivan, he and I can manage but we shan't do any drill yet."

"No, of course not, darling," said Olga. The others were gay, she was happy. Colonel Kirby wasn't going to marry Aleka Petrovna, he didn't have to go back to Karinshka, he could stay.

"Yes, Ivan, you're excused all parades," said Tatiana, "and you don't have to do a single thing for yourself. Anastasia will run about and fetch and carry for you."

"I'm his slave, you see," Anastasia explained to Olga, "and I'll probably be thrown to the lions unless I'm a proper minion."

"Improper minions will certainly be thrown to the lions," said Kirby.

"I should be sorry for the lions," said Olga, at which Anastasia began an impersonation of a Christian being devoured in a Roman arena. Marie said it sounded awful and begged her to desist.

"Oh, I'd be happy to," said Anastasia, "but I only take orders from Ivan Ivanovich."

"Throw her to the lions," said Kirby.

The uproar was compounded of shrieks and yells as Tatiana and Marie laid hands on Anastasia, pushing her towards Alexis who leaned forward and in simulation of a hungry lion aimed bites at her. Anna Vyrubova appeared, fulsome white garments accentuating her plumpness.

"Children, such a commotion," she said. "whatever is going on?"

"Oh, only some shocking pandemonium," said Tatiana, "you know how it is when Ivan Ivanovich is here, he always provokes the most riotous behaviour."

It was a magical morning. They sat around him, they talked, they listened, they laughed. He had never known children so addicted to laughter. They told him how they had spent their winter, he told them how he had spent his. They were awfully upset that he had had this accident and said his bruised head must be dreadfully painful. Alexis said he often had bruises like that himself and if they hurt Ivan as much as they hurt him, it was quite rotten.

Olga winced at this, knowing how often Alexis had been in agony, sometimes because of the most trifling knocks. But Alexis looked happy now, absorbed in all his good-humoured Ivan Ivanovich had to say.

Colonel Kirby had such a way with all of them, she thought. He reached out to them, delighted them, laughed with them. He did not seek the company of other men, compete for the attentions of some of the court ladies, he seemed more than happy whenever he was at Livadia to be with them.

Olga had thought Easter at Livadia might not be as lovely this year.

But now it promised to be the loveliest.

Kirby wondered, as he listened to Anastasia describing the things she kept in her room at Tsarskoe Selo, if Anstruther had received his message. If he had it would have arrived like a bolt from the blue. Very likely he would return the compliment. He would have Kirby out of Livadia quicker than a shell from a gun.

It had not taken Kirby long to find out what Aleka had meant. He had checked the only possible source of information. It was all neatly fitted into his hairbrush. The wafer-thin cards had been moved, their angle of lodgement different from that which he always used. And the cards contained in code brief but telling intelligence on agents and contacts in Russia. He did not doubt that the cards had been removed long enough for the data to be collated and the code broken. Not only had he, in complacent over-confidence, placed himself in jeopardy but so many other people too.

His only hope was that if Aleka's revolutionary friends wanted to use him they would hold their information over his head. They had little practical interest in espionage agents, it would be a matter of indifference to them whether the Okhrana knew or not. Information on such agents was for using not divulging.

Nevertheless, Easter for Kirby promised only days of uneasiness and anxiety.

The complicated creed of Russian Orthodoxy was something that Kirby, only a conventionally religious man, had never enquired about. He had always been far more interested in the schisms of Russian politics than in those of religion. There were innumerable political parties and every party suffered its secessionists like an inevitable disease. It was left to the church to bring the people together at Easter, to unite dissident Russia in celebration of Christ's resurrection.

For the Tsar and his family it was the holiest and most joyful of occasions, Alexandra immersing herself body and soul in the rites. In her devotion to God and her ecstatic adoption of her husband's faith, Alexandra found celestial happiness in the way Russian Orthodoxy celebrated the meaning of Easter.

Kirby was at the cathedral for the service. He knew the Imperial family took it for granted that he would attend, that he would participate when the Metropolitan, the highest Russian archbishop, would lead the whole congregation in a midnight search for the risen Son of God. He was accompanied by Karita, the Crimean girl in rapt exaltation. They saw the Imperial family in their places at the forefront, the Grand Duchesses vestmented in the white garments of Easter. Members of the court and officers of the Imperial Guard brought the splendour of high places to the crowded pews. The service was moving, impressive, and the choral litanies were sung with unrestrained joy and devotion. At midnight Kirby joined with all the other worshippers when the whole congregation took up lighted candles and in the measured wake of the Metropolitan circled the cathedral, re-entered it and there heard the Metropolitan announce the rediscovery of Christ.

Kirby could not help being impressed. And he was intrigued anew by the character of Russia. It was entirely typical of its people to be irreconcilably divided politically and socially and completely integrated on such religious occasions as this. He wondered what a hundred million Russians would do in a moment of supreme national crisis, whether they would form an indivisible whole or each turn a different way, each choose any path but that of his neighbour.

On Easter Day the Imperial Palace was thrown open to hundreds. Peace and tranquillity happily made way for feasting and celebrating. Livadia swarmed with the Emperor's subjects. Nicholas was delighted and Alexandra, never more content than when the people showed their love and esteem, was a fount of hospitality. She was always happier among the people than among the aristocrats. Catching Kirby's eye when she was dispensing the little Easter cakes to yet one more contingent of children, she smiled. He was talking to other children, shy village children, and the noise and the activities had set his head thumping. He interpreted Alexandra's smile as a request and went to her. She was in flowing white with a single necklace, elegantly beautiful. Always she gave him the impression that she associated majesty with humility.

"Imperial Highness?" he said.

"Colonel Kirby, Ivan." she said, "you've been so good, helping to look after so many of the children. I wish others might be as kind." He knew she referred to courtiers who were inclined to be too easily bored by "the people." "But you've done enough—yes, you have, I can see you have. You're excused. You're to go and sit outside and I'll have tea sent out to you."

"I'm not quite as done up as that, am I?" he smiled.

"Enough for you to be excused, so you are not

241

to argue." She returned his smile. He could not remember any time when Alexandra had not shown him kindness and graciousness. Whatever their faults, he believed in Alexandra and Nicholas.

He was, in fact, pleased to leave the festivities for a while. His head was a swine. The bruise had lost its external ugliness but occasionally, as now, it thumped out its sensitive reaction to noise. He went out into the gardens, found chairs and a table by one of the massed rose beds, the table under the shade of a tree. He sank into a chair, the Palace behind him rising in strata of tall, shining windows and sparkling white stone. The noise slipped away and there was only the warm tranquillity he loved.

"Tea, O Lord of a missing slave?"

That could only be Tatiana and it was. She herself had brought a samovar down on a tray, with a plate of Easter cakes. It would not be long, he thought, before undiminishable beauty invested Tatiana. She had a quicksilver grace now, grey eyes that were forever laughing, and the endearing enchantment of youth. He had a special affection for Tatiana, so responsive in her humour, so close to Olga.

"Tatiana Nicolaievna, how did you know I was in need?" he asked.

"Mama told me," said Tatiana, setting the tray down on the table. "Oh, it's no bother to slave for you, Ivan, especially when your official slave is so dreadfully busy flirting with boys. I'm to tell you that, you know, because then I can tell Stasha whether you're atrociously jealous. You'd better be, she'll be alarmingly put out if you aren't."

He looked up at her. He was very amused. She thought him devastatingly English with his lean, brown look, his military moustache and the smile that was always so quick to show in his eyes.

"Tell Anastasia I'm so jealous that I'm the one who's alarmingly put out," he said.

"Oh, fiddle," said Tatiana, "it's just not fair to

favour her when we're all equally devoted to you. Actually, I'm the most devoted."

"Tatiana, is it permitted to say I love you all very much?"

She lost her teasing look. She knew that he was far from teasing. She felt as if there were strange shadows falling.

"Ivan, we would all be terribly miserable if you did not," she said. She looked down at her hands. She said. "Oh, if only you were a Crown Prince."

"Fat or thin?" he said.

"It's not a joke, Ivan," said Tatiana. "you know it's not, don't you?"

"Tatiana?" He was vaguely disturbed. Tatiana looked up. There was just the suspicion of tears. This was alarming. She knew. He supposed there were moments when his love for Olga must have been obvious to someone as observant as Tatiana. There was nothing he could do, no declaration or denial he could make. Either would be futile. He shook his head. "One doesn't have to be a Crown Prince to love you all, does one, Tatania?"

"No," she said wistfully, "but—"

"I should be a great joke as a Crown Prince, I can't even stay on a horse," he said lightly. He saw there were two glasses with the samovar, two plates with the cakes. "Are you staying to drink tea with me?"

"I'd like to very much," said Tatiana, "but Mama wishes me to do a hundred things for a million people and I must simply fly. I think someone older and more entertaining is coming to keep you company."

"General Sikorski?"

"Do you wish him? Then I'll see. You are the dearest man, Ivan." And she bent to kiss his cheek before hurrying away. She met Olga coming round from the terrace. Olga was flying. She checked her pace when she saw Tatiana.

Alexandra had called her and said, "Olga sweet, I've sent Colonel Kirby to have some tea in the gardens. He's been doing too much. But I think he might like

243

a little company. If you can spare some time would you like to join him for a while?"

It had been difficult for Olga not to show pleasure. But she managed a little restraint as she said, "Mama, I think I could spare a little time."

Alexandra smiled. Olga was as readable as an open book. But it was Easter Day, a time for giving, not denying.

"Well, you deserve a rest too before the evening. Go along, darling."

Olga knew it was even more difficult to disguise her feelings from Tatiana. Her sister would know why she had been hurrying.

"Oh, dear," said Tatiana, "it's you. He said he was looking forward to seeing General Sikorski."

"Tatiana? Who said that?"

"Ivan. I've just taken tea to him. Mama asked me to, she said she would see if you could spare time to sit with him. Imagine him preferring General Sikorski."

Olga assumed a complete innocence of what it was all about. She patted her sister's cheek and said, "You mustn't go on so, darling, you'll wear your tongue out one day. I shouldn't mind too much but you would miss it dreadfully."

Tatiana laughed in delight. Olga was delicious at times. Oh, how remiss of Ivan Ivanovich not to have been born a Crown Prince. It would have put her dearest sister in heaven. Tatiana went back into the Palace in sighing wistfulness while Olga went on to join Colonel Kirby.

She was in a dress of Easter white, the sun caressing her and enhancing the golden overtones of her chestnut hair. He rose, his arm in a black silk sling.

"We received your message," said Olga, "but General Sikorski couldn't come, he's fallen asleep in a dish of cream cheese. So I came instead. Now I expect you'll fall asleep too. But I'll pour the tea first." She was demure in her humour. She began to fill a glass.

"General Sikorski? Well, I don't know. Olga, you look—" He checked himself. So often he almost committed the error of using words that Alexandra would consider unfortunately presumptuous. He could flatter Olga as others did, meaninglessly. He could not go beyond that.

"Oh, I look, do I?" Olga was smiling. "I know what you mean, but I've been rushing madly about. There are so many people being received and I suppose I do look rather like a broom in the wind."

He imagined the right meaningless response to that would be to tell her she looked as if she'd been sweeping them all off their feet. Instead he said. "I was going to say you look better at serving tea than General Sikorski." That was just as meaningless. He smiled wryly to himself.

"Thank you," she said, "you are as gallant as anyone, Colonel Kirby."

Her smile was not a mere pleasantry. It had its message. Because she was so young, seventeen, he sometimes forgot how intelligent she was. He knew that she knew his gallantry was meaningless. Safe. She did not mind. She understood.

"You aren't going to take tea standing up, are you?" she said. She waited until he sat down again, then seated herself at the opposite side of the table. "Isn't it lovely out here? We're in the best place, are we not? It's become so hot inside. Are you very tired?"

"Not a bit," he said, "I'd just begun to creak a little, that's all."

They laughed together at that. He relaxed over the tea. She pushed back a wandering tress of hair. Their eyes met and held. She was quite still, her back to the sun, her face softly shadowed. Time seemed in suspense. Suddenly she was suffused with colour, she dropped her eyes and stared unseeingly at her clasped hands. A bird called, sweet and piping. The scent of flowers magically distilled the air. Olga's head was bent, her hair a cascading curtain.

"Olga?" he said. She looked up. He felt pain. Her eyes were brimming.

"It's nothing." She shook her head. "It was just a

245

little hurt that caught me. But nothing, really. Will it relax you if I read to you? I have my Shakespeare with me." She indicated the white bag she had brought.

"That would be very pleasant as well as peaceful," he said.

She took the black-bound volume from her bag, opened it up and rifled through the pages.

"I haven't read all the plays yet," she said, "or even half of them. I like *The Merchant of Venice*. Shall I read something from that? Or there is *The Prince of Denmark*, which Monsieur Gilliard says is very highly favoured by the theatre."

"Make it a surprise," he smiled, "read from that page where you have your hand."

She lifted her hand from the page she had flattened, looked at it and said, "I don't know if you'd like this, it's *Romeo and Juliet*, which is all about terribly young people suffering miserably because of love."

"Mmm, yes," he murmured, "hardly the thing for terribly old people like you and me, Olga."

"Well, you will see," she said. The breeze lifted a strand of her hair and it brushed across her face. She pushed it back. "If it isn't to your liking," she said, "it will be your own fault for choosing so indiscriminately."

"Am I to be read to or not, young madam?"

"Don't be impatient," she said, "it will only make me nervous." She regarded the written word and he regarded her soft, wide mouth. "This is to do with Juliet's nurse," she said, "in conversation with Juliet, and I shan't mind if you fall asleep."

"Good," he said.

"Oh, you had better not," said Olga. "It's the nurse speaking, she's just returned to Juliet with a message from Romeo but all she says is,

I am aweary, give me leave awhile,
Fie, how my bones ache! What a jaunt have I had!

"Then here, a little further on, taking no notice of Juliet's anxieties, she says,

246

> *Lord, how my head aches! What a head have I!*
> *It beats as if it would fall in twenty pieces.*
> *My back! On the other side—O, my back, my back!*
> *Beshrew your heart for sending me about,*
> *To catch my breath with jaunting up and down.*

"All this while poor Juliet is dreadfully desperate to hear about Romeo and saying, let me see—yes—

> *Sweet, sweet, sweet nurse, tell me, what says my love?*

"And what does the exasperating old thing say to that? She says,

> *O God's lady dear!*
> *Are you so hot? Marry, come up, I trow,*
> *Is this the poultice for my aching bones?*
> *Henceforward do your messages yourself!*

"There, Colonel Kirby, what do you think of that for a most tantalising nurse and an indiscriminate choice?"

She looked up from the book. Kirby, entranced by her delicious humour, saw her smile. He had not known it possible to love a girl as he loved this one.

"Lovely," he said, and he knew that if Tatiana had been present she would have guessed he was not talking about Shakespeare.

"Well, at least you didn't fall asleep," said Olga. "Now I insist on *The Merchant of Venice*, I'll read you how Portia addressed Bassanio when he made the correct choice of caskets. It was a tender part of the play I liked very much." She turned the pages, found the extract she wanted and said, "See, this is what she says to Bassanio.

> *You see me, lord Bassanio, where I stand,*
> *Such as I am: though for myself alone*
> *I would not be ambitious in my wish,*
> *To wish myself much better; yet, for you*
> *I would be trebled twenty times myself;*
> *A thousand times more fair, ten thousand times*
> * more rich;*

> *That only to stand high in your account,*
> *I might in virtues, beauties, livings, friends,*
> *Exceed account: but the full sum of me*
> *Is sum of nothing; which, to term in gross,*
> *Is an unlessoned girl, unschooled, unpractised:*
> *Happy in this, she is not yet so old*
> *But she may learn; happier than this,*
> *She is not bred so dull but she can learn;*
> *Happiest of all is that her gentle spirit*
> *Commits itself to yours to be directed,*
> *As from her lord, her governor, her king.*
> *Myself and what is mine to you and yours*
> *Is now converted: but now, I was the lord*
> *Of this fair mansion, master of my servants,*
> *Queen over myself; and even now, but now,*
> *This house, these servants and this same myself,*
> *Are yours, my lord: I give them with this ring;*
> *Which when you part from, lose or give away,*
> *Let it presage the ruin of your love*
> *And be my vantage to exclaim on you."*

Olga read the passage slowly, evenly, ensuring no mistakes or hesitations to spoil the rhythm of the verse, although there was a catch in her voice that imparted a little breathlessness to the last line. Then the silence was soft. She glanced up. He was still, his eyes fixed on distant trees, verdant with new green, his expression so sombre that she thought he was locked in sadness. She trembled. Her teeth caught on a quivering lip and stilled it. When Kirby turned his head and looked at her she smiled brightly.

"You see, you were nearly asleep," she said.

"Bassanio, of course," he said, "knew he was undeserving of a love like that. So is any man. Olga, how well you read Shakespeare."

She closed the volume. And the only thing she could think of to say then was, "We heard you aren't to marry Aleka Petrovna, after all. I am so sorry." She had not mentioned the broken engagement to him at all until now. She did not know why she did so then. Perhaps because of Bassanio and Portia.

"It isn't a matter to be sorry about," said Kirby, smiling. "We weren't in love. It was a mutually happy parting. It's something better done before than left too late to be done at all."

"Aleka Petrovna could not have been as happy as that," said Olga quietly, "and you have to think about the future if you're to have grandchildren eventually."

"Olga, there are always other people's grandchildren to talk to. Do you think about your future or is it all written out for Grand Duchesses when they're born?"

"My future? Oh, I don't think about it at all," she said. "Well, I don't think about being a Crown Princess, I think about how happy I am now. It really is quite delicious to—well it is."

"What is delicious?"

"To read Shakespeare to you and almost send you to sleep."

In the quietness of the gardens, in the sunshine that caressed a happy Grand Duchess, a man and a girl laughed.

Alexandra observed the glow in Olga's eyes, the enchantment life held for her each day. But Alexandra said nothing. And when savage revolution struck its most terrifying blow perhaps Alexandra blessed her own forbearance in letting Olga, the most sensitive and modest of her daughters, have her limited happiness.

There was an Easter ball and Livadia that evening was crowded with brilliance and people. Both Olga and Tatiana attended. Olga, her shapely figure gowned in white, her diamond tiara regal on her piled hair, looked softly beautiful. Tatiana, also with her hair up and her tiara catching fire, wore a ball gown of pale, lambent green. The state dining-room, its chandeliers ablaze, was glittering. The more exalted officers competed for the privilege of dancing with the Grand Duchesses, but neither Olga nor Tatiana permitted their cards to be filled.

Olga's eyes kept searching everywhere. When she was

dancing and when she was not she was looking into corners.

"Tatiana," she said when they were pausing for breath after one dance, "isn't it strange that Colonel Kirby is missing? I can't see him anywhere."

"It's worse than strange," said Tatiana, fluttering her fan, "it's shockingly neglectful. I've saved him three dances and he isn't here for any. All my irresistible allure is being wasted on officers who want to introduce me to their favourite horses. There one quite nice young man, but he's so overcome by my unsurpassed loveliness that his mouth is open all the time."

"Well, be careful he doesn't swallow you," said Olga, "you are very unsurpassed tonight, sweet. Which dances have you saved?" They compared cards, their jewelled heads close. "Tasha, no! You're to dance the last with someone else, I've already promised that Colonel Kirby shall engage himself to me for that."

"How could you have if he isn't here?"

"Tatiana, you are not to argue."

Tatiana did not miss her sister's rising pink, but she only said with sighing woe, "Ah me, and I did imagine myself divinely waltzing with him. And Ivan wouldn't just have his mouth open, he'd say the most deliciously immortal things about my bewitching beauty. Oh well, with his arm still in plaster perhaps he couldn't manage to dance, anyway. Or perhaps the awful wretch has forgotten the ball is tonight and will appear tomorrow instead?"

"Darling, go and ask Mama," said Olga, "she'll know why he isn't here."

Tatiana eyed her sister. Olga looked adorable. Colonel Kirby really was a wretch. Olga had spent ages preparing for the ball and he wasn't here to appreciate it.

"Very well," said Tatiana, "and perhaps it's better that I ask."

Alexandra, seated because her limbs ached so, smiled as Tatiana approached. How beautiful the girl was tonight.

"Darling," she said, "you look quite the prettiest young lady, Papa and I are so proud of you and Olga."

"Yes, I am rather divine tonight," said Tatiana. "Mama, where is Colonel Kirby?"

Alexandra looked round. Her ladies-in-waiting were, however, chatteringly engaged with the Tsar's suite of officers. She did not want too much curiosity evoked about Colonel Kirby. There was enough of it already.

"My love," she said, "he has begged to be excused because of his arm. He felt he could only stand about and look out of place."

"But, Mama," said Tatiana, "he was playing in the gardens with us this afternoon and throwing a ball about. He wasn't standing about at all."

"Darling, he has begged to be excused and I could not refuse." Alexandra spoke with gentle finality. "I shall be going up soon, I'm a little tired and Papa says we aren't too formal tonight. Will you and Olga come up with me to say goodnight? Then you may return and enjoy yourselves and Papa will keep an eye on you. He says if he doesn't both of you are quite likely to be carried off."

"Papa is sweet," said Tatiana. She did not quite know what Olga was going to say now. Her sister had made herself as inconspicuous as possible near the buffet so that she could still keep her dance card free.

"Tasha?" She was a little anxious. "What did Mama say?"

"It's just as I thought," said Tatiana, "it's his arm. He thinks he would only be awkward with it, so he begged Mama to excuse him."

Olga looked incredulous.

"He's not attending at all?"

"Perhaps," said Tatiana gently, "it's because he isn't thinking of himself but Mama. Mama knows you've spent an awful lot of time with him and perhaps—"

"I see," said Olga quietly, "I see."

She danced. She smiled as she danced. So many people said how lovely she had become this last year, how modest she was, how unflirtatious. When Alexandra retired both her daughters accompanied her to her suite. Despite her aching limbs she moved gracefully through the state hall, acknowledging bows and curtseys with her nervous smile.

The three of them peeped in on Alexis. The Tsarevich was wrapped in childish slumber, peaceful and without pain. Alexandra stooped to press the lightest kiss on his hair. In her boudoir she said goodnight to her daughters, enjoining them to return to the festive ball. They kissed her warmly, affectionately.

Olga was very quiet as she and Tatiana left Alexandra's boudoir, she said nothing as they traversed a shining corridor. Tatiana put an arm around her.

"Sister, don't be doleful, it's such a splendid ball," she said. "And it isn't as bad as you think, Ivan is only trying to do what's right. Olga, you simply mustn't think about him so much. He is being good, you must be good too."

"Good?" Olga's whisper was almost fierce. "Is it being good to neglect us so, to stay away without even telling us? He didn't have to dance, he could have attended."

"Olga," said Tatiana, "he's doing this because it's sensible."

"Sensible?" Olga stopped as they reached a wide, shining landing. The noise of the ball reached them as a muted agglomeration of sounds and echoes. "Oh, that is a stupid, useless word!"

"You are going to get shockingly upset in a moment, I know you are," said Tatiana. "Olga, sweetest, dearest, he's doing it because—oh, because he's so much in love with you that he'll do nothing to make things impossible. You must help him, you must dance all night with everyone else—"

"Tasha, did he say that?" Olga trembled so violently that Tatiana caught her by the arms. "Did he tell you that he—no, he didn't, he could not, he must not."

"Darling, he didn't tell me anything, but he adores you, it's the most obvious thing I've ever seen." Tatiana gently squeezed her sister. "You must be happy with

252

that, he'll never hurt you, never do anything to spoil what there is. That's why Mama lets him stay, she trusts him. Darling, a ball is very romantic, it can weaken two people awfully—"

"I am not going to dance with everyone else," said Olga. She was very still now, her blue eyes dark. "I am not. You go on, darling, I'll come soon, I promise."

Karita answered the light tapping on the door of Kirby's suite. She opened her eyes wide to see Grand Duchess Olga, beautiful in her white ball gown, superb in her composed regality.

"Karita, where is Colonel Kirby?"

"Your Highness," said Karita apologetically, "he has gone out."

The light was failing by the time Kirby reached a woodman's hut half a mile from the Palace. But half a mile was little in the vastness of the Imperial estate. A man called Peter Prolofski was there, a man in a dark blouse, black trousers and black hat. His white face was round. The black hat looked as if it sat on a shining moon. Kirby was aware of a second man, a shadowy figure in the background of the dim hut.

"You're late," said Prolofski. His voice was flat, toneless. Kirby sensed that here was a man who did not care very much for people as they were or for the world as it was.

"Once I leave the Palace to look for a place like this I'm a stranger to the estate," said Kirby, "and your message did not give me much time." The message had been handed to him by a blank-faced male servant. "What is it you want?"

Prolofski had no time for preliminaries, for unnecessary words.

"I want Gregor Rasputin," he said.

"Take him for all I care, I'm not his keeper," said Kirby.

"Don't waste my time," said Prolofski, his pale face expressionless, "you're here to listen, to receive orders. Rasputin is the protector of Nicholas the Bloody. He

253

doesn't realize to what extent, but he is. The peasants believe in Rasputin the holy man, the holy man believes in the preservation of Tsarism. He believes in it because it enhances his own power. Without Tsarism he'd be nothing. But what Rasputin believes in the peasants believe in likewise. They're proud that a holy man who is also a peasant has the Tsar's favour. Therefore Rasputin must go. Therefore you, comrade, must see that he goes."

"I'm a small pebble, Rasputin is a mountain," said Kirby. "Tell me how a pebble can bring down a mountain. No, I'll do other work for you, find out things for you, but I can't touch Rasputin. My talent is for acquiring information."

The darkening hut smelt dry and woody. Prolofski smelt of soap and leather. He also smelt of cold fanaticism. He did not need information. The stupidity of such a suggestion made him softly spit.

"His death," he said, contemptuous of anything else, "must be seen as an act of the Romanovs. When the Romanovs eliminate Rasputin, the peasants will eliminate the Romanovs."

"That's not a fact, that's surmise," said Kirby. "I'm not a Russian, but I don't think anyone can correctly guess what the people would do under any given set of circumstances, or even guarantee that what they would do one day they would follow the next."

"You are a wriggler," said Prolofski. "We will see to the peasants, you will see to Rasputin. You will kill him with the good reasons of an Englishman, when you catch him attempting to outrage one of the Romanovs."

Kirby went cold and rigid. The round moon of a face was blank, so were the eyes. They were like the eyes of a dead fish, as Karita had said.

"Which Romanov is this?" he asked.

"There's only one who will suit our purpose," said Prolofski, "one whom Rasputin has looked at often enough. Olga Nicolaievna."

"Yes?" Perhaps his voice gave away his desire to

do murder here and now, for the shadow in the background stirred.

"You're very close to the Romanovs," continued black-hatted moonface, "and can arrange matters for us better than anyone else. It can be done anytime when Rasputin is in St. Petersburg again, visiting his German harlot."

"Who is she?" He surprised himself at his calmness considering the heat and violence of the hammer in his head.

"Alexandra the whore. If you say your talent is for acquiring information," sneered Prolofski, "you must have had your nose shortened recently. Or perhaps she has—"

"Don't say it. We need to work amicably. Go on with the relevancies."

"Simply, comrade, you'll kill Rasputin when you find him attempting to outrage Olga Nicolaievna. You'll hear her screams, go in, chase him out, catch him and kill him. That is all that is relevant, except that you'll need a pistol. Don't try throttling him or you won't live to see the revolution."

"What you mean," said Kirby, "is that I'll wait for him somewhere in the Alexander Palace and shoot him in the back. He doesn't have to be anywhere near the Grand Duchess."

"Of course." Prolofski permitted himself a shrug. "You aren't a complete fool, are you? Where you kill him won't matter, inside or outside the Palace. What matters is the story, the reason. Olga Nicolaievna may perhaps deny it, she's the type to prefer denial of truth or fiction rather than place herself in the public eye. Everyone knows this. Nothing will happen to you. Nicholas will be grateful to you whatever he thinks of Rasputin. The German whore will scream her head off, but you will be a hero. Who likes Rasputin apart from her?" He spat again. "The peasants will be told that the creature died because of a lying Romanov, since we will do the telling. It would be convenient if you could persuade Olga Nicolaievna to forget her

255

prudishness and co-operate. If she dislikes Rasputin, she doesn't dislike you."

Kirby felt a savage desire to blot out the face of the moon.

"You think that the alternative of having the Imperial family know about me would be worse than this?" he said. "You can forget about any possibility of the Grand Duchess co-operating in a plot to kill a man. She looks at the world in her own way and that sets her apart from people like you and me. When I tell my story of why I killed Rasputin she'll know I'm lying. You know that she'll know. So I might as well accept the alternative."

"We think not, comrade," said Prolofski. "You'll take the chance of reassuring Olga Nicolaievna that you acted for the best, even though you may have been mistaken."

"I see." Kirby still sounded calm. "But I must have time to think this out. When I leave Livadia I shan't be a free agent, I'm under the orders of my senior officer and have no idea when I might be in Tsarskoe Selo at the same time as Rasputin."

"All that is nothing." Prolofski rolled spit. "You're still under the orders of your friends in London, who are now pursuing a policy of co-operation with Russia. Your friendship with the Romanovs is encouraged, you may arrange to see them whenever you like as far as London is concerned. If you are simple, we aren't. However, we'll give you twenty-four hours to make up your mind. Come here tomorrow at the same time, spell out your decision and outline your own plan for this service to Russia. We'll want to know every detail and when Rasputin is back in St. Petersburg again, we'll arrange the day with you. You might try arranging it with Olga Nicolaievna. Who knows, she might not look at the world in quite the way you think."

Was the man as stupid as he sounded? No, thought Kirby, there was no stupidity here. Rasputin was to be executed and by an Englishman close to the Imperial family. The complicity of Olga, real or suggested, was unnecessary, superfluous. It was meant only to show him that if he wished to offer a reason for the killing, this was the one that, with Rasputin's reputation, had the basis of authentic possibility to it. It was also the one that would provide him with his best chance of escaping a charge of murder. Except that Olga would not, even to save his neck, support a story she knew to be horrifyingly untrue.

This was what did not fall into place. Simple as Prolofski had said it all was, this was not how Olga was to be used. They had some other role for her, some other tale of complicity that would involve her far more subtly and fix Rasputin's murder far more securely to the door of the Romanovs.

"I've never done this kind of work," he said, "and must tell you I may not be very good at it. I must think it over and see you again this time tomorrow."

They let him go, they watched him go. It was dark now.

"He has gone out?" Olga could not believe she had heard aright. "He can't have."

"Your Highness," said Karita, "he has gone for a walk."

"A walk? Tonight?" Something very close to angry resentment manifested itself in the young Grand Duchess. "If that is true—oh, it had better not be. Let me see."

"Your Highness——"

"Karita!"

Karita, in an unaccustomed fluster at the temper of the most equable of the Grand Duchesses, hastily moved aside to let Olga inspect the suite for herself. Olga simply swept in and Karita thought her quite sweetly magnificent. But what had come over her? She was never like this. Following her into the empty drawing-room Karita heard the sound of footsteps approaching the suite. She turned, saw Kirby entering through the still open door and hastened in a silent rush to him.

"What you have done I don't know," she whispered,

"but Her Highness the Grand Duchess Olga is here and seems very put out. Whatever it's about, you will need to think quickly."

Olga had gone through the drawing-room and was rapping on the bedroom door before the sound of voices in the entrance to the suite reached her ears. She swung round and met Kirby face-to-face in the drawing-room. Karita vanished, leaving the Tsar's daughter to deal with the Englishman in her own way. Karita had a feeling that whatever the cause of the confrontation, it was Ivan Ivanovich who was going to come off worse.

It would do him good.

Olga regarded Kirby with fierce resentment. While everyone else had taken so much trouble he was quite indifferent to the occasion. He was dressed so casually in flannel trousers and an old velvet jacket it was almost an impertinence.

He saw there was no diffidence of any kind about her, she was angry, she was beautiful, and her pride and her tiara gave her a tallness. He would have spoken but with a gesture of her hand Olga made it very clear that she would speak first.

"Colonel Kirby," she said, "will you tell me what has happened that you can't attend on us tonight? Will you tell me why it's safer for you to go out walking than it is to come to the ball?"

"Your Highness——"

"Oh!" For the first time in her life Olga stamped her foot. She did not like him like this, he was dark, serious and had no smile for her, none at all. She was near to tears but her anger saved them from spilling. "Oh, to call me that! Now I see, we are not to be friends, then. I have done something quite shocking and so you go walking in the night to be out of my way and call me Highness when you do see me!"

"That was only because——"

"I don't care to hear why! What does the reason matter? You wish to be formal." Olga was surprising

258

herself and Kirby even more. "Very well, we will both be formal. I can be so as much as you, and you are commanded, do you hear? You are commanded to attend on me. I will wait while you suitably attire yourself."

His darkness was transfigured into astonished delight. His shy Grand Duchess was actually being imperious. There was something new to be discovered about her every day.

"Suitably attire myself?" he said, his eyes mirroring the delight he felt. "I am commanded? I am commanded, Olga?"

"Colonel Kirby," she said, "are you laughing at me?"

"Indeed I'm not," he said, "I'm in great admiration of you. Am I in such positive disgrace because I cried off? Well, there was this arm of mine and there are always so many young officers devoted to you. I thought it a night for you to dance with them——"

"Oh!" Again she stamped her foot. She disliked his words intensely. Not only did they amount to no real excuse at all, but they had connotations of horribly dismaying condescension. Young officers! As if she were no older than Tatiana. "Am I not able to please myself? Are you to tell me you know what is best for me? Oh, I have done something worse than shocking, that is very clear!"

Karita was right, Olga was very put out. He had not seen her so upset. He had asked Alexandra to excuse him because of his arm, but the real reason had been connected with the message he had received. There was, however, also the fact that he knew Alexandra wished him to exercise restraint in his relationship with Olga. Restraint was one thing, hurting her was another.

"No," he said, "it's I who have offended, Olga. I have hurt you. I am very sorry, will you forgive me?"

Olga caught at a lip that was suddenly trembling. There was something more than contrition in his expression, something that reached out to her. She could not maintain a demeanour so foreign to her, not when

259

he looked like that, not when she was so unhappy. She melted in desperate appeal.

"Oh, you aren't commanded, but please come. Dear Colonel Kirby, what is the ball to Tatiana and me if you aren't there? We have saved dances for you but you need not dance at all, we can walk in the gardens instead or watch Tatiana. You've no idea how lovely she looks tonight, her hair is up and she'll never forgive you if you stay away, if you don't see her in her new gown, if you don't tell her how nice she looks. And see?" She was running on, breathlessly outside her limits now as with gestures of her gloved hands she drew his attention to her own gown, to her hair and her jewels. "This is all for you, I took so much care——"

It was a rush into silence then, and the uncontrollable colour surged as she realised what she had said. He could not help himself, he had to tell her that the care she had taken had not been wasted.

"Olga, you are always lovely," he said, "and now, look, you are more than that. You are quite beautiful tonight, has no one told you so? And of course I'll come, since if Tatiana looks only half as splendid as her sister it would never do to miss her." He smiled as he went on. "I'll suitably attire myself, then, but you shouldn't wait, I'll be there as soon as I can."

She was aflame with vivid colour, with the unspoiled richness of youth and innocence.

"I am not going without you, I am not," she whispered.

"You should, you know."

"Colonel Kirby, it isn't what one should do but what one does that really matters."

They went together in the end. He wore a white jacket and black evening trousers. Uniforms did not impress Olga a great deal, except that she thought her father looked Imperially handsome in his. The gaiety of the ball had become infectious and Olga was radiant now. Cossack officers were dancing, their sabres floored, the music compelling blood to take fire, the men spinning and leaping. Tatiana came in shimmering swiftness, her face alight to see Kirby.

"Oh, Ivan Ivanovich, you're disgraceful," she cried happily. She gave him her hand, he kissed it. "But how maddeningly gallant you look with your wounded arm and wooden leg, and how nice that you're here at last. Even Papa says his chicks are doleful without you. Tell me, do you like my gown, do you like my hair up, am I quite the loveliest thing?"

Tatiana, with her tiara adorning her gleaming auburn head, seemed crowned by silver and gold. Dear Heaven, thought Kirby, the beauty of this Imperial family. He would have spoken lightly, joked a little, and Tatiana's eyes were bright with laughing suspicion that he would indeed make fun.

Instead he said, "Yes, Tatiana, you are. Quite the very loveliest."

Tatiana laughed in delight. People were looking, people who found the Grand Duchesses' preoccupation with the Englishman much more intriguing than the dancing Cossacks. If Olga was sensitively aware of this, Tatiana did not give a fig.

"Olga," she said, "do you think he meant that, do you think he's serious?"

"I'm sure he's doing his very best, darling," said Olga.

"Oh, yes," said Tatiana, "he has a lot to make up for, staying away from us for hours and hours."

"Let Alexis give me a good talking-to tomorrow," said Kirby, "I can face up to it better when it's man to man."

Olga thought that richly amusing. And Tatiana thought how much more easily joy and laughter came to Olga when it was Ivan Ivanovich she was in company with. They watched the dancers. Tatiana slipped her arm through Kirby's.

"You're such good fun, Ivan," she murmured, "and the one we all love the best."

"I shall always love Livadia, Tatiana, always love the Imperial family."

Tatiana glanced up at him. He was smiling but his eyes were strangely dark.

"I know," she said softly.

Olga, on the other side of Kirby, could not hear their murmured talk above the noise of the stamping dance. But she saw that Tatiana had her arm in his and was exchanging the most affectionate of smiles with him.

Kirby danced, after all. He said that now he was here he was going to be extravagantly active. He took the cards of the Grand Duchesses. There were several vacant numbers on each card. He signed for two dances on each. Olga said nothing for a moment but when she returned to him after a mazurka with an elastic-limbed young guardsman, she remarked how safe his choice had been.

"Safe?"

"Why, yes," said Olga, "if you choose to dance twice with me and twice with Tatiana, that's very safe, isn't it?"

"I didn't think about it being safe, only rather greedy. Have I asked for too much?"

She framed a word with her mouth. He was sure it was, "Coward." Olga had grown up. He danced with her. His arm was no real problem. Olga was light and graceful, but she became a little concerned about the necessity of avoiding other dancers. He might get his arm knocked by some ruffian of a young officer, she said. The kind, she said, that he had thought she would like to dance the ball through with.

"Did I say that?" he asked.

"Oh, it was very clear that you were disposing of me in just that way," said Olga. "Colonel Kirby, please keep to the outside. If anything happens I don't know what Dr. Botkin will say. Not until he takes your plaster off can you be considered yourself again, then you can fling your arm about as much as you like."

She whirled, returned to him, whirled and returned

262

again. He said, "I'll have to be back in St. Petersburg soon, they'll take my plaster off there."

She would not let him disturb her happiness. She said, "I'll speak to Papa, you'll see. We are not permitting you to be in St. Petersburg while we are still at Livadia."

He danced with a lady-in-waiting who had a fondness for him because he liked the Imperial children so much. He danced with Tatiana, who thought he managed extremely well.

"Oh, goodness," she gasped as they circled, "for a man with a crooked arm and a wooden leg, Ivan, you are *so* adaptable."

"What's this about a wooden leg?"

Tatiana, unsparing of vitality on a night as gay as this, took in air before answering, then said, "Well, a crooked arm is no excuse for not coming to a ball, so it must be that you've got a wooden leg as well."

"Tatiana, you are very endearing."

"And you are just a little dark yourself, do you know that?"

"Surrounded by youth I have lost my own."

"Oh, poor old bones," said Tatiana. "Ivan, isn't Olga just beautiful tonight?"

They circled amid others. He said, "Preciously beautiful, Tatiana."

It was far into the night when the ball reached the final number. The orchestra sighed its way into the opening chords. Kirby, not engaged for the waltz, was talking to old General Sikorski. Tatiana appeared. Had the General forgotten he was obligated to her? The old soldier begged her forgiveness for his remissness, Tatiana put her hand on his arm and he led her proudly on to the shining floor. Tatiana had denied a score of young gallants and happily given the privilege of the last dance to the General. It was entirely within character.

Olga was talking to her father, Nicholas still resplendent and genial. He signalled to Kirby and Kirby went over. Officers were in attendance behind the Tsar.

"Ah, my dear fellow," said Nicholas.

"Your Highness?"

"It's been splendid, don't you think? So many delightful young people."

"Completely delightful, sir."

"But I shall be glad to get to bed."

This was friendly but meaningless. Kirby looked at Olga. She had her eyes on the dancers, on the colour and magic of the waltz. She should be dancing herself. He had thoughtfully avoided signing her card for the final number. He did not want Alexandra to shake her head. The Empress would be bound to ask.

Olga had one white slipper thrust forward, it was tapping. Kirby looked at the Tsar's officers. They were relaxed but oblivious.

"Highness?"

Olga turned her head. Her look plainly told him what she thought of that. He put out his hand, she laid her gloved fingers on his arm.

"With your permission, sir?" he said to Nicholas.

"Tatiana tells me you dance divinely for a man with a wooden leg," said Nicholas and burst into laughter.

Kirby faced Olga preparatory to leading her into the rhythm.

"I thought," he began but Olga shook her shining head.

"Oh, yes," she said calmly, "it's dreadfully risky to dance three times with me and only twice with Tatiana. I wrote your name in for the waltz. Do you think I'm a Grand Duchess for nothing?"

They danced the waltz. The light from the chandeliers seemingly reflected by a million jewels, soared in final brilliance as the flame of a candle soars just before dying. It bathed the dancers in incandescence. But Olga's radiance was muted, her lustrous head bent, her eyes lowered. She said nothing to all his attempts at light converse.

"Olga?"

She did not answer.

"Olga?"

264

Her hand tightened on his shoulder. They stopped. She took her hand from his shoulder and rested it on his arm, her eyes on the open glass doors that led to the terraces and down to the gardens. They walked from the heat of the ballroom into the cool quietness of the night. There was no moon, there was only darkness and silence. The Palace was warm with light behind them, Livadia velvet with night before them. Still she said nothing, but he felt her gloved hand moving down his arm. He took her hand, her fingers closed around his and clung.

"Olga, are you unhappy?"

She spoke very softly then.

"I am never unhappy when you are here." She hesitated and suddenly rushed into words jerky and impulsive. "But we were dancing and the ball was nearly over. I thought how you had been in such neglect of us, you wouldn't have come if—oh, did you think I'd consent to let you stay away, did you think I'd consent to dance the waltz with someone else? Papa had his own way of showing you that until I'm a Crown Princess I'm free to dance with whom I most wish. You did not dare to let me stand neglected in front of him."

He could not speak. The clasp of her fingers, the break in her voice and the intensity of his love bound his tongue. His arm was touching her shoulder. He was close, too close, to the warmth and softness of her.

"Colonel Kirby? Please?" Her voice was a whisper.

He looked down at her upturned face. The glitter of her tiara was subdued by the night, outshone by the glitter of her tears.

"What is it, Olga, what must I say?"

"That you'll never neglect me again, I cannot bear it."

He had hurt her more than he had realised.

"Neglect you? Olga, I love Russia as much as I love my own country, and I cherish the Imperial family more than any other. I shall come to see you and your sisters get married, I'll be there to see you become the loveliest Crown Princess of all. I shall be there on all these occasions, whether I'm invited or not. I can't be neglectful, Olga, though I can be imperfect."

She did not respond to that for a moment, then she said shakily, "And if I don't choose to become a Crown Princess?"

"Then you'll play another part for your country. I shall watch you grow into a most stately Grand Duchess, I'll come to all your birthday balls, and you'll still be dancing even when you're old—but only with those whom you most wish to. By then I'll probably have two wooden legs."

Her smile was tremulous. It flickered, was gone, and came again.

"Yes, perhaps we'll both become very old and doddering, but we shall still have fun, we shall still laugh together, and we will always be the dearest friends, will we not?"

"Always, Olga."

They walked in the night gardens and they talked until Olga was happy again. They stood on the terrace to watch the carriages drawing up to take away departing guests, and when the Palace was finally quiet they went in. The Tsar was just retiring with Tatiana, but Tatiana broke away to go swiftly and affectionately to her sister, saying, "Olga, how exciting it all was, but now, whew! I'm quite done up." She hugged Olga's arm and glanced up at Kirby. He smiled. It was the tenderest and warmest of smiles. And Olga was smiling too. But Tatiana thought her eyes were suspiciously bright.

Kirby went up the wide, shining staircase with them, Tatiana slipping her arm through his and talking her tongue away. The familiarity of the gesture, harmless though it was, gave Olga queer hurt. Kirby said goodnight to them. Tatiana extended her hand in the grand manner, he bowed and kissed her gloved fingers.

"Oh, you are quite delicious, Ivan," laughed Tatiana and came up on tiptoe to kiss his face. Olga turned away.

In their bedroom, simply furnished by comparison

266

with guest rooms, Olga took her sister by the shoulders.

"Tasha, how you can dare I do not know!"

"But, Olga, what is it I can't dare?"

"You know what. To truly hurt me. Oh, you're so much prettier than I am."

Tatiana stared.

Oh, goodness, Olga was unhappy again.

"Olga, oh, you silly, you must stop this," she said. "You should have heard what everyone, just everyone, said about you tonight, then you'd know who was prettier. And your Colonel Kirby, as you *will* call him, simply adores you, he said so."

The betraying crimson surged to Olga's face. She trembled, she gasped, "Oh, I told you, Tatiana, he could not—he must not—Mama will send him away."

"Goose, he isn't going to say anything to Mama. Shall I tell you what he said?"

"No!" Olga was desperate. It was all coming dangerously close to a confrontation with her mother. Tomorrow her mother would know that Colonel Kirby had attended, after all, she would ask affectionately-phrased questions and perhaps discover that she, Olga, had gone to his suite to persuade him to attend. Then there would be a kind but firm talk with Colonel Kirby and the following day he would announce he had been recalled to St. Petersburg or even to England.

"I'll keep it to myself, then," said Tatiana, "but no one else shall know, I promise. But how you can't want to know yourself, I simply——"

"Tell me. Tatiana, tell me!"

"It was lovely. I asked him what he thought of you and he said you were preciously beautiful. Preciously! There!"

"That isn't—Tatiana, that isn't to say he loves me."

"Oh, what a goose you are," sighed Tatiana, "you are afraid of him loving you, aren't you? You are afraid because of how worried it would make Mama."

"You are the goose," said Olga quietly, "it isn't his feelings I'm afraid of. Tasha, how wonderful it must be to be free to be loved."

Tatiana seemed to wake up almost as soon as she fell asleep. The dark bedroom was quiet. Why had she woken?

Because it wasn't quiet.

In the other bed Olga was weeping into her pillow. Love, thought Tatiana, must be awful.

He lay in bed, deep in thought. The light was without sun this morning, the sky cloudy. Karita brought him a late breakfast, singing to herself. Karita often sang to herself at Livadia. It was a divinely satisfying life here. At Karinshka there had often been so little to do for a good part of the year and then it would become all rush, confusion and scramble to see to the arrival of Princess Aleka Petrovna and to the wants of innumerable noisy guests.

She was full of pride and pleasure because Ivan Ivanovich stood so high in the affections of the Imperial family, and their regard for him was reflected in the friendly way they treated her.

She could speak quite a lot of English now and he never laughed at her when she pronounced a word wrongly. He only tried a mild correction.

"Not singk, Karita. Sing. Sing."

"Yes, I said that, singk."

"Well, you singk very sweetly, Karita."

He was very droll. She was so glad she had not married Oravio. It was far nicer to be with Colonel Kirby. Whenever he was especially pleased with her or she said something to make him laugh, he would put his hand under her chin and kiss her. That was always very nice.

But he did not seem especially pleased with her this morning. He lay there saying nothing, looking up at the decorative ceiling. He was dark and frowning. Well, it wasn't her fault if he had drunk too much at the ball last night and had got to bed too late. But she would have to bear the brunt, she supposed. She knew aristocrats. Whenever they woke up liverish they would

268

groan, and show how they disliked other human beings, especially servants. Ivan Ivanovich wasn't groaning, but he was brooding and far away. This was very unusual in him but she supposed it had to happen some time. The first thing that he would do would be to tell her to take his breakfast away. She would do no such thing. She liked to battle with Ivan Ivanovich. Besides, she herself had helped to prepare it in the Palace kitchens.

"Do you wish breakfast?" she asked, having drawn back the curtains to let in the cloudy light.

He blinked. Then he smiled. It took some of his darkness away.

"Hello, Karita. I didn't hear you come in."

"But you have been looking at me when you weren't looking at the ceiling."

"Oh, really? Well, that's a mark against me. How fresh you look. You make me feel jaded. How old are you, Karita?"

"Twenty," said Karita. He lay there with his right arm folded under his head, his mending left arm over his chest. She began to set out his breakfast on a glass-topped picture tray. When his magnificence was ready he would sit up.

"What happened between you and Oravio?" he asked.

"I told you, he found someone much more suitable."

"Did he, by God? I'd like to have a look at her, then. Karita, never mind about that, just pour me some coffee. Is it late?"

"It's the middle of the morning. Their Imperial Highnesses are up and so are the children. You are probably the only one still in bed. The Tsarevich said someone ought to pour cold water over you, he said that is how to get lazy soldiers up. He's so sweet, isn't he? Here's your coffee. No, you can't drink it unless you sit up." He sat up. He took the coffee. "The Grand Duchesses are all talking about the ball. How gay it was, I was allowed to peep in."

He looked at her. She would have graced the occasion in a ball gown of her own. But she never seemed to want more than life bestowed on her now.

"Karita," he said, "would it distress you if ever the Tsar and his family were in trouble?"

"No one who knew them could not be distressed," she said.

"Sit here," he said and she sat on the side of the bed. Once she would have considered that improper. She knew more now about what was and what wasn't. He regarded her thoughtfully, speculatively. "What do your own people think of the Tsar?"

"Most of them love him, as they should," she said. "The Tartar chiefs are all proud to be under his protection. Their ancestors were mine too, but now our family is Christian, the Khan and the chiefs and their people are Moslems. But all of us live together in friendship because of the Tsar, who is father to us all. And now that I know him I am as proud as the chiefs."

"The Crimeans are the best of the Russians," said Kirby. "Karita, do you know this man called Prolofski?"

"He's not a Crimean," said Karita, turning up her nose, "he's from the Urals where they're always making trouble. He's in the Crimea to make trouble here. He's against everyone who is better than he is, he's against everything that's above him, even the stars. He'd pull them all out of the sky if he could and make dust of them. Once he came to see the Princess Karinshka. That was the day they brought you here."

"If Prolofski conceived a way of pulling down the Tsar and his family, what would you do, Karita?"

Karita did not take long to think about that one.

"I'd have him put into a hole in the ground and keep him there, if he could be caught. But they call Prolofski the slippery one. He's never where you think he is." She wondered what this was about. Ivan Ivanovich was very serious this morning. "You went for a long walk last night," she said.

"And her young Highness did not think too much

270

of me for it," he said, but he did not smile. Karita began to feel disturbed.

"Ivan Ivanovich," she said, "if this man Prolofski is a bother I'll tell you something. If a time and a place were known and he came to that place at that time, I could catch him for you. Is he to be killed?"

She asked the question so calmly that he thought she could not know what she was saying. But her brown eyes were steady, cool and knowledgeable. It was a knowledge of men like Prolofski.

"I haven't killed anyone yet, Karita, nor have you. Have you?" She shook her head. "Do you really say you could catch them? There will be two."

"Two?"

"I'm sure of it. What shall we do with both of them? Prolofski is the prosecution, the other one the executioner."

"We'll find a hole for both," said Karita. "Abadah Khan will see to it. When are we to catch them?"

"Tonight. Don't you want to know why?"

Karita stood up. There was a strange burning in her eyes but she was still quite calm.

"If you say the Tsar and his family are in danger, then they are," she said. "If you say this or that is so, then it is. If you say Prolofski must be put away, then he will be. You would not take me to England if I asked too many questions. But you must tell me everything I need to know about the time and the place, everything that Abadah Khan needs to know. Then I must hurry or there won't be time to find him and have him arrange things."

Kirby told her of the woodman's hut on the estate and how he was meeting Prolofski there half-an-hour after sunset. He told her how he would signal the moment for action. He did not tell her why he was meeting the man, nor did Karita ask why. But he did say, "You can be in good conscience over this, Karita, I swear. Will you be back before sunset?"

"I shall be with Abadah Khan and his men," she said. "I shall only come back here if for some reason

271

Abadah Khan, can't help us. But if I can reach him in time he will, I know he will. If not, then you'll have to arrange another meeting with Prolofski."

"That might be difficult," he said with a grimace. "How will you travel?"

"By motorcar. Simeon Baroskovich will drive me. He's one of the chauffeurs, he'll get one of the motorcars out for me, you see, or I'll ask General Sikorski if I can borrow his and his chauffeur, though I like Simeon better. He is fond of me too, so it will be a nice surprise for him to have the day off with me, but he'll know nothing about Prolofski. If you'll tell his Imperial Highness I must go to see my mother, he'll give Simeon the day off to take me."

"Karita, do you run the Livadia Palace?"

"I only look after you," she said. He reached out a hand, she stooped and he kissed her warmly on the lips. Karita responded with an impulsive pressure of her mouth. His kiss was in gratitude, her response was simply because she liked being kissed.

"Be careful," he said.

"You're the one to be careful," she said, "you're to meet Prolofski." She went but turned at the door, a little smile on her mouth. "Why do you kiss me here but not in St. Petersburg?" she asked.

"In St. Petersburg," he said solemnly, "it would not be proper, little one."

He went into Yalta later. When he returned he had what he had never carried before. A pistol.

While he was away Alexis wanted to know why he had gone at all.

"I haven't seen him to ask him," said Olga, "but when he does come back you can give him a good talking to."

"He'll only say something to make me laugh," said Alexis, his leg still awkwardly stiff. "it's awfully difficult giving Ivan a good talking to."

"Yes, isn't it?" said Olga, feeling the day was a little empty.

It wasn't until evening when she was going with

272

Tatiana to dinner that she saw him. He was not dressed for dinner himself, he wore his good-tempered velvet jacket and brown trousers. His arm was in his sling. He was going to meet someone, he said, and had been excused taking the meal.

"Don't tell me her name," said Tatiana, "or I shall be disastrously jealous and stick pins into her."

"No, it's just a man I know," he said.

"Papa will not say no if you wish to meet your friends here," said Olga.

"He is not a friend," said Kirby.

"I must tell you," said Olga, "that when Alexis sees you tomorrow he's going to try to give you a good talking to."

"Why?" he asked.

"For neglecting us," said Olga and her blue eyes held his to remind him of words he had spoken.

"I shan't be too long," he said, "and when I come back will you play some Bach for me?"

"Olga," said Tatiana, "is dreadful at Bach, Ivan."

"Not to me she isn't," he said.

He whistled softly as he went, it was a tune Olga had heard before. It wasn't Bach. She smiled.

It was dusk as he approached the hut along the track. It stood in a clearing amid woodlands. Prolofski, standing in the doorway, watched him come, a tall shadow emerging from the trees. It had been cloudy all day and the dusk was a dark grey blanket. Prolofsky stepped silently aside to let Kirby enter the hut. A few moments later another shadow emerged from the same trees. Prolofski stepped from the hut to meet him.

"He came by himself, there are no others," said the newcomer.

Prolofski shrugged. He entered the hut, the other man following.

"You must permit this," said Prolofski and Kirby stood unmoving as the other man searched him, running quick hands over him in the darkness. He smiled sarcastically at Prolofski, whose round face shown white beneath his black hat. Prolofski shrugged again.

273

It was to say a man with a broken arm could still carry a weapon and could still use it. The searcher straightened up and gave a satisfied grunt. Prolofski listened. There was only the quietness of the grave outside. "In these times," he said," a man has to make sure."

"I understand," said Kirby.

"Can you? You can observe and you can pass opinions. But you're English, so how can you understand? It takes centuries and you have to be Russian. What have you decided?"

"First," said Kirby, "you must convince me you know enough about me."

"I'm to show you something? A piece of paper?" Prolofski's moonface was expressive of faint disgust. "My friend, I do not carry papers. It's all up here." He tapped his forehead under his hat. "It's committed and can't be forgotten."

"What you carry in your head isn't proof," said Kirby. "Remember my stake in this. It could be my life."

"Not if you kill Rasputin, only if you refuse to. As a spy they would shoot you because you've deceived Nicholas the Bloody himself. That, my friend, they'll consider unpardonable. To convince you that you must work for us I'll open my mind to you and speak the names of colleagues you have in Russia. First, there's a man called Anstruther of Yalta—though he is elsewhere now, comrade—and then there is a man called Burroughs of Moscow, also Borodin Jacovich of the same place——"

"They're enough," said Kirby.

"It wasn't a difficult code and it's all up here." He tapped his forehead again. Almost he smiled. "She has the piece of paper. You are doubly covered, my friend. By my head and her piece of paper."

"Princess Karinshka?" said Kirby. "Is she involved in this?"

"Not in this. She is useful in some ways, but is a woman with a woman's limitations. She won't be at your back, but I will. Now, Rasputin."

"Yes, Rasputin," said Kirby. On the face of it, Prolofski represented the biggest risk. He was merciless, Aleka temperamental. And Aleka did not yet know about the disposal of Rasputin. Or did she? Who could trust anything Prolofski said? Well, he would have to risk it. Prolofski had the names locked in his head. Aleka had them on a piece of paper. What would she do if she heard no more from Prolofski, if Prolofski disappeared into a hole in the ground? "This is how I propose to do it," he said and extracted a paper from his breast pocket. The watchful shadow moved. There was, thought Kirby, a familiarity about him. But he wore a cap, pulled well down over his forehead and the hut was dark. Kirby unfolded the paper awkwardly using his one hand.

"Am I a bat?" asked Prolofski.

"I know the interior of the Alexander Palace," said Kirby, who in fact did not, "and I must be sure you approve of what I suggest, because with a little luck I can kill him close to the bedroom of the Grand Duchess. The difficulty is that she shares this room with her sister. But look." He laid the paper on a rough table under the window of the hut. He took a box of matches and a thin wax taper from the righthand pocket of his jacket. Using his left hand that emerged from his plaster cast and his sling, he struck a match and lighted the taper. The dark bodyguard muttered. "There are no soldiers in this area," said Kirby.

"Even so, I don't like lights," said Prolofski. He bent over the table as Kirby played the light on the sheet of paper. The taper was in his left hand. Prolofski peered and shielded by his body from the watchful shadow Kirby slid his right hand under the table and withdrew the Colt automatic from its web of thread there. He stepped back. Prolofski looked up, the other man came forward and both saw the weapon at the same time.

"You are a fool," said Prolofski coldly.

"I brought it here earlier this evening," said Kirby. "Don't move. I will certainly shoot. I will have to."

"It won't save you."

The other man swore. The lighted taper in Kirby's left hand shone at the window. He kept it there. The gun glinted, pointing at Prolofski's stomach. It was steady but Kirby knew the other man would not hold back indefinitely. He did not want to fire, but there was always the chance that Karita and Abadah Khan had not arrived. Also, if they had arrived, at the first sounds of their rush Prolofski and his shadow, without the threat of the Colt to restrain them, might in the darkness slip the net.

It was infinitely preferable not to use the weapon. The sound would carry and on the Tsar's estate there were always patrols at night, although mainly around the perimeter.

Prolofski turned on the other man.

"If there were others and you missed them, fool——"

"I followed him as you told me to, he came alone," said the capped man, and suddenly in the light of the taper Kirby saw his face. It was Oravio, as unpleasant as he had always seemed pleasant. And Oravio shifted, poising himself on the balls of his feet.

At the doorway a voice spoke, a girl's voice.

"We are here, Ivan Ivanovich."

Prolofski turned slowly, deliberately. Oravio swung round. In the doorway, dark against the background of descending night, stood Karita, a rifle in her hands, a scarf about golden head.

"Welcome, little one," said Kirby and sighed.

Karita moved and into the hut poured dark, soundless men. The round white face of Prolofski was a mask of icy rage. He spat as they took him. Oravio struggled with a fury born of having been tricked. But they held him. Karita saw him, her mouth tightened, her eyes burned and she walked up to him.

"What did they ever do to hurt you?" she said.

"They oppress and murder my brothers," shouted Oravio, "and that's enough for any man." He spat. It flecked her dark blouse. "And it's more than enough for me."

Karita struck him across the mouth.

"You? Who are you?" she said. "Who made you their judge? You, you are only fit to live in a hole with the other assassins. Say no more or these good people will cut out your tongue and his too."

"Our comrades will remember you, whore!" roared Oravio.

Kirby took off his sling and stuffed it into the man's mouth. The dark men completed the gagging and they bound him. They gagged and bound Prolofski too. The black hat fell off. He was as whitely bald as the moon itself. For a moment he resisted, then suddenly quietened. The cold, protuberant eyes became blank and with his hands tied and his mouth stuffed he was taken with Oravio from the hut.

"Deliver them to Abadah Khan as quickly and as quietly as you can," said Karita. The dark men smiled. Kirby saw teeth flash. But none of them spoke. They vanished into the wooded depth with their captives, taking with them the rifle Karita had borrowed. Kirby extinguished the taper.

"We waited a long time," said Karita. "We thought you were never going to show the light, we thought perhaps things had gone wrong for you. It was very worrying."

"In my selfishness," said Kirby, "I wanted to find out first how much of my life Prolofski commanded. I'm still not sure. I'll tell you about it one day."

"It was good to catch him," said Karita, "he's an assassin, did you know? He doesn't care if he blows up ten innocent people as long as he gets the one he is after. Now he'll live in a hole with Oravio for as long as you wish. Abadah Khan will only let them out when you say. You are the Tsar's friend, therefore Abadah Khan says you have only to ask and his services are yours. You would like Abadah Khan, he is always laughing. You are all right?"

"I'm fine. You're extraordinary. Would you have used that rifle?"

"Of course," She sounded surprised that he should

277

ask. "I was very worried about you. Prolofski isn't a nice man and you had only one arm to use."

"That was a help, it put them off their guard a little, I think."

"I didn't want anything to happen to you," said Karita as they began to make their way along the dark track. "What would happen to me? I could not go back to Karinshka to work, I shouldn't like it there now."

"They'll wonder why Oravio doesn't go back."

"Nobody will find him, he'll have disappeared." Karita had only an incurable contempt for Oravio now. "We had better hurry, I have so many things to see to——"

"You've nothing to see to." He put his arm around her shoulders. "Karita, you are lovely. You are my pride and treasure. You've helped the Imperial family and you've helped me. Tremendously. Thank you."

He squeezed her shoulders. He began his soft whistle. Karita felt immensely pleased with herself. It was so satisfying to be regarded as a treasure and to walk with him along the winding track, the darkness a friendly embrace rather than a hindrance. He did not kiss her to show his gratitude for what she had done. She knew that here, where they were very much alone, would not be the proper place for him to do so. He would wait until they were back in the Palace. But even then he did not do so. As she removed her scarf in his suite and shook out her flattened hair he passed his hand over her soft, silky tresses and said again. "You are lovely, Karita. Thank you very much."

It gave her a nice feeling. But she would still have liked to be kissed.

He went down to the music room. It was empty. Square, spacious, with its upright chairs and its grand piano, it was put to frequent use in the evenings. Sometimes such evenings were informally family when the Grand Duchesses played, sometimes ambitious when everyone would gather to hear a maestro play. Kirby had heard the elder Grand Duchesses at the piano on

278

occasions. Tatiana had talent, Olga had creditable application. Old General Sikorski was surprisingly good with a violin tucked beneath his chin.

Kirby sat down at the piano. There was music on the stand. Bach. He smiled. He tapped out a light tune with one finger. He felt mentally relaxed, his mind free of its dark burden. Karita really was extraordinary, and more indispensable than ever.

Olga heard the tiny tinkling. She came and stood in the doorway. He did not see her, he was sitting at the piano, tapping single notes but making a tune, nevertheless. She watched him, her blue eyes soft, smiling to herself because he did not know she was there. How fit he looked again. And Mama had not been difficult, after all. She had heard all about the ball, had sighed gently at the mention of Colonel Kirby, but dearest Tatiana had quickly said how she and Olga had simply insisted on his attendance. And Mama had said, "Well, then, how could he refuse? And so he managed to dance, did he?"

"Not only with us," said Tatiana, "but with other ladies. Everyone likes him so much, he's so nice to have around. I wish you might invite him to Tsarskoe Selo, we could skate with him in the winter."

"I think Colonel Kirby would always prefer Livadia," said Alexandra.

"Yes, Mama, perhaps he would," said Olga. She did not dare press Tsarskoe Selo.

She wondered now how much longer he would be at Livadia, how much longer his British superiors would allow him to stay.

He looked up then and saw her. He smiled and Olga experienced a sensation of both pleasure and relief. Whatever had been troubling him, making him seem so remote, had gone.

"I am not disturbing you?" she said, entering the room a little diffidently.

"How can you be?" he said, rising. "This is your piano, Olga, and I thought you'd be playing Bach."

279

"You were longer than we thought you'd be," she said.

"I'm sorry," he said, "is it too late for music now?"

"No, of course not. What is that tune you were playing? I've heard you whistling it."

"Oh, it's something we sang when I was very young and at school."

"Sing it now," said Olga, standing by the piano.

"I'm dreadful at singing," he said.

"As I am at Bach," she smiled.

He sat down again, saying. "Well, I'll do the best I can. But I can't play, either."

"Well, do the best you can with that too," she said.

He played the tune with one hand. He could not sing, as he had said, but he did his best and Olga thought his voice passably pleasant considering. She listened to the song.

> What is her name, this maid so fair
> With flowers in her golden hair?
> Her name is Mary Out-of-doors,
> She has a cat called Pussy Claws.
> Where does she live, this pretty maid
> With eyes like bluebells in the shade?
> In a house by Dingle Dell,
> Though where that is I cannot tell.
> What does she do, this maid so sweet
> With slippers green upon her feet?
> She dances with the butterflies
> And that to me is no surprise.
> Whom will she wed, this maid so fair
> With flowers in her golden hair?
> She'll wed a country boy, you see,
> And give her Pussy Claws to me.

"Colonel Kirby!" Olga clapped her hands in delight. "Oh, that is a delicious song. Again, please."

"Together," he said.

"I will if you'll write the words down," said Olga.

He wrote the words on the back of a music sheet. She took the sheet, he did his best at the piano and they sang it together. Her voice was shy at first, but he didn't care how his sounded so she began not to mind about hers, either. Hers became clear and melodious then and they sang it through.

They laughed in triumph.

Olga was rapturous.

Kirby, looking up into her delighted blue eyes, was in hopeless longing.

ELEVEN

The clouds had gone the next day. Olga, with books under her arm, was about to leave her room to see her tutor when a lady-in-waiting came to ask her if she would please see her mother. Alexandra, writing letters in her boudoir, looked up with a smile as Olga came in.

How her eldest daughter was growing. And she was acquiring a quiet maturity that was entirely charming. She was for loving, cherishing, Alexandra thought. That wasn't difficult, to love her. Olga herself asked for no more than that.

"Olga, there, my sweet." Alexandra's voice was tender. "How summery you look. The sun is beginning to kiss you. Now, what is it I wanted to see you about? Oh, yes, Colonel Kirby—Ivan."

"Mama?" In a little apprehension at her mother's gentleness Olga's sunny look dimmed a little. "He is not going away?"

"Not until we return to St. Petersburg ourselves, perhaps." Alexandra was reassuring and rueful together. Olga was as transparent as the bright windows. "He's been to ask if you would care to ride into Yalta with him today. Would you like to go, darling? If so, I'm sure Monsieur Gilliard will excuse you. I am assured by Ivan that he'll take the greatest care of you."

"Oh, Mama, I——" Olga was about to say she would adore to go. She must not commit her feelings so. "Mama, that would really be very nice."

282

Alexandra did not know why she had consented to this at all. Unless it was that she trusted Colonel Kirby. But there was always the worry that the more Olga was in company with him the more impossible Olga's dreams became. Yet how could she deny Olga the sweet pleasures youth was entitled to before adult responsibilities turned those golden years into wistful memories?

"Then you may go, darling," she said.

"Oh, how nice you are," said Olga, "it is such a lovely day to go for a drive anywhere. Am I to go now? Is he waiting for me?"

"I expect so. Shall you take Sophia Boriovna with you?"

"Mama," said Olga carefully, "if Colonel Kirby has promised to take the greatest care of me, a lady-in-waiting might imply by her presence that we did not think he was able to."

Alexandra laughed.

"Well, you do make the suggestion sound stuffy, sweet. We had better trust Ivan Ivanovich, hadn't we? You're to have lunch in Yalta and be back this afternoon. Do you wish to change your dress? If so, don't be too long or by the time you're ready he *will* be waiting. And I should wear your spring coat, it may be cooler in Yalta than you think."

She permitted herself a little shake of the head as Olga flowed happily away. But perhaps it would all be over in a year or two when eligible suitors came courting her eldest. Olga would not expect her prospects to be less than her own. She herself had only been a minor Princess of Hesse and yet had married Nicholas, heir to the throne of All the Russias. Olga as the eldest daughter of the Tsar would not expect to become less than a queen. Future excitement would exorcise her present dream.

A question reached Olga as she was changing. Karita came to ask it. Would her Imperial Highness prefer to make the journey in a carriage or a motorcar? Colonel Kirby wished to know.

"Oh, in a——" Olga stopped to think. A carriage complemented idyllic Crimea in springtime, the ride would be leisurely and peaceful. Motorcars were exciting but so noisy. She supposed, however, that Colonel Kirby would be bound to have a man's interest in motorcars and all the young people she knew said that a carriage was dull compared with a motorcar. "Oh, I don't mind, Karita, tell Colonel Kirby he is to decide."

He was waiting on the drive below as she came down the steps from the Palace. She was clad in the palest blue dress with spring coat to match and carried a blue parasol. He walked up a few steps to meet her, she put her hand on his arm and let him escort her.

"You've ordered a carriage," she said, looking at the waiting landau, "I thought you would prefer a motorcar."

"I was sure you would prefer a carriage," he said.

Her smile told him how she appreciated that courtesy. He was in uniform, looking very smart. He wore no sling, he had managed to get his plastered arm into a sleeve. He seemed quite himself again. He handed her up, she seated herself in the open landau. Then she said, "Oh." There was another carriage in evidence. Sophia Boriovna was in it, and another lady-in-waiting, together with two officers of the household. So, her mother had decided that some protocol was to be observed. They were to take escorts. Sophia and the others would not intrude, they would simply be at hand if needed, and serve to remind Olga that a Grand Duchess of her age was not permitted to wander at will in the company of any man.

She did not speak until he had settled himself and the carriage was moving. Then she said, "You must know that I am quite overwhelmed, Colonel Kirby. I mean, I have actually been invited. Why am I so favoured today?"

"Perhaps because I neglected you all yesterday," he said. "I thought that as I had to go to Yalta today it would be more enjoyable if I had company. But General Sikorski said his back was stiff, Tatiana couldn't come,

Marie was too busy and I couldn't find Anastasia. Alexis wanted to but still has his bad leg and so I thought, well, there's still Olga——"

"Oh, how mean you are!" she exclaimed. He had not seated himself beside her but opposite her and his eyes were laughing under his peaked cap. "That is not a bit gallant."

"But it has turned out very well for me," he said. "The sun is out, the day is fine and here I am riding with the Grand Duchess Olga Nicolaievna who, the newspapers reported, looked most charming in blue despite a smut of wood ash on her nose."

"Oh no, it can't be!" Olga was mortified.

"But as usual you can never believe what the papers say."

"Colonel Kirby, you are teasing me abominably."

"I know. It's going to be that kind of a day, Olga. It's lovely."

She laughed. The horses trotted in equable togetherness. The carriage wheels sang. The vistas were glimmering with gold. To the right of the road the blue sea sparkled.

"Oh, I don't mind, you may tease me all you wish, it's so nice to be out," she said happily. "Thank you for asking Mama. I didn't think she—well, you see——"

"Well, you see," he said, helping her out. "I told her I'd take the greatest care of you in every way. You are a very priceless Grand Duchess."

She flushed. It was not that she felt shy, only emotional. She was in his care. She was priceless. That mattered very much. He did not have to tell her she was a Grand Duchess, though. She knew that only too well, and if he was trying to say that that was the foremost factor in their relationship, he must know that that was unnecessary too. She turned her gaze on lushly bursting magnolia blooms spraying flung branches. Spring was calling to summer in the Crimea, where the rich land knew little of man's despoiling ways.

"Tell me about England," she said.

"Again? I've told you so much," he said.

"Tell me more, tell me exactly what it's like where you live. We were at the Isle of Wight once when I was very young, and Mama and Papa had the most sumptuous time with King Edward. It was beautiful, I remember. Is it beautiful where you live? It must be because Mama was enchanted by it."

He told her about Walton, just a riverside village, where the swans glided by on the evening waters and boats were lazily rowed or punted to summer picnic spots overhung by willows. He told her about his Georgian cottage and his Aunt Charlotte who lived there and her sister Emma who had died, and how they had taken the place of his dead parents.

"They wanted someone to love," said Olga. "No one can do without love, can they?"

"No one," he agreed. "Love is a necessity and a creator. It inspires careless rapture in the young and is precious to the old. But it can also be very painful."

"How do you know that?" she asked, her eyes in absorbed wonder. "You have been painfully in love? Oh, I see—you did love Aleka Petrovna——"

He laughed.

"Aleka Petrovna? Oh, Olga, that would be like loving a beautiful grasshopper."

"You mean butterfly," she said.

"Grasshoppers talk," he said.

"We should not be unkind about Aleka Petrovna, I am sure she isn't as happy as she might be," said Olga. She wanted to know whom he had been painfully in love with, but if he wouldn't tell her it was not in her to ask questions. However, there was one question that need not commit him to telling things he did not want to. "Was she very beautiful, Colonel Kirby?"

"Aleka Petrovna? But you know her."

"No, I mean the girl you found so painful to love," said Olga.

He laughed again.

"Olga, how delightful you are," he said. "Who is this girl you've conjured up for me?"

"Well, that's a fine thing, I must say," said Olga, "it was you who said—well, I'm sure I just don't know what we are talking about now. Perhaps we had better talk about something else, and I'd like it if you were not so vague and I did not get so confused."

He enjoyed that. They laughed. The horses clip-clopped in tireless rhythm and the carriage swayed on gently-jostling springs. The other carriage was fifty yards behind them, but Olga neither heard it nor thought about it. She asked Kirby what his Aunt Charlotte was like.

"Matriarchal," he said. "She regards me as an unfulfilled person afflicted with wanderlust. Each time I return home I'm expected to arrive with a wife in my baggage. Aunt Charlotte supervises my unpacking and I know what she's looking for."

"Colonel Kirby, that is a dreadful way of talking about wives and baggage," said Olga.

"Oh?"

"All the same, it sounds deliciously funny," she said. "But one day perhaps you'll give your Aunt Charlotte a very nice surprise."

"Perhaps," he said. It was difficult to think seriously about nice surprises for Aunt Charlotte at this moment. Olga was lovely in the sunshine, as her hair flowed and rippled in the light breeze.

In Yalta they dismissed the coachman and groom for a few hours. Kirby explained he had to call again on a Mr. Anstruther. Olga did not mind what they did as long as he did not leave her standing outside in the street.

"You see," she said, "I should not like you to be forgetful of me."

"I can't add that to being neglectful," he said, "that would be terrible."

"Shockingly so," laughed Olga.

She waited happily and without fuss in the little office, as she had before, while Kirby went in to see Anstruther. Anstruther was not so brown, he was wearing a black jacket and striped trousers. That must mean something, thought Kirby.

"Thank you for coming," said Anstruther.

"Thank you for making your message so cordial," said Kirby.

"I got back here yesterday."

"I wrote you in St. Petersburg," said Kirby, "I didn't hear from you."

Anstruther looked at his fingernails.

"I received some disturbing news from you, if that's what you mean," he said. "Apparently you were careless enough to have your pocket picked."

"You could call it that, yes," said Kirby. "A man called Peter Prolofski broke the code."

"Yes, we've heard of him," said Anstruther. He polished a nail. "That, my dear Kirby, makes it more than disturbing. It's calamitous. I expected it when I first heard from you. But Prolofski, hum. The cat is amongst the pigeons with a vengeance. There's no telling what a man like that will do."

"I can tell you." Kirby described all that had happened. Slight relief smoothed the worst of Anstruther's worried furrows.

"Even so," he said, "there are two things we can't rely on. Prolofski staying down whatever hole they've put him in, which is probably halfway up some mountain, and your assumption that he alone broke the code and then kept it to himself."

"I don't assume that, I only hope."

Anstruther gloomed on the eventualities.

"You'd better be prepared for a quick return home," he said, "we all had. Damn it, did you have to be as careless as that?"

"I wasn't born for this work. I was persuaded—well invited—into it. There was always the possibility I could make a mess of it."

"Your modesty does you credit," said Anstruther with paternal heaviness, "but it doesn't help us. Look here, how involved are you with the lady outside?"

"I'm not involved at all. I can't be, not with a Grand Duchess. You know that."

"Damn it," said Anstruther again, "you're confoundedly useful with the contacts you make, you don't stop at the highest in the land. Now you muck it all up. Deplorable. Well, you had better stand by. They may recall all of us as soon as they hear from me. They don't like accidents, they like carelessness even less. I tell you, I'm very upset."

"I assure you, I'm not exactly exhilarated," said Kirby, "but I feel a bit better now that some Crimean friends of mine have put Prolofski away."

"There's that Karinshka woman." said Anstruther.

"Yes," said Kirby.

"Damn it," said Anstruther.

Olga was in conversation with the clerk. To remain silent in the presence of anyone made her shyness keener. She did not realise that the clerk, quite infatuated, was even shyer. When Kirby reappeared she rose quickly, a smile of gratitude on her face that he had not kept her waiting overlong, but she did not omit to say goodbye to the clerk as they left.

"I kept you waiting," said Kirby, "I'm sorry."

"Oh, you weren't at all long," said Olga as they emerged into the sunshine. There was a carriage drawn up a few houses down. Olga ignored it, though she knew the occupants descended to follow as she and Kirby went on their way. "What do you have to do now?" she asked.

"Ah, now I have my most important engagement," he said.

"Oh," she said in a little disappointment, "where do you have to go for that?"

"Wherever you like, Olga. All I have to do now concerns taking care of you, looking after all your wishes and making sure we don't forget to have lunch."

"Oh, I am very overwhelmed and favoured today," said Olga happily. "Shall we have lunch, then? Perhaps that will give us time to look at the shops. You don't mind if we look at the shops?"

"We did that once before," he said, "and it was very enjoyable. We'll do it again."

"Oh," she said impulsively, "you are so nice to be with."

Then, of course, she wished she could remember to exercise more restraint. Impulsiveness was so adolescent.

"Well, do you know," he said, "I think we're both quite nice on the whole, don't you?"

She could have taken his arm and hugged it for that. He had made her own remark fall easily and naturally into place. They walked to their lunch because the streets were mellow and pleasant, carriages looked gay and people looked sunny. It was warm enough but there was the occasional cool breeze from the sea and her spring coat was welcome.

They had lunch in a first-floor restaurant overlooking the pleasantest part of the harbour. It was so proud and exclusive an establishment that Olga thought the head waiter more vainglorious than a court chamberlain. She was not recognised, but her shy loveliness enchanted the courteous waiters who could not do enough to help her select from the menu. She and Kirby sat at a table in the far corner, with windows bringing sea views to them. There were deep red curtains and snowy-white tablecloths, polished silver and crystal glassware. The activity of the harbour was only a lazy movement of boats and boatmen. The steamer from Sevastopol was in, seeming to loll in idle obliviousness of its imminent departure.

They were served with smoked herring and sliced cucumber, and because Olga did not at all mind more fish they followed with a dish of salmon, hot and lucious in thick creamy sauce. Olga, accustomed to the simple fare favoured by the Imperial family, declared it a banquet and doubted if she could do it justice. But she did. She ate in unaffected pleasure and enjoyment. She did not ask for wine and Kirby did not order any. He had a waiter bring a carafe of diluted lemon juice, sweetened and cooled.

She had never dined out in public like this, and the sheer novelty of it was a delight. The restaurant became almost full. There were fascinating women in huge flower-bedecked hats lunching with immaculately-dressed men. The discreet ladies-in-waiting were there too, with the officers, but they were all as far from Olga as they could be and not once did they look inquisitively or knowingly at the Grand Duchess and her Englishman.

"Everything is to your liking, Olga?" he asked.

"Oh, I assure you, you are looking after me very well," said Olga in demure seriousness. He was quite himself again in every way and it was no wonder with his brown, sinewy look that women threw him covert glances. "Do you know, I think you're being looked at," she said. "I expect Tatiana would say it was because the ladies are finding you excessively handsome."

"Olga," he said, "they're looking at you, not me. What would Tatiana say about that?"

"She'd say it was because my face had turned black. You're teasing me again, aren't you? No one is really looking at me, are they?" The possibility disconcerted her. She coloured a little. He felt a tender incredulity that she could be so diffident. It did not usually take a growing girl long to realise it was a pleasure far more than an embarrassment to be looked at and admired. Olga seemed an exception. Which was one reason why he loved her so much. He might see very little more of her. London might recall him. Aleka might inform on him. The latter would be far worse.

"Well, you know," he said, "your hat alone is worth looking at." But his smile comforted her, told her she was not alone and did not have to suffer the curiosity of people by herself.

They had strawberries with sugar and cream. They were pink, succulent, delicious. She said. "This is quite the most enjoyable outing. I feel so free, just like any ordinary girl." Then she wished she had said young lady.

"But you're not like any ordinary girl at all," he

291

said, at which Olga's eyes looked as if they had been kissed by the sun.

After lunch they strolled around the shops. They inspected window displays, visited fashionable emporia. Olga was happy to look and to exclaim. He would have liked to buy her everything that fascinated her. But he knew Olga would not have let him and Alexandra would not have approved. In a bookshop, full of selected foreign literature which the Government had decided was not seditious, she examined titles and bindings. She loved reading. Her favourite authors were English, the language itself a feature of the Imperial family's life. Kirby extracted a Jane Austen novel, *Emma*. He leafed through it. He felt the lightest pressure against his arm as Olga peeped over his shoulder. There was the familiar delicacy of her scent.

"What book is that?" she asked.

"Have you read Jane Austen at all? She's a great favourite with Englishwomen."

"I'm very happy with my Shakespeare, you've no idea how I adore it," she said. He began to replace the book. Olga caught his arm and begged to see it, as if fearing she had been discourteous. He gave it to her. She opened it and began to read. The proprietor beamed benignly at them from his little desk. "Buy it for Mama," said Olga, "she will love it. I'll be able to borrow it. Oh, you see," she added in a little desperation, "what can I give you if you buy it for me?"

"Olga, we are friends and I have a treasure house of memories. Let us buy if for Her Imperial Highness, then."

"You must buy it, not both of us," said Olga quietly. She went to the shop doorway, waiting while he paid for the book and had it wrapped. When they were out of the shop and walking again she said in a whisper, "Oh, it is so unfair."

"Olga?"

"No, that was said to myself, not you."

She was strangely upset. He did not press her. And by the time the carriage had picked them up and they were trotting out of Yalta into the countryside she was happy again. The afternoon light was clear, picking out the distant mountains and the sweeping undulations of green valleys and blue hills.

"Oh, it has been immensely lovely, immensely," she said as they approached the soaring white magnificence of the Livadia Palace.

"Well, quite nice, at least," he said modestly.

Her hand in its white summer glove came to touch his arm, to slide down. The following carriage was at its discreet distance as he took her hand. The pressure of her fingers was of shy gratitude.

"Thank you for asking Mama, I have so enjoyed it," she said.

His heart itself seemed squeezed by her clinging fingers.

At the Palace he went up to his suite. Olga turned on the terrace and went in search of Tatiana. She found her in the gardens, lying on the warm, dry lawn, reading her French tutor. Tatiana quickened with pleasure to see her adored sister back at last.

"Olga, why, how famous you look. Oh, almost shockingly society. Tell me what you've been doing, we've all been green with jealousy. Anastasia is going about asking everyone what good is it being a slave when she can't follow in the footsteps of her master."

Olga sank down beside her sister. Suddenly sadness shadowed her face.

"Tatiana, oh, I don't ever want to be a Crown Princess."

"Don't you? Well, you just wait until the most adorable Crown Prince arrives to present himself. You'll take one look and swoon with longing."

"No, never, and I wouldn't be as ridiculous as that in any event," said Olga.

"Olga," said Tatiana, sitting up, "Ivan hasn't said anything to you, has he?"

"What could he say, what would he say that anyone couldn't hear? Oh, Tasha, he is so free, he will marry someone quite beautiful, he'll be free to be happy——"

293

"No," said Tatiana firmly, flinging back her auburn hair. "No, never. It's you he wants, it's you he can't have, but he'll always be tied to you even if he's a million miles away. How often, just how often do I have to tell you that? Dearest, you should believe more in yourself, you don't know how lovely you are, and you are, truly. Oh goodness, Olga, if you cry out here——"

"As if I would," said Olga, but she blinked a little. "I'm getting far too old to be as silly as that." She swallowed, her eyes dreamed. She said, "But oh, Tasha, I am so unbearably in love. It is so unfair."

"No, it isn't, you silly," said Tatiana, "it's lovely."

The younger Grand Duchesses came dancing from their lessons. There had been some overnight rain, now the clouds had broken and the expanses of blue sky widened. The greens were fresh, the flowers soft. Alexis was carried to a garden chair by Nagorny, the Tsarevich happy to see his friend Ivan Ivanovich there. The boy's leg was better each day, his colour healthier. Kirby was lazing, reading. He put his book down as the children claimed his attention. Anastasia and Marie curtseyed billowingly.

"O lord," said Anastasia, "thy slave fetching Fatima is here, what is there she can fetch you?"

"Well, let me see," said Kirby thoughtfully. "Yes. Fetch me five white horses and a donkey."

"You don't need a donkey," said Tatiana, "you have Anastasia. But what are the five white horses for?"

"One for each of you to carry you off to your heart's desire," said Kirby. "Alexis will be carried off to a mountain of ice cream, Marie to a beautiful prince, Anastasia to a slave auction, Tatiana to a magnificent ball and so on. The donkey, actually, is for me. I fall off horses."

As Olga arrived with all the sedateness of a young lady, Tatiana said, "But you didn't say where Olga would be carried off to, Ivan."

"To a railway station, I expect," said Anastasia, "she's always waving to engine drivers."

"Oh, no," said Marie, "that's only in gracious acknowledgement when they make their engines whistle at her."

A footman made his stately approach to advise Kirby that he was wanted on the telephone.

"Please may I come?" said Alexis. He put out his arms, Kirby picked him up and carried him. Olga watched them go and Tatiana watched Olga. When they returned and Kirby set the boy down in his chair again, Alexis burst out glumly, "Well, what do you think? They're going to take Ivan away. Just when I was nearly better and we could drill again."

Anastasia groaned, Marie sighed in dejection. Tatiana looked at Olga. Olga stood stunned.

"Ivan, it can't be true," said Tatiana, "you're to stay until we all go. Mama has said so."

"And I'm sure Papa *will* say so," said Alexis.

"What about me?" said Anastasia. "I won't be his slave any more, I'll be sold to a monster. Monsters are awfully capacious."

"Capricious," said Tatiana. "Ivan, it's only to St. Petersburg, of course?"

"I'm recalled to England," said Kirby, "and must go tomorrow."

"We'll hide you somewhere," offered Marie, "and if anyone comes looking for you we'll say you fell down a well."

"Let's go and see Papa," said Tatiana, "let's all go now and leave Olga to give Ivan a good talking to."

"Oh, yes, let's do that," said Alexis. Nagorny came to carry the boy in the wake of Tatiana, Marie and Anastasia, leaving Kirby alone with Olga. She stared unhappily at him, then turned away.

"No, you can't," she whispered fiercely, "not to England. Colonel Kirby, you can't."

"I must, Olga. I'm under orders."

She kept her back to him, the sunlight dancing on her hair.

"But England," she said. She sounded as if she could not understand his acceptance of such orders. "No, you can't," she said again.

"I love Livadia, I want to stay," he said, "but I've no alternative."

"If Papa asks—he is cousin to your King—there would be an alternative."

"Your father will know I must obey orders."

"Oh!" It was a little cry of frustration.

"Olga, I'm sorry," he said. If she found his acceptance of the situation inexplicable, he found the situation heartbreaking. He loved every moment he had shared with her. To be away from her, to know she was inaccessible, that was something he did not want to think about. It had been Brigadier Rollinson, not Anstruther, who had called him. He had been friendly but insistent over the telephone. He had said nothing of other things, he had merely advised him he was to return to England. It was an order. There would be similar orders given in other ways to other British agents in Russia. There was only one consoling factor about his recall. If Princess Aleka was in regular contact with Prolofski she would soon realise that he and Oravio had not disappeared to go on a pilgrimage to Jerusalem, and she might pass her piece of paper to someone else or to the secret police. In which case England would be a better place for him to be in than Livadia. In England he would not have to face the disillusioned Imperial family, he would not have to face Olga.

Olga was trying to contain herself but could not.

"Do you—do you say Papa could not have you stay?" She would not, could not look at him. "He could, but no, you are determined to go. You will never come back and I know why. It's because of me, because of us. But we have done nothing, nothing, we have only been friends. Colonel Kirby, you are deserting me to please them——"

"No, Olga."

"Yes. You're going to England and you'll forget us, and I cannot bear it, I can't!"

Olga ran. She ran blindly, her white dress whipping, her hair flying.

Karita did not know whether to be excited or sad. She loved Livadia as Kirby loved it, and she loved the Imperial family with all the intensity of the devoted. But she and Ivan Ivanovich would come back one day. Meantime she would at last go to England with him and see what it was like. It was strange how much she thought about England when it mattered so little compared with Russia. When she had been there a while and discovered what it was like, and when Ivan Ivanovich finally realised that only Russia was truly beautiful, he and she would return.

She sang as she packed. Then she was sad and sang very little. But excitement came again and she sang happily. Ivan Ivanovich was at the open windows. He had said he would help her pack. Karita had said that would not be necessary. All the same, he had said he would. But he was no help at all. He just stood there, looking out over the gardens and the sea. Livadia was soft with evening light, but he had seen it all before.

He had eaten with the Imperial family, a light dinner, and the Tsar had recognised he must obey his orders. Olga had said almost nothing. Alexandra remained in her suite as she invariably did.

There was very little left of the day.

Karita answered a light knock on the door. It was the Grand Duchess Olga, asking if she might see Colonel Kirby. Karita thought her unusually pale. She left them alone in the drawing-room.

"Olga?" He could not keep some tenderness from his voice. Olga seemed calm enough. The sun, going down, spread diffused light on her. She had her hand on the curtain, her eyes on the mountains.

"I'm so ashamed," she whispered, "please forgive me."

"Forgive you? Olga, I should have to be a saint to forgive anything in you."

"No, it was dreadful of me," she insisted, "I acted like a spoilt child. I shouldn't be here but I couldn't endure having you think badly of me."

"Badly? How could I? Olga, you have been the best and the sweetest of friends always. Would you like to walk in the gardens? We could talk but not be alone, as we are here."

"I'd like that," she said.

They went down to the gardens. The lights of the Palace cast their glow, holding back for a while the advance of dusk. They talked matter-of-factly for a while, about his journey home and the route.

And then he said as the distant night submerged the horizon, "I'm never sure whether I like Livadia better by night than day or vice versa. It's always peaceful by day, it's more so by night."

"Except when there's a ball," said Olga. They were walking slowly, the gardens darkening, the flowers closed and still. "I love it at all times, but I think it's the times when you——" She stopped. "Oh, it's only that you have always been so good for us, made us all so happy. We have all laughed so much, have we not?"

"Yes," he said. He was wrenched with pain. "Do you remember Juliet's cantankerous old nurse?"

"And your indiscriminate choice of Shakespeare? Oh, yes." Olga smiled. Then she said, "I am not going to disgrace myself again, but Tatiana is heartbroken. She may not seem so but she'll miss you so much. You amuse her excessively and she adores that more than anything."

"All the young like to laugh. You do."

"I'm not as young as all that," said Olga. "Alexis is quite down in the dumps about your going, but there, Papa says in your position you must obey orders as he would himself. I was very silly, wasn't I?" She went on feverishly as if to ensure there were no unendurable silences. "Alexis says that perhaps you'll write to him and tell him all about the British Army and how you

298

are getting on in England, and Anastasia says she hopes they won't give you any unmanageable horses to ride. And I shall have more time to read my Shakespeare, I'm trying to get through *The Tempest* now, but it's very involved, with Ariel under a spell and——" Her voice caught, she took a deep breath. "I think," she said, "that I'm trying to say everything all at once."

He owed Nicholas and Alexandra a great deal for their kindness, he owed Olga even more. She had shown him the priceless wonder of innocence, the joy and laughter of tenderest friendship, and all the values she held most dear. If his longing was hopeless, his pride in her was intense. He forced himself to say lightly, "I'll write to Alexis, of course I will, if I may, and you can tell Anastasia I'll stick to bicycles."

"Bicycles—oh, yes," she said. They stepped from a path on to a lawn. "Do you remember my sixteenth birthday ball? It was ages and ages ago."

"Was it? I remember it as if it were yesterday."

"Goodness, I'm much older now." She was over-bright. A man and a woman passed them, servants hand-in-hand. "But I did so enjoy it and Mama, you remember, was so interested to meet you. Oh, I wish I could give you something of Livadia."

"You have given me something, a photograph of you and Tatiana that was taken here. I don't intend to lose it, you know. And I also have your birthday ball dance card, that's very much of Livadia."

She stopped. He turned to face her. The brief twilight hovered, muting the rich lustre of her hair.

"That is for your grandchildren, isn't it?" she said. "You'll get married, I hope she will be very nice and that she will make you so very happy."

"Perhaps she will at least make Aunt Charlotte happy. And you, Olga, you will always be yourself, and that is something that makes you very precious to all your friends. You are the dearest and loveliest of persons, the finest of Grand Duchesses. I have been very privileged, Olga."

She was trembling. She put her hands to her face.

"We must go back," she said a little wildly, "they'll wonder about me."

"Yes, of course," he said.

But she did not move. Instead she said, "What will we all do, what will Livadia be when we are never to see you again?"

"Now who is being forgetful?" His one desire was to embrace her, his only salvation was smilingly to reproach her. "Didn't I promise to come and see each of you married? And so I shall. I can't be kept away forever. You'll have the most magnificent of birthday balls when you're twenty-one. Surely you'll invite me to that? I warn you, I'll be there all the same."

Her eyes shone.

"You really will come back to see us? Often? Mama and Papa are not really formidable and if you are able to come now and again they will invite you to stay. It's only that——"

"It's only that I must never outstay my welcome. I shall come, Olga."

"Oh," she breathed, "now I am happy again, you would never promise unless you meant it. Colonel Kirby, I am so fortunate, I have a wonderful family and I have you as my dearest friend. You won't forget to say goodbye to me in the morning, will you? You neglected to the last time."

"I have some very bad moments, don't I?"

"Oh no, you are excessively nice," said Olga. She slid her hand down to his and he took her through the fading twilight back into the Palace.

He and Karita left the following morning. Alexandra received him in her boudoir. There he thanked her simply but earnestly. Alexandra was all smiling kindness. She was, perhaps, relieved at his departure.

"It has been a pleasure to have you, Ivan," she said. "You've taken so much trouble with the children, especially Alexis. If you can come again at any time, you must promise to let me know. And you must write to Alexis, I hear you've said you will."

To Alexis. Not to Olga. He understood.

300

The rest of the family, including Nicholas himself, said goodbye to him on the terrace above the steps. Olga was steeling herself. Tatiana did not bother with any such reserve.

"Oh, you are a wretch to leave us at all," she said to him, "we're all going to be shockingly glum."

"It isn't awfully commendable, you know," said Marie.

"Oh well, men to their ships, you know," said twelve-year-old Anastasia.

The Tsar clapped Kirby affectionately on the shoulder.

"You have my best wishes, my dear fellow," he said, "but one day if I need a new general I'll beg cousin George for the loan of you. How will that do, you rascals?"

"That will do very well, Papa," said Alexis solemnly.

Kirby said goodbye to all of them in turn. Alexis, Anastasia and Marie kissed him. Tatiana gave him her hand. He saw tears in her eyes. But they were for Olga, not for him.

He took Olga's hand. Her blue eyes were frozen, her hand cold, trembling. "Goodbye, Olga Nicolaievna," he said and touched his mouth to her fingertips. He heard her whisper:

"Remember, you promised."

II
The Four
Horsemen

ONE

The summer came, smothering Russia with enervating heat. Immunised by seclusion against the diseases of corruption, ineptitude and injustice, the Imperial family felt no need to change any part of their daily routine. The sinews of Tsarist autocracy were being drained, but it did not seem so at Tsarskoe Selo or any other Imperial residence. It was a year when the might of kings and emperors reached its glittering zenith, when the panoply of monarchism had never shone brighter, and when revolutionaries began to harvest the seeds arrogantly sown by those who thought themselves indestructible.

It was a year when the gulf between aristocracy and the masses widened.

It was the tercentenary of Romanov rule in Russia, and such was the hold this dynasty had on the people that wherever the Tsar went he was greeted by the wildest enthusiasm. This further convinced Alexandra that the bond between the Tsar and his people was holy and unbreakable. Nicholas had nothing to fear from Russia. Russia to Alexandra was the people, not the ministers, not the Duma, not the Boyars. Paradoxically, since she was such a great believer in autocracy, she despised Boyars who followed its principles in the administration of their huge estates.

A letter reached Alexis. It arrived when he was recovering from another illness. He was still in bed and all the Grand Duchesses were there to share his pleasure in the letter. They knew who it was from.

"See, it has an English stamp," said Tatiana, "shall I open it for you?"

Alexis, pale but so glad the pain had gone, nodded his head. Olga sat by the bed, wiping the dampness that came to his brow from time to time. She reached for his hand as Tatiana opened the letter.

"Why," said Tatiana happily, "you'll never guess."

"Yes, I will," said Alexis, "Ivan Ivanovich said he'd write. It's from him, isn't it? You read it, Tasha."

But first there was a small snapshot with the letter. It showed a brick and timber cottage, taken from the wide sweeping lawn at the rear. Three people stood backgrounded by leaded windows. Virginia creeper climbed the wall and the sepia tint added its own mellowness. There was Colonel Kirby himself, looking very English and at home in an open-necked white shirt and white flannels. On his right stood a large, middle-aged lady, massively bosomed and nearly as tall as himself. He was smiling, while she was regarding the camera with apparent suspicion. And on the left of Colonel Kirby was Karita, looking so much herself with her fair, braided hair and a dark dress with white collar and cuffs.

"There, see? He has sent you a photograph, Aleky." Tatiana gave it to him and heads bent over the bed to share his perusal of it.

"It's awfully nice," said Alexis, smiling wanly.

"Goodness," said Anastasia, "that's Karita! Well! I say, doesn't she look pleased with herself. Is the other lady his wife? She seems rather—well, rather large."

"General Georgi would call her a fine figure of a woman," said Tatiana.

"I expect," said Olga, refraining from the general peering, "that that lady must be his aunt."

"Ivan looks terribly dashing," sighed Marie, "and *so* informal."

"Do read the letter, Tasha," said Anastasia.

306

Tatiana, sitting on the side of the bed, read it. Kirby had written,

Dear Alexis, I hope this reaches you without too much delay, I never quite know where you all are and there's a lot more of Russia than there is of England. I've missed you and I think I need some drill. I'm quite a dunderhead again. You had better come over and smarten me up a little.

Have you been well? I hope so. Tell Tatiana I've been very well myself apart from a tendency to fall over my wooden leg in the mornings. If you don't know about my wooden leg, Tatiana will explain. It's a red herring, and if you don't know about red herrings, ask Olga about them. I have great faith in her superior intelligence, which perhaps will come to your other sisters later.

Tatiana interrupted her reading to exclaim, "Oh, the beast!"

I'm sending you a photograph. It was taken by the boy who delivers our groceries. That way my Aunt Charlotte, Karita and I could all get in. The river is at the bottom of the lawn. You can see part of the lawn in the photograph but you can't the river. It was either the house or the river, but not both, so I decided you'd prefer to see the house, as one river is often just like another. It's the water, you know. The house is called White Cottage. It could really be called Why White Cottage as there's not much white about it. Ducks sometimes congregate at the bottom of the lawn. Karita seems to be a duck lover. She doesn't mind their quacking. I tell her not to give them food as they'll only quack for more.

When my Aunt Charlotte saw this photograph she said I looked like our postman off duty. She said it's regrettably Bohemian for a gentleman to be photographed without a collar and tie.

Karita is splendid. She's quite at home, but always the busiest of us, always finding something dreadfully urgent to do, so whenever I'm home it's better for me to keep out of the way if I don't want to be swept up. I go and sit in a wheelbarrow or something equally chastening. Karita has become quite fond of Aunt Charlotte. She isn't so

307

sure about England. She says it could be greatly improved if everyone spoke Russian, she is sure nobody can really understand English in the way it's spoken here. She speaks her own kind of English, which she says must be the proper one as she learned it from me, so why doesn't everyone else speak like she does? I'm in a constant state of apology, either for my countryman's strange English or for being in the way. Why White Cottage isn't quite as big as Livadia, as you can see.

The British Army isn't terribly busy at the moment but there are comings and goings at week-ends, when everyone likes to get home for Sunday tea. I work at the War Office in London, although I feel I'm on a shelf there. I'm regularly dusted down. At times I feel rather like a piece of old pottery. Karita says the time to worry will be when I look like it.

I'm taking her to the races tomorrow. She's in a dreadful state of suspense, mainly because she can't make up her mind what kind of hat to wear. Tell Olga how enchanted we'd be if she'd send one of hers, the one she wore when we lunched in Yalta. That was a lovely hat. Tell Anastasia I've found no one here who can slave half as well as she can. I've only the fondest recollections of her unimaginable servitude, which was so unobtrusive I never really knew when it was happening.

"Yes, I was rather invisible," said Anastasia proudly at this point.

Tell Marie I'm going to mention her to the Prince of Wales. That is, I will if I ever meet him. I hear he's looking for someone exceptionally eligible and exceptionally nice. Tell Olga and Tatiana I miss them very much, I miss all of you very much. I think of all of you every day. I am, yours affectionately, Ivan. In English it's John.

"Aleky," said Tatiana, "what did you think of that?"

"It's a nice letter, isn't it?" said Alexis.

"Divine," said Marie, "he says I'm very exceptional."

"Oh, I'm sure you'll get over that," said Anastasia, "it's nothing to worry about, Marie." Adopting a pose of humility she went on, "I suppose *I* shall always be

308

some good man's slave, I suppose that's what I'm best at. It's very chastening. What's chastening?"

"Sitting in a wheelbarrow," said Olga, casually borrowing the snapshot from Alexis.

Later, after they had all dispersed and left Alexis in the care of his nurse, Tatiana returned to his room.

"Alexis," she said, "shall we let Olga have the letter? She's very good at being tidy and keeping things properly, while you've always so much to catch up with when you're better."

"Oh, yes, let Olga look after it," he said in his agreeable way, "she'll be sure not to lose it. When I'm better she can help me write an answer to Ivan."

"She'll love helping you with that," smiled Tatiana. She lightly ruffled his hair, then sought out Olga to give her the letter and snapshot. "Olga, Alexis said you're to have it to keep it safe for him."

Olga was warm with pleasure. She hugged her sister.

"Tasha, how sweet you are to me. Thank you, darling. I'll keep it very safe and we can read it again to Alexis whenever he wishes."

"It was sent to Alexis," said Tatiana, "but it was written to you. It belongs to you. Aleky won't mind."

Left alone, Olga read the letter herself. It absorbed her, entranced her. It had come from England, where Great-Aunt Alix lived, and it had come from the place where her parents had spent their most blissful and carefree days. She put it carefully between the leaves of her Shakespeare, with the photograph.

The Russian Empire was sinking in a morass of its own inertia. In the arts, in music, poetry, literature and ballet, Russia remained pre-eminent. In system she remained archaic. What had been good enough for the 16th-century Boyars was good enough for the 20th-century too.

The Tsar's wiliest minister, Count Sergius Witte, was out of office. He was sixty-five and had less than two years to live. He would be dead when Nicholas had his greatest need of him. Even now, such was the Tsar's lack of faith in his own appointments that ministers came and went while still glowing from the honour of initiation. Few of them understood that under all the Tsar's unfailing charm was his unfailing determination to preserve absolute autocracy. Yet, unable to make any man unhappy in his presence, Nicholas always asked for ministerial resignations by letter.

Kirby was not in Russia when the Imperial family went to Livadia that autumn.

Livadia was as remote as ever. Russians in their millions were more distrustful than ever of ministers, more trusting than ever of their Father Tsar's intent to put things right. And at Livadia the Tsar thought about his people, talked about his people, and played tennis.

Alexandra, withdrawing further into cosy seclusion, was content to devote herself to prayer and love. Love of husband, love of family, love of God.

For Olga, the sensitive one, Livadia was not quite the same. She joined with the others in their games, but she sat often with her volume of Shakespeare, absorbed one minute in the complexities of plots within plots, dreaming the next with her eyes on the horizon.

Anastasia came dancing one day, waving a letter. She made for Alexis, the boy still with a slight limp.

"It's for you, Aleky, Mama asked me to bring it to you. It has a French stamp but it's from Ivan Ivanovich, Mama says it is."

Olga stiffened in her chair. She closed her Shakespeare, clasped it tightly. Alexis, as importantly as he could, opened the letter. But Tatiana did the reading. It was from Kirby to say he was with a British military mission in France, to tell Alexis he was vaguely busy at last and that the French 75 guns were masterpieces. They had so inspired him that he now knew his left from his right again. He wrote about France. There were some extraordinary creatures there in quite the most enormous hats. He had discovered they were women. Their gowns, he wrote, were enough to sweep the grass from the lawns of Livadia. They had great difficulty in climbing into carriages without hoisting their petticoats like sails.

Tatiana could not go on for laughter. Olga smiled stiffly.

Tatiana said, "Oh, the fickle wretch, I believe he's been flirting with the ladies of Paris."

"He had better not," said Anastasia.

"But is he coming to see us?" said Marie. "What does he say about that?"

Kirby wrote that Karita had stayed in Walton with Aunt Charlotte, which was just as well as she would never believe what there was to see and would be confused for the rest of her life. The Parisian modes were incredibly voluminous and there was enough material in a lady's dress to make a row of tents. One could hardly kiss any lady's hand without being smothered by her skirts.

"What a funny letter," said Alexis, "it's all about ladies' clothes."

"That's for our benefit," said Tatiana.

Paris was very French, Kirby said.

"That," said Olga, "is a most illuminating observation."

"Yes, who'd have guessed it?" said Anastasia.

For his part, however, wrote Kirby, he would rather be at Livadia. One didn't get smothered there. One might break one's arm but that was due to carelessness, and one was subsequently looked after like a hero. There were slaves who, when they weren't doing anything else, brought one cushions.

"That's me," said Anastasia proudly, "but I never brought him any cushions."

"It's to tell you that next time you should," said Tatiana.

"But is he coming here?" asked Marie, fifteen and with eyes as blue as Olga's.

Tatiana read swiftly on, murmuring the words to herself until she reached the final paragraph, which she read aloud.

311

I'm sending this letter to Livadia, assuming you'll all be there. Had I been able to join you, with Her Imperial Highness's blessing, how gladly I'd have come. How I envy you all, there is no place Karita and I talk more of than Livadia. I can see all of you there. Alexis, remember me to your sisters and tell Olga I wish her the happiest of birthdays. I love you all, think of you all. Perhaps I'll see you at Livadia next year, if I may. If so, I'll bring Karita. You are all as much in her thoughts as mine. God bless you all. Sincerely, Ivan.

"He isn't coming," said Alexis in disappointment.

Olga's eyes were dark.

You promised, oh, you promised.

A day or so later she helped Alexis compose a reply. Alexis found among other things that he was to pointedly ask Ivan when he was returning to Russia. He looked up to say that he supposed Ivan would probably be awfully busy with the British Army. Olga remarked that as he had said in his previous letter that he wasn't busy at all and was only spending his time in France watching ladies get into carriages with their sails flying, there was simply nothing she could think of to prevent him arranging a holiday at Livadia. Alexis said, "Good lord," and wrote down that as Ivan wasn't very busy why didn't he come to Livadia.

Olga laughed when she read the sentence.

"That is just like giving him a good talking to, darling," she said.

Easter 1914 was hot, the forerunner of an ecstatically beautiful summer that invaded the whole of Europe. But Kirby still did not come to Livadia. Olga's disappointment was intense. Worse, however, was the torment that came when she heard rumours that there might be a match between her and Edward, Prince of Wales. And what a match that would be, a union of mighty Empires. England was Russia's new friend. Marriage between Grand Duchess Olga Nicolaievna and the Prince of Wales would make the countries harmonious allies. Edward was handsome, debonair, the

312

most eligible man in Europe and the hope of every royal household with a daughter to spare.

Olga did not approach her parents or harass them in any way. She only waited. For days the rumours flew, growing louder, stronger. But neither Nicholas nor Alexandra spoke a word to her about them. Rumours were for ears that tingled to any social titbit. They were not for discussion. However, in the end Alexandra became aware of Olga's strained look.

"What is it, my love?" asked Alexandra.

"Mama," said Olga at last, "am I to be married?"

"Oh, dear," said Alexandra. She put her hands on Olga's shoulders, looked into the apprehensive blue eyes. "Darling, if we had arranged a marriage for you with each name that came with each rumour, you'd have twenty husbands by now. I know nothing of any marriage and nor, I'm sure, does Papa. We know it will happen eventually but we're in no hurry to precipitate it. My sweet, you would always be the first to know about such a matter, we would never discuss it without telling you and we would never make any arrangement that displeased you."

The relief on Olga's face was only too obvious, but all she said was, "Myself, I'm in no hurry at all."

"Sometimes," said Alexandra gently, "a girl thinks she'll never be in either hurry or desire, that her ideal doesn't exist. But she can change very quickly, darling. There, whatever happens, never believe that Papa and I would alone arrange a match for you. It would only be with your consent. We should not want you to marry anyone you didn't love."

Lenin was building his castles on mountains of ink. Trotsky was considering the likelihood of revolution by 1925, if things went reasonably well. Joseph Vissarionovich Dzhugashvili—so much a mouthful even by Russian standards that he called himself Stalin in the end—was recording assets and liabilities. Among these were a hundred million people and when he had given them an hour's thoughtful consideration he recorded seventy-five million as assets and twenty-five million as liabilities.

The Russian nobility, the Grand Dukes and Princes, still refused to make any real concessions. Unwilling to give up what they had in the way of privilege and power, they were as deaf to the sound of approaching tumbrils as their French counterparts over a hundred years before. They applied the same logic. One either worked the people or beat them, either locked them up or shot them. That was the best solution for any crisis.

It never seemed to occur to Nicholas that this was the summary justice peasants received at the hands of aristocrats and landowners. He approved just deserts for revolutionaries and assassins, but it was unlikely that he believed the ordinary people suffered cruelties. In his gentleness, man's inhumanity to man was out of his understanding. He could not, in any case, have conceived it existed in his beloved Russia.

It was a lovely day in June when Tsarism, Kaiserism, despotism and pomp reached the beginning of their end. With them were also to disappear magnanimity graciousness and dreams. A Bosnian student, Gabriel Princip, killed the Archduke Franz Ferdinand of Austria and, with him, over eight million other men. Franz Ferdinand took about fifteen minutes to die. The others the four years, an average of five thousand victims a day.

Nicholas declared war on behalf of the Slavs. And Russia, which had been seething and fermenting with discontent, became united in support of the Tsar. Of all the committed countries none opened the war on a greater wave of patriotism than Russia. Nicholas had never been better loved than on the day Russia began hostilities against its traditional enemy, Germany. Revolutionaries who declared against the war, against the Tsar, had to go into hiding from the angry people. The Duma was unanimous in its support. Its Bolshevik members were cowed by the intensity of the national feeling.

There were two prominent dissidents who were

neither revolutionaries nor Bolsheviks. Count Sergius Witte and Gregor Rasputin both opposed the war. Rasputin, recovering in his Siberian village from an attempt on his life, telegraphed Nicholas not to do it. Nicholas for once lost his temper and shredded the telegram. Rasputin responded by darkly prophesying that the Imperial family would be doomed by the conflict. Witte spoke his own case in more practical terms. Neither the prophecy nor the practicalities had any effect.

Answerable only to the Tsar in the field of hostilities was the Grand Duke Nicholas Nicolaievich, Commander-in-Chief of the Russian Army. His integrity was unquestionable, his ability undoubted. If he lacked armaments he did not lack manpower. Confidently, Russia awaited the outcome. The men marched and the women waved.

But who, when patriotism and zeal were at their highest, would have thought corruption and vanity in the shape of the Minister of War were to play a greater part than integrity and ability, were to be more influential than marching men and waving women? General Vladimir Sukhomlinov, who was inordinately jealous of Grand Duke Nicholas, was the quintessence of Russian double-dealing. He more than any other man was responsible for the abysmal shortage of everything Russian soldiers needed to fight the military might of Germany.

From the beginning to the end of their war Russians fought with each man's hands tied behind his back.

The Tsar took up residence at Army Headquarters, his family stayed at Tsarskoe Selo outside St. Petersburg which, because of its Germanic derivation, had now been renamed Petrograd. There were occasions, however, when Alexandra could bear no longer to be without sight of Nicholas. She travelled then with her children to stay with her husband for a while. She was suffering mental anguish at this time because of accusations that she was pro-German. She was not. She never had been. She hated Prussian Germans. She had

315

come from Hesse and Hessians were themselves, they han been forcibly unified with Germany by Bismarck in her mother's time. Wholeheartedly she prayed for an Allied victory, and nothing was sweeter to her than to have Britain as one of her allies.

The war changed many things, not least the daily routine of the family. Alexandra, with Olga and Tatiana, took up nursing. It was a vocation in which all three were naturally gifted, their love and compassion at last brought to bear in practical service to others.

The Catherine Palace at Tsarskoe Selo was turned into a military hospital. And there Olga worked each day, quietly and quickly efficient. Only at night did she have time to dream.

TWO

Kirby had at last had his resignation accepted. It had lain in a pigeonhole for many months. In the end they accepted it on condition that he remained in the Army for the duration of the war and joined the British military team in Russia. His knowledge of Russia and Russians was too invaluable not to be used at this critical time. He could forget Prolofski and a certain piece of paper. Neither meant anything now. Britain and Russia were allies. He did not argue. He could not, in fact, have been more satisfied. The extraordinary luck of the game was incredible.

His aunt, massively possessive, was very satisfied too. She was a Victorian, she dressed like one, she lived like one. She was entirely lovable but did her very best not to seem so.

"Good," she said when he broke the news, "its not before time. You've been kicking your heels. That isn't good for any man, especially a single one."

"But I'm leaving you again, dear thing," he said.

"You'll settle one day, I hope," said Aunt Charlotte. Her voice boomed a little when she allowed herself emotion. "Besides, my dear boy, you left something behind in Russia. I am not quite blind. Whatever it was, bring it back with you when you return. You're an incomplete man, quite unlike your father, who was the completest man I ever knew, bless him."

317

"That, I suppose, was because Father had Mother," he said.

"Father and mother, they make complete together always," said Karita, now like one of the family but still with a sense of what was proper.

"How right you are, child" said Aunt Charlotte. She wore a welter of deep grey garments pinned with brooches and dwarfed the slim Crimean girl. "I've begun to despair of his future. However, we're at war now and who knows what may happen? But I sincerely hope he'll not marry some flighty nurse simply because there is a war. Men do impetuous things in wartime."

"Flighty nurse, she is impetuous?" said Karita, not knowing whether the implications were inconsequential or dreadful.

"There's no such thing as a flighty nurse," said Kirby.

"You forget, I was a nurse myself during the Boer War," said Aunt Charlotte.

"You flighty nurse?" said Karita, brown eyes intrigued. She wore a white blouse and blue skirt, was the essence of attractive simplicity and, when she topped this outfit with a straw boater, a delight to the eyes of Walton.

"Good heavens, girl," said Aunt Charlotte.

"She not flighty nurse," said Kirby, shaking his head at Karita.

"Don't make such fun of her," said Aunt Charlotte, who adored the girl. "Karita speaks English very well, but that won't help her. She not flighty nurse indeed, what do you think you're at?"

"Oh dear, making fun, I suppose."

Aunt Charlotte smiled. Karita laughed.

"Well, I suppose you'll want to make your preparations," said Aunt Charlotte. "The Minister must think some good will come of sending you to Russia if he wants you there so quickly."

"He didn't say so himself," said Kirby, "he was elsewhere with serious matters on his mind."

"Your going is serious enough, do you say it isn't?" boomed his aunt.

"Only to you and me, dearest," he smiled.

"And to me," said Karita.

He had had some difficulty in making Them understand he must take Karita with him. He had promised that when he did return to Russia, even if not until after the war, he would take her with him. Karita had said that she would think he would. With her country at war she would not countenance being left behind now. They had given in gracefully in the end. Karita was ecstatic. She liked it at Walton, loved the old cottage with its mellow warmth, its oak and mahogany furniture, its crowded bedrooms, its pictures and its huge fireplace. She adored to stand by the little landing-stage where the lawn met the Thames and the ducks came paddling to her.

As a foreigner she was intrigued by everything being so different. It was not necessarily better, but it was different. There were so many chestnut trees and green hanging willows. It pleased her to wave to people gliding by in boats and punts, it delighted her when they waved in response. The road to the village was full of light and shade because of the many trees and she was amazed by the number of people who rode bicycles. The tinkle of bicycle bells was such a happy sound.

Kirby had bought her a bicycle and taught her to ride it, she in blushing confusion at times because her petticoats would fly and show him her legs. He only laughed at the flutter and swirl. It was all very well for him, he bicycled in trousers with clips to hold them in place. But it was such fun. She quickly became accomplished and looked very picturesque in her boater and fluttering skirts riding down to the shops for Aunt Charlotte.

Aunt Charlotte had been so kind. She had been intimidatingly suspicious at first. It did not seem right to her that Kirby should have a girl as pretty as this for his personal servant. But there was obviously only the right and proper relationship between them, and the girl

319

was a delight in her willingness to serve the aunt as happily as she served the nephew.

Young men came courting her. With her golden hair and her brown eyes Karita was a target for every bachelor in the neighbourhood. Karita was polite to all of them, walked out with those she liked the best, thought all of them very gallant—except one who tried to kiss her and received the point of her parasol in his stomach —but considered none of them with any seriousness. A most impressed young gentleman, a Mr. Hargreaves, astonished her by proposing to her. She recovered quickly enough to prevent him embracing her and told him in her delicious English that it was most hospitable of him, that she was quite ungoverned by his affection, but that it would never do, that Colonel Kirby would never approve. When he asked what Colonel Kirby had to do with it, Karita was astonished again.

"But I am his responsibiliky, he is my father and mother."

"Good grief," said the surprised young gentleman.

"He is having confusingk times without me and would not approve my marryingk no one."

"I don't like the sound of that," said Mr. Hargreaves.

"You are not asked to," said Karita as nicely as she could. Mr. Hargreaves was highly desirous of pressing his suit farther, thinking Karita a golden Russian rosebud who would beautify a little cottage he had his eye on at Shepperton, but Karita simply did not want to be either engaged or married. Really, it was only by fortuitous circumstances that she had not drifted into marriage with Oravio. An escape like that was a warning. Besides, Colonel Kirby would never consent. She might argue with him, she would never disobey him. Her mother would be furious.

She had come to call him Colonel Kirby now. Aunt Charlotte could not believe her ears when she first heard the Russian girl address him as Ivan Ivanovich. She said that that simply could not be allowed. It did not matter what obtained in Russia, it was not the thing in England. Karita, always willing to please

320

even if she did not understand—and who could understand the English?—bowed to one more strange English custom and thereafter refrained from what Aunt Charlotte thought was an uncomfortable familiarity.

Karita was delighted about the prospect of returning to Russia. Had it not been for the war she would have remained at Walton with pleasure; but now, seized by an excess of love and patriotism, she wanted to be in Russia, to see her country at work in the war against Germany. Germans were monsters. It was said that their soldiers were not averse to roasting babies.

"Oh, and eating them, I suppose?" said Kirby.

"Even that," said Karita.

"That, Karita, is against all your commonsense and you know it."

"I don't say it myself, but it's what I've heard," she said.

"Silly girl," he said, "I thought you'd given up believing anything you hadn't seen for yourself."

"Yes," said Karita, "but Mr. Browning has a brother in France who told him of this and was I to call him a liar?"

"Mr. Browning?"

"Yes. He is our new postman and I am walking out with him."

"Well, you can kiss him goodbye this evening, we are going tomorrow."

They arrived in Petrograd in January. The sea trip had been cold and hazardous. Petrograd was cold but more brilliant than ever, white with shining ice and snow, full of light and crowded with people. The familiar droshkies swished by, the sleighs jingled, and Karita wore again her sable fur and hat. Her eyes sparkled as they drove to a hotel, where Kirby was to stay for two days before going to the Polish front to join the British military team there. To Karita's astonishment, as soon as Kirby's British cap and greatcoat were recognised people on the street cheered him. She blushed with pride. That was something to write to her parents about indeed.

"Oh," she said, "you're very popular."

"I will be," he said, "if my arrival coincides with a great Russian victory."

Petrograd was exciting and gay. The gaiety did not seem to have much to do with earnest endeavour, only with the necessity for people to enjoy the atmosphere of the capital in wartime. Since there was a war, the citizens of Petrograd danced, celebrated and made love, for these were the activities they excelled at. To add to the glitter uniforms predominated and beautiful women sacrificed themselves in every way to amuse and entertain the heroes of the Admiralty and the War Office. The heroes responded with the social *élan* they were born with. At the front men and officers died in the snow.

The hospitals were overflowing, the casualties had been enormous. The trains brought the wounded in daily and it was difficult to get a hospital bed unless one was privileged. It did not help that anarchists and revolutionaries were beginning to toss bombs among civilians again, except that, as Trotsky said in so many words, this was for the good of the people in the long run.

Olga and Tatiana were working in the Catherine Palace. They blenched at times because of the hideous and brutal effects of war. Nothing they had been told, nothing they had heard about war and battles, conveyed the reality like wounded men did. Doctors and staff generously and tactfully attempted to protect the Grand Duchesses from too close a contact with the more distressingly wounded, but Olga and Tatiana firmly refused such protection. They did not want to play at nursing, to minister only when casualties had had their wounds dressed and hidden. Nor did Alexandra wish them merely to look the part. The Grand Duchesses were allowed to take their responsibilities seriously, and they shared as much of the distress and heartbreak of a military hospital as the rest of the nursing staff.

One morning Olga had been asssisting at the dressing of cases where amputation had taken place. The waste and tragedy of it all was beginning to show in the eyes of this compassionate young woman, awakening in her an awareness that life was so much more than Tsarskoe Selo or Livadia. She was nineteen, shapely and graceful, conquering her reserve and her shyness in ministering and talking to men whose suffering pained her.

With her figure waisted by her crisp, white uniform, she had been grateful for a few minutes' respite afforded by being sent in search of new lint and bandages. With the blue packets piled on to a tray she was on her way back to the ward. At the far end of the wide, shining corridor she saw a tall man in a khaki greatcoat. He was talking to an orderly and the orderly was gesturing and pointing. The tall man turned and began to traverse the corridor, coming towards her, his cap swinging in his hand. Olga stopped at the door to the ward. She started, her heart began to thump, her blue eyes opened wide and then her joy was pure but incredulous. Her limbs trembled, the tray tilted a little in her hands. He came with long strides, he saw the nurse standing by the door and suddenly he was looking into the bluest eyes imaginable. He checked and his teeth showed in a delighted smile.

"And I was so sure I'd lost my way," he said.

Olga was unable to speak. There was this numbing incredulity. They looked at each other. She could not hide her bliss and because of this the familiar tide of pinkness surged, suffusing her face with colour. Kirby thought her unchangeably lovely despite the austerity of her uniform, despite the snowy wimple that hid so much of her lustrous hair. How he denied himself the fundamental urge to touch her he did not know.

"How splendid you look, Olga Nicolaievna," he said.

"Oh, I can't believe it," she said, her voice a gasp.

"I mean it, you do look splendid."

"No, that it's you," she said, "oh, I simply don't know what to say."

He was still as she remembered him, still the man

323

with the fine eyes and the friendly smile whom she'd first seen on the station at Nikolayev.

"Well, what are words, Olga?"

"There are your words," she breathed, "and you kept your promise, you did, and just when I thought you'd never be able to because of the war."

"It's because of the war that I was able to." He smiled again, hiding feelings that hammered at him. He had never thought himself capable of the kind of love he had for Olga Nicolaievna of Imperial Russia. "Shall I hold that for you?" He took the tray. She relinquished it as if it were unreal. She could not take her eyes from him. "I went to the Alexander Palace to pay my respects," he said. "I saw Marie and Anastasia. Anastasia said I'd been a dreadfully long time coming. They told me you and Tatiana were here, so here I am." Orderlies passed by, followed by a nurse who smiled at Olga. He waited until they were out of earshot and then said, "Is it inconvenient?"

"Inconvenient?" She shook her head in swift reproach. "How can you say such a thing? Oh, I'm sorry, you must think me very stupid, but I really can't believe it, you see. I thought, we all thought—oh, Tatiana will be overjoyed that you've come. We talk about you so much." She looked at the tray he held, at the pile of blue packets. She came to. "They're waiting for these, I must take them in."

"Of course." He handed the tray back to her. "You're busy, I'd better not stay. It was enough——"

"Colonel Kirby, if you dare to go away, if you don't stay to see Tatiana, you'll never be forgiven. Please, if you'll go into the room at the end of this corridor and wait there, I'll come as soon as I'm free and I'll bring Tatiana with me. It's a visitors' room." Suddenly and for the first time her smile peeped. "For distinguished visitors."

He went to the room. It was vast. There seemed to be nothing of temperate or modest size in this place. The chairs and sofas were immense, offering comfort to a hundred visitors if necessary. But there was no one waiting at the moment. It made him feel as if he was alone in space. He sat down. He got up, discarded his greatcoat and walked about. He thought of Olga. That was nothing new. He couldn't recall a day in England when he hadn't thought of her. He had been restless by day, sleepless by night.

Russia had pulled at him, but They were unforgiving during his first months in England, coldly displeased by his carelessness. They had had to bring home every agent. But at least they had been able to do that. None of them had been arrested. Aleka Petrovna had kept her piece of paper to herself. Now that mattered no more and he himself was no longer in that branch of the service.

Kirby's thoughts were interrupted as the door opened. He turned. He saw Princess Aleka Petrovna. Palely, exquisitely beautiful in her furs, one hand deeply muffed, the other pushing the door wide, she regarded Kirby without surprise.

"My dear man," she said.

"Ah, Princess Aleka Petrovna, I presume?" he returned, and he bowed.

She smiled. Her white teeth shone. Her smile grew, it radiated and sparkled.

"Oh, my lovely infamous Ivan," she murmured. "How extraordinarily wonderful, how beautifully delicious." She closed the door and glided towards him in her black, glossy furs. "And how magnificent. Shall we kiss?" She put her arms around his neck, her muff dangling at his back, and she brought her tinted mouth to his. The kiss was warm, lingering, until suddenly her teeth nipped his bottom lip. She drew back, smiled sleepily at the tiny spot of blood she had drawn. "There, darling, that was to say how lovely to see you and how naughty you are. What did you do with Prolofski? With poor, burning Oravio?"

"I don't know. I met them once. I was to meet them again. They disappeared before I got there."

"You're a lovely liar. You always look so friendly when you're lying."

325

"It's not important now, is it?" he said. He was wary, cautious. She could still harm him, still make his old trade known to the Imperial family. "The only thing I really knew about Prolofski was that he was an elusive gentleman."

"But, darling," said Aleka, almost cooing, "one always knew where poor Oravio was. No one knows now. I am sure you were very naughty. How lucky you are that I'm not a spiteful woman."

"I'm grateful," he said, "and have given up adventure stories now. The war has changed everything for all of us."

"It hasn't for me," said Aleka. "It has for Andrei." She seemed very amused at that. "I came here to see him, poor dear."

"Andrei is here?"

"Oh, not as a battle hero," said Aleka, "he's to have his appendix out. But Ivan, darling, would you believe it, he's in the Army. Not to be aggressive, you understand, but to sit at a desk and sign papers. He's quite incapable of shooting at his fellow men. I do believe he realises this is only a war to preserve emperors and privilege, and the worry of it has given the sweet darling an inflamed appendix. It was immensely difficult to make arrangements, but I spoke to the Empress and she was kindness itself."

"What a strange creature you are," he said, "you despise privilege and yet you use it whenever you can."

"One must be practical, Ivan dear," she said, "and my motives are always the best. You know, I'm quite devastated to see you, it was Grand Duchess Olga Nicolaievna who told me you were here. What tender and merciful work she's doing, isn't she?" She was purringly malicious. "Oh, I shouldn't be sarcastic, I suppose, she is a sweet child. But, really, all of them are *so* useless on the whole. It will be better when Russia is a Socialist democracy, then the Romanovs can do a little work. When Olga told me you were here, I simply rushed. But why are you here yourself? Who have you come to see?"

Kirby dabbed at his lip.

"Oh, just a couple of people," he said.

"We can't talk here," said Aleka, "will you come to see me tomorrow? You must. We shall be friends again." She put her hands on his chest, her dark eyes a sly beguilement. "We shall have fun again, Ivan."

"I suppose some must dance while Rome burns," he said, "but will you forgive me, Aleka? I have to go to your Army Headquarters tomorrow."

"Oh, you disappointing brute," she said. Then she laughed. "As for Rome, it must burn. It will rise cleaner from the ashes. Now I must rush. You must come to see me when you return. If you don't, I shall get spiteful, after all. Let us fall in love all over again. Ivan, I'm the most susceptible creature and you are so magnificent."

She kissed him again and was gone in a swirl of black. A minute later Olga came in, Tatiana with her and also in uniform. She gave a little shriek of delight and, as Olga closed the door, came running. Tatiana had no worries about what was permissible and what was not, she flung her arms around Kirby and perched on tiptoe to kiss him.

"Oh, the time you've taken," she cried, "a hundred years at least. Ivan Ivanovich, you're a backsliding wretch but still shockingly handsome. Look at him, Olga, who would think he's ever worried about us?"

Olga was looking, seeing her sister hugging Kirby's arm. She wished Tatiana would not.

"I thought about you," said Kirby, "but worried mostly about myself. I thought they were going to tie me to a desk in Whitehall for ever."

"But they didn't," said Tatiana. She drew him to a red and gold sofa. "Let's all sit down, Olga and I have a whole thirty minutes to talk to you. I felt dreadful pangs when she first told me you were here, I thought she meant you were a casualty. You can't imagine my dread. Olga, come and sit." Olga responded to the expressive hand Tatiana put out, and the sisters sat one on each side of Kirby. Tatiana was vivacious, excited, her eyes alight. Olga let her talk while she herself shyly observed him from under long, dark lashes. Tatiana asked questions, answered them herself and then said, "Oh, I am wagging my tongue out of all proportion but it's so lovely that you're here, Ivan. We thought we'd never see you again until the war was over, but it just shows you must have faith, doesn't it? Why are you back again, have you come to fight for us?"

"Only at Headquarters," he said.

"I think I'm glad about that," said Olga, "there are more than enough men involved in the fighting already. Oh, there have been so many killed, so many wounded. Far too many. They're all so brave, the wounded. They lose an arm or a leg, or are even blinded, but they never complain, only thank us for the little we can do for them. Colonel Kirby, war is terrible. I wish it would end, I wish it would."

Her eyes were sad. He wanted to hold her, cherish her.

"It will end as soon as we've won," said Tatiana cheerfully. "England is on our side and everyone knows England never loses a war."

"Don't we?" said Kirby. "All the same we still manage to get ourselves deplorably knocked about." He could not bring himself to make easy remarks about a quick and glorious victory for the Allies. Already the Russian casualties had been enormous. To speak in comforting clichés about winning would not help anybody.

"Well, you must be sure that you don't get deplorably knocked about yourself," said Tatiana.

"Tasha!" Olga spoke vehemently.

"But we don't want Ivan——"

"You should not say such things," said Olga.

"I shall keep out of the way as much as I can," said Kirby.

"Colonel Kirby, some things are amusing," said Olga, "but that is not."

"Dearest Olga," said Tatiana, "don't let's be too

serious. He has come to make us laugh again, and so many things are quite serious enough. Ivan, tell us what you've been doing, all about England. Did everyone there get excited about the war? You should have seen how pleased Mama and Papa were when the news came that you would fight on our side. Mama was so joyful she wept a little."

He told them about England at war, about men flocking to enlist, the waving flags, the river craft hooting and the mood of the people. He told them about Zeppelin raids and how his aunt had condemned Zeppelins as infernal and defied one by going out on to the lawn at night and booming at it as it passed overhead.

"Oh, I should dearly like to meet her, wouldn't you, Olga?" said Tatiana.

"More than anything," said Olga impulsively, and then fought desperately not to let pinkness betray that her reasons were different from Tatiana's.

He talked about Karita, how well she had got on in England, how pleased she was now to be back in Russia. The Grand Duchesses were delighted to hear this news, they liked Karita immensely. Olga grew more relaxed.

Then Tatiana said, "I must go. You stay, Olga, there's another ten minutes yet." Mama might not approve but it was only fair that Olga should have him to herself for a little while. "Ivan, you must arrange with Olga when you can come again. And it must be soon, you stayed away far too long and it is so nice to have you back." She blew a kiss from the doorway and rustled crisply away.

Olga was immediately over-conscious of every imaginable implication and Tatiana's quite sudden departure seemed to have left a void wherein one groped for safe and mundane words. She looked at her hands, linked in her lap.

"Olga," he said. She almost jumped. She was so tense that she was perched on the very edge of the sofa and seemed prepared for instant flight. "Olga,

329

why did you tell the Princess Karinshka I was here?"

He did not sound very pleased and she went hot with mortification. She lifted her head, glanced swiftly at him. But he did not look displeased, only curious.

"Did I do wrong?" she said a little breathlessly. "I thought she would want to see you, that you might want to see her. It did not seem fair not to tell her you were here."

"Olga, do you think I'm in love with Aleka Petrovna?"

"She is very beautiful," said Olga, who felt that all men must find it easy to be in love with the Princess.

"Shall we get this clear?" he said. "I am not in love with her."

"Oh," said Olga inadequately. She regarded him wonderingly and saw that his smile was for her, not for Aleka Petrovna. She flashed into an instant of gladness, sheer and undisguised. Then she looked at a vase perched on a shining table as if detachment ensured that necessary margin of safety. "Was it embarrassing to see her, then? Was it silly of me?"

"Not a bit. We found we were very good friends." He wanted to push back her white headdress, to uncover her hair. He wanted to turn her face to his, to kiss the wide shapely mouth. "I think I had better be off," he said, "I've taken up too much of your valuable time. But I'm going to your Army Headquarters tomorrow and I wanted to see you before I left."

She flashed him a look of utter disbelief.

"Tomorrow? You're going to Baranovichi tomorrow?"

"Yes, that's why I'm in Russia, to join——"

"Colonel Kirby, that is ridiculous," she said. "It means you have come just to say goodbye again. You're always saying goodbye. Why, all you've done is give us thirty minutes of your time after nearly two years. That is a most ungenerous way of keeping a promise."

"Olga, I only arrived yesterday afternoon."

"All the same," said Olga. But she could not let her disappointment spoil the brief reunion. She smiled, she said, "Never mind, at least you're in Russia again and not terribly far away. Am I to remember you to Mama? And shall I tell her," she added with the demureness that cloaked her humorous asides, "that perhaps in another two years you'll call on us again?"

"Give the Empress my felicitations and tell her that if I may I hope to call as often as I can," he said.

"Oh, yes, quite as often as you can," she whispered. "It has seemed so long, you cannot imagine."

She rose. He stood up. He picked up his cap and greatcoat. He looked at her. Her lashes fell.

"Dear Olga," he said. It was the closest to an endearment he had ever permitted himself. It brought the pinkness to her face. "Olga, you are the Emperor's eldest daughter and Russia's brightest hope. Whatever happens, remember that you and all your family are very much loved by very many people."

"Colonel Kirby," she said faintly and was in desperate search for words again.

"You'll be late," he said gently, "I had better go."

She found some words.

"Please don't try to be a hero, wherever they send you," she said, "there are so many heroes and all of them dead."

"At Army Headquarters," he said, "it's not possible to be a hero."

When he had gone Olga stared blankly at the white door. She was late but she had to take another minute to compose herself before returning to her ward. She was at her most compassionate for the rest of the day and the wounded men thought her blue eyes amazingly beautiful. The Emperor's eldest daughter had no idea of her capacity for making people love her.

Later that day Kirby managed to offend Karita. She was to be sent home to her parents in the Crimea? Much as she loved them, she was not! How dare he try to get rid of her!

"I won't go," she said fiercely.

"I'll explain again," said Kirby. They were in his

331

hotel room. Karita had a room on an upper floor. "Tomorrow I'm off to Headquarters to join other British officers there. I can't take you, my sweet. And you can't stay in Petrograd alone. Therefore, little one, you shall have a train ticket home——"

"Therefore, I will not," she said.

"——and I'll come and put you on the train before I leave myself. When the war is over——"

"The war has nothing to do with it," said Karita.

"Ah," he murmured, "have we another Grand Duchess here?"

"Monsieur," she said primly to command his serious attention. As she hadn't called him that for years he knew a fine old argument was in the offing. "Monsieur, it's not at all proper for you to go to any headquarters in Russia without a servant. It might be proper in England, which I don't think it is, but it isn't in Russia."

"You minx," he said, "you got that from Aunt Charlotte."

Karita put her nose in the air.

"In Russia," she said, "officers always take servants with them. How would they manage otherwise? How will you manage? Who will see that you have clean shirts and socks? It would be humiliating if you had no servant. They would think you were nobody. What would Aunt Charlotte say to that?"

"I think you know."

"She would be most upset. She would not try to put me on some old train, she would insist that I came with you. You need only telephone the War Minister and he would tell you it would be disgraceful not to have a servant with you. He would have to find one for you and it would probably be some fat old thing nobody else wanted."

"Fat old things can be very comforting," said Kirby. "Fat old things don't argue."

"Who is arguing?" Suddenly Karita was very offended. "I have done something wrong? You wish to have another servant in my place?"

"Where would I get one like you?" he said. "You're

332

not my servant, you're my responsibility. I just thought you might like to see your parents, that's all."

"I will go to Crimea when you go there," she said.

He remembered Prolofski and Karita's unconditional participation.

"Well, I only hope it won't be too martial for you at Headquarters," he said.

"I am to go with you, then?" she said happily.

"Either you or some fat old thing."

She laughed up at him. He kissed her. It surprised and confused her.

"Oh," she said, "I thought it was not supposed to be proper in Petrograd."

"It isn't," he said, "that was a kiss from your mother and father."

She tingled a little, but not because of her mother and father.

"I hope that when we get to Baranovichi you won't have too many generals telling you what to do," she said.

Kirby laughed. But Karita did not consider it funny. It never seemed right to her that there were men who could give him orders. She had remarked to Aunt Charlotte how disconcerting it was that Colonel Kirby was not a lord, after all.

"Good heavens, child," said Aunt Charlotte, "he would look hideous in ermine."

What that meant Karita had no idea.

"Sometimes," she said, "I don't know what to proffer to people."

"Proffer them the information that he's a mystery to himself," said Aunt Charlotte. "All this wandering about, I really can't understand him. I wish to goodness you'd marry him. That would settle him down very handsomely and heaven knows, he could not do better."

"Aunt Charlotte!" Karita was in rosy shock. "Oh, hush! Such an improper consideration. If he heard you he would pack me off undressed."

"Undressed?" Aunt Charlotte was in booming shock herself then.

"Yes, he would pack me off immediately, as I am."

Aunt Charlotte's bosom heaved with laughter. The girl was a treasure and so charmingly quaint.

Karita was quite right, as Kirby had known she was. Russian officers had servants where British officers had batmen. Karita was accepted at Baranovichi by the Russians and viewed with raised eyebrows by the British. Kirby shared a railway coach with three British officers and Karita was housed with other servants in a mansion half a mile away. Headquarters itself was contained in a cluster of railway coaches screened by a wood, and Karita came every day to see to things. Within a very short time she had the coach compartments looking impeccable and the other servants thoroughly organised. She was always the most personable and irresistible of young women. As soon as she was introduced to the other British officers, all majors, she realised Colonel Kirby was their superior. She felt very satisfied about that.

Kirby's natural gift for liaison work was immediately obvious. He not only got on well with the Russians but seemed to understand them. British and French officers had a cordial enough relationship with their Russian counterparts, but found it almost impossible to understand the Russian character. The conviviality of the ebullient officer class was always in advance of their aptitude for being frank, so that one could get no real idea of how well or how critically a new battle was going, how a situation was developing.

A French officer whimsically observed to Kirby that he understood nothing at all about the Russians except that, frustrating as they were, it was impossible to dislike them.

"Is that what you really think?" asked Kirby.

"What I really think, mon ami, is that they turn their backs on all the bad news and that the worse the news is the more they smile."

"Then why despair? You're halfway to understanding them. When there's a crisis they clap you on the

334

shoulder and tell you not to worry. That's to let you know the sun sets and the moon rises, and you can no more change that than they can."

"But that is God's will. A battle is conceived, fought and governed by men."

"That's what you believe, my friend," said Kirby.

The one person who did not indulge in smiling ambiguity was the Grand Duke Nicholas Nicolaievich. Nor did he permit this in members of his immediate staff. He was not in a position, however, to forbid the Tsar to smile.

Nicholas did not let his concern over the progress of the war spoil his satisfaction in being at *Stavka*, as the Field Headquarters were called. The location was not far from the railway line connecting Moscow with Warsaw. Nicholas was happy to be at the centre of things. He did not interfere with the Grand Duke's authority in any way and was always in unaffected pleasure whenever the Commander-in-Chief consulted with him or engaged him in discussion.

Discovering that Kirby was among British observers present, he did not ask for the Englishman to be brought to him. He sought him out. He found him outside his coach talking to a Russian officer. They both saluted. Nicholas, his uniform plain and with decorations, returned the salutes. Then he took Kirby's hand and shook it vigorously.

"My dear fellow, this is extraordinarily nice," he said. "Well, who would have thought it? You will be a general yet. Are you comfortable? Have they given you suitable accommodation? I'm afraid we're not all that grand here."

"Everything is excellent, Your Highness," said Kirby. "May I express my own pleasure at seeing you again?"

"Ah, but it's not quite the same as meeting on a tennis court," said Nicholas. "What do you think of things?"

They strolled around the cold encampment and discussed the war. Kirby found that the Tsar's appreciation of the general situation was intelligent and keen, though his optimism was as obstinate as ever. Yet as always he felt it impossible not to have a warm, human liking for him.

Kirby and other Allied officers sensed the ammunition problem was already critical. But to speak of it to Russian officers was to invite the inevitable response that cheerfully led nowhere.

"Where did you hear that, old man? It's nothing to worry about. How is the bewitching Karita? Absolutely damned splendid girl you have there, Colonel."

Kirby was kept busy on translation work involving decoding.

It was when the early spring was softening the ground and turning frost into mud that one day the Grand Duke paid a visit to the divisional headquarters of a forward unit. Kirby, with another British officer and two French colonels, accompanied the Commander-in-Chief and his staff. They travelled in a galaxy of powerful staff cars, and it took them two hours to reach the division. They passed through various reserve camps on the way, the Grand Duke's car rushing through to the sound of cheers.

Not far from the divisional headquarters the Russians were solidly entrenched on their Polish soil, where their front ran for hundreds of miles. On this particular day the division had been under a bombardment that seemed erratic, the German guns switching from one sector to another. The limited Russian reply was symptomatic of their apparently incurable shell shortage.

As the Grand Duke's motorised cavalcade approached the divisional headquarters the distant bombardment increased, and the German cannonade intensified to a constant, rumbling roar. The house stood back about two hundred yards from the road. Kirby felt that the war had suddenly become very close, the noise of the guns impossible to shut out. There was activity inside and outside the house, the place full of guards, full of officers and men coming and going. The Grand Duke and his staff strode quickly up the steps, sentries sprang aside and presented rifles in

336

salute. Kirby stayed on the steps, and a Russian cavalry major, his boots grey with drying mud and his head bare, came out. He had a glass of wine in his hand. He looked at Kirby's British uniform with interest.

"The old man has come a bit close to things today, hasn't he?" he said.

"It was his own idea," said Kirby, "it sounds uncomfortably noisy here to me."

The Major, liking this frankness and the faultless Russian, grinned. He was square and rugged of face, thickset and powerful of body.

"Boris Gregorovich Kolchak, Fifth Ukrainian Cavalry," he said, introducing himself.

"John Kirby, British liaison."

Major Kolchak, looking not unlike a friendly bear, watched the road. More artillery appeared, riders lashing at the straining horses.

"That will make just about two hundred guns on this sector," he said, "outnumbering the shells by two to one."

Above the rumbling thunder Kirby said, "Is this normal or is there an offensive today?"

"Yes, it's noisy, isn't it?" said Major Kolchak. "But they're always at it, Colonel. The trouble with the Germans is that they can't fight a friendly war. Unless they're creating a little bit of hell for someone somewhere they're not enjoying themselves." A despatch rider driving a motocycle combination roared up the long drive and Major Kolchak waited for the engine to be cut before going on. "I don't know why they're raising hell today. They can't be thinking of making a move. With this thaw the whole country is like a bog."

"Perhaps it's a demonstration," said Kirby.

"Demonstration?"

"To acknowledge the visit of the Grand Duke."

Major Kolchak grinned again. "Come inside," he said, "it's just as noisy but at least you can have a drink."

Coincidentally, the guns stopped then and amid a

bleak silence they went into the stone-built mansion. In a large room full of tables, maps and men, the Grand Duke was making himself heard in an altercatory discussion with the divisional commander. It seemed that contact between headquarters and some forward sectors was dangerously tenuous and the Grand Duke was insisting on remedial action. Major Kolchak glanced at Kirby and shrugged as if to indicate confusion was a state familiar to division. He drew Kirby into another room, where a few officers were taking a cold lunch standing up. Kirby helped himself to a slice of cooked meat and some bread, leaving the more exotic food alone. Major Kolchak poured some wine. It seemed that the Major was in command of a cavalry troop bivouacked a mile away. He had been summoned to headquarters and told to wait for orders. He had been waiting two hours.

Outside the mess the corridor was suddenly alive with booted feet hurrying. The Grand Duke and his staff, after half-an-hour at headquarters, were on their brisk way out. Rooms began to spill men and papers.

"Orlovsky!" Major Kolchak, sighting a divisional staff officer, shouted at him down the corridor. "Orlovsky, my orders!"

"Damn your orders," the officer shouted back, "we're over-run. You'll have to pull back."

Major Kolchak swore.

"I think I'd better go," said Kirby.

"Russia," said the Major, "breeds more incompetents and lunatics than a bear breeds fleas. We'd all better go."

What had been a place of activity, overlaid with a hint of civilised anxiety—"Nothing to worry about, Your Highness, nothing at all,"—became metamorphosised into a bedlam of rushing panic. When they reached the top of the steps outside, with headquarters disgorging men in all directions, the Grand Duke, ramrod in his grimness, was already being driven away, his motorcar belching through the gates and on to the road. His staff were following in other cars. The foreign

338

liaison officers, two French and one British, were in the last car, waiting for Kirby. They beckoned him impatiently.

"D'you want to come with us?" Kirby felt he had to ask the hospitable and likeable Major.

"In that?" Major Kolchak raised a contemptuous grin at the car. "I've still got a horse somewhere. He's a brute but a reliable one."

The guns began again, opening up in a frightening roar of sound.

"God, they've burst through us!" Major Kolchak was in anger and despair.

A shell dropped a hundred yards away, and exploded crumpingly in soft ground.

"Come on!" roared the British officer to Kirby. Kirby hesitated, but Major Kolchak had gone to the open doors of the house and was bawling for a Captain Brusilov.

Kirby went down the steps two at a time to the drive. The guns seemed on top of headquarters, the cannonading roar an outrage to the ear. Another shell struck, hitting the roof of the mansion with a tremendous crack, and slate and stone rained down. Kirby, about to take his place in the car, already moving slowly forward, turned at the thunderclap and saw Major Kolchak at the moment when a slate struck his right shoulder. His knees buckled and he dropped. Kirby sprinted back up the steps, reaching the Major as he made to rise.

"That damned Brusilov," he said. He put a hand to his shoulder. He winced as Kirby helped him to his feet, his rugged face a little white. A cavalry captain appeared, spilling from the doorway in company with shoving men carrying divisional records of every kind. "You dallying idiot," shouted the Major, "get my horse!"

"Hold it!" shouted Kirby. He came down the steps, forcibly pulling Major Kolchak with him. The car was forty yards away. Before they reached the last step a shell smashed like the glowing iron fist of Mars into the bonnet of the moving car. The whole thing blew up, erupting into a blazing inferno of mutilated men and jagged metal. Kirby was hurled sideways over the steps, the Major with him. He found himself spreadeagled partly over the drive, his head and shoulders buried in the stiff wet grass of the verge. His breath whistled from squeezed lungs. He lifted his head and saw the fiery wreckage of the car.

"Oh, my God," he gasped.

Men were running in all directions. Horses were shrill with alarm, jerking at their tethers. He heard a groan. The Major came slowly to his knees, his injured arm dangling, his face whiter. Horses clattered. Captain Brusilov had returned. He rode one horse, led another. The Major grunted painfully and said painfully, "You'd better find one for yourself, Colonel." Kirby got to his feet, helped the Major into his saddle with the assistance of Captain Brusilov, and then ran to take the Major's advice.

The road was alive with retreating Russians, cavalry going pell-mell and cursing the advent of artillerymen riding sweating horses pulling salvaged guns. There was a thumping in Kirby's head that was familiar and made worse by the scream and crump of shells. His horse was a pounding, bony beast that carried him through the turmoil of retreat with the enthusiasm of an animal only at its best in a riot. Major Kolchak, riding with one arm useless, kept bawling questions at cavalrymen and the grey-faced men bawled hopeless answers back at him.

The road was becoming clogged, the gun carriages a lumbering impedimenta. The German guns were ranging, they had the road and its immediate environs under fire. They appeared to have divisional headquarters pinpointed now. Kirby heard explosions rocking chimneys, buttresses and roofs.

"Ride over the fields," said Kirby, "you're in no condition to charge through this little hell."

"Damnation," said the Major, but turned his horse. There was a whine, a sense of catastrophe and a

340

vomiting belch of gravel and stone as a shell struck the road itself. It took the legs from horses, smashed men into eternity by blast or shrapnel, and a gun carriage danced, lifted and crashed. The blast itself reached far enough to engulf Kirby and the Major with rushing heat that almost sucked them from their saddles. Kolchak groaned. A man staggered up from a kicking, dying horse. It was Brusilov. The next salvo whistled, earth on either side of the road was torn from its bed and hurled in mighty clods. Kolchak swayed in his saddle and blood dripped from the sleeve of his jacket. He began to fall sideways. Kirby flung himself from his saddle and caught the Russian as he limply fell. Men and horses were flying from the road, galloping in all directions to escape the salvoes.

This is hell right enough, thought Kirby, and one I wasn't born for. He dragged Major Kolchak away from the road. Something thudded into his right arm at the same time as he felt the numbing shock of white-hot shrapnel smashing into his left leg above the knee. He was flung violently downwards over the collapsing body of Major Kolchak. The thumping ceased and he lay still amid the uproar of German guns pounding retreating Russians.

THREE

Olga sat in the room she shared with Tatiana at the Alexander Palace of Tsarskoe Selo. It was bright today, even if cold. The snow had gone and the sun was doing its best to bring life to long-frozen green. It had been a bad time at the hospital for two days. The Germans had almost broken through in Poland, it was said. But Grand Duke Nicholas Nicolaievich had stopped them, thrown them back.

Today had been frenzied, so many casualties again. She had worked without stopping until four o'clock, and then they had insisted that she take a rest. She would go back for a while this evening.

She longed for peace, for the world to be sane again. Livadia was an impossible dream away now. How remote was its sunshine, its flowers, its gardens, its happiness. How far away was the pleasure of seeing Papa playing tennis with Colonel Kirby.

He might have written. Only to Alexis, of course. But he hadn't. Mama would not mind a bit how much he wrote to Alexis. He had said he would come to see them when he was on leave. Oh, he had better.

"Olga?" It was Tatiana in her hospital uniform. She sounded a little tentative.

"Tasha, have they sent you to take a rest too?"

"Olga, perhaps you should come," said Tatiana.

"Now?" Olga looked up at her sister. Tatiana tried to smile. It was so unlike her to make hard work of a smile. "Tasha?" Olga rose, gripped by intuitive fear. "What has happened?"

"It's Colonel Kirby. Olga, he's rather bad, but perhaps not dreadfully bad—oh, I thought you'd want to know and to come, but don't tell Mama I came for you, she would think it too pointed."

Olga snatched up her headdress. She said nothing, but she was pale and her fingers made fumbling work of the simple task of fixing it.

Then, as she went with Tatiana, she said, "Is he going to die, Tatiana? Is he going to be a hero?"

"Don't be so dramatic," said Tatiana matter-of-factly, "that isn't like you at all, that's silly."

They had brought him off the hospital train two days after he and Major Kolchak had been carried to the nearest base in a waggon. Nicholas himself had sent a message saying that whatever the best was, he would like Colonel Kirby to have it. Alexandra had received the message, dashed off in a hurry by Nicholas. Because the Tsar himself had interceded, the hospital staff did their initial best in respect of a bed. The Catherine Palace was overflowing, every ward crowded, so they took Kirby to an upper room that was the smallest in the vast place. It was a room used for storing truckle beds and the beds had been re-stacked and space found to accommodate the patient.

Alexandra had been appalled by his condition, his greatcoat dirty and muddy, thrown around him and buttoned to keep it on. Beneath this his uniform was just as dirty, and it was ripped and slashed where field medicos had attended to a smashed right arm and a badly wounded leg. Dried black blood caked his khaki, the field bandages solid with it. His forehead was bruised and he was unconscious, his pulse erratic. It was while Alexandra was taking his pulse rate that the shocked Tatiana slipped away.

She came back accompanied by Olga, by which time Colonel Kirby had been stripped. He lay on top of the blanketed bed, a sheet and other blankets over him. A doctor was examining his right arm. Olga, seeing the

343

extent of the wound, the gashed flesh, the seeping blood, paled to stricken white.

"Oh, Mama," she gasped.

"What are you doing here?" Alexandra spoke kindly enough but was a little disapproving.

"I couldn't rest with so much to do," said Olga, blue eyes frozen as she stared at the stillness of the Englishman. "I came back, I heard about Colonel Kirby— Mama, it's only his arm, isn't it? He's not really as bad as he looks, is he?"

"His leg has been hit too," said Alexandra, "but Dr. Bajorsky will see to him. You had better go to your ward, my love."

"Mama, please——"

"Hush now," whispered Alexandra, concerned at Olga's distress in the presence of the doctor and a nurse. The nurse, at a nod from the doctor, gently pulled aside the coverings to reveal the injured leg. Olga turned to ice. She had seen many wounds, many victims of bullet and shrapnel, and she knew the consequences of some wounds. Colonel Kirby's shattered arm was bad enough, his leg was dreadful. The flesh from the knee upwards was an angry, swollen blue, the wound itself was of torn and contused muscle and sinew, and how the bone itself was affected she dared not think. Dr. Bajorsky examined the leg as he had examined a thousand others, with the knowledge of his profession and the experience of concentrated months in this hospital. Experience of this kind was often a greater decider than knowledge.

Kirby's stillness was a help to the examination. He remained deeply unconscious. Dr. Bajorsky straightened up. Young less than half a year ago, he was old-looking now. He turned to the Empress.

"Your Highness," he said, "even giving him the very best help we can, his leg will have to come off, but with luck we can save his arm."

Tatiana stifled a cry, Olga trembled.

"God is with him and with you, Dr. Bajorsky," said Alexandra quietly, crossing herself.

344

"No," said Olga wildly.

"Olga!" Alexandra was inexpressibly shocked.

"God is always with us, I know that," said Olga, "but if his leg is amputated Colonel Kirby will die. Mama, you have only to look at him."

"He will die if it isn't amputated," said Dr. Bajorsky. "You will excuse me, Your Highness? I will make the theatre arrangements."

He left the room. Olga hesitated, then followed him.

"She's very distressed," said Alexandra, "but we can only put our trust in God."

"Yes, Mama," said Tatiana palely, "but I am distressed too."

Olga caught up with Dr. Bajorsky.

"Dr. Bajorsky, I beg you," she implored. "I know why you're going to take his leg off. It's because there are hundreds of other cases just as bad and you and the other doctors are so desperately pressed. It's easier to take off a man's leg than spend hours trying to piece the bone together. Amputation is swifter, isn't it?"

"Nurse," he said, for this was what the Grand Duchesses insisted on being called in the hospital, "the Emperor himself has asked us to do all we can, and we will. However pressed we are, do you think I'd allow myself to be governed by expediency and not by compassion? You do me an injustice."

"Truly, I don't mean to," said Olga desperately. "You've worked harder than anyone else here and done so much for so many, and you're terribly tired. But Colonel Kirby deserves more than compassion even. He's an Englishman and we can't let Russia take his leg off when he's given us so much of himself, he's been the truest friend Russia could have. He'd give his life for us. He *will* give his life for us if you amputate, because if you do he'll die, I know he will."

He was moved by her desperation, but he shook his head tiredly.

"He may die either way," he said, "for an operation such as you suggest will take many hours. In his condition would he survive that?"

"Yes, he would, he would survive the longest hours but not an amputation." Olga did not know if she really believed this, she spoke more in faith and hope than professional conviction. She begged and pleaded, detaining him in the corridor, and finally she said, "Dr. Bajorsky, try, oh please try. We will all be eternally grateful—oh, that must be what hundreds have said to you about other men, but give Colonel Kirby time, your time. Save his leg, God will do the rest. It will exhaust you, I know, but Dr. Bajorsky, dear Dr. Bajorsky, please?"

He had never realised just how lovely this Grand Duchess was, how earnest and urgent with faith she could be, how striking her intensely blue eyes were.

"You're asking the impossible," he said, "but when we get him into the theatre we'll have a longer look at the impossible. I can promise nothing beyond that."

"You will try, I know you will," she said.

"I will see, I cannot promise," he said. He smiled to give her some hope as he went on his way.

Olga returned to the room. It looked uncomfortable and depressing with its stacked bed frames and other stores. The nurse had applied temporary new dressings and enclosed Kirby in blankets. He lay very still, his breathing quiet. Alexandra had gone but Tatiana was there, sitting by the bed. She looked strained. Her day had been quite full enough without this. The nurse, carrying a bucket full of stained, dirty bandages, left the room.

Olga looked down at him, at his thick, tousled hair, his bruised forehead, his closed eyes. The nurse had cleaned his face, only the bruise discolored his features.

"Tasha, I told him," whispered Olga, "I told him not to be a hero."

"Men don't always listen to women," said Tatiana.

"Oh, Colonel Kirby," said Olga, "how very very silly you are."

His lids flickered, he opened his eyes. He saw her. The train was moving, the window dancing with light,

346

the sun was in her eyes and her hair was a bright cloud.

"Nikolayev," he said as if his mouth was full of cotton wool. But she heard him.

"Colonel Kirby," she whispered, "oh, how badly you have let us down."

He frowned, trying to understand why everything was so curious. The shining cloud of bright hair became a whiteness flowing around her head, her face, her shoulders. She was all whiteness. Then he remembered. It came quite clearly from out of the fog.

"I told you we manage to get ourselves deplorably knocked about," he said.

Tatiana put a hand to her mouth. Olga smiled brightly, brilliantly through wet eyes.

A spasm of pain came. He closed his eyes and slipped away again. Olga stood there, silently imploring him not to leave them.

"Olga," said Tatiana, swallowing, "if he loses his leg how shall we bear it? How will he ever play tennis with Papa again?"

"I'll sit with him," said Olga in a tense voice, "you go and rest, darling."

The moment belonged more to Olga than any of them. Tatiana rose, clung to her sister for a second and then went. Olga looked around the room. That they could have brought him to so depressing a place. It was a room for dying in, not living. She leaned over him. Lightly and hesitantly she touched his hair, smoothed its disorder.

She remembered Livadia, his health, his strength, his smile that always seemed so much for her. She remembered the feeling of ecstatic freedom when she had gone with him to Yalta, how he had taken such good care of her. She bent lower and touched his face with her fingertips. Then, in a breathlessly soft caress as fleeting as her shyest smile, Grand Duchess Olga Nicolaievna brushed his mouth with her lips.

"I love you, I love you."

He too dreamt of Livadia.

347

They took him into the theatre an hour later.

He was still there when the evening became cold and dark. A message came for Olga. It was from her mother. She was to return to the Alexander Palace immediately. For the first time in her life Olga wanted to disobey her mother. She wanted desperately to wait until it was all over, when they would be able to tell her what chances he was left with.

She returned to the Alexander Palace, she could not disobey the command. She did not think she could even close her eyes that night, let alone sleep. But she did sleep. She was in a fever at breakfast, wanting to know why no one had telephoned from the Catherine Palace. The chatter of the others was subdued, everyone knew that Ivan Ivanovich was very bad. Even so, it strained at her nerves. But she could not go to the hospital in advance of her mother and Tatiana. To wait and to look composed, to hide her tense anxiety, was an ordeal.

As usual, the three of them went together in the end. The warm spring sunshine was like a burst of bright hope. Tatiana said that she wondered how Ivan was. Alexandra said nothing about him until they reached the Catherine Palace.

"Olga," she said then, "we must find out how Colonel Kirby is this morning. While I see the doctors perhaps you'd go up to him.

"Yes, Mama," said Olga. She wanted to fly up the stairs but walked them. At the door of the room she tried to let her pounding heart slow down before entering. She went in. All the lumber had been removed, the curtains were opened wide and the sunshine beamed. The room was bright and clean. Colonel Kirby lay in his bed. The nurse sat by his side. She smiled at Olga.

"He hasn't wakened yet," she said, "he was in the theatre for such a long time."

But he was still alive. Olga wanted to ask questions but could not. Her throat was dry, tight.

"It's amazing," said Nurse Nicola Bayovna, "they thought he might lose his arm and his leg, but he still has both."

Oh, how wonderful. Dear dear Dr. Bajorsky.

He came in then. He was tireder, blue shadows ringing his eyes in his thin face. He managed a smile.

"Well, we gave him all the time we could," he said, "and he has survived so far."

"God is good to us always," said Olga, "and sometimes very good. Is he going to be all right?"

"That I don't know yet," said Dr. Bajorsky, going to the bedside. "It's impossible to put either his leg or his arm in plaster yet, the wounds are so bad. We've had to strap him, it's going to be very uncomfortable and unpleasant for him, and not very easy for the nurses." He lifted the coverings and Olga saw the bulkiness of heavy bandaging, the straps that bound the right arm to the body and long splints to his leg. He wore hospital pyjamas, the left leg of which had been cut away. She saw that the bandages ran thickly from his knee to his thigh.

But she was happier now. It did not matter what Dr. Bajorsky thought. She knew that Colonel Kirby was going to recover. She knew.

"You're a wonderful man, Dr. Bajorsky," she said in gratitude.

"Exhausted is the word," he said.

"Yes. But thank you."

"Yours was the faith," he said, "and we'll see, we'll see." He did not seem dissatisfied. He looked at the temperature chart, his lids heavy. He glanced at Nurse Bayovna. "Remember," he said, "he is not to move or have his dressings touched until I say so."

"Yes, I understand, Doctor," said Nurse Bayovna.

"Good, he'll be safe with you," he said and with a smile for Olga he left. He had had only ten hours rest in three days.

Olga did not want to leave herself. But the duty here belonged to Nurse Bayovna. She had her own duties elsewhere. She turned as her mother came in.

349

Alexandra had found out that there had been no amputation, after all, and she did not know whether to be in concern or relief.

"Mama, he's better already," said Olga, seeing Colonel Kirby's face turned peacefully into the pillow.

"Olga, how can you know that?" Alexandra looked austere in her white uniform and although she was always kind, the nurses were often in a little awe of her. Nurse Bayovna effaced herself a little.

"Oh, I'm sure he is," said Olga. "Mama, I will nurse him——"

"No, darling," said Alexandra firmly, "you can't. How would it look if you devoted all your time to one man alone?"

"But he's our friend."

"Olga, we aren't here to only nurse our friends."

"I'll share the nursing then." Olga tried to speak casually but could not disguise nervous appeal. "Speak to Dr. Bajorsky, Mama. Just for a few hours a day. Papa would say we owe it to him, wouldn't he?"

"Oh, lamb, you'll make it so hard for yourself in the end," whispered Alexandra. But she could not deny Olga completely. Her heritage would deny her so much as it was.

So Olga shared the duties with Nurse Bayovna. But it was Nurse Bayovna who was present when at last the patient opened his eyes. He regarded her dreamily, wonderingly.

"You weren't here before," he said faintly. Nicola Bayovna understood. Patients were peculiar in the way they conceived an immediate affection for certain nurses. She had had a hundred wounded men fall temporarily in love with her. This one had chosen the Grand Duchess Olga Nicolaievna as the object of his affections. How ambitious.

Nurse Bayovna smiled and said, "Someone else will not be long."

She sent for Dr. Bajorsky. He came as soon as he could. He and his patient regarded each other. Dr. Bajorsky looked whimsical, Kirby as if the business

350

of being awake was only for the contemplation of more sleep.

"Ump," said Dr. Bajorsky. He listened to Kirby's heartbeats, looked into his pupils and moved the big toe of his left leg. "Ump," he said again. He ignored the swathed arm and leg. "If he stays awake," he said to Nurse Bayovna, "he can have some soup. If he doesn't stay awake it doesn't matter, sleep is more important than food at the moment."

When he had gone Nurse Bayovna, a strong, vigorous-bodied young woman with a gift for remaining calm when others could not, sent a message to Olga. Olga came flying, bursting into the room with a rush.

"He's been looking at me as if I don't belong here," said Nicola, "so if you can stay a few moments I'll see if I can fetch him some soup. Dr. Barjorsky has seen him and said he might have some."

As she left on her errand, Olga could hardly contain her desire to run to the bedside. But she approached without any apparent haste. His sleepy eyes looked wonderingly up at her.

"Colonel Kirby, you're awake," she said. It was very trite, very obvious, but it was said gladly, happily.

"Am I?" he said. His voice was slurry. "Let me see you." He seemed in abstracted contemplation of a stranger. "How odd," he said, seeing blue eyes when Nurse Bayovna's had been green.

Olga felt sudden panic. If he were to go into delirium. But there was no flush, no perspiration.

"Nicola Bayovna has gone to find you some soup," she said as calmly as she could.

He closed his eyes. He opened them again. He smiled. She wondered when the pain would return to him.

"Good," he said dreamily.

The panic went, beautiful relief flooded her.

"Oh, you're better, I know you are," she said. "Don't you dare be anything else after Dr. Bajorsky has done so much for you. Do you hear me?"

"I hear you, Olga Nicolaievna," he said.

He went to sleep again. He would not want the soup now. But what did that matter? She sat down by the bedside and waited happily for Nurse Bayovna to return.

There were complications but none so serious that Dr. Bajorsky could not deal with them. And when visitors were allowed Karita came to see the patient. She had returned to Petrograd from Baranovichi and had found a small apartment for herself.

Paul Kateroff, a handsome student, accompanied her to Tsarskoe Selo. He was twenty-two and had been a student for many years. He did not want to be anything else until Russia had been turned upside-down and made a fit place for a worker. His lank, black hair fell carelessly over his forehead, his eyes held the bright, burning light of the zealot. He refused to enter the Catherine Palace, saying he would wait outside until Karita had finished her visit.

"I'll not put one foot inside such a place," he said, "it's a marble symbol of a libertine and an oppressor. I'll only enter it when good Russians have cleansed it."

"How anyone so nice can be so silly, I don't know," said Karita. Paul lived in an apartment above hers, sharing it with other impecunious students, with whom he talked and argued far into every night. No wonder he looked so thin and pale. But it was a look that appealed to certain women, for when he emerged he looked like a poet who had spent the night starving in his garret. Karita thought he would be very attractive when he had grown up. She left him pacing in restless contemplation of Russia's problems. With help she found her way to the sick room. Her knock was answered by no less a person than Grand Duchess Olga, looking clinically efficient in her uniform. Olga smiled, Karita opened her eyes in surprise, then dipped in a curtsey as she entered. This seemed to startle Olga.

"Karita, what on earth are you doing?" she said.

"Your Highness———"

"Oh, no, you shouldn't curtsey or call me that here, Karita. I'm the same as all the other nurses."

Karita, who had no idea just how much Olga wanted to be like everyone else, thought the comment graciously modest but extremely inaccurate. Grand Duchess Olga Nicolaievna was herself. Nearly everyone else was very ordinary.

"You're his nurse?" said Karita in astonishment.

"Oh dear," smiled Olga, "do you think me too inadequate?"

"Goodness, no!" Karita blushed, then quickly found an avenue that pointed in a better direction. "Indeed, I only think Colonel Kirby very fortunate, I'm sure he could never have anyone nicer or more adequate than you to look after him."

"What's all that muttering?" It was a masculine voice. Karita peeped and there was Colonel Kirby, head and shoulders comfortably propped on heaped pillows. But he looked very drawn.

"He's better than he looks, you know," said Olga, observing Karita's concern. "One can tell he is, he's grumbling all the time now."

"Only about Nurse Bayovna's hot broth," said Kirby.

"There, go and talk to him," Olga said to Karita. Karita thought her surprisingly cool and professional, and yet there was something about her as if she were singing inside. She supposed the Grand Duchess very much enjoyed being a nurse.

"Well?" Kirby said. His stitched wounds had knitted, the torturing discomfort of strapped and anchored limbs eased by the application at last of plaster. The remorseless pain of splintered bone skillfully joined by Dr. Bajorsky had finally retreated. There had been many days of pain and Kirby knew there must have been times when he was neither a pretty nor an admirable patient.

"Well indeed," said Karita, seating herself on the bedside chair, "you're a fine one."

"Do you think so?" he said modestly. She smiled. There was a look in his eyes. She was not sure what it

353

meant. Perhaps it was to say he expected more from her than that kind of greeting. So she leaned forward and kissed him. Olga stiffened and turned abruptly away. "That, I suppose," said Kirby, "was for your mother and father?"

"It was from Aunt Charlotte," said Karita and Olga relaxed. "There's a letter from her, it's very old, it was given to me by one of your officers at Baranovichi and is addressed to both of us, see? Her English is very funny. I'll leave it for you, she says the ducks are still very noisy at times." She put the letter on the locker.

"Her Highness will read it to me," he said.

Karita whispered to him, "It seems very improper to have Her Highness nurse you when you're not even a lord."

"Don't tell Her Highness that," said Kirby.

"Don't tell me what?" said Olga from the window.

"It's nothing," said Karita hastily. She rushed on to speak of her apartment, the friends she had made and how Paul Kateroff was being extremely attentive and kind. Kirby asked who Paul Kateroff was and Karita replied that he was a student and that she was helping him to grow up. Olga laughed. Karita had always been deliciously quaint. Colonel Kirby was smiling and Olga thought how good it was to see his smile. Karita was a very refreshing person. How attractive she had become, with a flair for styles that suited her.

Karita said that she was working in a hospital herself.

"Well, I never," said Kirby.

"I must do something while you're in here," said Karita. "I work in the kitchens. The hospital food isn't very good, but there's the war, you see. It's better than twiddling my thumbs, isn't it?"

"Much better," said Olga.

"Much," said Kirby.

Karita, however, wished him to know that she hadn't left the Crimea to work in hospital kitchens for the rest of her life. She did not mind doing this for a while because of the war, she said, but he was to understand that she desired to resume her proper position with him

354

as soon as he was better. Kirby assured her that she could not desire this more than he did himself.

This was not her first visit since he had been out of danger, but they would not let him receive visitors until he was out of his sweating pain. It was a great relief now to see that he was obviously going to be quite well again eventually. But not until her visit came to its end did she let him know she was not exactly pleased with him.

"Ivan Ivanovich," she said, "I hope you aren't going to make this sort of thing too much of a habit."

"It only happens when I get on a horse," said Kirby.

"You should be more careful, you should think of others," said Karita, "it's distressing for people."

When she had gone the room, lacking her refreshing brightness, seemed obtrusively quiet. Olga was so silent as she busied herself with little activities.

"Olga?" he said, sensing she was quiet for a reason that had nothing to do with her work.

"I am busy," she said in a suppressed voice, keeping her back to him.

"Are you tired? I haven't been easy for you and Nurse Bayovna, have I?"

She swung around at that.

"I'm not tired and you've been no trouble at all, you aren't even to think such a thing. Only——" She stopped. There were so many words but always she had to search so carefully for the right ones. "Only Karita was telling you the truth," she said, "you should not be so careless, you should think of how others will feel if anything happens to you."

"Sometimes it's not carelessness, it's circumstances," he said.

"There, you see, that is it," said Olga, "because of the war and because of the circumstances, you should be very careful. Oh, it's nothing to smile about——"

"No, of course not," said Kirby, "I was only thinking how pleasant it was to be alive and to listen to Olga Nicolaievna being a Grand Duchess."

"Colonel Kirby, I shall get Nurse Bayovna to talk to you," she said.

"Oh, lord," he said. Nurse Bayovna did not suffer nonsense from any patient.

Olga smiled.

He would not be able to get up and go away and be careless again for a long time yet.

She felt happy about that.

Kirby had another visitor a week later. Andrei came to see him. He was in the uniform of a major. It was exquisitely tailored, it adorned him rather than clothed him. Kirby congratulated him. Andrei begged him not to mention it. The uniform made him shudder, he said, each time he put it on. But a man not in uniform these days had little appeal for ladies and none at all in the eyes of impressionable maidens. And one got into exhausting arguments with patriots. Patriots were frightfully aggressive people. But he hadn't come to bore Ivan with his own problems.

"No, my dear man," he said, "I was distraught to hear you'd been cut to pieces in some barbaric skirmish and I had to see if the surgeons had cut you to more pieces or put you together. How delightful to see that your head is still where it should be."

"My remnants are knitting together nicely, thank you," said Kirby, while Nurse Nicola Bayovna eyed Andrei's tailored languidity quite hungrily. "How is the Princess?"

"Aleka Petrovna," sighed Andrei, "is currently revelling in her natural role as the most beautiful bitch in St. Petersburg. Or is it Petrograd now? I forget from time to time. You're to blame, dear friend. She was only inclined to be enjoyably exhausting before. Now she's like the kiss of death. The merest word out of place and she'll destroy the most decent chap by ridicule. Fortunately, I'm able to turn a deaf ear. That is my only real talent, you know. It was extraordinarily obtuse of you not to have married her. I'm sure it gnaws at her. She'll claim a pretty revenge one day."

356

"Aleka and I are the best of friends," said Kirby. He stretched, rested his head and shoulders comfortably on the heaped pillows and assumed, it seemed, an attitude of complacency. Andrei raised an unconvinced eyebrow.

"Ah, my dear Ivan, this is your story," he said. "But has she been to see you? No. Have you asked her to come? No. What is to be inferred from that?"

"That you've acquired another talent," said Kirby. "You're making speeches. What has happened to you? Are you taking iron tonics?"

"Please," said Andrei, "let us refrain from being gruesome. You forget, my brave brother-in-arms, you forget the hidden reserves any man must have to survive what I survive at the War Ministry. Paper, dear Ivan, mountains of it, positive avalanches day after day. And all of the most beautiful quality. I really don't know where they get the money to pay for it when there's none to be spared to buy rifles, or so I hear. General Sukhomlinov is a pretty villain, his wife a quite devouring hostess. There's a woman with the real kiss of death for a fellow, if you like. Shall I give Aleka Petrovna your love? Be generous, dear friend."

"Tell her I hold her in eternal gratitude."

"Heavens," murmured Andrei. He looked around the room. It was bright, the windows open to the warm air. There were flowers. He smiled lazily at Nurse Bayovna standing by the windows. She blushed. "If you appreciate her as much as that," he said, "do marry her. She needs to have her mind taken off other things. She has now decided the war is a sham. She'll find herself in Siberia yet."

"Andrei, old scout," said Kirby, "why don't you marry her? You're the only one able to turn a deaf ear to her kiss of death."

"Much as I adore her," said Andrei, "I'm already married. To peace and quiet. My angel," he said, raising his voice to reach the ear of Nurse Bayovna, shapely and full-bodied, "will you dine with me tonight?

I should be enchanted to discuss my appendix operation with you."

"How irresistible," said Nurse Bayovna, faint with rapture.

Karita was at a students' meeting. In a large room on the top floor of a house in the workers' district, the smoke from students' pipes was as thick as the packed bodies. Karita thought it uncomfortable and unhealthy, but knowing a little about students now she suspected an unsalubrious environment lent authority to their politics. They did not like comfort when they were agitating on behalf of the poor. They were all very earnest and none more so than Paul Kateroff. She had come with him because she thought it as well to find out the extent of his interests in her desire to help him become an adult. He was a nice boy.

Everyone wished to address the meeting, it seemed. There was such a noise as they all argued about who should be first.

"I can't hear a word," said Karita, rather wishing she was back in England and feeding the ducks by the landing stage. The war was terrible and everyone in Russia was at odds with everyone else again. The majority of students in Petrograd had long got over the initial flush of patriotic excitement.

"No one's speaking yet," said Paul, "we're debating order of precedence."

"I thought only aristocrats worried about that," said Karita sarcastically.

She was disgusted when the first speaker was allowed to address the smoke and the peering faces. He made no sense at all except, she thought, to show how ignorant he was. And how deplorable. He was capable only of a ranting, hysterical hymn of hate, of asking for the destruction of so many Russians that she wondered if there would be any left. She was sure the students would shout him down. But they didn't. The faces glimmering through the smoke shone with infected passion. There was a man standing against the wall to

358

one side of the speaker. His arms were folded, his head bent. He was certainly not a student himself. He looked like a workman dressed for church, his dark suit ordinary but neat, his boots clean. His eyes glittered with approval as he listened.

The second speaker was an echo of the first, except that he was hoarse whereas the first student had been shrill. He said much the same as the first as far as Karita could make out. Which was that Russia belonged to the people, that the aristocrats and bureaucrats should be exterminated, that the aristocrats were monstrous because of their inhuman cruelty and the people were despicable because of their abject cowardice. Monsters and cowards should all be exterminated, only in rivers of blood could Russia be cleansed. And the war must be stopped.

The applause was rapturous.

"How silly they all are." Karita murmured to Paul, "wishing to stop this war so that they can start one of their own, and against their own people."

"Hush," said Paul sternly.

The man in the neat, dark suit was next. He was introduced anonymously as Comrade Worker. Comrade Worker began in level, unranting tones which Karita appreciated. The shrill and the hoarse voices had made the room hotter. Comrade Worker seemed intent on cooling it down. He was articulate, intelligent and persuasive as he outlined reforms that would eliminate injustices. He tabulated injustices one after the other, using his fingers. But when he had the rapt attention of every student he became passionate, sweeping them along on a tide of words full of the hatred that Karita despised. Waves of saliva-flecked invective washed the smoke. Karita was horrified as she found herself listening to a spitting denunciation of the Romanovs. The enmity Comrade Worker felt towards them was terrifying and it was reflected on faces shiny with heat.

"Stop him," she gasped to Paul.

"Hush," he said again. He had spoken to her many

359

times about injustices, about the necessity of revolution, but Karita had heard the same things from others. She could listen when anyone spoke of injustices, but she could not listen to lies and she could not tolerate it when lies became calumny. Her brown eyes began to burn.

Suddenly Comrade Worker became quiet again, suddenly his voice was hissing sibilantly through his sweat.

"My young comrades," he said, "you are the intelligent youth of Russia, the future strength of Russia. But are you to have a future? Who has control of your destinies, your minds, your bodies, your hands, your tongues? Why, Nicholas the Bloody, Nicholas the Butcher. Who has the power to deny you bread? Nicholas the Autocrat. And who sows the rotten seeds of corruption in his Imperial guts, bloated with the blood of students and workers? Alexandra the German whore. Who'll succeed the butcher and the whore? Why, the pox-poisoned Tsarevich and the fat, bow-legged daughters as they eat off gold plates and learn to become bigger whores than their mother——"

"Liar! Filth!" Karita burst through wedged bodies, her eyes burning, her face white. "You," she shouted at Comrade Worker, "you are an obscenity! You speak of people you've never met, whose love for Russia would shame you if you could be shamed, which you can't. You know nothing of our Father Tsar, of his family, and your lies are as disgusting as you are! Am I to follow obscenity? What would you do for people but poison their minds and fill them with hatred? Give me truth and I'll listen to you, give me disgusting lies and I spit on you!" And in the white heat of her anger Karita did spit.

"Get her, stuff her mouth!" shrieked the student who had spoken first.

Karita was roughly jostled. She was appalled at the violence of the hatred she could sense and see. Paul shouldered his way through to her, his thin body brist-

360

ling. He thrust off a girl student attempting to grab Karita by the hair.

"Don't touch her, any of you," said Paul, putting his arm around Karita's shoulders. His expression was fierce, he flung back his lank hair. "She has her own opinions and has a right to express them. Otherwise, what is this freedom we all talk about? Is it the freedom only to listen to ourselves?"

"It's the freedom to do away with her kind!" shouted someone. "Are we to listen to her telling us we must love the Romanovs?"

"The right of free speech must not be denied to anyone," said Paul, having to shout himself in order to be heard. "If it is denied then we'll be no better off than we are now. Everyone must have that right, everyone."

"My young comrades." It was Comrade Worker trying to regain command of the meeting. "Listen to me, let me deal with her———"

"Yes, let them listen to more lies," said Karita loudly and clearly. "I would prefer to go."

She was too contemptuous to feel afraid. She turned her back on the speaker. Paul began to escort her to the door. They let her go. They were angry but they stood aside for her.

"We'll remember you, lover of Romanovs!" called the first speaker, his voice shriller.

When she was in the street with Paul she said, "Thank you, Paul, you were at least more grown-up than the rest of them. It's simply no good hating people."

"There are some individuals I can't help despising," said Paul, "but hatred, yes, that's the least commendable of all human emotions."

This part of Petrograd was grey and ugly. It had become so because of encroaching industry. Karita disliked it intensely. It made the Crimea seem like God's garden. She longed for Colonel Kirby to be out of hospital, for the war to be over so that she could return to the Crimea with him or go back to England with him. Her rightful place was in service with him, she did not feel ambitious beyond that. One day he would marry, have a wife and children, and then her role would be more satisfying than ever. She would have a whole family to look after.

"Paul," she said, "do you despise the Imperial family? Are they among those you resent?"

"I despise all autocrats, Karita," said Paul, "I reject all forms of autocracy, everything which denies fundamental human rights."

"We're all the children of our Tsar," said Karita. "I love the Tsar, I think nothing of your Comrade Worker. Shall I tell you about the Tsar and his family whom you despise so much?"

"What can you tell me about them that I don't already know?" he said, smiling at her pretentiousness. He knew nothing of the happy times she had spent at Livadia, close to the Imperial family. Karita had never spoken of Livadia to him.

"I don't think you know anything about them," said Karita as they walked to the tram stop. "But you're a nice boy and it will help you to know something."

"Boy?" Paul had a warm longing for this golden-haired Crimean girl, and her casual definition of what he was to her dismayed him. He had studied everything there was to study on Russia and was academically mature and politically adult. A boy? From this young woman? Ridiculous.

"Before you believe what some people say about others, you should find out about others for yourself," said Karita. A tram rattled by. They did not run to catch it at the stop. Trams were frequent. "I taught myself that, I discovered it was only fair to others. You must be fair too." And she went on to tell him about the Imperial family. He listened but did not believe. How could the Romanovs, directly or indirectly responsible for so much suffering and oppression, be the kind of people Karita said they were? If she had met them at all she had been dazzled by their outward

362

magnificence. Some people, especially young women, were like that. They would express contempt for the Tsar but if by chance they came close enough to him to receive a figurative pat on the head they reacted as if they had been blessed by God.

"Perhaps they're not as bad as some people make out," he said to humour her as they stood waiting for their tram, "but they're still autocrats and in the end they'll perish, Karita."

It was strange how uncomfortable he felt then. He could not understand it, unless it was that the brown eyes she turned on him were without their usual softness. It was as if they burned.

"If you were responsible in any way for harming them, if you helped to destroy any person I loved, I'd kill you, Paul," she said.

He was shocked but did not believe this, either.

He did not know Karita.

She went to see Colonel Kirby again the following day. She could forget the growing hatreds outside when talking with him. He was like her. He did not believe in people hating each other. He liked people, he put up with their faults.

The summer had burst into excited splendour because of the magnificence of Russian victories against the Austrians in Galicia. The Tsar paid tribute to his heroic troops in person. He reviewed the wildly enthusiastic soldiers in the captured fortress citadel of Przemysl on a golden day. His visit inspired further triumphs, for a few weeks later the Russian steamroller advanced over the Carpathian mountains and, despite terrible losses in men, threatened the Danubian plain and Vienna itself. Europe trembled and politicians on both sides made great speeches. Almighty God received a mention in all of them.

Nicholas for once was held in considerable esteem by friend and foe. It was not to last, of course. He was too convenient a whipping boy.

Typically, it was Winston Churchill who, when all

other prominent Allied statesmen were speaking slightingly of Nicholas on his abdication in 1917, declared him to be the inspiration behind all the heroic endeavours of his armies. He summed the Tsar up as a man of average ability but incomparable integrity and loyalty, as a simple man who accepted the titanic burdens of his vast responsibilities without complaint. And Churchill was frankly contemptuous of those who belittled him.

Churchill did not suffer small men lightly.

He did not consider Nicholas small.

Aunt Charlotte sat in the garden. It was shady under the old pear tree. Beyond the lawn the river glimmered through the delicate fronds of the willows. It was quiet. There weren't the boats and the punts there used to be, except on Sundays. Everybody was so busy doing their bit. She herself was involved, helping with Red Cross work and knitting for the troops. Her knitting lay in her lap now. She was reading a letter from Karita. Her nephew John had written too and both letters had arrived in the one envelope, the envelope stamped OHMS.

Dear Aunt Charlotte. It is good and bad here, Colonel Kirby has been wounded that is bad, but it is good he is now more better. I go to see him in the hospikal where he was not sitting up last week but he is now so he is fine. I am cooking food in another hospikal it is not very good and I think it was more nice food when we gave the ducks to eat. How is ducks, good I hope and I speak very masterful English now Colonel Kirby say so. So now ducks understand me better when I see them again, also the postman and Mr. Harris in the grochery. It is very bad war but will not be long to be over and then we come and see you again and be proper family. I am looking for someone very nice for Colonel Kirby to marry, then it be more family. Your loving Karita Katerinova.

The adorable girl, thought Aunt Charlotte.

It would not do to tell her that the ducks had

vanished. Aunt Charlotte suspected they had been nefariously abducted to augment the rations of people whose greed was greater than their scruples. Who but the unscrupulous would slaughter innocent ducks in order to fill their stomachs for a brief period? One did not like to admit it, but the war brought out the worst in so many people.

What on earth did the child mean, she was looking for someone very nice for John to marry? Was he so remote from his responsibilities as a normal man that he couldn't look for himself? Indeed, he didn't have to look at all. It was about time he saw what was in front of him.

Convinced on that score, Aunt Charlotte took up her knitting.

"From the east to western Ind
No jewel is like Rosalind.
Her worth being mounted on the wind
Through all the world bears Rosalind,
All the pictures, fairest lin'd
Are but black to Rosalind.
Let no face—

"Are you listening, Colonel Kirby?"

"Intently," he said. He was in a wheelchair out on the balcony, the Russian sun a balmy caress. Olga sat nearby, her Shakespeare open in her hands. She regarded him suspiciously over the top of the book.

"I'm not sending you to sleep?" she said.

"You read beautifully, Olga. I'm fascinated by the promise of Rosalind."

"Are you? You looked to me as if you were about to nod off."

"It was the look of suspended bliss," said Kirby. "A natural state when one is under the spell of sunshine, and a transient Grand Duchess."

"Transient?" said Olga, intrigued.

"Yes. Here one moment, gone the next."

"That's nothing to do with being transient," said

365

Olga, "that's to do with my being busy elsewhere."

He did not need a nurse in attendance now. He had not needed one for quite a while. Olga only came to see him when a break in her ward duties permitted, when she would bring fruit to eat for her lunch and be with him while he ate his. She did not do this every day. She was too well aware that her mother considered she was stretching friendship with Colonel Kirby to the limit. She did not want her brief, irregular visits to be forbidden.

"I know how busy you are, Olga," he said. The Germans had reinforced the Austrians in Galicia, the battles were bloody and serious, the Russian hospitals full again with casualties. "I know how limited your free time is and I can't tell you how much I appreciate every minute you spare for me." It sounded stilted, ordinary. He wanted to say, he could have said, much more. He could have said that he loved her so much it might be better for his peace of mind if she didn't come at all. Sometimes his desire to cherish her became what perhaps it was, an impossible chivalry, a virtuous fantasy. That often happened when she was close to him, stooping to tuck the hospital blanket around his knees, when she would look up at him, her smile asking him if he thought she was fussing him too much. Her mouth, unkissed in passion, offered a promise that her status denied him. It was on such occasions that tender desire to cherish seemed anemic and unreal beside desire that was an ache, a longing, a pain.

Olga could have told him that he was her only escape from the tragedy and suffering all around her in the Catherine Palace. She could have told him that only in this room was she happy. But by now she too was beginning to cover her emotions with lightness, to ward off the dangerous moments with whimsy.

So she said, "Well, yes, I'm really being very generous with my favours, you know."

"Oh? To whom?" he said. "Is there a wounded Crown Prince here?"

"Oh, there are a hundred," she said, "and all of

them dashingly handsome. There's one with a moustache that turns up, one with a moustache that turns down, and one with divinely white teeth who wants to eat me."

"Dear me," said Kirby, stroking his own moustache, "a royal gourmet of very fine discrimination."

"I don't think being swallowed whole for dinner would feel like very fine discrimination to me," said Olga, "but since we're speaking about them—Crown Princes, I mean—at least they don't get themselves deplorably knocked about. One doesn't have to worry about Crown Princes in wartime. They aren't allowed to be fired at."

"I don't like the sensation myself, I must admit," he said. He thought for a moment, then smiled as he said, "Yes, I wish I'd been born a Crown Prince."

"Oh," said Olga. She looked at her Shakespeare, closed it. That was a very dangerous moment. She had nearly rushed into the most impulsive response. She steadied herself and said, "Oh, I don't know if it would have suited you, Colonel Kirby. And you'd have had Marie and Tatiana following you about in the most embarrassingly ambitious way."

"I could have dealt with that," he said.

"Please don't be modest," said Olga, "tell me how."

"I'd have eaten them. I presume all Crown Princes have the same appetite for tender Grand Duchesses."

"Colonel Kirby—oh, you are—do you know what you are?"

"What am I?"

"Greedy," said Olga.

And, as they so often did, they laughed together.

"Excuse me."

Startled, Olga looked up. At the open windows stood a young, fair man attired in a formal morning suit and carrying a well-used Gladstone bag. He smiled apologetically. Olga rose.

"How charming," he said, taking a longer look at this blue-eyed nurse. "Do forgive this intrusion, but I knocked and no one answered and I'm afraid I came in without being asked. I'm here to see Colonel Kirby, if I may." His Russian was awful, his accent English.

"Oh?" Kirby regarded the young man from his chair on the balcony. "You have the advantage, I think."

"Oh, are you Colonel Kirby?" He spoke in English now. "Delighted to meet you, sir. I'm Ronald Vine from the British Embassy. What a lovely spot in which to recuperate. The view of the Park is wonderful." He looked at Olga again. "By Jove, I almost envy you, sir. Charming, charming."

Olga blushed a little. Mr. Vine's admiration was very frank. Kirby smiled. Olga, for all that she would be twenty this year, could still not deal sophisticatedly with strangers.

"I'll leave you to talk to Colonel Kirby, Mr. Vine," she said. Her perfect English, with its softest of accents, shamed his execrable Russian. He almost blushed himself. He glanced after her as she left the balcony and entered the room.

"Quite stunning," he murmured.

"Quite," smiled Kirby. "Sit down, Mr. Vine."

Vine took the chair Olga had vacated. He was a cheerful, confident young man.

"They thought someone ought to come and see you, sir," he said. "You're so well thought of. His Excellency is most impressed."

"Really?" Kirby spoke drily. "What about?"

"Oh, everything," said Vine. "By the excellent relations you maintain with our hosts, for one thing, and then there's a copy of a letter he's seen from a Major Kolchak."

"What letter?"

"Why, the one in which Major Kolchak asks that due recognition be given you for heroically saving his life."

"For heroically trying to make a run for it is more like it," said Kirby. "Major Kolchak and I were blown up together and when it happened I had my back to the enemy and the enemy was still miles away. Good

368

God, you don't mean someone's thinking of giving me a medal?"

"Well, a citation, perhaps."

"Rubbish," said Kirby, "I'd never be able to look Karita Katerinova in the eye again."

"Who is she?" asked Vine.

"Someone who knows I shake in my shoes when there are heroics going on. Tell His Excellency that Major Kolchak didn't know the truth of it."

"Just as you like, sir," said Vine breezily. "By the way, His Excellency said that if it hadn't already been arranged by your superiors, he'd do his best to see that as soon as you're fit he'd get you back to England for your convalescence. By George, think of the theatre in London and the hunting in Berkshire." He checked his breeziness, aware that Colonel Kirby was looking thunderous. He coughed. "By the way, sir, we wondered if you'd like some work to do? Entirely up to you, of course, but I hear you don't like being idle even as an invalid."

"I'm not an invalid, I'll be running about in a week."

"Jolly good. Well, look, sir, there's an awful lot of translation work which I hear you're superb at, much of it right in your class. Nothing confidential, of course, but something just to keep your hand in. If you'd care to, of course."

Something like a grin softened Kirby's scowl. It was a relief to the cheerful Mr. Vine.

"Leave it on the bed," said Kirby. It was work he liked. It would help the hours go by.

"Oh, that's damned good of you, sir," said Vine, "we're so short of staff at the embassy. I must say," he went on happily, "that's an extraordinarily charming nurse you have. Rather makes a fellow want to stay on, don't you think?" This time he thought Kirby was looking at him as if he wore all the hallmarks of incurable idiocy. "I say, have I said something gauche?"

"How long have you been in Petrograd?" said Kirby.

"Ouch," said Vine, "does my inexperience show up my immaturity?" He gave an engaging grin. It made

369

Kirby like him. "I'm very new, I'm afraid, I've only been out here two months. The shine hasn't worn off, has it?"

"I'm sorry," said Kirby, "I think I must have been a bit pompous."

"No, not at all," said Vine, "but with all due respect, sir, I still think your nurse quite delightful."

"Yes, she is," said Kirby. "Tell her so on your way out."

"I will, by Jove. Um, you wouldn't know if she is formally attached at all? I mean, one doesn't meet———"

"I shouldn't overdo it, Mr. Vine," said Kirby gravely. "After all, this the first time you've seen her. Just be acceptably complimentary on this occasion. As a diplomat you could handle that well enough, I'm sure."

"Leave it to me, sir, and thanks awfully. One can always call again with more work. A pleasure to have met you, I assure you."

As soon as he had gone, and not without telling Olga he considered it a pleasure to have met her too, she came out on the balcony. Kirby didn't know whether her flush was born of laughter or confusion.

"Well," she gasped, "it was a wonder you didn't arrange for him to take me to the ballet. I wasn't listening, you understand, it was just that I couldn't help overhearing. You did not bother to whisper."

"Olga, he was so impressed that———"

"And what did you mean, he wasn't to overdo anything?"

"Well, if you had had to call for help, what help would I have been with my wooden leg? Young men who are very impressed can also be very impetuous."

"Colonel Kirby, you are deplorable." Olga shook her finger at him. He looked up at her from his chair. The sun was in his eyes. And she knew he was laughing. "But oh, you are silly too. You are *not* going back to England. How ridiculous to sit there and let that young man try to arrange things for you. Dr. Bajorsky won't allow that, I promise you. And what are those files that have been left on your bed?"

"Some translation work."

"I see." If Olga could not quite cope with strangers, she could deal very composedly at times with Colonel Kirby. "What are you going to write with, your left hand?"

"How stupid of me," he said. His right arm was still encased in its plaster. "Oh, I still might manage a little writing."

"Yes, if Dr. Bajorsky says so." She stood there, her head and shoulders outlined against the blue sky. The hospital work had made her face a little thinner, her eyes bigger. She was lovelier. "Colonel Kirby," she said quietly, "you're not going back to England. If you even think about it, do you know what I'll do? I'll ask Dr. Bajorsky to take your leg off, after all."

"Dear Olga Nicolaievna," he said, "when you do marry a Crown Prince——"

"Oh, no!" She was distressed to the point of anger. "You of all people to say that! I won't be disposed of by anyone, not even by Mama or Papa. I shall please myself and make my own decisions. If there are certain things that restrict my freedom of choice, do you think this means I must marry someone I'm told to? I will never do that. Or, perhaps *you* would like me to marry some fat French pretender just because you think a Grand Duchess should? How would you like it if I said you should marry some fat Italian countess?"

"Would she have to be fat, Olga?"

"I hope she'd be very fat and very horrid, that would pay you out very well," said Olga.

"Olga, Mr. Vine was right," said Kirby, "you are quite stunning."

"Oh, Colonel Kirby, how gallant you are," said Olga, demurely fluttering her long lashes and laughing herself into happiness again.

Two days later Tatiana found time to visit him. She brought Anastasia and Marie with her. He was in his usual place on the balcony, with some work in his

371

lap. The daily sunshine had restored his colour. His limbs were mending fast. Anastasia was now fourteen, Marie sixteen, and both had the good looks so characteristic of the whole family. They turned the visit into an occasion, into an exhilarating reunion. Romantic Marie sighed rapturously and longingly over the handsome wounded hero and Anastasia indulged her talent for ecstatic theatricals.

After kisses had been bestowed and greetings were over, she sank low in a billowing curtsey.

"Oh, great and corpulent Sultan," she began.

"You mean opulent," said Tatiana. Her vitality was undimmed by her hospital work. She was like her mother only in her willowy elegance. She had a zest for life and an animation in company that had escaped the dreamful, introspective Alexandra.

"Oh, great lord and commodious master," began Anastasia again, "I have been dreadfully distraught by your incapability——"

"My what?" said Kirby, his hand in Marie's.

"She means your incapacity," said Marie, "she's so awfully ignorant at times that she makes us all blush."

"I'll pinch you when we get home," said Anastasia. "Oh, reverend alabaster——"

"Stasha, you horror!" Tatiana choked on her laughter.

"Well, I think reverend alabaster sounds perfectly lovely," said Anastasia, "it suits Ivan beautifully."

"Thank you, my little warbler," said Kirby.

Anastasia shook back her ribboned hair and curtseyed again.

"Alas, it is long since I slaved for my master——"

"What a cheek," said Marie, "you never slaved at all, you only ever talked about it, and whenever Ivan wanted you you were never there."

"Only because I was already slaving on an errand for him," said Anastasia, "and to show him I'm not adamantly peeved about him being so long away I've brought my master an inexperienced gift. It's a moon of solid gold."

And with a beamingly generous smile Anastasia presented Kirby with a fat, round, glowing orange.

"Thank you excessively," he said, "but—er—inexperienced?"

"Yes," said Anastasia, "it's not how much a present costs but the loving thought behind it, as Mama always says."

"You goose, you mean inexpensive," said Tatiana.

"Actually," said Marie, "I've just brought you a nice orange, Ivan." And she produced an even plumper fruit.

"Thank you too, Marie," said Kirby, "I shall have a very juicy time with these."

"You can spit the pips over the balcony," said Anastasia. "Alexis is away with Papa but I remembered to bring you something of his. It's a rather nice piece of string, it's for tying up things."

"My word," he said, accepting the length of twine, "if I can think of some things that need tying up when I'm not too busy, this could be the very thing. What a comfort it is to have friends like you young ladies."

"I should think it's a shocking headache to have one like Anastasia," said Tatiana.

"I shall now perform a slave dance that will make you sit up, great Sultan of the Seven Suns," said Anastasia.

"I am sitting up," he said.

"She means it will make you goggle," said Marie, "she's the most frightful show-off."

Anastasia was always willing to accept such remarks as compliments. She smiled graciously at Marie. She began her dance, gliding around the balcony and describing what she considered were Arabian pirouettes with whisking swirls of her white dress.

"Ah, a Spanish flamingo," said Kirby. "Yes, very goggling. Olé."

"Would you believe it," said Tatiana, "Ivan's at it now."

"At what?" said Marie.

"Flamingo when he means flamenco," said Tatiana.

373

"What's a flamingo?" asked Anastasia, breathless from a final pirouette.

"Oh, just a pink goose on long legs," said Kirby.

Olga arrived. She had managed to snatch time to bring his lunch and her own. She heard shrieks of laughter outside, went to the open windows and saw her three sisters around Colonel Kirby on the balcony. They were hilarious and he, infected by their gaiety, was helpless with laughter himself.

For ecstatic moments there was to Olga no war, no bitterness, no suffering. There was only a warm, beautiful feeling that the happiness of Livadia had reached Tsarskoe Selo.

Tatiana looked around. She saw Olga at the open windows with a tray in her hands. Tatiana smiled, then caught her breath on a little dart of pain. Her adored sister's eyes were brilliant with tears.

They sent him away soon after. After the Russian advance over the Danubian plain had been checked, the Germans began to inflict massive defeats on the Imperial Army in Poland. They took Warsaw. Russia was stunned, bleeding. The need for more hospital beds became so critical that the very walls of the huge Catherine Palace seemed to bend outwards as wards were crammed to the limit of their capacity and beyond. They put five beds into Kirby's room and sent Kirby himself to convalesce among Russian officers on an estate some thirty miles from Moscow.

Dr. Bajorsky apologised for the suddenness, the inconvenience, but there it was, the circumstances were such that there was no help for it and Colonel Kirby was to be evacuated immediately.

Whatever Alexandra might have had to do with it, the fact was the hospital needed every inch of space and Kirby saw that this removal was a reasonable consequence of circumstances. He did not argue, only took the opportunity to thank Dr. Bajorsky for all he had done. Dr. Bajorsky, a tired ghost of a man now, shook his head.

"I'd have taken your leg off, Colonel, as it happened," he said. "It was Her Highness the Grand Duchess Olga Nicolaievna who prevented me. You owe more to her faith than you owe to my surgery."

"Dear God." It was an involuntary exclamation from Kirby. Dr. Bajorsky, involved in so much of the frenzied activity of the morning, glanced at the Englishman and saw, perhaps, something of what he felt for the Grand Duchess. "Is she here?" Kirby asked.

"No. I think she has a late duty today. But if you wish to thank her then leave her a note. I'll give it to her."

Kirby wrote it stiffly with his right hand.

Olga knew nothing of his removal until she arrived later. She was stunned. Dr. Bajorsky, explaining the reasons, was conscious of blue eyes looking frozen. He gave her Kirby's note.

My dear Olga. Thank you so much for everything. Thank you and bless you.

They had taken away her escape to happiness. Now there was only the war.

FOUR

Karita was in splendid spirits. Kirby had written to her and she had gone to the convalescent retreat to join him. Paul Kateroff was astonished and angry. When he realised there was no thought in her mind of not going he told her that her subservience degraded her. She put her chin up.

"Is it subservient to do what one wants to do?" she said.

"You're no better than a serf, running when he says run, going when he says go——"

"We are family, he's my mother and father," said Karita.

"You stupid girl, what does that mean except a lot of archaic nonsense?"

"It means that I would rather be family with him than stay here and pull your silly nose," said Karita.

Paul was so bitter that he made the mistake of saying things that made her blood rush and her body burn. But she let him finish, she was only thankful that Ivan Ivanovich was not present himself to hear what was said.

Then she spoke. "I thought you better than some of the others, but when you insist on listening to so many lies and so much hatred it's to be expected that you end up speaking obscenities yourself."

He had lost his golden-haired girl. He never saw her again. He died in the revolution, executed by Bolsheviks because he opposed their denial of free speech to all.

On the estate given over by a patriotic landowner for accommodating convalescing officers, Karita lived among other servants. She was sad at times because the war was going so badly for her beloved Russia. But she would not have been less sad elsewhere, and elsewhere she would not have had her moments of warm satisfaction. Ivan Ivanovich was frankly delighted to have her there. He was so generous in his appreciation of all she did for him, her attentions liberally augmenting the cursory ministrations of the limited medical staff, that Karita was almost embarrassed.

"There's no need to thank me so much for everything," she said, "after all, we are really family."

She had begun to say things like that. It amused him, endeared her to him. He laughed.

"Karita, little one," he said, "I adore you."

"Oh, not improperly, I hope," said Karita.

He shook with laughter.

Karita was not only his comfort, she was his ally. He needed one here. The Russian armies were being battered and pounded on every front in the west, and the Russian officers were becoming bitter. Colonel Kirby was English and therefore the natural target for their bitterness. What was England doing apart from allowing Russia to make nearly all the sacrifices? The British sat safely in their French trenches and no doubt gambled only with cards while Russia lost thousands of lives a day. It was no wonder England could always win the last battle when every preceding battle was fought by her allies. Kirby used maps to try and explain the British case, he used population figures to show why Britain could not put such massive armies into the field as Germany or Russia. But he knew he sounded apologetic rather than convincing. Karita soon became aware of how he was being assailed by her countrymen and showed her resentment by actually arguing with them. They were astonished at first, then always they roared with laughter, smacked her on the bottom and told her to go and put ribbons in her hair. Karita was tempted to smack some of them back but one could not do that to men who had lost an eye, an arm, a leg. But they were very unfair. She knew that her Englishman loved Russia as much as they did.

Kirby was using a crutch. He hopped about on this like a wooden-legged sailor, she said. She also said he was not to take too much notice of what the Russian officers said.

"They're trying to blame you," she said, "and you couldn't have done more for Russia unless you had been blown completely to bits. Oh, why are people so stupid? And why is it the Germans are winning? It's very sad, isn't it?"

"It isn't because the Germans are better or braver, Karita," he said, as they sat together on a terrace overlooking a landscape of brown fields, "it's because we've cared less about guns than they have."

"Why do you say we? You aren't a Russian, it isn't your fault."

"We all hide from reality if we can, we all tend to say it was the other fellow." His expression was sombre. "I may not be a Russian but I've had everything from Russia a man could want."

"Oh, you are nice to say that," she said. "So many people say terrible things about their own, but I've never heard you say anything at all terrible. And there's so much trouble again, so much of people throwing bombs again. We put Peter Prolofski into a hole but there are more like him every day, all coming up out of different holes."

It was the first time she had mentioned Prolofski since that dark night at Livadia. They shared the secret very easily and with a great deal of mutual respect.

"I remember Prolofski, Karita," he said, and put his arm around her shoulders. It made her feel warm and wanted. It was an extraordinarily nice feeling. "Now the Tsar is going to take over command of his armies from Grand Duke Nicholas. What do you think of that, Karita?"

They looked out over the landscape of sunlit brown. It was pleasant enough but without the colours and contours of the Crimea. The war was not so far away here. The Germans had over-run Poland. The atmosphere was unhappy.

"The Tsar will beat them, you see," said Karita.

"Perhaps, if they'll give him guns and shells," said Kirby. She looked at his profile. She had never seen him so sombre. Her heart sank. If Ivan Ivanovich could not smile any more, what had happened to Russia? What was happening to it?

"I wish he'd take you with him," she said, "you could think how to beat them."

He turned his head. Her brown eyes were full of trust in his infallibility. He shook his head. He laughed. Karita smiled in return. Anything was better than to have him gloomy.

"Karita, I know nothing of how to move armies, I'm really only a desk soldier," he said. "All I know at the moment is that I don't like the Tsar being so committed to isolation from his capital. Every enemy he has will move against him."

They were moving, but not so much against Nicholas as Alexandra. Totally unequipped to take on the role of autocratic regent, Alexandra nevertheless attempted it. Immediately she was attacked on all sides, and the attacks were venomous. Particularly hateful to her were the renewed accusations that she was pro-German. The slanders that attached implications to her relationship with Rasputin were unbearably crude and vicious. Because of her faith in the holy man and her devotion to God, she suffered every calumny with spiritual a strength that was unbreakable.

The Russian retreat slowed down and a defensive line was established. But the loss of Poland had been a shock, and it was one from which the armies and the nation never really recovered. Alexandra did nothing to improve morale at home. All that she did do seemed to worsen things, yet she was utterly sincere in her conviction that all she did was for the good of Imperial Russia.

Meanwhile Kirby found an ally with a more authoritative voice than Karita's. Major Kolchak suddenly arrived. He seemed to have one shoulder awkwardly lower than the other and his arm threatened to be permanently stiff. He had the look of a man who had nearly been hanged. He was delighted to renew his acquaintance with Kirby, and on his first visit to the mess listened with his square, rugged face gradually darkening as fellow officers attacked Kirby for England's shortcomings.

"Gentlemen!" Major Kolchak's voice startled them all into silence. "You're forgetting yourselves. Colonel Kirby is our guest. He's also my friend. Shall we talk of women we have known?"

Yet in his own way Major Kolchak was the bitterest of them all. He directed his anger not against the Allies, however, but against Russian incompetence and corruption. He foresaw more than the possibility of Russia's defeat, he foresaw the complete collapse of civil administration and the plunge into revolution. He had long conversations with Kirby. He was convinced that the first to go would be the Tsar himself.

"Those who hate Nicholas or are envious of him include certain Romanovs," he said. "But if they contrive to destroy him then they themselves will be eliminated by the revolutionaries. The revolutionaries, once they have got rid of the reigning Romanov, will make sure they aren't saddled with another. What an inglorious mess we're in, my friend. And look at me, I'll be lucky if I can draw a pistol in defence of the Tsar, let alone fire it."

"Stand behind me," said Kirby, "I'll fire for both of us—but with my eyes shut."

Major Kolchak liked that.

"Ah, we are two of a kind," he said, "I am a coward too, by God. And a useless one now."

But the human body being the resilient machine it is, Major Kolchak was declared fit enough to return to his unit in August. And not long afterwards Kirby returned to Petrograd.

Alexandra, on one of her periodical visits to Headquarters, casually mentioned what a remarkable recovery Colonel Kirby had made. He had written to Alexis, telling the Tsarevich he would soon be back in Petrograd where he expected to receive orders that would return him to the British military staff at Headquarters.

"I couldn't be more pleased," said Nicholas. The strain of his new responsibilities as Commander-in-Chief showed in the new lines around his eyes. But he seemed relaxed at the moment. He always enjoyed Alexandra's visits. To the stark militarism of *Stavka* she brought the luxury of trivialities, the news of friends or relatives. There was no time during their married lives when these two people were not happy to see each other, no time when Nicholas did not listen attentively to her ingenuous opinion of a minister's failings or her homely recital of a domestic happening.

"Colonel Kirby is a fine man," she said, then went on to talk about the children. She touched on Anastasia's tendency to favour things that made her fat, then on to the wretchedness of circumstances that were spoiling the most exciting years of Olga's life. "She works so hard, Nicky, and is under so much strain with her nursing. She will do more than she should. It's such a shame that it should all be like this at a time when life ought to be at its sweetest for her. We must do all we can to see that the most important things don't pass her by."

"Marriage, for instance?" Nicholas mused on that subject, always a complicated one, always governed as much by politics as anything else where any of his children were concerned. "I don't think she's in any great hurry, my love, and I don't think she will be while we're still at war."

"Oh, my dear," said Alexandra, close to him in the austere comfort of his railway coach, "I only feel we

381

shouldn't use the war as an excuse to overlook the matter or we may find we shan't want to lose her at all. We must be fair to her."

"My feeling is that Olga would prefer us to leave it to happen rather than have us contrive it," said Nicholas. He could not quite see the point of Alexandra's concern. There were simply no eligible suitors in the offing with the war situation as it was. Indeed, most of such suitors were on the side of the enemy.

"But it would be unwise and unfortunate if she wanted us to leave it for the wrong reasons," said Alexandra. Never in the best of health now, she too had her other worries. There were dark shadows under her eyes.

"Well, there's little we can do except pray for victory and peace," said Nicholas in his philosophic way. For Nicholas there was always the hope that things would be better tomorrow. "Nobody will be happier then than Olga. She'll think of marriage then, my love."

"I pray to God for victory, peace and Olga's happiness," said Alexandra earnestly. Then for some reason she said, "As to Colonel Kirby, I'm sure he'll be fretting for more active service when he returns from convalescence. It would be nice to be able to help him. What a pity we can only do so indirectly. If he were in the Russian Army we could do so much more for him."

Nicholas's smile brought back some of his youthful charm. He was forty-seven and beginning to age. But his smile was still irresistible.

"No, my sweet Alix, I can't make him a general. That's only been a joke between us. He knows it."

"My love, I know it too," said Alexandra. She was still as slender as she had been as a young woman, still used reserve to armour her shyness. "I only meant that when he's quite fit again he might relish a new role. He's always said how much he'd like to serve you, Nicky, and he could do this very well as a staff officer in our own Army. It only needs a word from you to the British authorities to have this arranged."

"Mmm," said Nicholas. He rubbed his beard. "He could come back here. He's uncommonly useful to have around and the most congenial chap as well."

Alexandra observed very pleasantly that she had actually been thinking just how much Colonel Kirby might appreciate a complete change of scenery, and that to keep him close to them might be considered rather selfish and indulgent. Everyone liked him immensely and they themselves ought not to make too much claim on his company.

This time the Tsar's smile was a rather wan recognition of the roundabout way Alexandra had travelled to make her point. He knew she suspected Olga of forming a totally unwise attachment which could prejudice his eldest daughter's outlook when the possibility of a suitable alliance did arise.

"Mmm," murmured Nicholas again, "I wonder if he'd like to come over to us? We could use him in Armenia with our Caucasian Army. He'd be very useful there, especially with the British operation in the Dardanelles going on."

"Armenia?" Alexandra measured the distance in her mind's eye. She smiled gratefully. "I'm sure that's an excellent place for him to be, darling. You know, you always arrange things so well when you're not being harassed by others. It's a great pity that so many people think they're being helpful when they're only interfering. I know this is only a minor matter but it still needed thinking about."

Nicholas knew it was not a minor matter to her. He leaned forward and caressed her cheek with his fingertips.

"I'll have a word with our British friends," he said.

Kirby was back in Petrograd. He limped a bit and there were furrows in his right arm deep enough to carry rivers of water when he was in the bath. But his convalescence had browned him, he looked fit again and the limp would go in time with exercise.

As soon as he and Karita arrived in the capital he

received a visit from a spruce senior Russian officer. He had come from the War Ministry and wished a few friendly words with Kirby. In short, His Imperial Highness the Tsar sent his felicitations on Colonel Kirby's recovery and wondered if Kirby would care to serve him more directly. A rank equivalent to his British one awaited him at Third Corps Headquarters in Kars on their southern Caucasian front, where it was hoped the Russians would in due course link up with the British when the latter forced the Dardanelles. Did Colonel Kirby think that a suitable appointment? His Imperial Highness would consider it an honour if he agreed. The British authorities had signified their approval of the transfer. What did Colonel Kirby think?

Kirby knew exactly what to think.

He could either go to Kars, south of the Caucasus, as an officer in the Imperial Russian Army or decline and almost certainly be returned to the United Kingdom. There was no other alternative when one knew what must have actuated the offer.

Kirby accepted. For one reason alone. He wanted to stay in Russia. He had to maintain some communication with Olga, even if only that of treading the same soil, even though they would be a thousand miles apart. Having accepted he received orders to proceed to Kars on Monday. It was now Saturday. He had two days grace. Karita was nearly speechless. What were they doing with him, sending him there, bringing him here and now this? He was just being ordered about. He was to join the Russian Army? But why? It was absurd. Now he'd be ordered about by the Russians as well as the British. Aunt Charlotte would never stand for it.

"Yes, I am simply speechless," she said.

"Are you?" he said. "When?"

He told her the British would no longer have the right to give him orders. Just the Russians. Karita said orders from some of the Russians she knew would confuse the saints themselves. Kirby told her to stay in Petrograd if she wished——

384

"Oh, no, you're not going to try that again," she said. She would go with him to this place wherever it was. He told her that Kars was nearer to her home in the Crimea than Petrograd was. It was in Armenia. Karita shuddered. Armenia *was* the end of the world. It was where you froze to death in the winter and scorched to death in summer. Its people were still barbarians. Nevertheless, as he had to go she would go with him. Her mother would certainly insist on it and it was no use arguing.

"I know that," he said, "I'm wiser now."

The following day, Sunday, he went to the Alexander Palace, arriving there at a time when he felt the Imperial family would have returned from morning service. Tsarskoe Selo seemed at peace, the Palace in quiet, majestic contemplation of the Sabbath. He asked for audience with the Grand Duchess Olga Nicolaievna. His own name brought a flicker of acknowledgement from a court official. He did not know the man, but the man seemed to have heard of him, and no doubt in association with Olga. It would be this sort of thing that would bother Alexandra.

He did not have to wait long before he was escorted through the Palace to one of the drawing-rooms. Olga was there, and imprudently or not, she was quite alone, without any lady-in-waiting. She wore a dress of purest Sunday white, satin-sashed, and her hair, caught by the light of the windows, was as bright as if the sun had poured gold into it. If the realities and tragedies of war had awakened her consciousness of the world as it truly was, yet they had also given her complete maturity, turning a sensitive girl into a compassionate woman. She was a girl no longer. But never, he thought, would she ever lose for him that which had first come to his eyes. The enchantment of unkissed innocence.

She was a little tense, a little pale, but as he came towards her the warm blood quickened and her eyes shone. He was so brown again, so much himself once more, despite a slight limp as if his leg had a stiffness to it. He took the hand she extended.

"I haven't been so long this time, have I?" he said, smiling.

"Dear Colonel Kirby, no, not long at all," she said, a little breathless and very happy. "Oh, it's good to see you looking so well again, you cannot imagine how pleased I am." Her hand trembled in his, she curled her fingers tightly to steady them. They looked at each other. Her mouth began its betrayal, her bottom lip would not be still. He felt the urgency of his desire to kiss her, to lay his lips on the soft bed of her mouth. Each time he saw her it became harder to deny the urge. Now it was frightening. She was emotional, the long lashes quivering, wanting to hide what was in her eyes. They flickered, fell and lifted again. He knew he must not, she knew he must not, but her mouth was tremulous with appeal, her clasp tighter.

The door opened, the moment of danger precipitately broken as Tatiana came in. Olga drew hastily back, her face burning as she turned to hide herself, her hand on the heavy curtain drawn back from the bright window.

"Ivan Ivanovich! They said you were here and you are! Oh, how lovely!" And Tatiana swooped and flew to him. "Olga, may I?" She threw her arms around Kirby's neck and kissed him in glad, impulsive welcome. Olga swung round and a little gasp broke from her. The despair of being denied that which Tatiana took so uninhibitedly showed in her stricken expression.

"Oh, Tasha," she said in pain, "am I to say you may not?"

Tatiana, oblivious of her sister's distress, drew back to survey Kirby with shining delight.

"There, you see," she said, "you're put together again and even better than before. Oh, how grand you look, Ivan. Olga, whoever would think he had been so knocked about. Are we to sit, may we talk?"

"Shall I go or stay?" said Olga.

Tatiana turned, saw that Olga was in some way hurt and went swiftly to her.

"Dearest, I'm sorry," she whispered, "but I was so

386

excited. Let me stay a minute or two, let us all talk for just a little while."

Olga could never resist Tatiana. The three of them sat and talked. At first it was all about what each of them had been doing, then about the war. The war could not be escaped from. The Grand Duchesses had their own anxieties about it and were all too obvious in their desire to hear Kirby say the situation was not really serious, that the Allies would ensure it would all be over by Christmas at least. He could not paint that kind of picture, especially not for them. He could only suggest that time was on the side of the Allies, although he knew that time by itself was likely to be tragically expensive for Russia.

Olga began to wonder. There was something about him that made her suspicious. Had he come to only say goodbye again? Men were always doing that in wartime. Worse, he had a tendency to do it all the time. A little fierceness took hold of her. When Tatiana said she must go, it did not surprise Olga in the least to hear him say he was going away tomorrow. But she was astonished, and so was Tatiana, when he said he had accepted a commission in the Russian Army.

"But Ivan," cried Tatiana, "how ridiculous! Oh, and how famous. You're really going to fight for Papa and all of us?"

"It isn't a bit famous," said Olga, "but it is ridiculous. What does it mean, does it mean something good?"

He told them it meant he was to join the Army of the Caucasus.

"The Caucasus? Oh, do you call that good?" Olga sounded angry. Tatiana wondered if Olga realised there was an implied possessiveness about her attitude that was regrettable.

"Nothing is very good for anyone in this kind of war, is it?" said Kirby. Tatiana liked him so much, he refused to get emotional or dramatic, he kept things as matter-of-fact as he could even though she knew he cared deeply for Olga.

Olga rose. The Caucasus? That was a million miles away.

"It's an utterly beastly war," said Tatiana as she and Kirby rose too, "but you have all our blessings, all our prayers, and when it's over there'll be a wonderful victory ball. We'll be there and so will you. Ivan, make it come to an end soon. It's not so bad for us but it's dreadful for our soldiers. Don't be away too long, come back to us. Dearest Ivan, God bless you." She kissed him, squeezed his arm and went quickly from the room.

Olga, pale with accusation, faced him.

"Why have you done this?" she asked. "Why have you joined the Russian Army and volunteered for the Caucasus? Do you know how far away that is?"

"Olga," he said, "Russia has been good to me and I owe her a great deal. The Emperor has given me trust and friendship and I owe him even more. If this is the best way I can serve him——"

"If?" Olga's suspicions clarified into conviction. "I see," she said, "it's someone else's idea. And you have consented to it. Colonel Kirby, I never thought you would let them send you to the Caucasus without fighting them a little."

"But you see, Olga," he said, "being sent to the Caucasus is for me infinitely preferable to being sent back to England. I want to stay in Russia, I want to see the war through here."

"The Caucasus isn't here!" Olga was so upset that she turned her back on him. "Colonel Kirby, you're going to make me so unhappy. We need our friends, we need them close to us."

"Olga, you have thousands of friends in Petrograd alone." He saw that her back was very straight and felt a pride in her.

"Have we? Tatiana and I are beginning to wonder about that." She moved to the window, looked out over the summer-dry grass. "I mean true friends. Oh, you are the unkindest of men to do this."

"What?" he said in astonishment.

"You are." Her voice was muffled, defensive. "You know I can't bear goodbyes, yet you're always forcing them on me. That's unkind, isn't it?"

"Oh, my dear sweet Olga," he said impulsively and tenderly. It did little to steady her nerves. Desperately she kept her eyes on the view, though she saw nothing of it. She was close to betraying her parents' trust. "Olga, do you think I like goodbyes any more than you do?"

"No, but ——" She lapsed into helplessness. She turned to him. She tried to smile. "Oh, I do have bad moments, don't I?" she said. "It's I who am being unkind. And I'm complaining about something thousands of people face every day. Please forgive me. But it would be heavenly to live in a world where there were no goodbyes, where one's friends were always close. Don't you think so?"

"I expect a few of us would still find something to complain about," he smiled. "Probably about how our friends were always on our doorstep."

"Yes," she said. She seemed unconvinced. She twisted the sapphire ring she wore. "I'm very selfish, aren't I?"

"No, you are not," he said firmly.

"I am, you know." She tried another smile. It was not a great success. "I want things I can't have. That *is* selfish in a Grand Duchess, isn't it, when so many other people are in far greater need, when they have so little of what I take for granted, like bread? Please, you'll ignore my little tantrum, will you not? You must go to the Caucasus, you must go wherever you're sent, of course you must. Only—only I do wish you did not seem to be saying goodbye so often."

"There have been different times, Olga, especially at Livadia."

It was in her eyes then, the memory of golden days and laughing children.

"Oh, yes," she said. She went on in her softest voice. "Colonel Kirby, please don't think me too foolish, but I have so cherished our friendship, so treasured all those times. You made Livadia so happy for us. It isn't wrong, even for me, is it, to cherish a friendship?"

"Or for me?" he said gently.

"Oh, it's so difficult," she whispered. Suddenly he saw the brightness of tears unbearable to him. "But I wish there were other words, not just the ones to do with goodbye. I wish there were."

He shook his head, unable for a moment to speak. Then he said, "There aren't so many other words, Olga, only these. I shouldn't say them but I must. I love you, I love you with all my heart. I loved you the day I first saw you, I loved you when you were sixteen. I love you now. I will always love you."

She flamed into rich, radiant colour. She trembled, she put her hands to her face, pressed her eyelids with her fingertips. Her head bent, her hair fell forward. She fought emotions that threatened everything for which she was predestined by heritage. She searched her being for words of her own. She lifted her head, uncovered her eyes and looked up into his face.

"Now, whatever happens," she said, "nothing can take that away from me. Now I shall always be happy. Now I shall never be a Crown Princess, there's no Crown Prince I could ever love because all the love I have is already given. Now you and I will always be the dearest of friends, as we said before, but now the very dearest. And we shall never forget each other, shall we? Oh, I would so like it if you would always remember me, wherever we are, whatever happens."

"I can never forget Livadia, and you are Livadia," he said.

Olga smiled then, her eyes moistly brilliant. They had spoken their words. There were no more. She put out both hands. He took them, he raised each to his lips in turn. And that was all they had, Grand Duchess Olga Nicolaievna of Imperial Russia and John Kirby of England. That and all they had shared in the tranquillity of Livadia.

If, apart from her nursing work, Olga's life was confined and sequestered, if she lived mostly in guarded

390

security, this did not make her an unimaginative or shallow Grand Duchess. She was always herself, thoughtful, observant and understanding, longing to love and be loved. She was the personification of all that was best in the graciousness of her disappearing world. Because she was herself she kept her promise to her mother, she kept faith with her father. All that John Kirby ever touched of her were her hands, all he ever kissed were her fingertips. She was true to her heritage.

It was only her heart she denied.

Tatiana slipped back into the room when he had gone. Olga was at the window, gazing out at the sunshine wherein danced all her dreams.

"Olga? Don't be sad, dearest," whispered Tatiana, cherishing and envying the wonder of her sister's love.

Olga turned her head. Tatiana saw the reflected dreams.

"Sad? Oh no, Tasha, I'm not sad. You don't know how beautiful it is to be loved. I have almost everything I can have now, and it doesn't matter how often or how far they send him away, he'll always be where we are, always."

"No, darling, he'll always be where you are."

FIVE

Karita went with him to Kars. He was commissioned a colonel in the Imperial Army, a staff appointment was his. The arrival at Third Corps Headquarters of an Englishman in the uniform of a Russian colonel was a mystery, an amusement and an embarrassment. They had not been notified of his appointment and did not know what to do with him. True, his papers confirmed his appointment, but they had no papers themselves. However, mystified or amused, they did not lack hospitality and having broken open a bottle or two they declared him a fine fellow and said he must be quartered somewhere. They found him a first-floor apartment in a commandeered house. Karita thought little of Kars and even less of the apartment. It was too small, there were only three rooms and a kitchen. She turned her nose up at the crowded living-room, full of the most uncomfortable furniture.

"You must tell them," she said, when they had moved in, "you must tell them the Tsar himself is your friend. He would never permit you to be lodged in such an ordinary place as this."

Karita was exaggerating. She was always apt to expect more for him than he was entitled to.

For the first few days he was entirely unwanted by Third Corps staff. They were charming enough but were not disposed to use him. However, his fluent and easy command of their language, his adaptability, his

392

equability, his love of Russia and his liking for its people, made them look differently at him after a week. They began to explain the campaign to him.

Kirby became involved in heavy and complicated staff work. It was more than welcome in that it compelled his mind to focus on things other than his hopeless love. Yet even during his busiest moments he would suddenly think of her, his mind drawing its picture of her, making it an effort to concentrate on figures again.

As for Karita, in her golden charm she was the delight of every Russian officer and man who set eyes on her. For her they would fight a million Turks. Karita asked only that they would dispose of the few they faced at present. That would help to get rid of what was only a nuisance and then they could all go and dispose of the Germans. Intrigued and infatuated officers slapped her and tickled her and pinched her. Karita would have retaliated if she hadn't known they would consider this an encouragement. She wondered how Colonel Kirby would react if he knew she was subjected to these familiarities. She thought she had better tell him. Perhaps he could do something about it. He listened very soberly. He knew the inadvisability of showing amusement when Karita considered that something not quite proper was going on at her expense.

"And I am black and blue," she finished.

"Where?" he asked.

"Where?" She was shocked. He seemed quite serious. Did he expect her to show him? "Where? What does it matter where? That's my own business, I should hope, and certainly nobody else's."

"Good," he said, "you take care of it, little one." And he patted her.

"Well!" Karita could not believe it. Not only was was he indifferent to her problem but he had actually patted her where she had been most often pinched. It was like setting his approval on the familiarity of others. "Well, that's very nice, isn't it? I'm to be pinched black and blue while you look the other way."

He rubbed the nap of his cap with his sleeve. It

served to remind her that he was due at headquarters.

"Don't you like it?" he said. "It's their way with pretty girls, you know that."

"It's their way with *some* girls," said Karita, "and what I should like to know is, do *you* like it? If you're in favour of it perhaps you wouldn't mind if I took my clothes off to let them see what they're slapping and pinching."

He put his cap over his face. His voice came hoarse and muffled.

"Heaven preserve me, you'll be my death," He put his cap on. Karita, seeing the trouble he was in to keep his face straight, tossed her chin disdainfully. "All right, sweet one," he said, "I'll bring the subject up. Well, I'll do something. In broad daylight I can't imagine what and they're not going to take me seriously. I'll have to pose the question when is a pinch not a pinch and go on from there."

Karita was quick to see what that might mean.

"Ivan Ivanovich," she said, "don't you dare discuss my person with those roaring bullfrogs."

"I wouldn't dream of it," he said, and then pinched her on his way out.

"Well," she gasped, outraged, "well!"

But behind the closed door she fell into fits of gurgling laughter.

Subsequently she suspected he had forgotten or dismissed the matter as soon as he left the house because it was still happening days after.

So she put pepper in Kirby's soup one evening and laughed until she cried when after only three spoonfuls he became hotter and hotter, redder and redder.

Karita had a sense of fun but it was always advisable to take her seriously.

The war went on. Christmas came. There were several non-festive outbreaks of violence in cold, icy cities. Kirby sent greetings to the Imperial family. Alexandra replied with a letter of thanks, gracious and kind for all its brevity. During the first week in January he re-

394

ceived a card, posted in an envelope. It was a religious card, a print of the Nativity. On the reverse side were three penned words.

"*I love you.*"

There was no signature.

He understood. He treasured it.

Daily Karita polished the small oval gilt frame that contained a snapshot of Olga and Tatiana. He kept it on a table in his bedroom. Often Karita pressed her warm mouth to it.

The Russian winter had closed down the Western front but Grand Duke Nicholas, a stimulant to the whole of the Caucasian front, did the unexpected by launching his attack in the ice and snow of mid-January.

By this time Kirby, restless for action, had relinquished his position as a staff officer and applied for service with a unit of Caucasian Cossacks. Headquarters had been amazed. It was too much vodka. His eccentric request was granted. He told Karita that if he rode with the Cossacks he could get out of the way quicker on a horse.

"Why do you have to get on a horse at all, why do you have to be so foolish?" she said. "Is it because of people saying your country wasn't doing enough?"

"I'd forgotten that," he said.

"Then is it because you want to get yourself killed? Sometimes you look as if you're thinking of doing something dark and stupid." She was cross with him.

"Not as dark and stupid as that, I hope. But I must do something more than desk work, Karita."

That upset her.

"You should not be thinking only of yourself," she said. She had washed her hair the night before and it was still unbraided, a mass of flowing gold. "You should think of me too. What will become of me if anything happens to you? Do you think of that?"

"You'll go back to your village, your parents," he said. He had no intention of getting himself killed or losing the pleasure of Karita's company.

"And who is to go back to Aunt Charlotte?" It was plain that for once Karita considered him thoughtless and selfish. "My mother and father have each other, Aunt Charlotte would have no one at all. Someone must go back home to her from Russia. I'll have to."

Her outlook on this kind of thing was fascinating.

"Karita, you are quite the loveliest person," he said affectionately, "but there's no need to worry. Perhaps we'll both go back to her together. We'll see what happens. Meanwhile, you can return to your parents now——"

"I will not!"

"——or you can stay here and keep the apartment for me. At the Army's expense, of course, until I get back on leave. You can have whatever money you need."

"I shall stay here," she said. "How would it look if no one was around when you came on leave?"

"Not very proper, I suppose," he said. She regarded him unsmilingly. He wore his Russian uniform with its high collar naturally enough now. It was rather nice of him, really, to want to fight for Russia but, ah, just wait until he had ridden with those Cossacks for a while. He would soon want to get back to his desk.

She was surprised at the warmth of his leave-taking. He not only kissed her very affectionately, he even embraced her. The firm physical contact created sensations so confusing that her face turned fiery.

"Oh, goodness," she gasped when he released her.

"Sweet and dear Karita," he said.

She sat down heavily when he had gone. Emptiness rang hollowly through the spotless apartment.

"Oh, no," cried Karita, horrified to find she was weeping.

It was dreadful to feel so lonely.

Grand Duke Nicholas Nicolaievich, as redoubtable a soldier as any in the war, attacked Erzurum, about one hundred and fifty miles west of Kars. The infantry swarmed in the wake of bursting Russian shells, going in with the bayonet against Turkish positions in the valleys and on the heights, their massed waves reducing redoubts and enveloping gun emplacements. The cavalry followed on, often riding through their infantry to cut down scrambling, retreating Turks. It was a fine affair for the Caucasian Cossacks, always at their most dashing when the enemy was on the run.

Kirby rode with them. The Cossacks were tough, wiry men who rode small horses like ponies. They took little notice of Kirby. He had no doubt been dumped on them by some obtuse general who wanted to get rid of him.

In an attack on a ridge the Turks suddenly abandoned their positions. Cossacks charged at the heels of triumphant infantry up the slope. The foot soldiers yelled at them. Trust those thieving Cossacks to try and get to booty first. Bullets from retreating Turks flew and Kirby had his horse shot from under him. Miraculously he sprang clear before the wounded, screaming animal rolled on him. A Cossack pulled up. He watched Kirby mercifully shoot the agonised beast.

"Are you hurt, Englishman?" His grin was sarcastic, he was oblivious for the moment of Turks and sorrier for the horse than Kirby.

"I've fallen off more horses than I care to remember," said Kirby, his coat belted, his peaked cap pulled tight over his head.

"Ah!" A wider, more appreciative grin. "Go back and get yourself another. Ayeiah!" And he was away, flogging his mount up the slope.

The battle for Erzurum was bitter. The Russians lost men in such numbers that Kirby frequently wondered how soon it would be before his own body rode into a bullet or shell-burst. But it was the infantry which bore the greatest brunt, the Cossacks engaged only to complete a rout or hasten it.

The battle did not completely erase his thoughts of Olga, however, for at night, cold and exhausted, his mind gathered its pictures and tumbled them into kaleidoscopic fantasies until at last he fell asleep. Only by day, when there was smoke and noise, guns and bullets and whistling sabres, when fear took hold of all the senses, were memories thrust violently aside and thoughts turned solely on survival.

Erzurum fell and the Russians won a short breathing-space.

The Grand Duke began the re-grouping of his forces. The Turks began the assembling of their Second Army for a massive counterstroke. The Grand Duke anticipated it and before the Turks knew what he was about he had smashed their Third Army. When the Turkish Second Army did attack the Russians were in positions of strength, and held on to all the ground they had captured.

Both armies were content to take up defensive lines for the winter, although winter in these regions, with temperatures skating around the thirty degrees below zero mark, was almost as unwelcome to entrenched thousands as a barrage of red-hot steel. The conditions were as bad as men could endure and Kirby, frozen day after day, wondered if he would ever be warm again. There had been no leave, no real respite, except for the wounded, only brief rest periods behind the lines. And only the dead were at peace.

The casualties mounted here and in Europe. Germany, Austria, Turkey, France and Britain poured in their fodder. Their dead lay in heaps. And Russia? Her dead made mountains.

Lenin sat in Switzerland, calculating what the Great Powers were doing to each other.

On the European front, the German generals could not ignore the Tsar's armies, however poorly supplied they were. It had been their intention to concentrate on the defeat of the British and French while merely holding their Eastern line. But the weight, intensity and fervour of Russian efforts circumvented every German attempt to bring this plan into full and effective being. The Tsar, constant in his loyalty to the British and French, could not have served his allies better than he did.

The politicians dwelt in their temples of discourse

and attacked the men they had sent to direct the battles. If they had emerged from their debating chambers to fight the battles themselves, while the soldiers went home, the war would have been over in days.

Imperial Russia moved from heartbreak on the fronts to disillusionment at home. The people had long begun to disbelieve Government propaganda. Disorders increased, civil unrest flared. There were strikes in the factories at times when the military situations demanded maximum effort at home. The war was becoming less and less popular. Women, utterly appalled by the losses, wanted their men back. It was demoralising to listen to soldiers on leave, when they could get leave.

Rasputin was on the way to becoming a greater fool than ever. Almost everything written about him, even by his enemies, gives the impression that he was an awesome mystic. But in reality he was simply psychic, a random quality given to ordinary or extraordinary persons alike, even to idiots. The idiot Rasputin was thrusting the Imperial family to the brink of tragedy. He womanised, boasted and belched, he bandied the royal names about.

He gave Alexandra the wrong political advice, undermined the Tsarism he desired to preserve and took no kind of advice himself, for he lacked all humility.

In his alliance with Alexandra he engineered the removal of any minister he took a dislike to. As no minister of any integrity could stomach Rasputin, one by one they all went. And in their places Rasputin recommended men who were greater fools than he was.

It was in early December 1916, when a unit of Turks, irritated by pin-pricking sorties from booty-collecting Cossacks, launched a quick, furious attack in the miserable grey of an icy dawn. They surprised the Cossacks, bayoneted a few, shot a few, and hauled off a number of prisoners to strip them of everything of value, even their boots. Included among the prisoners was Kirby.

He spent the next twelve months in a prisoner-of-war camp, where he found the Turks very casual and indifferent observers of the conventions.

Karita, used to hearing regularly from him, began to wonder why she now heard nothing at all. She pestered Headquarters. Headquarters enjoyed her visits. She received extremely generous offers from some of the most splendid members of the staff, each man promising to dress her in diamonds at least. Karita did not want diamonds and she did not need a bed. All she required was information concerning Colonel Kirby.

It was a long time coming. He was missing.

Missing? Did that mean he was dead?

It meant he was missing.

It numbed Karita. She had always realised something might happen to him. But this. It could mean he'd never come back. It could mean he was lying out there in the snow, stiff, frozen.

She felt as if they had taken off her right arm. It was two days before her numbness thawed out and she was able to face reality. Reality was a devastating loneliness but not complete despair. There was always hope. She would not leave Kars, not unless he was officially listed as killed. So she stayed on. When Headquarters tried to introduce another officer into the apartment she refused point blank to allow this. She would not co-operate in any way. She would not budge. The apartment was held in the name of Colonel Kirby, a friend of the Tsar himself, and until she heard from him or the Tsar, she would continue to hold it for him. Headquarters surrendered gracefully.

Karita worked in the military hospital and waited. She counted her beads and she prayed. She wrote to Aunt Charlotte, telling her only that the weather was awful and that Colonel Kirby was still making things unpleasant for the Turks. She thought of the Crimea and its sunshine, she thought of Walton and the river, of the cottage, the ducks and the nice old postman.

She had made many friends in Kars, and had more than a few admirers. She felt, however, that with things as they were she had to worry just as much about Aunt

Charlotte's future as her own. It was no time to become involved with any admirer.

Aunt Charlotte, busy, bustling and booming in Walton on behalf of the glorious war wounded of Britain, would have been amazed at Karita's concern. She was quite enjoying the war in a way. There was so much to do for the heroes.

Whatever talents Rasputin had he set them all lower than his gifts for roaring buffoonery. He uttered his last belch at the end of December. On a very cold night in Petrograd he was silenced by Prince Felix Yussoupov and other conspirators. They poisoned him, shot him and drowned him. His bullet-ridden, arsenic-filled, lung-swamped body was found under the ice of the Neva a few days later. If this did not mean the end of Imperial Russia to Alexandra it did mean the end of her peace of mind concerning Alexis. Without Rasputin, who had had such a mesmeric hold on the boy's life, she did not know how Alexis would survive future illnesses. Rasputin's death was her personal disaster.

They buried him in the Imperial Park at Tsarskoe Selo. The Emperor and Empress were there, also the Grand Duchesses and a few intimates, including Anna Vyrubova. Alexandra wept. Her tears were for the holy man and herself and Alexis. They should have been for Russia.

Yet despite her grief she displayed astounding resilience, an outward calmness and dignity that impressed ministers, ambassadors and friends alike. It was a dignity compounded of the resignation and sadness that were to be with her for the rest of her days.

In March Russia catapulted into revolution. On the 15th of that month Nicholas abdicated, not in favour of his haemophiliac son, whom he wanted to keep with him, but in favour of his younger brother Michael. But when Tsar Michael hastened to Petrograd from Gatchina he encountered such belligerent opposition that he abdicated immediately. The Romanov rule had

401

reached its end. Workers' councils renounced the dynasty and rejected all forms of autocracy.

The Provisional Government locked the Imperial family up in the Alexander Palace at Tsarskoe Selo, partly for their own safety. The Emperor himself arrived there on March 22nd, having taken an emotional farewell of his Army. Weary but calm he met Alexandra in their private apartments.

They had nothing left then but their love for each other.

Olga, now twenty-one, knew at last just how few friends they had. She could not believe they were as few as this. But she did not indulge in self-pity. They still had each other, they would always have each other. And no one could rob her of her dreams. She and Tatiana were closer than ever, made so by experiences shared in the joy and laughter of growing up, in the triumphs and defeats of war, and in their hospital work. Now they shared the humiliations and indignities of a family rejected by the country they passionately loved. They had never dreamed they could be hated.

"Papa is growing so thin," said Tatiana one day in May, two months after the abdication.

"He hasn't been blessed by things which help a man to grow fat," said Olga, "but at least he's a little happier now that they have let him plant a kitchen garden."

They were outside, venturing on a permitted but restricted walk. Soldiers, as always, were never far away, suspicious of every move. Nicholas had been allowed to dig a kitchen garden in the lawn of the Imperial Park, and on this day he was enjoying the pleasure of sowing seed. There were a few soldiers with him, willing to help with the work. Suspicious though they were, their willingness was typical of the effect the Imperial family had on most of their guards throughout their captivity, which was to last sixteen months. Their refusal to show bitterness or to complain, their total lack of airs and graces, and their

402

insistance that it was not they who mattered but Russia, all helped to soften men surly and hard to begin with. At all stages of the captivity there were some men who would have liked the Imperial family to go free.

Perhaps the only man who would have been totally impervious was Lenin. Lenin was Russia's sea-green incorruptible. Such men permit themselves no emotions. Lenin was able to sit up writing one of his interminable treatises on a night when his wife's mother lay desperately ill in the same room. He could do nothing for her, she could do nothing for him. Therefore, it was logical for each of them to pursue their separate ways, she towards death and he towards the completion of his manuscript. He did not bother to call his wife when the death rattle came. She could have done nothing, either.

Olga and Tatiana would have found Lenin utterly incomprehensible.

"Alexander Fedorovich," said Tatiana, referring to Kerensky, head of the Provisional Government, "has told Papa we might be sent to Livadia, to stay there indefinitely."

"I know," said Olga, "and he means what he says, I think."

"Livadia," said Tatiana wistfully, "would be infinitely better than here."

"More than that, much more," said Olga earnestly. "Livadia would be worth praying for every minute of every day."

Tatiana's expression of bright hope matched Olga's earnestness. Tatiana was nineteen, willowy and by now the most classically beautiful of the Grand Duchesses.

"How I'd love to be watching Papa playing tennis, seeing Mama in the sunshine," said Tatiana restlessly. She glanced at her sister as they slowly walked, then at soldiers who were lolling but watchful. "Olga, do you know where Ivan is now? Does he write to you?"

Olga looked straight ahead. The Park was lovely in May.

"We've never exchanged letters," she said.

"Olga, how stuffy that sounds," said Tatiana. "Is it because Mama wouldn't approve? But perhaps she would now. We're nobodies now, you know. You should write to him, he'll be so concerned about us. You should tell him we're all well."

"Mama is even prouder now than she was before," said Olga quietly.

"That isn't to say you shouldn't write to a friend, especially now that we don't seem to have so many. Oh." said Tatiana with a sigh, "if it were me I'd be dashing off pages and pages every day. Olga, you're silly to be so sensitive, to be as proud as Mama in wanting to do exactly what's right when everything is so different now. Well, tell me, is there anything sillier than any of us now saying this or that shouldn't be done because someone isn't a Grand Duke or a Crown Prince? If you feel that because of Mama and Papa. Ivan isn't to be concerned about what is happening to us, aren't you concerned about what might be happening to him?"

"Tasha!" Olga was fierce in her hurt. "Tasha, how could you!"

"Well, you should write to him," insisted Tatiana.

"He is supposed to have written to Mama and to Alexis," said Olga. "He did last Christmas but not this. Mama hasn't had a word from him, nor has Alexis. Tatiana, do you think he's gone back to England? They say it's awful in Armenia, worse than Galicia was or anywhere else."

Tatiana did not answer that. They turned away from guards posted at the limit of their allowed exercise and retraced their steps. Tatiana could only think of one reason why Ivan Ivanovich hadn't sent Christmas greetings to the family. It was a thought she pushed fiercely aside, a thought she could not put into words in front of Olga.

She said, "I think Mama would like to go to England even more than Livadia. Papa says he'll never leave

Russia, but Mama thinks he'd be safer in England than anywhere."

"England?" Olga caught her breath. "Are they talking again about sending us there?"

"Mama often talks about it and Alexander Fedorovich nods his head and says he'll see."

"Oh, it would be the best thing until people come to their senses here," said Olga eagerly, "it's the only place Mama and Papa would live in outside Russia. There'd be Great Aunt Alix and Grand Mama—she'd go too—and all our English cousins and——"

"And perhaps Ivan Ivanovich too," said Tatiana.

"Tasha, it's not for myself, truly it's not."

"All the same, if he were there," said Tatiana teasingly, "it would be rather nice, wouldn't it?"

"Colonel Kirby——"

"Colonel Kirby?" Tatiana laughed a little. They could all still laugh. "Olga, oh, how modest and coy you are. When you do see him again I suppose you're just going to say, 'Colonel Kirby, you've been rather a long time again, but you may kiss my hand.' Dearest, don't you see, we really are nobodies, and Mama simply could not refuse your marrying him now, could she?"

"Tasha, don't," gasped Olga, "oh, that would give her one more worry when she already has so many."

"But that is what you're thinking of if we go to England, isn't it?"

"Tasha, don't!"

The guards watched them, two brightly-attired young women walking in the sunshine of the Imperial Park, the Alexander Palace a looming edifice of cupolas and domes. One soldier followed them with sleepy eyes. His mind stirred his tongue and he coarsely expressed his preference. A comrade looked at him, spat softly and turned away.

In August, Alexander Kerensky, sympathetic towards the Imperial family, had them moved to Tobolsk in Western Siberia. He did not consider them safe while they remained at Tsarskoe Selo and was doing his best to negotiate their eventual exile to England.

In November, the Provisional Government was overthrown, Kerensky had to run for his life and the Bolsheviks took over. Lenin, who wasn't quite the prophet Rasputin was, arrived only just in time to participate in the Bolshevik putsch. If it hadn't been for the accommodating Germans and the shortsighted Kaiser, Lenin might easily have missed it all. However, he did arrive full of words and pamphlets, and was in time to take his place with Trotsky as a fount of inspiration. Stalin was there too but did most of his work unobtrusively and in the dark.

The autocracy of Tsarism had gone. Now the Provisional Government, which was to bring democracy to Russia, went too. The glorious Bolshevik revolution triumphed, and there emerged the new despots, no less intolerant than the old. Men fighting for the cause of Bolshevism died. But not Lenin, not Trotsky, not Stalin. Like all politicians theirs was not to die but to encourage others to. They attacked the citadels of authority from the back. The citadels fell and they at once began to establish as cruel and oppressive a system as that which for years they had denounced. Stalin proved as merciless and bloodthirsty as any Tsar, but more hypocritical.

Such were the men who called the Imperial family butchers.

Andrei was one of the aristocrats they came for on the last night of November. He came down the stairs of his Petrograd house as they burst in. He was immaculately casual in a silk dressing-gown and slippers. His hands were in the pockets. It was the usual untidy crowd. Sailors, soldiers, civilians and women, and all of them hungry-looking.

"What is it you want, food or blood?" he said.

"We want your bones," said a man, "we want them for the dogs."

Andrei saw his own servants among the intruders. They would not look at him. Nor, he knew, would they help him. The hungry ones rushed. Andrei's right hand

406

came out of his dressing-gown pocket and lazily, but with a little flicker of satisfaction, he shot the first man. Then, to please himself and to frustrate the rest of them, he very successfully shot himself. He was quite happy to depart. It was their world, not his. There'd be no peace for anyone.

Aleka came later. She strode into the smashed-up hall wearing a coarse black serge coat, her booted feet tramping, her hair scragged back and bound by a ribbon of revolutionary red. But for her fine pale skin she could have been a worker's woman. She had Bolshevik comrades at her back. Tucked into a leather belt around her coat was a pistol.

She looked at the body, at the pool of blood on the shining floor.

"Andrei, oh you fool, why didn't you go?" she said, but only to herself. Aloud she said, "Well, they all have to go in one way or another, comrades."

But he could have escaped. She had telephoned him, implored him to get away and at once. He had preferred to stay. It was sad. She had loved him. He had loved her. But for the sake of the revolution one had to suffer some heartache.

She began to abuse the short-sighted comrades who had damaged what was now the property of the people.

SIX

In December they said that Lenin smiled.

Among things that actually did happen was the conclusion of an armistice between the Russian Army of the Caucasus and Turkey. The Turks were only too pleased, their own Ottoman Empire was falling apart. The prisoners they held were one more drain on their vanishing resources. So they began to open the gates.

"That way," they said to the Russian prisoners, pointing north, and the released Russians began their long walk home. It was a last walk for some. The sky hung each day like a frozen grey blanket. the earth was soundless and without life. Only warmth could make the soil breathe again and warmth seemed as if it had gone forever. Some of the men reached Russian lines by Christmas. Kirby was one of them.

In early January he was back in Kars. The place was bleak and brooding, icy and bitter. Men moved indifferent to each other. The Russian forces were breaking up under the demoralisation brought about by a terrible war and a Bolshevist revolution. All these wasted years when each savage battle had only paved the way for another, and the death of one day led to the suicide of the next.

Kings and queens, emperors and empresses were at the top of the long slide down.

Headquarters in Kars was not very interested, all kinds of prisoners were turning up. There were still dinners, dances, women. There was still wine. There were still elegant, well-dressed officers. If they knew they were dancing while the flames came closer they did not seem to be bothered. He was to come and see them when he felt better. It was good to know he had survived, of course. His name had not been included in any prisoner-of-war lists.

He asked them about the Tsar and the Tsar's family.

They shrugged as if to indicate Nicholas had brought it all on himself. And there was no real news except that the whole family was now reported to be in To-bolsk in Western Siberia. They would not be there long, of course. The place was full of loyalists who would rescue them any moment.

Kirby thought of the family as he trudged through the icy streets. There had been scarcely a day since news of the abdication reached his prisoner-of-war camp when he had not thought of them. He thought of Alexis the boy, Anastasia the gifted. Marie the ro-mantic. Tatiana the intelligent. And he thought night and day of Olga the sensitive, now in the hands of people who, embittered by oppression, would take pleasure in humiliating the whole family.

He reached the house. It stood in hard grey-brown defiance of the biting cold. He had no key but the door to the first-floor apartment was not locked. Head-quarters had said Karita was still here. The apartment was empty, but it was warm and lived-in. The fire was laid but not lighted. Timber was in the grate. A small oil heater burned and spread comfort. A samovar stood on it as if someone had known he was coming. He poured tea from it, drank the golden liquid slowly and gratefully. He put a match to the fire. The flame sprang. His fur coat, his ear-muffed fur hat and his worn brown boots were stiff with ice.

Removing cap and coat he sank into a chair. He wondered about Karita. Headquarters had said she had anchored herself to the place as stubbornly as a sailor's mule. Yet she hated Kars. He began to pull tiredly at his boots. His thin face was dark with the stubble of beard, he looked like a cold, unshaven tramp. There was someone at the outer door. He heard footsteps and seconds later Karita came into the room, pinkly glowing in the sable he had bought her in old St. Petersburg, when the capital had been gay and alive, when he had been alive too. She was carrying a paper bag.

She stopped, she stared. He managed a smile as he looked up at her from the awkwardness of loosening boots he hadn't had off for weeks. Karita gave a wild sob, threw the bag down and ran to tumble to her knees in front of him. She hid her face as she pulled at his left boot. She was crying noisily. He put out a hand, pushed back her hat and teased her golden hair.

"You should have gone home to your parents, little one, but thank you," he said.

"Ivan Ivanovich . . . oh, you're disgraceful, disgraceful . . . all this time and not a word from you." She put her hands to her face and sobbed into them.

"Now look here," he said mildly because of physical lassitude, "I haven't been lying around enjoying balmy Arcadia——"

"Arcadia? Who is she?" Karita's voice, wet with sobs, managed to sound outraged.

"It's a kind of rustic heaven. Well, I haven't been there. Didn't you get any of the cards they let us write?"

"I've heard nothing, nothing. Oh, it's easy for you to sound as if everything has been quite ordinary, you knew you weren't dead, but I didn't." Her voice burst through her tears. "It's the most disgraceful thing I've ever heard of. A whole year and I haven't once known what was to become of me. But you would go off, you wouldn't listen to me and see what happened."

"What did happen?" He felt he was home again. Karita, like Olga, was always herself.

"I don't know," she cried indignantly, "nobody knew. Oh, those stupid people at Headquarters. It's no wonder Russia is in such a state when there are so many people like that about."

"Didn't you guess I was in a prisoner-of-war camp?"

410

Karita, still on her knees, lifted her head. She was so happy that the tears ran sparkling with joy. Her long loneliness was over.

"There, that's it," she said, "you would go. But you were supposed to do away with Turks, not let them put you in some awful camp. Oh, look at you," she gasped, "you're so thin, so cold. What have they been doing to you? What have you let them do?"

"Nothing," he said, "this is just wear and tear. Still, I suppose it does show I'm pretty inadequate without you." His eyes, dark in their hollows, were more alive than the rest of him. They were warm with affection because she was here, because she had waited. Karita was hot with gladness.

"Why didn't you say you were coming?" She began to pull at his boots again. "Oh, they're stiff, are they frozen to you?"

"I hope not, otherwise you'll have both my legs off. I'm not putting you out because I didn't let you know, am I?"

"Ivan Ivanovich, doing silly things is bad enough," she said, "but saying silly things is even worse. There." She had loosened the boots. She sat back on her heels for a moment, surveying him with quite possessive pleasure. She pulled the boots off, sat back again and then gasped. She stared in horror. In the flame of the fire, a brightness in the darkening room, the condition of his grey woollen socks was unspeakable. His heels and toes emerged from mere woollen rags. The dirty rags were indescribable, but for Coloney Kirby to have such disgustingly filthy feet, well! There were simply no Russian words she could think of.

"They're stinkingk," she said in English.

"I know," he said. "Just be grateful that you haven't had to live with them for as long as I have." She surveyed him again. How drawn he was, how tired. But at least his eyes were bright. Karita felt the strangest emotions. Her heart hammered. Her blood rushed. Moistness took renewed possession of her eyes. She got up, her face flaming.

411

"Stay there," she said breathlessly, "I'm going to bring some hot water and then some hot soup. Later you can have a bath. Oh, it's disgraceful, everything is." She rushed out. In the kitchen she stamped a foot at herself because of the stupid tears. She took him a bowl of hot water, put the bowl on the floor at his feet, picked up the woollen rags and threw them disgustedly into the fire. Kirby slid his feet into the bowl.

"Oh, so this is the unbearable bliss, is it?" he murmured. "Karita, you precious lovely girl."

Karita stifled a sob and rushed out again. She began to prepare soup. She went back when the pot was on. He was still there, very relaxed, his feet immersed. The water was muddy.

"Karita."

She stood beside him. He looked up at her. There was something in his eyes, a reflection of thoughts painful and intense.

"What is it?" she asked.

"Is it true? They've taken the Imperial family to a place called Tobolsk?"

"Yes," she said. There was a burning in her brown eyes he had seen before. "Yes, that's what we've heard. Ivan Ivanovich, if they harm them I shall still love Russia but I shall despise its people."

"Not all of them."

"All of them, because there'll be those who will have done it and the rest will be those who have let them. The Tsar is a good man, a kind man. They're blaming him for everything, for the stupidity of politicians and the wickedness of others. I know nothing about how to govern Russia, but I know people and I know our Father Tsar, I know his family. If they are harmed, oh, I tell you, Ivan Ivanovich, I'll do some harming myself. And I've something better to use than my tongue."

She pulled open the door of a tall corner cupboard in which was displayed china and ornaments. From it she took a polished, shining rifle. It was a British Lee-Enfield.

412

She showed it to him and the burning in her eyes was reflected in his.

"As soon as we can, Karita, we'll go to Tobolsk," he said.

Karita put the rifle away. "The soup won't be long," she said, "but I wish I'd known you were coming, then I'd have had something much better than soup to give you. I wouldn't have wasted so much time walking with Captain Kalinin."

"Walking? In this weather?" His voice was drowsy. "And who is he?"

Karita smiled a little slyly.

"Oh, someone very nice," she said. "I've been working at the hospital. Captain Kalinin is one of the medical officers, he's from Georgia. I'm to meet his people when I go there."

"Well, at last," murmured Kirby.

"At last? What is that supposed to mean?"

"Everything, I imagine, if his people approve. I can't imagine them disapproving of a perfect treasure. When are you going?" Had he not felt so tired the wrench of disappointment at the obvious prospect of losing her would have been stronger.

Karita slipped off her coat, she sank to the floor beside his chair. The fire tossed its flames, reached out its light and heat.

"It hasn't been very nice without you," she said, "it's nice now. I'm so glad you're here again. I'm not going to Georgia. Goodness, do you think I'm to marry Captain Kalinin? You'll be going back to England when the war is all over and what would Aunt Charlotte say if I let you go by yourself? She would ask where I was and make it uncomfortable for you."

"There are other things to do first, Karita."

"Yes, I know." She put her arm on his knee and rested her face there. "Captain Kalinin is just very nice and sometimes he gets food for me. Sometimes it isn't very easy to come by, especially meat or flour. Oh, I forgot, do you know what I have?"

"Something I like very much, Karita," he said.

"You're the loveliest kind of person to come home to."

"You're saying that because I'm making hot soup for you. I have some beef."

"Beef?" He stirred out of his drowsiness and sat up. "Beef?"

"Yes." Karita sounded as if she were in happy possession of a fatted calf. "Boris—Captain Kalinin—gave it to me. He wouldn't take any money. He never does. Was it proper to let him kiss me instead?"

"It happens all the time, I suppose. It sounds a fair exchange. Yes, it's proper enough. But beef?"

"Yes." She jumped to her feet, flitted through shadows and found the paper bag. She extracted a square tin and showed it to him. By the light of the fire he recognised it as a tin of British Army bully beef. "There, it's in a tin to keep it fresh," she said, "and I think you make a hole in the tin, then put it in the stove and bake it."

"Ah, mmm, yes, but I shouldn't do that," he said, "it'll probably blow up. I'll show you what to do with it later. Would you have potatoes and an onion?"

"Potatoes, yes. But an onion. Oh, I'll get one, you'll see. Our neighbours are all very nice. I'll go and look at the soup."

She went into the kitchen again. She was singing. He stretched in the chair, his body rapturous in its tiredness and its absorption of warmth. He thought of Olga. The memories came bright and clear. The pain was there, and the longing. But fear too now. Fear of what the Bolsheviks might do. If Karita had received none of the prisoner-of-war cards he'd sent, then Alexandra had probably not received the two he'd sent her. He closed heavy eyes. Despite the thoughts, the fear, he fell asleep in the chair.

Karita came back, carrying a bowl of steaming soup. She looked down at him. His head was on one side, his hair thick and untidily long. It needed trimming. He was fast asleep. His drawn face was in quiet peace. She tiptoed away to keep the soup simmering. She returned with a blanket and put it over him.

414

She stooped and kissed his forehead.

Ivan Ivanovich, she thought, it's about time you took a wife and went home. A fire is not enough to come back to, it's ridiculous that you have no one but me. Why didn't you marry the Princess Karinshka? That, I think, was something to do with Prolofski and Oravio. When I next see our Aunt Charlotte I'll ask her if it's not too improper for you to marry me. You must have someone.

She sank down in front of the fire. She watched the flames. It was lovely not to feel lonely any more.

It was cold, so cold in Tobolsk.

The fuel allowance for the Imperial family permitted only one fire to burn, that in the drawing-room.

Sometimes the soldiers were friendly and sometimes, because of political happenings, not so friendly. The Bolsheviks had not swept Russia, after all, they were having to fight for their lives to keep what part of it they did have. Opposition was against all logic. It made them tremble with fear and frustration, it turned them vicious. One felt it. The soldiers felt it.

On a morning when those guarding the Imperial family were not so friendly, one of them a hard and cynical veteran of the campaigns in Galicia, placed himself in the path of Grand Duchess Olga as she crossed the hoar-frosted yard to retrieve a small spade belonging to Alexis. The girls had been using it to pile snow and shape it. The frost glittered on the man's heavy eyebrows, on his fur cap. His gloved hands held his rifle across his body, blocking her.

"I'm sorry," said Olga gently, "is it because I'm not permitted to be out here today?"

It was like that sometimes. Such meagre privileges as they had would be suddenly withdrawn and without apparent reason.

"No," the man said gruffly. "Is there anyone behind me?"

"Nobody," said Olga. She was heavily wrapped and muffed, her fur coat a welcome warmth about her cold

415

body. She was thinner. Her skin had lost its kiss from the sun and she was pale, as they all were.

"Then take what you see in my right hand and swear your ignorance of it coming from me," he said. He spoke growlingly. It was for the benefit of any suspicious comrades. His right hand covered his rifle butt. She saw a tiny triangle of white showing. She reached, pulled it free and slipped it into her muff. It was a crumpled envelope.

She knew she must not thank him or smile at him. Everyone watched everybody else here. But she could not refrain from showing him eyes warm with gratitude. It was a letter she clutched inside her muff and how welcome it would be to Mama and Papa. The soldier brusquely turned his back, stamped to strike the cold from his booted feet and Olga went back into the house as if rebuffed. Her heart was beating, thumping. Letters sometimes came for them, but always they were censored first unless they were smuggled in. This one had come furtively. Was it for Papa?

For some reason she did not go into the drawing-room but hurried up the stairs as quietly as she could, she wanted to see to whom the letter was addressed before producing it in front of the others. The bedroom was icy. She pulled the envelope out. It was addressed to herself at Tobolsk, Western Siberia. She knew the writing. It was the same as that on the fly-leaf of her Shakespeare, the same as that in letters sent to Alexis. She herself kept those letters for her brother. Her eyes swam. She heard Anastasia's clear voice from below.

"Where's Olga? Someone is to tell her we're all to go outside for exercise. Marie, don't stand on my foot, you elephant."

But no one came up the stairs to look for her. Olga sat down on the edge of her bed. She opened the letter. It was difficult to read at first because the ridiculous agitation of her heart seemed to affect her eyes.

Dearest Olga. I don't know if this letter will ever reach

416

you but I'm told by a certain person that it will. And I pray that it will so you'll know how much I and others are thinking of all of you. I wrote two cards to the Empress from a prisoner-of-war camp in Turkey, but fear she may not have received them. I'm back in Russia now and on my way with Karita and others to Tobolsk, and to do all we can when we get there.

I know that as I write you are in Tobolsk. I know that Russia has gone mad. I can't think of your present circumstances without anguish. What can I or any man say to comfort you? I could say that a family which deserved love and understanding received none at all, but what comfort is that? I pray that things are not too unbearable for you, although I know it isn't necessary to tell you or any of your family to have courage.

Men who found fault in the Emperor but none in themselves have become his judges. I can only remember him as the kindest of men, I can only remember the Empress as the kindest of women. Who can judge them without setting aside their own imperfections? Dearest Olga, if there are such men there are also others, others who still love their Tsar and will have nothing to do with deposing him, or judging him. I'm with many such people now.

If you're surrounded by bitterness and hostility that you can't understand, remember it can't last, it must come to an end when they begin to know you all. I know you'll be happy again. I know I'll see you again. I have a promise to keep. The Emperor has not betrayed Russia, only trusted inadequate men too much and been too generous to his allies.

Karita begs you to accept her love and loyalty. We think of you, of all of you. Remember me to Alexis, to the Grand Duchesses and to your well-loved parents. I cannot forget them, I cannot forget you. You are always in my thoughts, always in Karita's prayers. You are very dear and very lovely, and I must say so.

I love you. Sweetest and most beautiful Grand Duchess, I love you. God be with you. John Kirby.

Olga sat there on the bed. The room was freezing. The world outside was brittle with hard, glittering frost, the voices of Anastasia and Marie high and clear with the resilience of the young.

417

He had not forgotten them, after all. He had not forgotten her. Nor was he lying in an icy grave in bleak, wintry Armenia. He was on his way to her.

Olga Nicolaievna smiled, her eyes huge pools of blue in her pale face. The letter in its preciousness she hugged to her as she went down the stairs and out into the tingling, frosty yard. Tatiana looked up from the snow they were all helping to build into a huge pile to keep themselves warm.

What did it matter if the guards were so moody and unfriendly today when her dearest sister looked so happy?

They were in Western Siberia with the White Army, the formidable Czech Legion spearheading the counter-revolutionary war against the Reds.

Karita was as hard as delicately-tempered steel, Kirby as lean and bitter as a starved wolf. They had left Kars in late January and, with a motley collection of Bolshevik-hating ex-Imperial Army men, joined forces with the Czech Legion. They themselves were in an improvised cavalry unit of four hundred, and the horses they rode they had had to buy. Mostly the unit was comprised of Kuban Cossacks, who foresaw anonymity clothing their nation under Bolshevism, but Karita was not the only woman who rode with them. There were other Amazons only too willing to fight the Reds. And Karita not only had her rifle, she had a nose for Reds. She could smell them a mile away.

She always had one question for strangers she did not like the smell of.

"What would you do, my friend, if you had the Tsar in your hands?"

They either replied stupidly or with hatred.

She turned her back on the stupid ones. She blew off the heads of the others. She had Tartar blood in her veins and appointed herself the executioner of all those who dealt in violence and hatred. They were destroying the Russia she loved, repaying injustice with worse injustice. She knew the kind of Russia they wanted. Well, some of them would not live to enjoy it, she sent them to discuss it with their ancestors.

She wore a Cossack uniform, including baggy trousers and boots, much to the roaring delight of her Kuban comrades. She had acquired a sabre to go with her British Lee-Enfield. She kept the sabre sharp, the rifle clean. She made good use of both weapons. If she and the other women were not allowed to attack Bolsheviks head-on, they were always there when the men had the Reds running. But sometimes it was harder to survive the admiration of the Cossacks than the dangers of anything else. Sometimes it was even necessary to shout for Colonel Kirby. They had a respect for Colonel Kirby, not because he was for their Tsar but because Karita had told them he was related to the King of England. That was something to Kuban Cossacks. They were admirers of Imperial power.

Ivan Ivanovich worried her a little. He had become so hard and so obsessed by the need to reach the Imperial family before it was too late. He had lost his good humour, his tolerance, his smile. She was horrified at the risks he sometimes took when they were smashing Bolshevik infiltrators out of villages or towns. She harangued him passionately on occasions.

"Will you let the scum of Russia take your life? Don't you ever think of what's to become of me?"

"You'll survive." His brusqueness was typical of his moods now.

"Oh, yes, I'll survive and you'll fight your way through a whole Red army, I suppose. And I'll have to follow on to bury each little piece of you until only your stupid head is left."

"Stop wagging your tongue," he said, "use your bottom instead. Put it on your horse. We're moving."

"There's no need to be improper," said Karita icily.

He stared at her. She had survived vicious Reds and amorous Cossacks, she lived each day within earshot of blaspheming men and she had seen sights he did not care to think about. Yet here she was acting the prim puss of the drawing-room.

"For God's sake," he said impatiently. He was consumed night and day by urgency and fear. Any advance was always too slow, and every Bolshevik who stood in his way, he wished to hell. He had neither time nor inclination for the kind of conversation he and Karita had had in the past.

"Aunt Charlotte would blush to hear you speak like this," she said.

"She'd blush for you. You look like a thieving Cossack."

"Oh, yes, a nice clean skirt would be better, wouldn't it?" She was furious with him. "Aunt Charlotte would like that, of course, with every man leering at my legs and petticoats."

He smiled then, Karita, tanned by sun and wind and ice, her golden hair plaited and bound, smiled too.

"Come on," he said.

If she sometimes worried about him, he sometimes wondered about her. Whenever prisoners were taken Karita unforgiving in her contempt for those who were turning Russians against Russians, sons against fathers, disclosed a streak of cruelty. She could watch without pity as the Cossacks put many captives to slow death. It was an anguished dance the Bolsheviks performed in the middle of a village before the Kubans finally dismembered them or broke their limbs and knotted them around their necks. Karita could smile at such things, her eyes burning.

Kirby, hating the cold, fanatical face of Bolshevism, the creed of men dedicated to the political liquidation of millions, did not care much whether men like these were executed or not. But he did not like torture for its own sake. He did several captives a good turn by shooting them as soon as they began their tormented writhing. This displeased his Cossack friends, but he was an Englishman with an Englishman's eccentricities which they humoured, though sometimes with a scowl.

Advancing towards Western Siberia the White Russian units were incorporated into the Czech command, and from then on had the umbrella of organized Czech efficiency to protect them from their own waywardness. But although the combined Czech and White Russian force began to hammer opposition into the ground with increasing speed, nothing satisfied the hurry Kirby was in. He had been blown up by the Germans in Poland and had been fortunate to survive the campaign in Armenia and his year as a prisoner of the Turks. Now he had more luck than a cat with nine lives. Stiffened by the Czechs, the White Russians were more formidable, the Cossacks more savage, and Kirby rode with them as they hurled themselves at Reds like the intoxicated Assassins of Hasan-i-Sabah. His disregard of risks and his apparent indifference to them appealed to men to whom life was not something to cling on to at the expense of so much else.

The Czech Legion, made up of fifty thousand men who had deserted from the Austro-Hungarian forces, had been promised safe conduct across Russia by the Bolsheviks. They had intended to join the Allies in the continuing war against the Germans. But at station after station the Czechs received anything but help from local soviets. The soviets had already taken on the trappings of fiddling intolerance and bureaucracy that they had disliked so much under Tsarism.

Finally, the Czechs, sensing treachery, took matters into their own hands. They struck first. Disciplined, well-organized and well-led, they were the real power behind the campaign to shove Bolshevism back into the obscene obscurity from which it had sprung. By the spring of 1918 they had helped to turn over the eastern half of Russia to White control.

They drove on into Western Siberia, towards Tobolsk, Kirby feverish now. He almost loved the Czechs for their inspired tactics, for their masterly and imaginative flanking movements which enabled them to isolate objectives and then easily reduce them. Russians would have gone for a massed frontal attack every time. The Czechs would take Tobolsk their own way, minimising the Reds' chances of removing the Imperial family in time.

They had fought through ice and snow, then through rain and howling wind. They had seen Russia at its most fearsome, but there was a day at last that was warm and sunny. It was a day when Karita and Kirby came close to quarrelling. It was late April. The Russians were saddling horses, men spitting and coughing, clearing their throats. Kirby was bristly and dark, the bitterness of civil war, of fighting that had no end, combined with anxieties that never left him, had hardened him body and soul. He was tightening the saddle girth when Karita, the skirt of her coat frayed and worn, her Cossack-style hat swinging in her hand, came up to speak to him.

Not for the first time she asked him how his head was. It was no wonder, she said, that he'd been captured by the Turks when he always went into action with his head empty. He, for the first time, told her to shut up.

She flushed with anger.

"That," she said, "is the voice of a very empty head. I know what will happen to you, you'll reach the Imperial family without any head at all. But what will it matter? You don't use it, anyway."

His eyes glittered. He wore an old coat over a patchwork of garments that had comprised a reasonable uniform when he left Kars. His trousers were tucked into black boots. He looked intense impatient.

"What are you complaining about?" he said. "I don't complain about you. If I lose my head, that's my worry. If you turn into a savage. that's yours."

"Savage? Who is a savage?" she cried.

"You are. You gloat over the agonies of men."

Kubans leading horses down the village street grinned to see Karita Katerinova in fury at her Englishman.

"Men! They aren't men!" She was loudly scathing. "They're animals. Do you know what they're doing to our people? Hanging them, shooting them, burying them alive! You wish me to laugh about this? You wish me to be kind to them? You want them to die so that they don't feel anything? They are animals who demand that we betray our own mothers, who have brought hatred to the whole of Russia and say it's for the good of Russia. What is good about that?"

"Nothing," he said, "but shut up."

"I'm to say nothing when you call me a savage?" Karita could have wept with fury, with unhappiness. "What a fine thing that is, coming from someone who is supposed to be related to the King of England!"

"And who is supposed to be that?"

"Well, do you think I could tell the Kubans you were nobody?" she said, angrily scornful. "They would probably have murdered you long ago if you had been. It would have made me look a nobody too, they'd have cooked me for supper. I'm disgusted with you. Never would I have let you take me away from my parents if I'd known you would call me names—oh, a fine father and mother you are to me!"

His irritation vanished. He gave a shout of laughter. Watching Kubans grinned happily to see him kiss her on the nose and slap her bottom. But it did not mollify Karita. She was bitterly disappointed in him. She knew he was suffering because of the Imperial family, but so was she. And what with so many other things her nerves were constantly at breaking-point. He was always trying to get himself killed. That would be fine for him, he would be peacefully dead, but what about her? She would have to go back to her parents and either be a servant to some village headman now that all the aristocrats had been murdered or marry some Crimean wine-treader who never wore clean clothes except on Sundays. The thought made her shudder. It had only been by the merest accident and her own intuition that she hadn't married that infamous Oravio.

And now Ivan Ivanovich thought her a savage. She looked at him with hot and angry brown eyes, turned on her heels with a swirl of her skirted coat and went to saddle her own horse.

"Kill yourself, then!" she called over her shoulder. "Get your head blown off!"

"Karita! Come back!"

She heard the insistence of the command. She would have gone on with angry strides but suddenly thought of her mother. Her mother would be horrified. She was bound in service to Ivan Ivanovich. Under no circumstances would her mother have permitted her to defy him. She stopped. She heard his footsteps behind her. The unit of cavalry was beginning to mill up and down the dirt surface of the village street. Villagers were coming out, some offering the men what food they could spare. The Cossacks grinned and asked for wine.

"Karita." His voice was kind. His hands on her shoulders turned her round. His face was burned by the wind, his eyes tender. "Forgive me, Karita. Everything I said was unkind. Everything is my own fault. I think too much of other things and not enough of you. It would be a sorry day if you and I came to blows. There's too much of it going on all over Russia now without my bad temper inciting more of it. There, I'm sorry. Am I forgiven?"

Karita was mortified. She had been ungenerous. She looked at the fur hat she held. It had been glossy once. In an excess of unusual embarrassment she spent the next few moments tugging it on over her head. Then she said, "Ivan Ivanovich, it's only that I don't want you to get yourself killed. Oh, as if we would fight each other, you and I. But it'll be better when all this is over and we can go to England again. You don't shout at me there."

The quaint absurdity of this nearly had him laughing again. But Karita was in such obvious seriousness that he knew she would not take kindly to any lack of it in himself at this moment.

"England is a long way off in more ways than one, Karita."

"But when we take Tobolsk," said Karita, "that will bring it a great deal nearer."

"Yes, it will," he said, "for us and for them, I hope."

He put his arm around her, squeezed her.

Tobolsk fell to the Czechs and the Whites two days later. They made wide, sweeping thrusts that pincered the town. Pounded and pulverised. the defending Reds broke and fled in panic, knowing only too well how the Whites dealt with prisoners they suspected of being active Bolsheviks. The cavalry burst upon the fleeing Reds. Karita lost Kirby in the smoke and confusion. She found him later. The Czechs were pouring into the town and the Cossacks were playing murderous tag with Bolsheviks around the streets and houses. Amid all the wild movement Kirby dismounted, stood with two other officers in the centre of the town. They were talking to a frightened civilian.

Kirby's face was grey. The Imperial family were no longer in Tobolsk. They had been removed some time ago to Ekaterinburg in the Urals.

The advance westward continued. The Czechs and the Whites did not intend to stop until they had taken Moscow and Petrograd. The Bolsheviks had transferred the seat of Government to Moscow.

They entered the Urals and approached Ekaterinburg. It looked like a fortress in its position on the hills that rose before them. It was a grey. industrial place. It could take time to capture. The Czechs began sizing up the most economical means, the Whites were for a direct, impatient assault. Kirby himself was not interested in anything but getting to the Tsar and his family before the Reds cheated him again.

At dawn one morning he left the White lines, Karita with him. She was sure he was making a noose for his own neck and she would prevent that if she could. Kirby was driven by a hammering urgency. He could not remember the last time when he had slept well. Even when his mind and body were exhausted he awoke night after night as nightmarish visions jerked him into sweating consciousness. He knew enough about Bolsheviks now to suspect they would never let the Romanovs go.

It was July. It was hot. The dawn itself was a brooding stillness, awaiting the advent of the fiery sun. Kirby and Karita rode until they reached the foothills, and then Kirby indicated they should ride openly into Ekaterinburg by the road.

"Are you mad?" asked Karita. Her rifle was slung, her skin damp. She was bareheaded and wore blouse and trousers. Kirby wore shirt, trousers, cartridge belt and pistol.

"We'll just ride in," he said, "it will be less suspicious than creeping in. If we're stopped we're deserters carrying information on the Whites."

That was not too unreasonable. People were constantly changing sides all over the areas of combat. It was the only way for some people to keep their lives.

Surprisingly, as the sun rose to tip the hills and the wooded slopes with morning gold, there was an atmosphere of utter quietness. There were no manned defences, no outposts, no guns, no bullets, no Reds. There was nothing to be seen on the road, nothing to be seen on either side of them except the silent slopes. They entered the town, riding their horses leisurely. Ekaterinburg itself was quiet too. Or so it seemed. Karita stiffened as a woman's voice suddenly pierced the early morning air. Kirby smiled humourlessly. It was a woman shouting at a lazy husband.

"I think we're very noticeable," said Karita.

"Crowds feel safe, individuals feel isolated. There'll be people soon, Karita."

"How will we find the family?" she asked.

"We shall probably have to ask."

"Madness," she gasped.

They turned a corner and found themselves riding towards an oncoming platoon of Red soldiers. The platoon was marching quickly, the men still had sleep in their eyes. Karita and Kirby drew aside, the soldiers marched by, taking no notice of them. The town began to wake up. Then they heard the sound of horsemen behind them. They looked round. A band of Reds

426

came up, their purpose as clear now as the risen sun. One silent house had had eyes.

Kirby put his hands up, Karita followed suit but with a look of disgust.

"Who are you?" asked one of the horsemen.

"Friends," said Kirby, "we've come over from the Whites. We have information."

"Very original." The man smiled cynically. "We've had that kind of pleasure a thousand times and they were nearly all liars. We'll see whether the District Commissar thinks the same about you. That way." He jerked his head.

They were taken to a deserted kindergarten school. Their weapons were confiscated, with their ammunition, and they were searched for other arms. Karita minded very much about the loss of her Lee-Enfield and she minded just as much about the way she was searched.

"Pigs," she said, but she spoke in English.

They were taken down a flight of stone steps from the ground floor and flung into a cellar. It had the smell of other human beings about it, wretched human beings. The door was locked on them. There was no furniture. They sat on the floor. They had been in worse places. Karita made what cheerful conversation she could and Kirby maintained an attitude of hope. It was only a question of convincing some locally-elected commissar that they loved Lenin. And it was from him that they might find out where the Imperial family were.

An hour passed before anyone came. Then the door was unlocked. Two men stood there. They wore civilian clothes but carried rifles. Members of the local soviet, thought Kirby. Bolsheviks on the whole were easily recognisable. Like Cromwell's Roundheads they looked like men who found joy in self-denial.

"You. You. This way."

They were taken up to the ground floor. The school seemed lonely, empty. There were hollow echoes. A door was pushed open and they were prodded into a large room whose only furniture consisted of two desks

427

and several chairs. A man sat at one desk, his capped head bent over a sheet of paper. He was writing. He did not look up as Kirby and Karita were brought before him. He continued writing. The two men retired to the door and stayed there. There was a slight nervousness about them and they seemed to be listening for something they would rather not hear.

The moving hand stopped. The commissar lifted his head. He had a round, white face and in the darkness of any night it would have looked like a pale, glimmering moon. There was mutual recognition. Inwardly Kirby heaved a deep sigh. The cold expressionless eyes of Peter Prolofski flickered and a smile like a white cheese splitting parted his mouth.

"Ah," he said very softly to Kirby, "there's always some light on a dark day. I'm surprised to see you, my friend, but very happy." He said to Karita. "Who are you?"

"She's with me," said Kirby, "we left the White Army together."

"She has her own tongue, I suppose?" said Prolofski. "Let her use it. Who are you, woman?"

"A deserter, like he is," said Karita.

"Oh?" Prolofski leaned back, his fingertips drummed the desk lightly. "I could not be sure if I remembered your face but I know your voice. So, you're both here. Extraordinary. It was very uncomfortable for me for a long time. But you have your friends, I imagine. I have mine. It was dark in that hole. But it was only a question of waiting. One year, two years, ten." He shrugged. "It made no difference as long as we stayed alive."

"That was necessary at the time," said Kirby, "things are different now."

"Very different." The moonface looked unhealthy but complacent. "And so you've deserted and come to me. It could not have been better arranged by Satan himself. He at least has proved his existence. It's amusing, don't you think?"

"Not to us," said Kirby. "And you could be wasting

428

time. Do your people want information on the Whites, where they are, what——"

"We know where they are." Prolofski interrupted flatly. "They're knocking on the door. They want Ekaterinburg. They shall have it. We'll take it back later. Your information is useless. It would have been useless, in any case. I know you, my friend. I'll give you some real facts. Our comrades of the Red Army have already pulled out. I have a few more things to see to and then I shall be gone too. I shall leave you and your hellcat last on my list. I shall think about you, both of you. You shall think about me. I hope——"

The door behind him opened. Two people came in, a man and a woman. The man was Oravio, the woman Princess Aleka Petrovna. Oravio was gaunt, his earnestness a hungry glitter. Aleka was thinner, her pale skin a stretched tautness over her cheekbones. She wore the blouse, skirt and boots of a female commissar. She stared at Kirby, at Karita, her body stiffening, her black eyes ringed by shadows. Oravio stared too, then looked as if the fates had brought him his most satisfying day.

"I think," said Prolofski, "that you all know each other."

"What are they doing here?" asked Aleka. Her husky voice, once a purring pleasure to the ear, was emotionless.

"Comrade Commissar," said Prolofski, "their investigation is mine. I shall deal with them."

"Well, you have the appetite," said Aleka. She shrugged. "It's his revolution," she said to Kirby, "and you were very unwise to have finished up here in view of other things. But you always had a stupid streak."

"One either wins or loses, Princess," said Kirby. He felt desperately sorry for Karita, he was drained of everything else now. It was the filthiest bad luck to be hit by this one in a million chance. Prolofski would take more than his pound of flesh.

"Princess?" Oravio sneered. "She could get her throat cut for that."

Karita's heart was like ice but she said very lightly, "There's an awful smell about this place."

Oravio took that badly. He cracked her across the face with the back of his hand. Kirby, hardened by every kind of experience and indifferent now to any other, almost broke Oravio's jaw with a fist that felt like a hammer to Oravio and sounded like one to Aleka. For a moment her tired eyes flashed into glowing life. Oravio crashed to the floor. The two men at the door ran forward, beating Kirby with rifle butts. Karita spat at them. Aleka's eyes relapsed into indifference.

"Yes, yes, all right," said Prolofski, gesturing the men back. "But he's mine, comrades, and I don't want him spoiled. They're both mine. Take them away."

They were locked in the cellar again. They sat on the floor, their backs against the wall. There was a bruise on Karita's face.

"Prolofski," she said, "was very bad luck, Ivan Ivanovich."

"Very bad luck, Karita. I'm sorry."

"You aren't to worry about that," she said. "But Prolofski, he's quite a worry. Someone let him out."

"Yes. The sort of thing that happens in times like these." He spoke calmly enough. He did not like the thought of what Prolofski was going to do to him, he liked even less the thought of what the moonfaced ghoul might do to Karita. They would both finish up very dead, that was certain. But it was not going to be swift and clean, that was also certain.

"They're going to kill us, you know," she said.

"Yes." He smiled. Karita was able to smile too, then. "I don't know what Aunt Charlotte's going to say," he said.

"She'll be very upset." Karita sighed a little. "Ivan, you're not blaming yourself too much, are you? I should be happier if you did not do that. I do not regret anything, I'm glad to have been with you and I'm not sorry to be with you now. It's better together, isn't it?"

430

"No, it isn't," he said, "it's damned silly. You shouldn't be here, you're the last person who should suffer from my stupidity."

"I'm not looking forward to it," said Karita frankly, "but, you see, Ivan, it's been very nice being with you for so long. It wouldn't be at all nice without you."

He looked at her. She was smiling. He felt wholly, completely undeserving of her. He put out a hand and lightly teased her hair, something he had often done.

"Well, together, then, little one," he said.

His eyes seemed so dark.

"You're still thinking of them, aren't you?" she said.

"Of them and of you. I'm praying the Czechs and the Whites move quickly enough."

They were both thinking the same thing. If the Reds had pulled out they would probably have taken the Imperial family with them, moved them again. If so, he and she had thrown their lives away for nothing. She became very quiet.

There was the tiniest sound of the key being carefully and slowly turned in the lock. The door opened and Aleka came in. She closed it with extreme care. She put a finger to her lips. She listened, then she came forward and dropped to her knees close to Kirby to whisper to him.

"We must talk very softly. Oh, you are such fools to have let Prolofski of all people get you. But that's how it is, life is for you one day, against you the next. It's against me now. Dear God, the things they have done, the things I have seen. Some had to go to begin with, I even excused them for Andrei. But they go on and on, they'll drown Russia in the people's blood in the end. You must listen. If I help you, you must help me. Prolofski means to kill you this afternoon, it will be the last thing he'll do before we leave this place. There are only a few of us here now. They're letting the Whites have Ekaterinburg——"

"Aleka," said Kirby, "where are the Imperial family?"

Her eyes went blank.

"They've gone," she said.

"Where to?"

"I don't know. There's no time to talk about them." She was urgent, desperate. "I'll help you deal with Prolofski as long as you take me with you. I want to go with you, I must. The Russia I wanted lived only a few days, then they murdered it. It's dead now, but still they do these things, they're murdering a corpse. Russia will be dead for a long time. I've been sick a thousand times. It won't be long before they murder me too." Her whispered words poured out. "I wasn't wrong, Ivan, what I wanted was possible, now they've made it impossible. This is not my country, this isn't what was to be done. The revolution has been betrayed by animals. Listen, Prolofski and Oravio mean to execute you in this cellar. I shall try to be here too. Take this." She reached into her calf-length boot and drew out a small pistol. "You must kill Oravio first. Prolofski never carries arms, he always uses others to kill for him. Ivan, you'll use this and you'll take me with you, speak for me to the Whites when they come?"

"I owe you that much," said Kirby, "and you and I, Aleka, can always be the best of friends."

"More than that," she whispered passionately, "much more." She leaned, she pressed her mouth to his. Karita froze and as Aleka rose and slipped noiselessly out she looked after her with the burning back in her eyes.

It was a long wait from then on. They spoke very little. The afternoon had come before Karita suddenly said, "Aleka Petrovna is a bitch."

"We'll see," he said. He checked the small pistol. There were six shining bullets.

It was five o'clock when Prolofski and Oravio entered the cellar. It was unbearable to Karita to see that Oravio had her rifle, her beautiful Lee-Enfield. She knew the potential of that blue barrel. She was not too proud to feel humble in the face of it, and silently she began to say her prayers.

432

"My friend," said Prolofski, "why did you come by yourselves to Ekaterinburg?"

"It doesn't matter now, does it?" said Kirby. He and Karita were still on the floor, their backs against the wall. His hands were in his lap.

"No, it doesn't matter now," said Prolofski. "For crimes against the State the Romanovs were executed two days ago. They're all very safely dead now. You're going to follow them, only you will take longer."

Aleka came in. Kirby seemed transfixed, Karita was white. Aleka smiled.

"Still talking, Comrade Commissar?" she said. "You will have your preludes and overtures, won't you?"

The diversion, casual and inconsequential on the face of it, was enough. Kirby, madness in his eyes, uncovered the pistol and shot Oravio from where he sat. He fired repeatedly and one after another four bullets thudded into Oravio's chest and stomach. He fell, his screams choking in blood. The rifle clattered. Prolofski moved like a striking snake. But Kirby thrust out a long leg, Karita sprang and the rifle was in her loving hands. Prolofski shouted. There was the sound of two men quickly descending the steps. They were the men who had been listening nervously all day for the sound of the first shells from the Czech guns. Karita let them both rush in before she pulled the trigger. The noise was a blasting roar in the low-ceilinged cellar. The first man's face seemed to disappear behind a glistening red mask. Kirby, two small bullets left, shot the second man. The cellar reeked, the noise of the firing ran around the walls for long seconds before dying away.

Prolofski stood in the silence of the grave.

They listened. The moonface was wet with sweat. Cold blank eyes protruded. There was only silence.

Then Aleka said, "That's all of them, Ivan. There are no others. Everyone else has gone. I wonder how many bodies there are in Russia?"

"What has happened to the Tsar?" asked Kirby.

"I don't know. Deal with him." Aleka nodded at Prolofski, covered by Karita's rifle. Karita held it with

433

burning gratitude. God had been good, giving to her a man egoistically symbolic of the hatred that had destroyed a good and beautiful family. Karita believed what Kirby did not want to.

"What has happened to them?" His hand shot out, he took hold of the neck of Aleka's linen blouse and pulled her forward. Aleka found herself looking up into eyes that were murderous.

"Ivan, what has happened to *you*?" Because of his wrenching grip Aleka choked on her words. "Have you let them turn you into a savage too?"

"Tell me what you know," he said, and his hand shook her so that her head jerked.

"They're dead, shot," she gasped. "Oh God, they murdered them too."

"All?" His voice was a harsh whisper. "All? Olga too? Olga?"

"All of them," she breathed.

He let her go. He covered his face with his hands.

"Sweet Jesus Christ," he whispered.

"Don't you see, that was when it all ended for me?" she said feverishly. "I didn't want that, I never wanted that. I put my trust in people worse than assassins. There hasn't been a day since Lenin seized power that I haven't seen someone butchered or hanged or shot. Ivan, they killed them all, the whole family, all the children. Oh, dear God, all of them."

Kirby uncovered his grey face. He shuddered. Karita was weeping. Prolofski was stiff, only his eyes moving, glancing at the open door beyond the sprawled bodies. Kirby turned, took the rifle from Karita and jammed the point of the barrel hard into Prolofski's stomach. It brought an involuntary escape of hissing breath from Prolofski.

"No!" It was a cry of anguish from Karita as she saw Kirby's finger tighten on the trigger. "No! You've never done such a thing, only you have stayed sane while everyone else has gone mad. Ivan, no! Oh, I will do it, but not you, not you. Wait, there's another way, a better way. Give him to the Cossacks."

Kirby smiled into the white, sweating moonface. It was a smile that made Prolofski sweat more and it turned Aleka's blood cold.

"Yes," said Kirby softly, "we'll give him to the Cossacks, little one."

"And it's over now," said Karita, "we can go to England. Aleka Petrovna is right. Russia is dead. We will go home, Ivan."

"Yes," said Kirby.

"Ivan, you'll take me with you?" Aleka seized his arm, held on to him. "I still have money, jewels, I'll give you all you need to get us to England. Ivan, anything, anything."

Prolofski was a disgusting embarrassment to Karita in her grief, Aleka Petrovna an irritating encumbrance. She took the rifle back from Kirby and used the butt to smite the embarrassment unconscious. Prolofski fell heavily. That left only the encumbrance, the irritation. Coldly Karita pointed the rifle at Aleka.

"Get away from him," she said, "he is not yours. We are family, he and I and Aunt Charlotte. What are you to do with us? You're frightened now, frightened that we'll leave you and that the Cossacks will get you as well as Prolofski. But tomorrow, if we take you with us, you'll be laughing again."

"Oh, Karita, no, I swear," pleaded Aleka. "Karita, I shall never laugh again. Ivan, I did help you, now you'll help me, won't you?"

"Yes," said Kirby. He was not looking at her, he was not looking at anybody. He felt only freezing pain. Russians in their madness had murdered a whole family. For the sins of the worst of the Romanovs they had murdered the best of them.

The children. Oh, great God, where was *your* compassion?

They stayed in the school until the Czechs and the Whites swarmed into the evacuated town. Then they gave Prolofski to the Cossacks and he danced macabrely and in agony. Karita did not look on. Neither

435

did Kirby. But Aleka did. It was the one act of butchery she wanted to see.

Ekaterinburg had been worse than Tobolsk. The Imperial family were not merely locked up, they were practically boarded up.

Alexis, unable to walk, had been ill for months. The four girls, wistful for happy days gone, bore their final imprisonment bravely, their humiliations quietly. The coarseness of their Ekaterinburg guards shocked them. Brought up in an atmosphere of protective love and devout Orthodoxy, they regarded love and compassion as the finest of human emotions. But however much they were shocked by their guards, however often their minds were distressed and their hearts saddened, they did not fail their parents.

They never ceased to give each other affection and comfort, to do what they could for the suffering Alexis.

The attitude of Nicholas and Alexandra during those weeks at Ekaterinburg, the most despairing of their lives, was an example to shame an ignorant, indifferent world.

Of all statesmen, only Winston Churchill cared.

Nicholas and Alexandra thought first always of others in that place. They were harassed, bullied and threatened, but they showed concern only when the hatred was directed against their children or the few loyal servants who still remained with them. It is difficult to grasp the extent of their courage in conditions of horrifying adversity and even more difficult to weigh it against their frailties when they were Emperor and Empress.

Lenin and Trotsky were in command, but great and glorious as their revolution was they went in fear of opposition, in fear of the deposed Tsar and his children. Trotsky wanted the Imperial family disposed of. He wanted a public trial in Moscow, where justice could be seen to be done. The fact that the verdict would have been arrived at in advance did not have to deprive the people of the chance to witness Trotsky's presenta-

436

tion of an unanswerable case. The Ekaterinburg soviet told him in effect, however, to immortalise himself in some other way. They did not intend to let the Imperial family be taken to Moscow.

If there was unlimited fortitude in that house there was not quite so much laughter. But Anastasia still had her moments and Marie still described her dream prince (who had altered with each year she had grown). And Tatiana still had precious hours with Olga, when they talked of days that were golden and beautiful.

"Olga, are you ever afraid?" asked Tatiana one day. It was the afternoon of July 16th 1918, and it was hot. They were in their bedroom. It was one place where they could escape the eyes and tongues of the guards, although even here they could never be certain.

"I sometimes pray harder," said Olga with a slight smile.

"They dislike us so, worse than any of the others we've had," said Tatiana.

"Perhaps they've suffered more," said Olga.

"I shouldn't think they'd ever know whether they were suffering or ecstatic," said Tatiana sarcastically. She went on a little vehemently, "I can't bear the dreadful way they treat Mama and Papa."

"Oh, Tasha, Mama and Papa deserve so much better than this," said Olga, "but oh, I'm so proud of them, so proud they are our parents. They've given us so much love and happiness. And when you think of poor Alexis, you and I can't complain, can we?"

"We might later on," observed Tatiana, "because I'm sure Anastasia is going to become dreadfully bossy."

"Darling, you will hold your own," smiled Olga. Then very softly, "Tatiana?"

"Yes?" said Tatiana.

"We have all been very happy, have we not?"

"Oh, dearest Olga, we've been immensely, beautifully happy," said Tatiana, "we've all had so many wonderful times, and if you've had a little more it's because you're the dearest of all of us."

"No, I've been the luckiest," said Olga, her smile

437

tender, "but for all of us there's so much, so very much, that they can never take away from us."

"Especially from you, darling, especially from you."

It was in the cellar of that Ekaterinburg house on the night of that same day when a man called Yurovsky valiantly identified himself with the Cause. He was valiant in that there were few other men willing to do what he did. He did not do it with his bare hands or even by himself. He had his guards to help him, as well as an array of brave rifles and his own courageous revolver. Nevertheless, the credit is his, for he took the bold initiative and he fired the first shot.

With it he killed the Tsar, with it began the execution of the whole family and their servants.

Nicholas died immediately.

Alexandra died making the sign of the cross.

Alexis, crippled, died in his father's arms.

Marie died in incredulous astonishment, Tatiana proudly and in contempt of the executioners. Anastasia died twice. She came to as the first echoes of death faded and hearing her moans they bayoneted her into lasting silence.

Olga died quietly, as she had lived, her dreams vanishing. There was just one last moment, a moment of stark, tragic reality.

Now he would never know just how passionately she had loved him, adored him, never know——

She fell forward.

They finished off a screaming maid with bayonets.

"Well, that's the lot," said Yurovsky, Russia's man of the moment, as he stirred a crumpled dress with his booted foot. "Well done, comrades."

Such was the stuff of which the heroes of the revolution were made.

The lesson to be learned, but which we refuse to learn, is that they are all the same, heroes of revolutions. The fact that we refuse to learn, that there are always some of us who will give help, comfort and bread to the violent ones, means that the children of Nicholas died in vain.

The grey British warship steamed its way through the turgid November waters of the Black Sea, heading south from Sevastopol. Its decks were crowded with refugees, most of them Russian. From the decks silent men, women and children were taking their last look at their native land.

Kirby stood in the lee of the solid mounting of a huge naval gun. Karita was close to him. Princess Aleka Petrovna lay emotionally prostrate in quarters assigned to the most exalted of the refugees.

Kirby's eyes were on the receding domes and cupolas of Sevastapol, their brightness dulled under the grey canopy of the wet, wintry sky. The pain was unbearable. He was leaving her. She would remain in Russia forever. She would never grow old now, never become a stately, grey-headed Grand Duchess. Nor would she ever be a Crown Princess.

The hills of the Crimea were rain-shrouded, rising in the distance to merge mistily with hanging clouds. It did rain often in the Crimea. It was rain that gave it its rich greens. But in the spring, in the summer and autumn there was so much sunshine, so much. It was there, in her beloved Crimea, that she would always be. Not in the bleak, unfriendly Urals, not in Ekaterinburg, but there, in the peace and beauty of Livadia where she, where all of them, had spent their happiest days. It was there that she would find again the tranquillity she so loved, there that she would for ever rest. But every dawn, every rising sun, would bring her spirit from its sleep and she would dance again over the green lawns and come lightly to the pools. She would be laughing, happy, and always hand-in-hand with Tatiana.

In her gentleness and innocence she had gone from life unkissed. She had gone with those she loved. They were all at peace now, dearly together in spirit as they had been so much in life.

My sweet, my beloved, my precious Olga.

Karita's eyes were swimming. The tears misted the damp shores for her and blurred Sevastopol. Beyond that fading coastline Russia lay like an endless waste, and the cold bitter ashes of useless war and savage revolution, blown by the winds of stupidity and hatred, covered her earth.

It was not Karita's Russia. Others had it. They had even taken her God-fearing parents and shot them because neither would denounce the Tsar.

"Ivan?" she whispered.

He did not answer. He could not take his eyes from those clouded hills, his mind from all he had known. He thought of his marriage with Russia, the period of deceit, the years of discovery, the years of loving, the years of endurance. Finished.

The decks swayed to the roll of the warship as it veered sou'-sou'-west. The British sailors did not for the moment harry the mass of refugees, they let them see all that they could before Russia was lost to them in the rain mists. The faces of men, women and children were still, their tongues were still, and they paid their last, despairing farewells in silence. They had become exiles the moment the ship weighed anchor.

Karita desperately wanted to be comforted, desperately wanted to be loved. But Kirby was quieter than the silence itself and more remote. It was as if he stood not on the steel deck of a warship but in a place of his own, inaccessible to all others. But when at last the land was obscured and they could see no more of Russia she spoke to him.

"Ivan, I'm so cold, so unhappy."

"Yes, I know." He turned to her at last, he put his arm around her shoulders. Their garments were little better than those they had worn for the last year and they drew together for warmth as the cold, wet sea wind bit into their bodies and stung their faces. "We're leaving them all, Karita," he said. He remembered words Olga had spoken. "There were so many heroes, and all of them dead. Will they forgive us for going, do you think?"

440

"I think, if they could, they'd come with us," said Karita. "They did not die for this kind of Russia, not those we knew. But, Ivan, we can't mourn them for ever. We shall always remember them."

Do not forget me, Olga had said. The pain wrenched him.

"And the children, we shall always remember the children," said Karita. "How could we forget them and all those brave men and women we fought with? They were the best and most beautiful of Russians. But you and I have to live, and we have to speak for them. Ivan, we can't go home to Aunt Charlotte looking as if we are dead too. Life is for today and tomorrow, not for yesterday."

"Yes, we have tomorrow," he said, "we at least have survived."

"God has been very good to you and me," said Karita.

He was not sure of God's benefaction, not now.

His arm tightened around her shoulders. She pressed closer. They stayed there, oblivious of other people slowly drifting away to find warmer places or places where they might weep unseen. They stayed there with the sea wind tugging at their worn, belted coats, watching the wake of the steel ship as it took them from Russia and carried them home.

Everyone was on deck again to see new shores and to get in the way of the crew. The December afternoon was misty bright, the winter sun drawing up the vapours of melting frost. They saw the land, the greens as deep as those of the Crimea, they saw a multitude of anchored ships of war. In an hour they would step ashore.

"I'm so glad to be here," said Karita.

"Because it's here that I don't shout at you?" said Kirby.

"Oh, no," she said.

They heard the laughter of men above the buzz of excited refugees. Princess Aleka Petrovna was delight-

441

ing some of the ship's officers. She was fur-clad, she was brilliant and beautiful. She had bought the fur from a woman who had little else. She had received half-a-dozen proposals. She had laughed at all of them. She had loved only two men and one of them was dead. The other she had lost, she knew she had lost and restlessly she looked for other stimulants. Officers would do for the time being. But at a pause in the laughter she excused herself and made her way over to Karita and Kirby.

"Ivan," she said, "we're to see each other in London? You'll not desert me altogether?"

"We'll always be the best of friends, Aleka."

"I wish you'd stop saying that," she said. She smiled, her dark eyes sly. "I've arranged to buy a house in London. You must visit me often. Whenever you need love and not friendship I'll be happy to make you happy, darling."

Karita clenched her teeth.

"You must think of yourself, Aleka, not of me," said Kirby. He owed Aleka something she did not realise. She had led him to Olga Nicolaievna. He would not desert her altogether.

"I am thinking of myself, you fool," said Aleka. "But I shan't sit around waiting on your magnificence, I shall join the British Socialist Party."

"Good God," said Kirby. He was a little sly himself as he added. "You must get to meet Sidney and Beatrice."

She laughed. It was too spontaneous, he thought. Too brittle. The dark smoky eyes recaptured for him the moment when he had first met her at Nikolayev. But they were not the same eyes. And he knew she was haunted too. But not by the same things, the same people, as he was. She was haunted by disillusionment, by having lost all and gained nothing. Her revolution had lacked manners. That she could neither forget nor forgive.

She turned to Karita. Impulsively she put her arms around her, embraced her and whispered, "Oh, don't be angry with me for ever, Karita, you don't know how lonely I am, how I envy you." She pressed her mouth to Karita's cheek and then went back to the stimulation of the officers. She was merry in moments.

"Aleka Petrovna is laughing again," said Karita.

"No," said Kirby, "she isn't. We all lost something, Karita."

"But the war is over now, now we have tomorrow, don't we?"

It was over, except in Russia, where they still fought each other and murdered each other. Here in England and Europe the politicians were already preparing to write their memoirs, which would be full of reasons why it was all someone else's fault. Pageantry and glitter had gone, empires had disintegrated. Republicanism in a plain suit was claiming its turn. There would be less privilege, more equality.

There would be less poverty, less oppression and less blindness.

The beauty and the graciousness had been too expensive.

The world would be painfully reborn.

The land was closer, they could see the harbour, the roof-tops, everything soft and hazy in the winter sunshine.

"Ivan," said Karita, her eyes on the flowing sea, "did Grand Duchess Olga Nicolaievna love you?"

The pain was there, the longing, the sadness.

"She wasn't an ordinary girl, Karita, she wasn't allowed to love like other people."

"That's not an answer," said Karita, "but I didn't really need to ask. You're luckier than so many men, aren't you? Olga Nicolaievna did love you. There were so many things that I saw but didn't think about at the time. And Aunt Charlotte loves you. I love you. And Aleka Petrovna wants you."

"Karita, my sweet," he said in affectionate concern.

"Oh. I would so like to be loved myself," she said.

Heedless of the crowded deck he turned her, he lifted her face up to his. He felt shock. Karita Katerinova,

443

with whom he had shared so much, endured so much, and to whom he owed so much, was crying.

"Karita, can you think I don't care for you? We have been together so long, you and I, shared joys and sorrows, tragedies and love. When I look at you I see everything I've had from life, everything I've had from Russia. In you I see Russia, I see Livadia and yes, even Olga. You are everything I love about your country, you're my life, my happiness, my tomorrow. In you I see the sun and the snow, I hear the children of the Tsar, I hear their songs and your songs, I see Russia as I loved it, as I still love it. I dearly wish you'd marry me, Karita. If not, then I'll have nothing, no beauty, no peace, no tomorrow. What Olga meant to me was a cherishing of innocence, what you mean to me is yourself. Karita, my little one, I love you very very much."

Karita was sobbing as if all the tears of Russia were drowning her. People were looking, gaping.

"Karita, will you marry me?"

The grey warship was gliding through calm, sunlit waters. Karita's golden head lifted and she smiled through her tears.

"Oh, I would like to so very much," she said, "we should be such a proper family then."

He kissed her on the lips.

Kirby took Karita's hand as they stood side by side and watched England come to meet them. He did love her. She was very dear to him. He would never tell her how close Olga would always be to him, however, never tell her how Olga would always be first in his heart. He would live with that and in such a way that he would not cheat Karita of love.

Her hand was warm, her fingers long and slim, loving and possessive.

He looked into the sun, and it was Olga's hand, soft and clinging, that he felt around his.

She came out of the sun, her blue eyes dancing, her flowing lustrous hair tipped with deep gold.

"Colonel Kirby, you have been a very long time again . . ."

At Livadia, when summer day is done and evening softens the warm shadows, the ghosts of innocents scamper over the green lawns, their laughter caught as whispers in the trees, and every still pool reflects the deep blue eyes of a dreaming girl.

Dear Reader:

Charity Woodstock, the passionate heroine of THIS LOVING TORMENT, is irresistable. Just as the men that surround her are unable to leave her alone, you will be unable to put her story down.

From the moment you meet her in the arms of a famous highwayman as she escapes burning as a witch, until many adventures later, when she is once again on trial for her life, you will follow Charity with fascination.

Until you've read THIS LOVING TORMENT you'll have no idea what the words "tempestuous historical romance" can mean: Charity is loved and lied to by a Dutch Patroon's son. She has an idyllic affair with a frontiersman, another affair with a handsome rogue of a smuggler, is enamored of a plantation owner, properly hated and plotted against by his wife, sent off to Barbados, kidnapped by pirates and, finally, finds love in the arms of a man she first knows only as a voice making secretive deals with the Patroon early in her adventures, but who reappears in several disguises throughout the tale—and is, in the end, her undoing.

THIS LOVING TORMENT marks Valerie Sherwood's first appearance on the Warner list. And we haven't been as excited about an author since Jennifer Wilde.

The Editors

This Loving Torment

by Valerie Sherwood

In her cell, unable to eat the bit of tasteless gruel the jailer had brought her, Charity finally drifted off to an exhausted sleep, only to wake with a start at a small sound outside in the corridor. She tensed. The jailer had an evil face. Could that be him shuffling around outside her door?

She sat up, thoroughly awakened now and saw in the dimness a shape outside the bars of her cell. She opened her mouth, determined to scream loudly, but closed it as Tom Blade's voice murmured, "Shush, witch."

Was she dreaming or was the door to her cell opening. She stood up uncertainly.

"Well, come on," he muttered. "Don't just stand there!"

And she stumbled through the door and into the corridor where he put a hand over her mouth and whispered in her ear, "Walk soft and we'll be out in no time!"

Clutching his hand, trying to still the mad beating of her heart, she tiptoed along the dark corridor, waited while he felt in his pocket for another key, turned it gingerly in the lock. Then they were outside, breathing in the cool damp air of the summer night. She lifted her head; she had thought never to breathe the air as a free woman again. She turned to look questioningly at the man who had set her free.

He was beckoning, moving away like a shadow into the night, and she followed to where two horses were tied beneath a tree.

As she reached the tree a short broad fellow

stepped out of the shadows and clapped a hand over Charity's mouth, silencing her.

"She were going to scream," he grunted. And then, "Why'd you bring a wench, Tom? You know we've only got two horses!"

"We'll steal one for her then," said Tom.

The short man had inky black hair, a swarthy complexion and small black eyes. Taking his hand from Charity's mouth, he shook his head vehemently. "These farmers around here might not follow the likes of us," he said, "but they'd follow their horses clear down to Carolina!"

"She can ride with me," said Tom shortly, boosting Charity up to the saddle. "If I'd left her, they would have burned her as a witch."

"She'll be our death," muttered the other glumly, climbing aboard his own mount.

"Charity, this is Bart Symonds," said Tom. "If bribery hadn't worked, he was going to try to break me out."

Charity looked at them both with new respect. Plainly she was in the company of bold men. But her fastidious nature was repelled by the slovenly Bart; nor did she like the way he looked at her.

A moment later they were walking their horses over the soft sod, and moving quietly through the streets of the sleeping town. When they reached the last house there was a shout from a sentry who leaped up and fired a musket shot into the air.

"Ride!" cried her companion grimly, to Bart, giving his horse's flank a whack, and they were off like the wind into the summer night.

She didn't ask where they were going. She didn't care. Away, that was all she cared about. Away from vile relatives and filthy jails and bigoted judges and derisive townsfolk. She dashed cold water over her face at the stream and rose up, still stiff from her unaccustomedly long ride.

That night they seemed to be riding in long slow

curves. She guessed they were skirting little hamlets that had sentries who might be alert to challenge two men and a woman riding through the dark. Twice they crossed water, going downstream and out upon the opposite bank each time, and she guessed the men were considering that they might be tracked by dogs. It was a terrifying thought.

As the moon waned in the sky and a false dawn appeared, Tom reined in his horse and found them shelter in a cave behind a waterfall. Charity woke feeling painfully hungry. The jail fare had been terrible, but she had now been without any food for two days.

She staggered to her feet and looked around for Tom.

He was gone.

She ran from the cave and rushed out from behind the waterfall—and gasped as Bart appeared from nowhere and caught her arms, pinioning them to her sides.

"Don't go running out like that," he growled. "Look where you're going first."

"I was looking for Tom," she said. "Let go, you're hurting me."

His mouth curled in a nasty smile. His swarthy face was very close. "And if I don't let go," he said, "what will you do about it?"

"Let go of the lady, Bart," said Tom's voice. It had a cold ring to it.

Bart's hands dropped to his sides. He stepped aside and Charity saw that Tom was carrying some berries in his hat.

"Best I could find," he said briefly, proffering some to Charity. "But tomorrow we'll have us a feast."

Bart grunted. "We'd have had us a feast today if you hadn't been carrying double and slowed us down."

Charity hoped they would have a feast. She was certainly ready for one. Wearily, she dragged herself back onto the horse, and Tom swung up behind her as they started off through the gathering dusk. She was more aware than ever of Tom's sometimes tightening arm beneath her bouncing breasts. She wished fervently the dresses material weren't so thin. She wished she weren't so aware of him, tingling at the touch of his lean thighs against her legs.

By morning the trio had reached a little out-of-the-way inn, which they studied from a distance and then approached quite openly. It was a small stone edifice with its chimney already smoking, telling the world the scullery maids were up and about.

"I've friends here," Tom said with a merry smile. "Here they know Tom Blade for his generosity—not for his misdeeds!"

He lifted her gallantly off the horse. Swaying against him, her eyelids heavy with fatigue, she followed him inside.

Only the innkeeper was in the public room as they arrived. His face lit in a broad grin as he saw Tom and Bart, and they nodded amiably in response.

"We'll be wanting two rooms," said Tom. "Food. Feed for our horses and currying—and the wench here'll be wanting a bath and a comb and to have her clothes washed and mended. Can you manage it?"

"Indeed I can," said the innkeeper, rubbing his hands together as if already they felt the jingling gold. "First room on your right upstairs, Mistress. Bath'll be right up."

Charity came out of a deep pleasant sleep to feel something warm against her, a body. To feel hands gently stroking her breasts, sliding down her back and along the curve of her hips. She sighed happily. Suddenly she jerked awake, opening her mouth to scream.

Instantly a big warm hand was clapped over her mouth.

"You wouldn't be wanting to wake the whole inn,

would you?" murmured Tom's lazy voice. "Not over a bit of lovemaking!"

Charity made inarticulate sounds against his hand and continued to struggle violently.

"In case you should decide to scream," muttered Tom, "I should tell you first that one of the king's men has just come into the inn; he's drinking ale with the landlord downstairs. It may be he's never heard of Charity Woodstock, the condemned witch who's just escaped, or then again maybe he has. He rode in from the north."

Charity stiffened in horror. If she screamed, if she attracted any attention, she might well be returned to Dynestown to burn!

Cautiously Tom took his hand away from her mouth but retained his firm grip on her body.

"I thought you'd be sensible," he said.

Charity struggled grimly in silence.

With ease he turned her toward him and climbed on top of her. Charity looked up at him murderously, her eyes wild, her naked white breasts rising and falling with fear as she fought him.

Tom lifted his head and looked down at her, his long golden hair swinging down so that it lay along her cheek.

"Is rape the only thing you're used to, Charity?" he muttered with a frown. "Don't you ever give yourself fully to a man?"

Her teeth caught in her lower lip and she fought back a groan of rage, but he laughed and held her fast. His golden mustache tickled her face as his mouth closed over hers forcing her lips apart.

Her struggles increased as she felt his hand pry her legs apart, felt his tongue part her lips again insistently, felt his hands move leisurely. He held her arms steady, as one hand slid down her back and caught one cheek of her writhing bottom, holding her still as he thrust deep but gently within her, probing, exploring.

It was different from that other time. She realized

at once and was startled. She was gasping as he took his mouth from hers, whispered soothingly into her ear. Against her will, she felt her body respond to that rhythmic pressure, felt her flesh burn and tingle as his hands caressed her. And then the banked fires within her own self burst loose and she was aflame against him, straining toward him, moaning, thrusting her breasts forward to flatten them against his chest, raising her hips wildly against his, panting with exertion, burning with desire.

When they had finished, she lay panting beside him, raging inwardly that her body could thus betray her, hating herself that she had responded so fully to him and that he had known it, had enjoyed it.

"You were supposed to sleep in the other room with Bart! If I hadn't trusted you, I'd have locked my door!"

"You'd have had a hard time locking the door," Tom said, "since the inn has no keys. The keys were all lost long ago, the landlord tells me." He grinned. "Possibly so he can move about the rooms at night if he wishes, and make a fat purse leaner when he has a mind to. And anyway," he added, "Bart's got him a wench to warm his bed. She's from the kitchen. Mine's from the parlor." He chuckled.

He leaned on one elbow and studied her naked body, tracing little patterns with his hand across her stomach. Charity quivered.

"How could anyone think you a witch?" he murmured. "Except a beguiling one. Tell me, how did they happen to charge you with witchcraft?"

"My Cousin Matthew raped me," said Charity bitterly. "And Aunt Temperance, to cover up his crime and secure my inheritance charged me with witchcraft. At my trial, they all testified against me."

"I see." His fingers moved lower along her stomach, gently stroked the triangle of gleaming pale gold hair that grew there. "So I take it I'm the second man in your life?"

She turned and looked him full in the face. "No,"

she said honestly, "you're the first. Matthew was an animal."

She thought he looked pleased.

"Well," Tom said. "Two people so made for each other should take advantage of it, don't you think?" And rolled over on her again so that she gasped at his sudden weight. She felt a flare of passion as his lips trailed down her throat and across her bosom to nestle in the valley between her breasts, then slowly, deliberately to climb those small soft hills and nuzzle their pink summits. Under his touch she felt desire racing along her body tinglingly, felt her arms open and her legs seem to spread themselves wide of their own volition, to allow him to enter her gently. She shivered in his arms, reaching a crescendo of passion that shook and surprised her.

With a sigh, Tom flung himself off her and fell asleep almost at once. She looked at his lean muscular shoulder, at his gleaming tawny gold hair that mingled with her own on the pillow, at his newly trimmed Van Dyke beard that gave him a devilish look, at the whole naked length of him that lay sprawled beside her, one buttock touching the soft curve of her hip as she lay on her back. Troubled, Charity asked herself if what she felt was love?

Did she love Tom Blade that her body could respond so fiercely to his lovemaking?

At a baker's, a hard-faced woman who spoke English turned her away.

"Could be, she'd have been good at the work," the baker said wistfully.

"Nonsense," said his plain-faced wife in a resentful tone. "She'd be good only to ogle the men, with a face and a figure like that. Back to the oven—your bread is burning!"

Charity wandered on, past close-set row houses of Holland brick, with their small windows.

It seemed little use to inquire at a smithy, or a

wheelwright's. She turned away, sickened, from the squeals and smells at the butcher's.

She was about to inquire at a dry goods shop when she saw that not one but two girls were lolling in it, looking bored. Since neither of them had anything to do, it seemed extremely doubtful that the management would add a third to join them in their idleness. With a sigh, she turned away.

By now she was tired, for she had had practically no rest in two days, but hope rose in her because she had come to a dairy. Although she was unfamiliar with cows, they had gentle eyes and milk was a clean wholesome thing. She thought she might enjoy a season of being a dairy maid.

Thankful that the owner——whom she found shoveling manure in his big spacious stone barn with its massive beams——could speak English, she inquired about work, too honest to pretend she knew anything about cows.

He thought it over, looked at her several times, seemed to consider and then nodded his head. Her heart leaped. She could get away from Bart!

"I'd take ye, if ye'd sign articles of indenture," he said slyly, "and consent to be bound, so that I'd know ye'd not be runnin' off with the first likely lad to walk by, leavin' me with the time wasted I'd spent trainin' ye."

Charity's heart slumped. Bound! To be a bound girl. It had a sad ring to it, almost like slavery. Still . . . it might be the only way.

For how long? she asked anxiously. For seven years, she was told, at the end of which time she would receive a calf and a respectable dress and in florins she would receive——

But Charity had already fled. Even the thought of getting away from Bart did not seem so tempting that she would sign away her freedom for seven long years. Seven years! A lifetime to one who was only nineteen.

She had no way of knowing that the crafty dairyman had only meant to bargain with her; assuming she knew that three or four years was the usual period of indenture, and had hoped to strike a bargain at five. Regretfully, he saw the girl hurry away; she'd been a healthy, rosy-cheeked maid, she had, and well spoken even if it was only English she spoke —far different from his own surly vrow. He sighed. Ah, well, times being what they were, perhaps the girl would be back.

But Charity sped away, thoroughly upset by his offer.

The light was fading and so were her spirits, though she had started out so resolutely. Discouraged, she plodded back to the inn, her shoulders drooping, her mind filled with worry over Tom's fate, wondering whether he was still alive. In silence, she walked across the plank flooring and sat down to dinner with Bart, who was getting soddenly drunk in the inn's public room. Somehow during the day he had acquired the companionship of a foursome of trappers. The trappers were having a high time in town before they departed once again for their life in the remote forests where they trapped the woodland animals for their pelts. The noisy men were also getting very drunk and one of them kept grinning inanely and pinching Charity's thigh under the table.

She kept edging away from him and, eventually, he took the hint and began talking to the barmaid, a buxom Dutch girl with a coarse full-bodied laugh, whose big breasts nearly popped out of her low-cut blouse as she leaned over to bang down the flagons of ale.

Charity knew that there was no longer any hope of finding a job this day. She also knew with certainty that Bart had her staked out for a romp in the room upstairs. But she was determined not to go upstairs. She would simply sit at the table all night, seated on the hard wooden bench, and when everyone either passed out or left, she would fall asleep on the wooden table, and try again tomorrow to get a job. She had already decided that tomorrow she would take anything—even as a last resort the seven years' indenture. Bart's woman she would **not** become.

The trappers pressed drinks on her but she shook her head. She must not become giddy. She'd need her wits about her if Bart suddenly decided to drag her upstairs.

Numb with fatigue, she sat silently listening to the men talk. Sometimes she found their conversation interesting. One of the trappers told Bart that Manhattan was an Indian name which meant "the island," and that the Iroquois had named the Albany area **Ska-neh-ta-de,** which meant "beyond the pine trees."

Bart was curious about the Indians. Were they friendly?

Not always, was the reply. They blew hot and cold. Those in the Hudson Valley were the friendliest of the lot. The fiercest tribes, all agreed, roamed to the west of Albany—the Iroquois, the Five Nations.

One heavyset trapper who had been in the area longer than the others said that the friendly Algonquins of the Hudson Valley had given the Iroquois their name, which meant "real adders," but that the Iroquois called themselves the Ogwanonhsioni, which meant "long-house builders." They called their land the "Long House," since that was the shape of their territory, presided over from east to west by the Mohawks, Oneidas, Onandagas, Cayugas and Senecas.

Bart had heard of the Mohawks.

The Mohawks were so fierce, they had once forced the Delawares to lay down their arms and to dress as squaws. They exacted tribute from the Hudson River tribes. And it was their enemies who had named them the Mohawks.

Bart pounced on that. What did Mohawk mean?

His informant grew grave. The Mohawks called themselves "people of the place of flint," which was the meaning of their musical name for themselves, Kanyengehaga, but their enemies had christened them "Mohawks" meaning "those who eat people" —as indeed they did.

Bart laughed uneasily, but Charity's smile wavered. Cannibals!

"Ye're scarin' the girl," objected another trapper. "She'll be afraid to come along!"

Bart gave him a fierce look and he subsided.

Come along. . . . Charity was very tired. She certainly wasn't going anywhere, she told herself. Furthermore, she intended to stay awake and make certain that nothing untoward happened.

But she was even more tired than she knew. Gradually the men's voices became a drone in her ears and, resting her head on her arms on the table, she fell fast asleep. A furtive pinch on the thigh from the trapper on her right woke her so that she stirred ever so slightly, but she didn't raise her head from her arms.

Bart was rolling drunk by now, but not so drunk as to miss the main chance; he was having a low-voiced conversation with two of the trappers—the two who were still sober enough to talk—and the drift of that conversation froze Charity's blood.

They were talking about her.

"That's my lowest price," Bart was saying. "I'll sell her to you for that, no less, to warm your beds in the wilds."

Charity tried not to move, not to let them know she'd heard.

"Where would you find a woman like this one?" Bart wheedled. "Look at that shiny hair, those round breasts—well, you can't see them now, she's lyin' on the table, but you should see her naked! Skin like silk!" He paused to let them drink that in.

"You seen her naked?" asked one of them eagerly.

Bart's voice had sneaky laughter in it. "By the riverside," he said. "She belonged to my friend Tom then, and they used to roll in the grass there. I seen them there more than once."

Charity writhed inwardly. Bart had **watched** them! He must have hidden in the bushes waiting for them to appear!

"But tonight? What about tonight?" cut in a hoarse voice.

"Tonight's mine," said Bart in a surly tone. "Tom never'd let me get near her, but tonight she's mine. Tomorow you can have her."

"Where is this Tom?" asked another. "Will he come after her? And try to kill us maybe?"

"Tom's dead for all I know," said Bart heavily. "He were bleedin' like a stuck pig when I saw him last. Anyway, he's on his way to Barbadoes. If he comes back, you can sell her back to him when you've done with her——and make a fair profit!"

"Hell, we can always buy us a white woman from the Indians at their slave market up north on the lake. The Indians catch plenty of 'em, and they sell 'em up there——those that last that long. Some's real good lookin'. Hard for us to get in there, but we can always make a deal to have one brought out to us by the Frenchies——"

"But this one's English!"

"There's lots of English women at the slave market. Thought you knew that."

"But if the Frenchies have to go in and buy one for you," Bart pointed out craftily, "you got no guarantee what she'll look like. And you don't know how many painted savages has had her. Or what they's done to her. This girl was a virgin when my friend took her——and that was only a few days ago."

Charity's nerves shrieked as she digested it all. She sat tensely, her head on her arms, waiting for them to stop talking, so she could make her escape.

"A virgin you say?"

"Yep. And educated. You heard her talk."

"That ain't the kind of education I'm interested in," sneered one trapper. "The kind of education I want in a woman is all got thrashin' around under a blanket."

"At your price we oughta have her tonight," grumbled another. "I still say—"

"Why, ye'll thank me for beddin' her tonight," declared Bart intensely. "I plan to teach her some tricks twixt now and mornin' that'll make her worth more to ye."

Glad to go with them! Teach her tricks! Warm their beds in the wilds! Horror washed over Charity in such an engulfing flood that she almost fainted. First Bart —loathsome Bart—and then this coarse crew.

"Another round here!" roared someone at the next table, and with her nerves taut as a drawn bowstring, Charity jumped. She sat up, deliberately yawning. "That man woke me up," she declared pettishly. "I'm going to bed. Bart, you can stay down here until you fall off that bench for all I care!"

Bart laughed. "I'll accompany you!" He winked at the others.

"No, you won't," snapped Charity. "I'm going to take a bath first and comb my hair." She hoped he did not know she had already taken a bath; it would make him suspicious.

Bart shrugged. "Time for another round of beer then." He watched her lasciviously as she moved away from them. She could almost feel the naked lust in that stare.

Very pale, but moving with apparent purposelessness, she reached a point midway between the stairs and the door. She did not think there was a back stairway. At least she had not seen one. She knew if she climbed those stairs she would be trapped.

She took a deep breath and strolled toward the door.

"Ho there," yelled Bart, his voice suddenly sharp. "You're goin' the wrong way!"

"I want a breath of air," she called back over her shoulder, moving steadily toward the door.

There was the sound of a table going over as Bart

leaped up, as she streaked through the door and went flying up the street. She had turned down a dark narrow alley when she heard them come thundering and cursing out into the street.

"You go this way, I'll go that way!" she heard Bart yell. "She can't have gone far!"

Her heart sank. If the trappers were looking too, they would surely catch her. She nearly tripped over a sleeping dog in the alley. He moved with a growl as she jumped away, and she tiptoed on. If the dog had barked, she would have been lost. It brought home to her how dreadful was her position. These men were used to trapping animals—animals far more wary than she. They would have little trouble trapping a friendless woman alone in a town that was strange to her.

Turning a corner she gazed into an empty street that led straight down to the docks. Before her stretched a maze of boats and ships—there was her hiding place!

She slipped off her shoes and, holding them, ran silently toward the docks. Many of the smaller craft were drawn up there, side by side. Some would have cabins, all had sails and gear—she would find a place to hide.

Behind her there was a drunken shout. "She's headin' for the docks!" Footsteps pounded behind her.

THE BEST OF BESTSELLERS
FROM WARNER BOOKS!

THE BEST OF BESTSELLERS
FROM WARNER BOOKS!